RESURRECTIONS

BELDEN CRANE JOHNSON

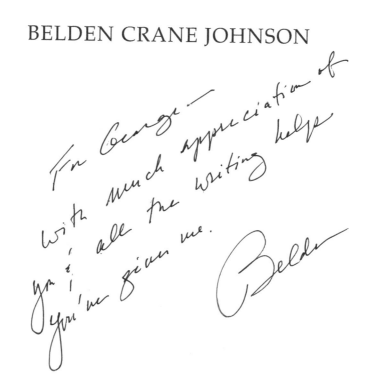

For George —
with much appreciation of
you & all the writing help
you've given me.

Belden

In loving memory of

BURT BELDEN IDE

who gave me unconditional love

&

taught me the Trick to Everything

CONTENTS

PART IV

PART V

ILLUSTRATIONS

PREFACE

This novel has been over a half century in the making. Mostly, it's a true story.

On my eighteenth birthday, my great-aunt Emily Ide passed on to me the diaries, letters, and photographs of her uncles, Belden and Ira, and the diary and a drawing of Helen, who was her mother. I had, of course, been regaled throughout childhood with the legends surrounding Belden's remarkable life.

At that time I was an undergrad at Harvard concentrating in American History and Literature. Part of that department's many requirements for graduation was to write a mini-dissertation, called a thesis. I petitioned the History & Lit department for a waiver to write not an academic thesis but a historical novel based upon original research.

What a wonderful way to combine history and literature, or so I thought.

Harvard appointed a faceless committee to "consider your proposal." I imagine it was one or two faculty members. After six weeks of considering, the committee wrote me a long letter saying, basically, that they liked the idea but would have to nix it because, and I quote, "We wouldn't know how to grade it."

I was gobsmacked, though I didn't know that word yet.

But I let go of the idea, wrote a passable thesis on Ernest Hemingway, and graduated.

That fall I drove with my new wife in our black VW Beetle halfway across the country to the Writers' Workshop at the University of Iowa, which had kindly given me a teaching assistantship, and wrote my first novel during my first year there. It was not, however, this novel but a dystopian work set in an America invaded by foreign powers, which my first agent said was the best first novel of the decade. Rather than getting it published, however, he gave it to his brother-in-law, who turned it into a B-grade movie you've probably had to suffer through and which neglected to give me a credit line.

After that novel, I wrote rough drafts of six more over the next thirty years, though I didn't work very hard at getting any published. Having been badly betrayed by my first literary agent, I tended to stick completed manuscripts in bottom drawers. I was content to see my short fiction and poetry manifested in the "little" magazines. I also very happily raised two sons and entered into the new career of psychotherapy.

Finally, around 1996, I went back to research and craft the novel I'd hoped to write in 1965. I was about 100 pages in when a brilliant new writer named Charles Frazier published *Cold Mountain*. I read it with my heart in my throat. Except for the fact that *his* great-grand-uncle had been a *Confederate* soldier, our two stories were so alike that any reader would assume that I had plagiarized him. Like Mr. Frazier, I even had taken Homer's *Odyssey* as an organizing structure. And I must say that Mr. Frazier had written like an angel, a far better maker than I.

I was, as we used to put it, bummed. I played with radical structural changes to distinguish my story from Mr. Frazier's, but in the end I put yet another novel in another bottom drawer.

However, this remarkable story was never far from my mind.

In fact, my ancestors, in the form of my characters, pestered me, insisting that I had a duty to tell their story. I felt very Japanese, imbued in Shinto culture. I went to visit the graves of my ancestors and, as I wrote, surrounded myself with their pictures. Great-grandmother Helen, with one of the saddest faces I've ever seen, broods down at me from the wall above my writing desk. They began visiting me in my dreams, giving me support and direction.

I went back to the simpler story.

In this book, that I am happy to have lived long enough to complete, I hope that you will discover in it someone to love, as do I. These "characters" were real people. Much realer in many ways than I find myself and my contemporaries. While I know that people of any age are just people, the Americans of that era were cut from a different cloth. They were, I believe, better than we are now. They certainly had better penmanship. The tragic conflict that killed 800,000 of them, put an end to institutionalized slavery, and preserved a fragile Union that is still, in many ways, re-fighting those old battles, broke something in the American psyche. We have yet to heal that wound and repair that break, if it is reparable. To do so, I believe we must imbibe the lessons of our history.

As the great Spanish-American philosopher George Santayana put it, "Those who cannot remember the past are condemned to repeat it."

PART I

BRADFORD, NEW YORK, 1862

Belden

1

A FALLOW FIELD

As the two big Percheron horses pulled the steel plough through the green of the alfalfa-covered field, turning the sod and revealing a snaky furrow of moist dark earth, a flock of blackbirds followed, cackling like Harpies at the bounty of plump red-and-purple worms that were suddenly exposed to their beaks. The crisp morning air was rich with the smells of upturned humus and crushed flowers.

The young man at the ploughshares had that sense of easy competence at his task that comes of long practice. He had a mass of dark brown hair, arresting blue eyes, and a clean-shaven, pleasant face. A bit over average height, his well-knit body spoke of both exuberant good health and years of hard physical work.

At the edge of the field he whistled a command, turning the team, lifted and re-set the gleaming point of the plough, and, with a "Hup!" started the Percherons down the new furrow. He loved the big black horses, progeny of the destriers who once bore fully-armored knights.

He glanced up at the blackbirds, which had scattered out of the path of the horses, and grinned at their screeching protests.

"Watch out there, blackbirds!" he called to them. "Belden Crane is coming through!"

He didn't really mind the blackbirds—they kept the timber rattlesnake population down. This field had lain fallow all year, however, and might have drawn some rattlers. He'd tied hay bands around his lower legs to protect himself from their bites.

Despite the threat of snakebite, plowing was Belden's favorite job on the Crane family farm. It was a small farm, comprising a gently sloping forty acres of south-facing hillside above Mud Lake and the town of Bradford in the Finger Lakes region of western New York State. Pa—William Crane—had come out from Massachusetts Bay as a young man to clear the land, converting many of the trees into lumber to build house and barn. He had pried the terminal moraine of boulders from the soil and built solid fences of them. Ma—then Emily Sutton--had taken a fancy to the post-and-beam construction of the house as well as the man who had built it and agreed to his marriage proposal in 1837. They had produced three children: Ira, 22, Belden, 20, and Helen, 16.

The other Bradford farmers had at first shaken their heads at Pa's concept of field rotation. While they tried to squeeze as much out of every field they had, Pa left one field fallow every year, seeding it with alfalfa and then plowing the legume back under in the late summer. Once the others saw how much more his thus-revitalized fields produced, they began imitating his practices, which also included fertilizing with aged manure and composted leaves and grass trimmings.

While Belden plowed, Pa and Ira were loading the wagon with manure and compost from the piles behind the barn that would be spread today and then mixed into this field when they harrowed it. Belden was glad not to be shoveling manure, happy in the freshness of the cool air coming down from Mt. Keuka, and delighted in the colors of the dark birds, cerulean sky, brown earth, and the palette of greens in the summer foliage. He was mapping out in his mind's eye the picture he'd paint this evening after supper.

"Persian blue for the sky...Vandyke brown for the earth...mix yellow lake with the blue for the leaves of that tree and brown and burnt sienna for the trunk. I'll try the colors on a piece of glass before laying them on canvas. Oh, and black-brown for the horses. Gee up, Castor!"

The Percherons' names were Castor and Pollux.

That morning he'd arisen an hour before even Ma was up, as was his custom, to start a fire in the cookstove and to light a candle on the kitchen table, where he read his Blackstone, making notes on the law in a leather-covered notebook: "A bill of attainder is an act of the legislature to pass sentence of death without a trial...." He had hopes of being an attorney one day. Or he could join Charlie Ide at the blacksmithing trade—he'd made himself a new ramrod for his musket at Charlie's forge that had turned out straight and true. Let Ira take over the farm.

More immediately, though, he'd be a soldier.

Today he and Ira were going to tell Pa. Again. They'd been eager to enlist when the Rebels had started the War by firing on Fort Sumter last April, but Pa had said the War would be over in a few months and he needed them for the planting. Then he needed them for the harvest, and then to buck up the winter firewood and tap the sugar maples and then again for the spring planting. They could see that Pa was stalling them. Which didn't make much sense, since Pa was an ardent abolitionist Republican who had worked hard to get Mr. Lincoln into the White House and fiercely supported Honest Abe's decision to fight to preserve the Union. When Abe had attempted to compromise with the slave states when he first came to office, by supporting their good friend Henry Seward's constitutional amendment allowing the slavers to hold onto their "property" if that preserved the Union, both Ma and Pa had had a hard time accepting his priorities. They had preached the evils of slavery since their children were knee-high to grasshoppers and now that their boys were ready to step forward and do their duty they were having qualms. Belden and Ira, on the other hand, were eager to free the slaves and preserve the Union.

And, if truth be told, to see the Elephant, as the saying was. War was something big, awesome. It gave a man a chance to find out what he was really made of. Although he believed he could face gunfire and a bayonet charge as well as any man, Belden couldn't know for certain how he'd bear himself till he'd done it. Enlistment would also give him a pert blue uniform that the girls loved and a chance to see some of the rest of the country. The furthest he'd been from home was Albany, when Pa had taken the family with him to meet the then-Senator Seward, who was now Lincoln's Secretary of State. Belden thought that if he had to stay cooped up in Bradford for the rest of his natural days he'd go stir-crazy.

Now that Eugene Gasscone had arrived from Quebec to help Pa on the farm, it seemed to Belden that Pa could no longer say no to their plans to enlist. Sure, Ma and Helen would cry and say they were afraid they'd be killed, but that's just what women did. Cinder was doing the same ever since he'd been stupid enough to mention that he was enlisting one time after they'd made some really sweet love. Cinder. She'd be the hardest to leave. He really did love her. He'd need to remind her when he saw her at the dance tomorrow. He suspected that she'd throw a fit again.

"Haw, Castor, haw!"

Of course they were all frightened for him and Ira and didn't want to lose them. That was understandable. But he couldn't just stand by when his country was fighting to end slavery and preserve her very foundations. He wasn't going to profiteer like Jesse Munsen and make himself rich selling the War Department shoddy shoes for absurd prices. And he knew for a fact that Jesse Munsen would be bird-dogging Cinder the minute he left town. Jesse had been a yellowbel-lied rat since the day Belden punched him in the nose for making Cinder cry when they were all in the first grade in the one-room schoolhouse. Well, he'd see Cin at the dance tomorrow night at that same schoolhouse and reassure her he'd be back for her. He hoped she'd understand, but he felt a growing uneasiness about it.

* * *

When Belden finished turning the last furrow on the field, he unhitched the horses and led them to their drinking spot on the brook. As they sucked in water he squinted up at the sun and reckoned it must be close to dinnertime. Walking upstream a few rods, he squatted at the brook's edge and washed hands and face in the cold rushing water. Then, cupping his hands together and dipping them deep before raising them to his lips, he sucked in several handfuls of what he judged must be the clearest, freshest water in the world. Its origin was a spring bubbling out of the mountainside a half mile from where he now drank. Pa had fenced the brook off from domestic animals, at least, till it reached this field. Pa had also laid pipe from the spring itself to the holding tank at the house. Pa was that handy.

Wiping his cold hands on his pant legs, Belden lay down on his back in the brookside grass with his hands clasped beneath his head and looked up at the puffy white clouds billowing in the sky like great ships. Actually, the one right above him looked like one of those bison out in the Wild West.

Charlie's uncle William B. Ide had gone West with the 49ers and had gotten himself elected a judge and then the President of the Bear Flag Republic, which then became the state of California. Belden and Ira had often talked of heading out there to try their luck. Like many young men, they wanted to see what was on the other side of the mountain. And back then the women who loved them had persuaded them not to leave. Seemed to Belden that the men wanted to travel and have adventures and the women wanted to feather a nest and have babies. Cinder wanted babies. With him. That made him uneasy as well.

He heard the creak of the wagon and rolled over to see Tom, the red ox, waddling into view, towing the wagon like a barge. Pa and Ira sat up on the seat in their shirt sleeves, the dinner basket between them.

"Whoa!" Ira said, halting the wagon at the south end of the field. He got down to unhitch Tom so the ox could join the horses grazing on the bits of grass left around the edges of the field. Though two years older, he was a slighter version of Belden, an inch shorter, a few pounds lighter. "Two peas in a pod," Ma liked to say.

Pa stepped down with the basket and Belden felt his stomach rumble. When Pa headed for the shade of the big oak, Ira came over to Belden and gave him a hand up. They followed Pa and the lunch basket. Pa's white hair gleamed in the sun just before he stepped into the cool of the shade. Belden found his hand touching his own dark hair. Pa's had started turning white in his early thirties. Some people said it had turned after he'd fought in the Indian raids, but Pa said the men in his family all went white early. "White, but never bald," he liked to say, with a grin flashing out of his darker beard.

Belden often marveled at that: How was it that his beard had stayed dark when the hair on his head had turned? It did give him a distinguished look.

By the time Ira and Belden joined him in the oak's shade, Pa had the basket open, spread the cloth, uncorked the cider jug, and laid out the fried chicken, sliced red onions, and hunks of bread and cheese Ma had packed for them.

Pa greeted them with a warm smile.

"Let us pray," he said, and they clasped one another's hands to form a small circle and bowed their heads. "We thank Thee, Father, for these Thy gifts. Help us to use them to do Thy good works. In Jesus' name, Amen."

Belden and Ira echoed the amen and the three men sat down, reaching for bread and chicken.

"Belden, this is a job well done," Pa said, indicating the plowed field with a nod of his head. His blue eyes were penetrating and warm at the same time. "You lads would do well to consider the life of a farmer. A man can be his own master and will always be able to feed his family when he is a farmer. There's sufficient acreage here for both of you to be prosperous on."

"As you have always been, Pa," Belden replied, before setting his teeth into a drumstick.

"You can persuade me, Pa, but leave him Bel be," Ira said, pouring the cider into three wooden cups. "He may be handy, but he's got a poetic soul. He's destined for greatness, is our Belden."

With that he gave Belden a playful punch in the shoulder, which his brother returned in kind. When Ira handed him a cup of cider he accompanied it with a wink. Belden ducked his head to hide his grin.

"I don't pretend to greatness," Belden said. "I just want to go out and see a bit of the world and try my hand at other instruments than the plough and scythe."

"Such as the musket and bayonet, you mean," Pa said. His tone had gone serious. "Yes, I knew you'd be raising the issue once again any day now. So let's get to it. There's nothing wrong with seeing a bit of the world, lads, though truth to tell, while east is east and west is west, coming home is always best. And I know that's a truth each man must learn for himself. Nevertheless, traveling's one thing, soldiering's another. Soldiers get killed."

"Not us, Pa," Belden said. "We'll stand in the back."

"The day either of you ever stands in the back, I'll eat my hat without salt," Pa said. "That's one of the problems of soldiering. The brave die young. The cheats and cowards survive, even if they do die a thousand deaths."

His sons fell silent. They knew Pa's best friend Amos Knapp had been killed in the Indian raids while acting as rear guard to cover the retreat of men Pa barely nodded to anymore.

"When you were boys we read you the tales of the knights of the Round Table and King Arthur," Pa said. "In those stories brave men fought with sword and shield, face to face. Warfare has changed since then. A musket ball can pierce your heart in an instant at a hundred paces, and you never see the man who killed you, or him you. Cannon-fire cuts down men like the scythe fells the wheat, scores at a time. This terrible war will consume the flower of our manhood, North and South. I pray I do not end my life wearing black."

"It's not just that we want to be like the Knights of the Round Table," Belden said. "We want to help free the slaves. We've been hearing you speak about the evils of slavery since we could walk, Pa.

You'd read us to sleep with chapters from *Uncle Tom's Cabin* when we were boys. When the war began, I remember you quoting from Alexander Stephens' speech saying, and I think I can remember this exactly, 'Our new government's foundations are laid, and its corner-stone rests, upon the great truth that the negro is not equal to the white man; that slavery, subordination to the superior race, is his natural and normal condition.'

"And that shocking line from John Marshall of Texas," Ira added. "'It is essential to the honor and safety of every poor white man to keep the negro in his present state of subordination and discipline.' It is patently clear that this war is about slavery. Like you, we believe that the abolition of slavery is a cause worth fighting for."

"Fighting for, yes," Pa said. "Dying for, no. If one of you doesn't make it back it will break my heart."

He stood, brushing crumbs from his shirtfront and clearing his throat. As Belden got up he thought he saw a tear in the corner of his father's eye.

"Well, lads," Pa said, "let's spread some of the farmer's gold onto this fair field. We must feed that which feeds us, in balanced reci-procity. We are the stewards of this Earth. Hold a moment and look down and tell me what you see."

Ira and Belden exchanged a quick glance. They knew what was coming.

"Mud Creek, Pa," Ira said.

"Do you see any boats in Mud Creek, plying their way down to the markets of the larger cities?"

"No, sir," the two boys said, in unison, feeling like actors speaking their lines.

"And why is that?" Pa asked.

"Lack of proper stewardship," Belden said. "The Good Lord gave Man dominion over the land, to preserve and replenish it, to pass it on to future generations, yet Man has used it carelessly."

"The early settlers, yourself excepted," Ira said, "cut down almost all their trees, leaving few to hold the earth steady. Erosion of the hillsides commenced, filling Mud Creek with effluvia and rendering it impassable. So now we must send our produce to Hammondsport by horse and wagon."

Pa looked at them, one after the other.

"I've told you this before, haven't I?"

"More than once, Pa," Belden and Ira said together, grinning.

"Just wait till you get white hair," Pa said.

2
———

THE DANCE

I ra and Belden lolled in large tin tubs of warm water in front of the parlor fireplace. No fire this evening, which was still sultry. The tubs had been hot for Ma and Helen, then Pa. The boys always bathed last. They'd added a couple buckets of hot water to that which was now lukewarm.

"In those Mahometan countries of the East," Ira said, soaping up his underarms, "it's the women who bathe last. I believe the same is true of the Hindoos and the Japanois."

"Well, that makes no sense at all," Belden replied. "It's us men that get the dirtiest. Helen doesn't even leave a soap ring."

"I believe, brother dear, that it's a question of what these peoples perceive—and this is them, not something I countenance, mind you--as the inner dirt rather than the outer."

"You're making that up."

"Sadly, no. In many foreign lands, women in their moon cycle must leave the village and live in a separate hut."

"How do you find out such peculiar facts, Ira?"

"I read widely. Are you blushing?"

"No, that's all the inner dirt in the water suffusing me."

"Must you always be so disgusting?"

"Me? You're the one fabricating such fantastic lies," Belden said, laughing. Ira was so easy—and so much fun--to tease.

They were quiet for some time.

"Ma hasn't said another word about us enlisting," Ira said at last.

"Oh, she will," Belden said, submerging his head as if to shut out the words he feared were coming. He hated having Ma mad at him. He'd rather be stung by a hive of hornets. He rubbed his scalp fiercely for a bit before resurfacing.

"Charlie Ide says his pa, old Julius, maintains it as a fact that if you massage your scalp a minute every day you'll never go bald," he said.

"The Cranes don't go bald anyway," Ira said. "Nor do the Ides. So Charlie and Julius are bound to be right. I think it's the way we are born rather than how we effort."

"Charlie wants to sign up, too," Belden said, "but his Ma made him promise to wait till he's at least eighteen."

"He's Helen's age."

"Same grade, but I think he might be a year younger."

"Charlie's a good egg," Ira said. "Make a good brother-in-law."

"The best. You know something I don't?"

"Nope. But they get on. How's Cinder taking it that you're enlisting next week?"

Belden sighed and dunked himself again before answering.

"Haven't told her yet. Tonight's the night. About signing next week, I mean. As you know, we've been arguing about my enlisting for at least a year. She's dead set against it."

Ira gave a low whistle.

"Boy, you're gonna get boiled in oil."

"I understand she's afraid I'll get killed. Why can't she understand that I owe my country and the Negro this service? She's as fierce an abolitionist as any of us."

"She doesn't want to lose you, Bel. Tell her you understand that."

* * *

Scrubbed and brushed and dressed in crisp white shirts and their best and only suits, Belden and Ira walked down toward the brightly-lit schoolhouse, from which the strains of fiddle and bow floated up to them.

When they came in through the doorway together, several familiar faces turned to them with shouted greetings. These were the boys and girls they had known their entire lives. They'd attended church and social functions together since before any of them could remember and then gone to school in this same building from first through eighth grade. By the time any of them had been old enough to think about pretending to be something different, it had been too late. Everyone knew everyone pretty well and viewed major character change with skepticism.

Micah Silvernail's daughter Lucia, who everyone called Cinder for reasons no one could recall, popped out of the crowd and seized Belden's hand. She was dark-haired and slim, with arresting dark eyes and a warm wide smile.

"You've come at last!" she said. "Dance with me! Evening, Ira!"

With that she pulled Belden out onto the floor and came into his arms with an eagerness that always excited him. Ira smiled and slipped away from the dance floor, which had been created by pushing the students' desks to the far side of the room. He edged up to where the two man band of Harry Merriman on the fiddle and Jim Givens on the penny whistle were doing their best to carry the tune. Jim stopped fingering the whistle long enough to greet him with handshake and grin. They put their heads together for a moment, laughing as if at some joke, and then Ira headed for the punch bowl.

Standing over the bowl and scooping himself what was clearly not his first cup of punch was Jesse Munsen, Jr., his face a floral red. Ira had never understood why the people of Bradford called Indians "red-skins" when he'd never seen an Indian who wasn't some shade of brown. Only whites' skin actually turned red, from the sun or from drink, as Jesse's had now. Rather than scooping another cupful for Ira,

Jesse purposefully dropped the scoop into the bowl so the handle was deep into the punch.

"Well, well," he sneered, "if it isn't some of the dumb cannon fodder of Bradford. Have you accepted the King's sovereign yet?"

Having grown up with Jesse, Ira was accustomed to his jibes, though he had never liked them, or him.

When they had attended this very school, Jesse was the kid who brownnosed the bigger kids and bullied the smaller ones. Belden and Ira had more than once chased him off from tormenting some younger, smaller boy or girl. And God help the girl whose mother braided her hair before school. The day Jesse had yanked Helen's braids, Ira, normally never a scrapper, had knocked him to the ground.

Jesse came from a family of shrewd Danes who owned half the town: the mill, the only dry goods store ("Dry Goods, Crockery and Glassware, Boots, Shoes, Yankee Notions, &c."), large tracts of land, several rentals, even the cemetery. They drove hard bargains on all their dealings. The joke was that when the Munsens buried you, they saved sewing costs since there was no need for pockets in your shroud.

His father, also Jesse Munsen, had been the State Senator since Ira could remember, a Democrat and Pa's principal antagonist at town meetings. Old Jesse was a firm believer in letting the Confederacy secede and stay slave. "Let 'em go and good riddance!" he'd said more than once.

"We enlist next week," Ira said, reaching for the scoop with two fingers. "But I don't think they hand you a sovereign any more, and certainly not the King's. When Abe institutes the draft, how much will you have to pay to buy a substitute?"

"As much as it takes," Jesse said. "I won't throw my life away for a bunch of ignorant niggers. They aren't even human."

"So you say, like all racists," Ira replied.

"I recognize I am a member of the superior race, unlike you and Belden. You're nothing but Levelers. Is he going with you?" Jesse asked, pointing to the couple on the dance floor with his chin.

"Unless Cinder talks him out of it."

"I hope he's man enough to say no to her, cuz once he's out of the picture I'm gonna swoop in on her like a chickenhawk."

"You always did have delusions of grandeur," Ira said. "Please excuse me."

And with that Ira walked away to join a circle of friends.

* * *

Cinder and Belden spun like a top across the roughhewn oak boards of the schoolhouse floor, their faces shining. Couples moved back to give them space to maneuver, beginning to clap in time to the music, enjoying the grace of two of their favorite young friends, who they all expected to marry up soon, so perfectly matched did they seem. When Harry and Jim brought the jig to a ragged close, the onlookers erupted in applause for both music and dance.

Belden tugged at Cinder's hand.

"Let's step outside," he said.

Without hesitation, she ran out through the doorway hand in hand with him into the night.

The fresh air cooled their faces after the heat of the schoolhouse stuffed with revelers. The nightsky was festooned with stars. Slowing to a walk, they navigated by the starlight around the schoolhouse. Beyond the schoolhouse was a storage shed, its door secured by a padlock. They went behind the shed, which put it between them and the schoolhouse, and kissed with a terrible hunger. Belden pushed Cinder up against the back wall of the shed and ran his hands down her sides and flanks. Cinder reached down and pulled up her long skirt. She wore nothing beneath it. Her thighs gleamed white in the starlight, framing the dark triangle between them. She was hot and wet to his touch. He unbuttoned his trousers and thrust himself into her. Her body bucked and trembled and a small scream escaped her open mouth. He clapped his right hand over her mouth and she screamed more fully into it, again and again, her body writhing against his, her eyes squeezed tightly shut. With a sudden intake of breath, he pulled himself out of her and his seed pumped in spasms against her thigh. Then they both collapsed onto the ground as if the sinews in their legs had been severed. They held each other tight, panting like long distance runners.

After what seemed a long time, Cinder murmured something, her lips moving against his cheek.

"Couldn't make that out," he said.

"I long for the day when you needn't pull out of me," she whispered.

"That will be a blessed day," he said.

"Let's not wait any longer," she said, suddenly animated, taking his face between her hands. "Let's get married and have children."

He sighed, a long exhalation

"Cin, you know I want to marry you one day and have lots of babies. And you know that I need to do my duty to our country first."

She pulled back and looked into his eyes. Hers seemed to redden.

"I thought you'd given that up!"

He looked at her for a long moment. His jaw hardened.

"We've been over this a hundred times," he said, a note of sad determination in his voice.

She scrambled to her feet and roughly slapped the debris from her skirt. He got up more slowly.

"Is being a soldier more important than a life with me?" she spat. Though he couldn't see them in the dark, he knew her eyes were full of tears.

"Of course not," he said. "You know how important both are to me. I just have to do the soldiering first. Ira and I are going to enlist next week."

"You're going to...well, don't expect me to be waiting for you when you get done, if you're still alive!" she said, her voice breaking. "For how long are you enlisting?"

"Three years."

"Three years? *Three years?!*"

He tried to take her into his arms but she fended him off.

"I hate you!" she hissed.

"You do not," he said. "You love me, and I you. But we are not the only people in this tormented world. Our Negro brothers and sisters need us to fight this fight for them, for now and for all time."

"I won't wait for you!" she said again and, sobbing, ran off into the darkness.

Belden felt his anger rise. The next to last thing he ever wanted to do was to hurt Cinder. The last thing he wanted to do was to shirk his duty, as he saw it. He felt as if his guts were being yanked from him by two teams of horses pulling in opposite directions.

He was ashamed to find tears running down his own cheeks.

* * *

"Knock, knock," came Ira's voice from the other side of the shed.

"*Viens*," Belden said, whipping his face. Ira sauntered around the corner.

"Where's Cinder?"

"She ran off, probably home. She hates me."

Ira chuckled.

"You told her? She hates you for the moment. She'll love you again tomorrow."

"I doubt it," Belden said. "She seemed pretty sure this time. Let's go back to the dance."

"Okay," Ira said, "though you might want to button up first."

Belden glanced down.

"I think I'll take your advice," he said.

"Or not," Ira replied. "I have it on good authority that the eminent creator of the first dictionary, Dr. Samuel Johnson, who was a great drinker of the claret, necessitating many trips to the loo, would grow weary of unbuttoning and rebuttoning at a long party and simply leave his trousers unbuttoned. On one trip back from the loo he even forgot to put his member back into his trousers. A high-toned lady of the nobility intercepted him and did him the courtesy of informing him of his oversight.

"'Dr. Johnson,' she said, "I must inform you that your penis is sticking from your trousers!'

"Unfazed, Dr. Johnson looked down at himself, then back up at the good lady.

"'Madame,' he said. 'You flatter yourself. It is not sticking, it is hanging.'

"And with that *bon mot* he returned to the claret table."

Belden completed his task. He brushed his clothing with both hands.

"Ira," he said, "you are getting to be worse than Pa. That is a marvelous story, which you have told me at least half a dozen times. I know you are attempting to cheer me, but I am beyond cheering. In fact, I think I'll just head home. Go back to the dance and enjoy yourself."

Ira looked at him for a moment.

"As you wish," he said. "If Cinder is there, what do you want me to tell her?"

"She won't be. But, on the off chance that she is, don't tell her anything unless you want your face slapped."

"The fiery gypsy lass."

"She is all of that. Goodnight, dear brother."

* * *

When Belden got home, only Helen was still up, working by lantern light at the kitchen table on a charcoal drawing of her mother's face. Gently holding her shoulders, he gave her a kiss on the top of her head. Her hair always smelled like a baby's, he thought.

"Good job!" he said. "I can tell it's Ma. Why weren't you at the dance?"

"Charlie wasn't going to be there."

"You're sweet on Charlie Ide."

She looked up at him over one shoulder.

"How many other choices do I have? And, yes, I am sweet on him."

"Point taken."

"How're you and Cinder?"

Belden sighed.

"She's mad at me. Says she won't wait."

"She won't. She's not the waiting kind."

"You would."

"Doesn't make me better. Just different."

Belden nodded slowly.

"Yes," he said.

He took down his painting-in-progress from its hook on the wall and placed it on the table across from his sister. From his shelf he took the Persian blue and took off the cap, set it beside the painting, then pumped a tin cup half full of water from the small pump at the sink.

"How do you feel about it?" he asked, sitting across from her and dipping his horsehair brush in the cup of water, then in the paint.

"You and Ira enlisting? Two ways. I'm proud of you both...and I scared I'll lose you."

"Don't be. You know we're invincible."

He began filling in the sky of his painting. Where would he place the clouds to give the composition balance? One would take the shape of a stag.

"I know you think you are," she said. "And I've heard that pride cometh before a fall."

"Ouch," he said.

3

BREAKFAST

The following morning when Ma came in she gave Belden a kiss on the cheek as she usually did before pumping water into the coffee pot. Belden watched her from beneath his brow to get a sense of her mood. He knew Pa had probably told her of their discussion. After grinding the dark beans with the old hand grinder, she dumped the grounds directly into the pot and set it on the stovetop with a bang. Uh-oh. Yanking open the door to the fire, she shoved more split pine kindling onto the coals. She detached the big cast iron skillet from its hook in the overhead beam, clattered it down onto the castiron stovetop, and threw in slabs of bacon. Soon the bacon was crackling and she poured off some of the grease into the smaller skillet and began cracking in eggs with ferocity.

Belden looked up from his Blackstone at the unusual level of racket Ma was making. Her back seemed stiff as his new ramrod. He sighed. He knew what was probably coming.

When the coffee began to boil, she moved the pot to a cooler part of the stove and broke an egg into it to gather the grounds from the liquid.

Helen came in, yawning, and kissed first Ma and then Belden

before beginning to set the table with the silverware that bore her mother's name and the date of 1847. Her father had parted with a goodly sum to the Rogers Brothers silversmiths for his wife's tenth anniversary present and insisted that they use the beautifully-crafted utensils for everyday use. Helen loved the heft of them in her hands.

Pa clomped down the stairs next. He kissed everyone all around.

"Where's Ira?" he asked in his deep voice, always deeper in the morning.

"Slug-a-bed," Helen replied.

Pa turned back and shouted up the stairwell: "This is a day which the Lord hath made! Let us rejoice and be glad in it!"

Ira stumbled down the stairs in his bathrobe, hair poking up in twenty directions, rubbing sleep from his eyes, and kissed everyone before taking his seat at the table and accepting a mug of coffee. This family tradition had earned them the sobriquet of "the Kissing Cranes" in the county, to distinguish them from the many other Cranes. This sobriquet was not always used with admiration, for it was, truth to tell, a custom strange to many of those descended from the original Puritans. The Cranes had made the Atlantic passage neither on the *Mayflower* with John Alden nor on the *Arabella* with John Winthrop but on a later ship whose name no one could remember. Finding the Plymouth Colony too rigid for their liking, most of the Cranes had soon begun moving westward, purchasing land from the Indians with fathoms of wampum.

These Indians, who did not share the palefaces' concept of private property, signed their X to the scraps of parchment on which the whites seemed to place such value and happily received their kind gifts of wampum and steel knives. A few months later, when they walked into a "land owner's" well-chinked cabin and lifted the lid on the cooking pot bubbling over the fire to see what was for dinner, they were surprised that their new neighbors seemed so upset. They concluded that the palefaces must all be crazy.

Belden put a bookmark in his Blackstone and set it back on the shelf beside the huge family Bible and *The Collected Works of*

William Shakespeare as Ma and Helen began placing plates with bacon and eggs on the table.

There was a polite knock at the kitchen door, which then was opened by a young man of eighteen or so. He had dark hair and eyes and an olive complexion.

"*Bonjour!*" he said.

"*Bonjour!*" the Cranes sang back.

"*Comment t'allez vous?*"

"*Tres bien, et vous?*"

This was Eugene Gascone, the French Canadian who had apprenticed himself to the Cranes as an indentured servant. He slept in the small bunkhouse near the barn that would fill up at harvest season with another three field hands. Part of his job was to teach the Crane children French, though only Belden seemed to have any facility with the nasal accent. He took his place at the foot of the table.

After Pa sat down at the head, everyone sat and took their neighbors' hands, forming a circle. Heads bowed.

"Father, we thank you for this which we are about to receive," Pa said. "We ask that these Thy gifts give us the strength to do those things which we ought to do and to shun those things we ought not do. In the name of the Father, the Son, and the Holy Ghost. Amen."

The last word echoed around the table and everyone looked to Ma. Only when she lifted her fork did they pick up theirs to dig in. Ma was a stickler for manners. Though her children might be living in the wilderness, she wanted them to feel comfortable in the social circles of New York or Boston.

Having grown up with these little rituals, Belden had taken them for granted. Only recently had it dawned on him that not everyone followed the same formalities. At his friend Lew Whitehead's family meals, each person clasped their own hands for a moment of silent prayer. While he knew that the Rebs prayed to the same God, he had begun to wonder how they did it—and whether they asked Him to protect their human property. It didn't make sense that the same God could be both for and against slavery at the same time. Yet the Rebs maintained slavery was sanctioned by the Bible and therefore their God-given right. Belden had read his Bible and, yes, found mention of slaves, for slavery had been the custom back in those ancient days, but he saw no commandment supporting it and there were several stories featuring freeing slaves. If you truly practiced the Golden Rule that Jesus had articulated, how could you treat anyone as a slave? Only if you defined the Negro not as human but as animal, as many South-erners did. That seemed to Belden as the crassest and most self-serving kind of rationalization.

Ira had defined "rationalize" for him: "You must understand, Bel, that it's really two words—'rational lies.' It's the lies people tell them-selves that they pretend are rational."

As these sundry thoughts paraded through his mind, Belden was aware of a nagging feeling of guilt pushing up: He shouldn't have made love to Cinder before telling her that he was going to enlist. At the least, he should have told her first. He'd been selfish.

He tried to dismiss the feeling, but it continued to gnaw at him.

"I am sorry," Ma said, "but I cannot hold my tongue any longer."

She glared first at Ira, then Belden, while moving the ring with the tiny diamond up and down her finger. Though she never took the ring off, when she moved it up toward the top of her ring finger, her chil-dren became anxious. What would happen if it ever came off? It was a symbol of her dedication to her marriage and the whole family. Both of her boys set down their forks. Belden stared at the name "Emily" inscribed on his.

"Mr. Crane has told me that you two are bound and determined to go off and get yourselves killed. Well! Well...just remember the mouse!"

She stood abruptly, knocking her chair over backward, and, sobbing, ran from the room.

Shocked, Ira and Belden looked at Pa. They had seen their mother weep only once before in their lives, and that had been from joy.

"Remember the mouse?" Belden asked.

"I'll go see if I can comfort her," Ira said, getting up.

"Leave her be," Pa said. "She'll be back."

Ira sat back down.

Pa sighed.

"When you lads were quite small you made a pet of a mouse. When it died you were heartbroken."

"We had a pet mouse?" Belden said. "I don't remember."

"I do," Ira said. "We'd named it Sir Lancelot, though we were never quite certain of the gender. He—or she—lived behind the baseboard of our room and would come into bed to sleep with us on cold nights. We fed it bits of cheese. Ma said it would give us the plague like the one that was raging in China."

"So is Ma saying that as we were heartbroken over Sir Lancelot's death, so she would be over ours?" Belden asked.

"The trope may be less than exact," Ira said. "I don't think she sees us as small and flea-infested."

"Do not mock your mother," Pa said in the quiet voice they all knew meant they were treading on dangerous ground.

"I'm afraid for you as well," Helen said, rising to fetch the coffeepot and fill their mugs. "The numbers of the dead and wounded I read in the paper are beyond my comprehension. 460 of our boys and 387 of theirs killed in one day! That would wipe out the entire population of Bradford!"

Belden and Ira looked at one another across the table. Ira gave a tiny shake of his head. Belden knew what he meant and kept his mouth shut.

Though Eugene never looked up from his plate during the entire discussion, he listened carefully to all that was said. His superiors in Quebec had sent him south to gather information about the attack on Canada that some in the U.S. Congress were agitating for. How he was expected to discover such plots on a small farm in the Finger Lakes region of western New York even he could not explain. But Captain Maurois had been very clear in his sibilant Quebecois French: "Seek work as a laborer with William B. Crane, an important spokesman in the Republican Party and a close friend of Secretary of State Seward. Keep your ears open for any talk of an invasion."

* * *

There was a knock at the back door. At first Belden thought it was Ma, then realized how silly that was. Of course Ma had no cause to knock at her own door. Helen rose to see who it was. She came back with a strange expression on her pretty face.

"It's Cinder for you, Bel, and I don't think she's happy. I invited her in but she said no."

Belden sighed and rose from the table. Ira shot him a look of compassion. Pa was studying the bottom of his coffee cup as if the swirls held prophecies.

He found Cinder pacing back and forth in the back yard between Ma's herb garden and the outhouse. She looked angry. There was no sign of Ma.

She turned to face him and spoke in a harsh voice he hardly recognized as hers. It sounded as if she were possessed by a witch of Salem.

"I assume that you haven't changed your mind about enlisting?"

"Cinder, please..."

"Have you or haven't you?!"

Belden took a deep breath.

"I have not."

"Then hear me: I will marry Jesse Munsen."

"You would never do such a thing."

"Oh, you don't know me, Belden Crane! The day you leave here I will give him my consent. Do not write me letters, for I shall burn any I receive. Go and serve the damn country and do your damn duty and forget about me!"

With that she turned and ran down the path to the road. He stood immobilized for a moment, stunned by her language: He had never heard her use a curse word before.

"Cinder!" Belden yelled after her. He didn't try to pursue her for he knew well that she could outrun him—or anyone in Bradford. He felt his heart pounding in his chest. He felt awful. He had hurt her so deeply that she only wanted to hurt him back, and she would marry a man she—and just about everyone in town--despised. Though he had never seen it before, he had heard of cases of what was coming to be called "temporary insanity," in which seemingly normal people did insane things for a brief period. He could only hope that she would come to her senses before doing anything rash.

He heard the door to the outhouse creak and looked around to see his mother walking towards him. Cinder was not the only one he had hurt.

Ma came up to him and placed a gentle hand on his cheek. Her face was twisted with agony for his grief, not just her own.

"I heard it all," she said. "She'll change her mind. She's not a flighty girl."

"God, I hope so," Belden said, and fell into her arms as he had so many times as a little boy.

The next day, he and Ira left to enlist.

4

THE DEATH OF UNCLE JIM

The tragedy occurred almost a month after Ira and Belden had left Bradford. The harvests were mostly gathered into the barns and root cellars. There was a coolness to the night air that hinted at the approach of autumn.

The cry of "Fire!" woke many in the town around midnight. The bell at the Fire Station tolled and all the able-bodied men who heard it tumbled out of bed and into their boots. Pegasus, the old nag who drew the wagon carrying the buckets, ladders, and shovels comprising Bradford's defense against fire, was put in her traces and led by means of a lump of sugar in a backward-jogging volunteer fireman's palm to the blaze. Uncle Jim's shack was pretty much a sheet of flame by the time the bucket brigade attempted to form a line and toss water on it, but at least the B.F.D. prevented the inferno from spreading.

No one was more thankful than old Micah Silvernail, Cinder's father, who lived in the house next door to Jim's in what was known as "South Bradford." Although the lots in this section of town were smaller and cheaper than those in the town's center, the Munsens collected the rents on most of them. The house that Cinder had grown up in was a white clapboard, like so many in the town, with a steep roof designed to shed snow. Micah had paid for it with gold when he arrived in Bradford with his pregnant bride Bildad. The town fathers had debated the wisdom of allowing a Jew to buy real estate until old Jesse Senior, who acted as mayor when he wasn't representing the district in the State Senate, had argued that Micah Silvernail was really a Gypsy and not a Jew. William Crane believed that Jesse Senior's sophistry had less to do with Micah's supposed ancestry than the gold ingots that he had conjured as if by magic from his weathered saddlebags.

"You should have seen the way his face lit up when he saw those ingots," he told Emily and Helen. "At that moment he forgot what he'd been saying about Jews being responsible for the death of Our Lord, which argument never made a lick of sense to me, or to Rev. Atwill, for what it's worth."

Emily nodded.

"It was the Roman pontiff, Pontius Pilate, who railroaded Him in a sham trial," she said. "The Jews were powerless in Israel of that time. The Romans put down their occasional rebellions with an iron fist. Small-minded people have from time immemorial had a need to divide humanity into us and them, Jews and Gentiles, black and white, North and South."

William smiled at his wife.

"How did you get so smart?" he asked.

"Someone made the mistake of letting me learn how to read."

"Yes," Helen added. "Some people even try to make a similar political division between men and women. It's high time we get the vote."

Her father turned his smile upon her.

"And you are just the young woman to help lead that cause," he said. "When you were a mewling babe we took you with us to Seneca Falls to hear Elizabeth Cady Stanton speak. Oh, she was eloquent and persuasive! You must have imbibed her words with your mother's milk. I have been fortunate indeed to know so many brilliant women. Any one of them makes Jesse Senior seem an imbecile."

* * *

Gold had swayed Jesse Sr. and thus the council in Micah's favor and when, a few years later an escaped Negro slave had appeared in town as if he had leapt fully formed from one of the larger trees in the surrounding forest, that same council was not opposed to allowing him to rent the shack next to the Silvernail residence. The neighborhood had already gone downhill.

"Uncle Jim," as he came to be known, was, when sober, a gentle and peaceable soul who earned his bread by hiring himself out to do odd jobs. He was a tireless worker who could do anything on a farm, and he was also adept at carpentry—a good man to have at hand when you were raising a barn.

But there was another side to Uncle Jim, a side that made a good argument for the many temperance movement people in Bradford, including Emily Crane: When Jim got drunk, he seemed to transmogrify into a different person. Although he'd take his jar of Munsen white lightning into the privacy of his shack, it wasn't long before all of South Bradford would hear him. He began with Negro spirituals that he sang basso profundo with an enthusiasm that the Silvernails, at least, found to be entertaining. Soon, however, the singing gave way to the most blasphemous cursing that anyone in South Bradford had ever heard—it sounded to Mrs. Morse as though "the Devil himself had escaped the fires of Hell." Next could be heard the sounds of breaking furniture and unearthly growling.

Uncle Jim was always penitent the next morning. He'd go round to his neighbors and apologize, saying he didn't know what had gotten into him. (Mrs. Morse knew, of course, that it was possession by the Dark Lord himself.) He'd spend the rest of the day repairing the furniture he'd broken in what he called his "fit," and then he would seem his usual soft-spoken self for a week or a month, when it would all happen again.

At the Silvernails' request, Emily Crane decided to pay Jim a visit. She put on her white gloves to do so.

"Jim," she said, once they'd discussed the weather, "you're a good man when you're off the demon drink."

"Yessum," Jim said, looking down at his feet, which were shod in a castoff pair of William Crane's boots.

"But when you imbibe white lightning, you cause a terrible ruckus."

"Yessum. And I'm terrible sorry for it."

"So why not just give it up?"

"I tries, Missus Crane, I tries. But somethin' just builds up and builds up inside of me and I just gotta let it out. It rides on that white lightnin' right out my mouf."

"Oh, Jim, there must be another way."

"If you cipher out what that be, you let me know, Missus Crane."

"Jim, forgive me if I'm being too forward—but what happened to your wife and children?"

When he looked up at her his eyes were black with grief.

"Oh, Missus Crane, massa done sold my wife and chilluns down the river. Don't know where at. That's why I done run off."

* * *

After much debate about the cause of the fire, popular opinion concluded that Uncle Jim must have been drunk and knocked over a coal-oil lantern. But why, Emily wondered, had he stayed within a burning building? Popular opinion had a ready answer: too drunk.

Emily talked to Helen about it.

"I need to hear myself think," she said. "I just need a good listener."

"Sure, Ma. Can I knit this sweater while you're talking? I'm making Bel and Ira each one."

"Good idea. They'll warm the boys this winter and idle hands are the devil's workshop."

She paused and seemed to consider, then pressed on.

"I'm quite perturbed by Jim's death. I can't believe that he wouldn't flee a fire. Certainly, he might have been inebriated. But that's never prevented him from being able to break up the furniture. If you can bust up a chair you can open a door and step outside."

Helen nodded. Her fingers flew with the clicking knitting needles.

"So," Ma continued, "if it wasn't a drunken accident...someone must have killed him."

Helen stopped knitting. She looked up into her mother's startled eyes. Ma must have not realized that until she said it out loud.

"I can't believe what I just said," Ma added. "We haven't had a killing in this town since Mrs. Knickerbocker shot her husband when he was trying to sneak in the back door. And the jury let her off scot free."

"But if Jim was killed," Helen whispered, "who would do such a thing?"

Emily shook herself, like a dog ridding itself of water.

"Who would benefit from Jim's death?" she asked. "We must think like Pinkerton detectives."

Now Helen's eyes grew wide.

"The Munsens?" she asked. "They'd set fire to their own property?"

Ma's face was white. She nodded, then stood and began pacing the floor.

"They'd benefit in several ways," she said. "First, they'd remove the nuisance Jim was causing to their other renters in South Bradford. Second, they'd be able to collect on the property insurance on the shack—and you know they'd overvalue it. Pa told me they recently bought coverage for all their properties from the Philadelphia Contributorship, the company Ben Franklin started back in the middle of the last century. You know the insurers wouldn't send an agent to check the value of buildings up here in western New York. So, like they always do, the Munsens would make a profit. Third, they now have a cleared lot where they can rebuild a better rental and gouge some other family that's too poor to buy their own place."

"No one likes the Munsens," Helen said, "but whoever dispatched

Jim had to have killed him or at least knocked him unconscious first. Hard to believe they'd do that to him."

"Let's talk to Cinder," Ma said. "She lives next door and might have noticed something."

Helen grinned.

"We'll be the Lady Pinkertons," she said.

"Come up with a better name," Ma said.

* * *

Cinder met them at the front door. If she was surprised she didn't show it.

"I've just put the kettle on," she said. "Let's have some tea. Who wants raspberry honey in theirs?"

Everyone took raspberry honey.

"What news of Belden, and Ira?" Cinder asked.

"They were mustered in on the 11th of August," Helen said, "and took the train down to the District of Columbia on the 13th. Belden's in K Company with Lew Whitehead and Jack Knickerbocker."

"I pity their commanding officer," Cinder said.

"They elected Alan Sill their captain," Helen said.

"A good choice. And Ira?"

"He's applied to become a male nurse," Emily said. "He wrote that he'll receive training at a hospital in Baltimore. And what of you, Cinder? We heard you're going to marry Jesse Junior."

Cinder looked out the window.

"We're already married," she said, very quietly. "In a private ceremony."

Neither other woman said a thing for a long moment.

"We hope that you'll be very happy," Emily managed at last.

Helen nodded. Cinder said nothing.

Everyone took a sip of sweet tea.

"We wondered," Emily began, "if you heard or saw anything the night of the fire. Before the fire, I mean."

Cinder stood and walked to the window that overlooked the spot where Uncle Jim's shack had stood. Black ash and a stone foundation were all that remained. Even the stick-and-wattle chimney was gone.

She shivered, as if someone had walked over her grave.

"That was awful," she said. "He really was a very kind man."

"We think someone might have killed him," Helen said.

Cinder didn't blink.

"Of course someone did," she said. "But we didn't see or hear anything unusual that night. It's a mystery."

Helen smiled.

"Would you like to join the Lady Pinkertons?"

"What an awful name!" Cinder said. "It sounds like an underwear store. How about, hmm, the Bradford Sleuths?"

* * *

The Bradford Sleuths walked from the Silvernails' over to where Uncle Jim's shack had formerly stood.

"There's not much to work with," Cinder said.

"Just a lot of yucky black ash," Helen said, "which I have no intention of wading into."

"They took away what was left of his body," Cinder said. "And started right off debating the propriety of burying his remains in the heretofore all-white cemetery. That'll keep them busy for a week or two."

"Them," of course, meant the all-male, all-white town council.

"They keep us from voting or being a part of governing," Helen said, "but they can't stop us from solving crimes."

Emily Crane was walking a widening gyre around the burned area. She stooped to pick up a square tin, the kind used to store coal-oil, from beneath a rhododendron.

"Looks like someone was an arsonist," she said. "And their name is stamped right on it for God and everyone to see."

"The Munsens," Helen said. "They burned his shack and him in it."

"Oh, I can't imagine that they'd do such a thing," Cinder said.

Helen caught her mother's eye. Cinder was already protective of her new family.

PART II

SAVE THE UNION, FREE THE SLAVES

5

SPIES

For the first week, Belden enjoyed Army life. Being issued a bright blue uniform and a shiny new Enfield .577 musket with an even shinier bayonet, sleeping in a tent, eating Army chow and sitting around a campfire at night—it was all a lark. He'd even bought himself a pistol—an Army Colt .44--with a chunk of his enlistment bonus.

"It's good to have back-up," he told Lew Whitehead. "Once you've fired your musket and stuck your bayonet into someone, you can bring out a pistol for the next Reb."

"Yeah," Lew said, "but what about the one after that?"

"It's a six-shooter. I can take down an entire squad."

The second week was all Drill: Forward March, To the Rear March, Port Arms, Fix Bayonets...they were all sick of nothing but Drill, from sunup to sundown, which, during these late summer days meant more than twelve hours. Drill and more Drill, but they had yet to fire their muskets once. So what that his Company, K, had won first place in the regimental drill contest. He'd signed up for a three year stint to save the Union and free the slaves and he wondered if he'd spend the entire time drilling.

He was sick of Drill, sick of sleeping in a muggy canvas tent with a low roof, sick of the food, sick of the Virginia mosquitoes, sick of being ordered around like a dog. He missed Ma's cooking, he missed Cinder, and now he missed Ira. And it hadn't even been three weeks since they'd enlisted back in Hornellsville. A bit more than two weeks down, one hundred fifty-four to go. He hadn't felt so trapped since he'd gotten lost in Peterson's Cave as a boy of six. It was Ira who'd pulled him out that time. Good old Ira.

Then one evening Belden apprehended a Rebel spy. That perked things up.

The spy wore a clever disguise: that of a chicken. A Rhode Island Red, to be exact, which besmirched the name of that Free State. He'd slipped into camp before supper—salt pork and beans again—and Belden had caught him with the sure hands of a farm boy, holding him upside down by his feet so he'd calm.

"Gentlemen," he said to his squadmates, who were already laughing and cheering, "I have apprehended this Rebel spy and I affirm that he has a right to a fair trial. You must sit in judgment. I charge him with entering our encampment without a pass, wearing a cunning disguise, and counting both our numbers and our weaponry. How say you? Guilty or not guilty?"

"Guilty!" they roared.

Belden tapped one of the log rounds they used for chairs with the butt of his pistol.

"Sir!" he intoned. "You have been found guilty by this court of disinterested citizens and are hereby condemned to death by bayonet. May God have mercy on your soul."

He set aside the Colt pistol—which he'd wisely not loaded yet—and took his bayonet from its scabbard on his left hip. He was surprised to find that it had a dull edge. He replaced the bayonet, wondering if it needed to be honed, and took out his clasp knife. Laying the chicken's head on the log chair, still holding the legs high with his left hand, with his right he drew the knife blade across the neck, separating head from body.

Spurting blood from the open neck, the chicken kicked free and ran, headless, around the campfire twice before collapsing into a twitching heap.

"*Sic semper tyrannis!*" Belden intoned. They were, after all, in Virginia and that state's motto seemed apt. "Now, who will volunteer to fashion this fine fellow with a coffin of clay?"

"I so volunteer!" said Jack Knickerbocker, who took a pail down to the riverbank to gather some clay.

Meanwhile, Belden gutted the chicken, tossing the offal onto the campfire.

When Jack returned with the clay, they caked the body, feathers and all, and set it among the coals to bake.

An hour later, when they nudged the now-baked clay coffin from the coals and broke it open, the smell of fresh chicken intoxicated them. Most of the feathers came away with the shards of clay.

"Now," Belden said, "though this be but a corporal disguise, I see no reason for us not to enjoy the fruits thereof."

And they set to work divvying up the tasty corpse among the former jury.

After they'd eaten, Lew said, "I move that we now visit the local tavern to drown our guilt from this terrible cannibalism."

* * *

The next morning when the bugler tried to roust them out with a spirited if somewhat jagged rendition of Reveille, Belden groaned and turned over on his cot, pulling the rough wool Army blanket up over his aching head despite the humid heat. Lew and Jack had introduced him to Busthead last night, purchased with their enlistment greenbacks from a disreputable shack not a mile from the training encampment. He was glad now Ira had chosen to leave K Company to join the nursing corps. Like his mother, Ira had strong opinions about the demon drink.

"Anyone who drinks strong liquor is a damn fool," Ira had said, more than once.

This morning, Belden tended to agree.

Ira wasn't even that Puritan about drink; he made an exception for wine. He was fond of quoting Ben Franklin's famous dictum that "The existence of wine is proof that God loves us and wants us to be happy."

Sergeant O'Malley stuck his red Irish face into the tent.

"Up, ye lazy louts! Or you'll feel the back a me hand on an ear! Up, up, up!"

Groaning in unison, four men in long johns rolled out of their cots and began pulling on their blue uniforms and Army-issued brogans. These "bear-traps" were constructed of rough, ankle-high leather with identical square toes, You could wear them on either foot, neither comfortably.

"Christ on a cross," moaned Jack Knickerbocker. "That's the end of drink for me."

"Don't take the Lord's name in vain," said Jacob Zimmerman.

Belden caught Lew Whitehead's eye. He nodded.

"Christ have mercy up-ooon us!" they sang in a counterpointed harmony. They had been in the choir together at St. Andrew's Episcopal Church. Belden was a baritone; Lew possessed an angelic tenor. Jacob was a member of a more austere Calvinist sect with vague origins in the High Alps of Germanic Switzerland. Its few members convened in the Zimmerman house on Sundays and adhered to incomprehensible tenets.

Jacob shook his head in disgust. He alone had refused the Bust-head and could shake his unsullied head without agony.

Together, they stumbled out of the gray canvas tent, pulling on their caps. It was another cloudy, muggy day. The sky looked like the greasy underside of one of the lids on the huge pots in which Cookie heated up their daily swill over the open fires. These fires, burning with green wood both day and night, poured out clouds of smoke that made them all cough, as many were doing now. Some Rebel wag had said that you could always tell where the Union soldiers were by listening for their coughs.

"Fall in!" shouted Sgt. O'Malley. "Dress right, dress! Ten-shun!"

Here we go again, Belden told himself. Another start to another boring day.

He could not have been further from the truth.

* * *

In Formation, Colonel Van Valkenburgh informed them that they would be packing up that day to move to Fort Lyon, in Alexandria. Any change sounded good to Belden.

After Formation, when Belden about-faced and was headed for the chow line, O'Malley shouted at him:

"Private Crane! Get your lily-white pretty boy's ass over here!"

Uh-oh, thought Belden. What have I done amiss now?

"Yessir?"

"I am no 'Sir,' Private. I am your Sergeant! Report to the HQ tent, Private Crane! Double-time!"

Yes-s...Sergeant."

I must be in big trouble, he thought as he jogged across the flattened grass of the encampment on the gentle hill. He could see the Potomac River and the Whited Sepulchers, as he thought of them, of the Government buildings across it. When he arrived at the Headquarters tent, which was five times the size of the one he slept in, he came to attention in front of the three-striper at the tent flap and, remembering not to salute a sergeant or call him sir, said:

"Private Belden Crane reporting as instructed."

"At ease, Private. The general is busy at the moment."

Belden gulped. The general! That would be Gen. Slocum, in charge of the entire 107th New York Volunteers. What could the general possibly want with him?

What seemed like an hour was probably only five minutes. Belden rehearsed how he would enter the general's tent, come to attention, salute, the words he would say. He found that his palms were sweating. It was this blasted Virginian humidity, he told himself.

"You, Crane! The general will see you now!"

Removing his cap and placing it in the crook of his left arm, Belden pushed past the tent flap into the dim interior. As he saluted Gen. Slocum and nearly shouted "Private Crane reporting as instructed, Sir!" he noticed from the corner of his eye that a second man, this one in civvies, stood a few feet to the right of the general. As his eyes flicked to this man, he realized with a start that he knew him. The prominent nose and brow distinguished him. He was Belden's idea of what a Roman Senator must have looked like. It was his father's old friend, William Seward, Lincoln's Secretary of State. A staunch Republican and strong anti-slavery man who had almost won the nomination for President.

"Secretary Seward!" he blurted, feeling like a fool for not knowing the protocol in this circumstance. He dropped his salute and reached out his right hand. Smiling, the Secretary shook it. Gen. Slocum cleared his throat.

"At ease, Private," he said.

Taking the clue, Belden went into Parade Rest, feet apart, hands clasped behind his back holding his cap, eyes front.

"Secretary Seward has asked to speak to you without me being present," Slocum said. "I will go take a pipe."

Ignoring Belden's salute, the general pulled a leather tobacco pouch from beneath a pile of maps on his table and left the tent.

Seward chuckled.

"Relax, Belden," he said. "You don't need to stand on ceremony with me. You've known me since you were in knickers."

Belden remembered the day his father had taken him and Ira to Albany to meet the then Senator. They'd all worn their best clothes and brushed their cowlicks till they mostly lay down.

"Yessir. How are you, sir?"

Seward sighed.

"I'd be a passel better if our generals could win a battle or two. That's why I've asked to speak to you. I want you to help us win the next one."

Belden's mind reeled. How could he possibly help win an entire battle? Well, if Henry Seward, as his father had always called him, had faith in him, he probably could do whatever was necessary.

"What I'm about to ask of you is highly dangerous and of the utmost secrecy. You are under no obligation to take what I am about to propose as an order of any kind. Do you understand me, Belden?"

"I think so, sir. You're going to make a proposal I am free not to accept."

"Exactly. How would you like to be a spy?"

Belden actually grinned, thinking of the chicken.

"Love to, sir. Just tell me what you need."

Secretary Seward pulled one of the maps on Slocum's table toward them.

"We are here, in Arlington Heights."

Belden bent over the map. He had always loved maps and now relished looking at a bird's eye view of the territory he'd been in for several days without knowing even the name of the hill he was camped on. Arlington Heights. On the map he could see the big islands in the Potomac and the precise grid of streets in the District of Columbia, with the numbered streets running north and south and the alphabetical streets east and west.

"I have a very important mission for you. For it, I want you to remove your uniform and dress in civvies. Then take a horse we shall provide along this road" —pointing a long forefinger at the map—"and make your way toward Manassas Junction, here. You will report to Gen. Pope there and present him with this sealed envelope, which you are to deliver to no other eyes but his."

Seward handed him a standard brown envelope with the words:

GEN. POPE'S EYES ONLY

written in cursive lettering across its front.

"General Pope will provide you with a rough map of the area he wishes you to explore around Bull Run. You are to leave your horse with his attendants and proceed on foot. Your mission is to find out how much of the Rebel artillery is actual, and how much is logs painted black, to mimic cannon. At our first engagement at Bull Run, back in '61, the Rebs fooled us by making us think they had twice the artillery they actually had. Here—"

Seward reached into a bag and brought forth a leather container.

"--are field glasses so you'll be able to ascertain which are fake from a distance. Stay far enough away so you are not apprehended. Any questions so far?"

"No, sir. I go in civvies on horseback, report to Gen. Pope, give him this letter, and count the number of cannon, actual and fake, in the area he sends me to, and report back to him."

"You've got the gist of it. Now, here's the hard part. Under the customary rules of war, spies may be shot. So don't get caught. However, in this so far 'civil' war, most spies are treated as enemy combatants and simply imprisoned. So, if you are caught, you can hope for that. Just don't count on it. I advise you not to get caught. If you are, we will say that you went off on a lark on your own, AWOL. Leave your weapons here with a friend. Is that clear? That is the tale you will tell if captured."

"Yessir. I was bored with Drill and wanted to see the Elephant."

"Excellent. Just please be clear. If you are caught you will be imprisoned, or shot. If you are successful, you will save hundreds, if not thousands, of Union soldiers' lives, but you will never be officially commended for this heroic act. Gen. Slocum left the tent so that he can have deniability. So far as you are concerned, he knows nothing of your escapade. Only you, I, and Gen. Pope will know. Are we clear?"

"Perfectly, sir."

"Private Crane, do you accept this mission?"

"Yes, sir. With all my heart. Thank you, sir, for this opportunity."

The Secretary chuckled and shook Belden's hand.

"I knew I could count on you, Belden. And when you return, I'd like you to drop by the State Department to visit me and tell me how it went. I wish you Godspeed."

It was only much later, as he trotted down the Warrenton Turnpike on an Army nag after packing up his kit and entrusting it to Lew Whitehead, that Belden wondered why his mission had come not from

Ed Stanton, the Secretary of War, but from the Secretary of State. Then it seemed obvious: Send the man whom he knew and trusted. Though he would have said yes to whoever had offered him this mission.

Not only was he going to get out of Drill, he was going to do something important. He was going to be a hero. Ira would be green with envy.

* * *

He finally found Gen. Pope's HQ late in the afternoon. The day had remained overcast and sultry, until a midday shower cooled the air a bit. Not having an oilskin, Belden was soaked, but had passably dried by the time he found the HQ tent. There, Pope's numerous aides badgered him to give them the envelope, one after another. Though Belden felt like a lone scout besieged by a host of sappers, he refused to surrender the envelope to anyone but the general. Perhaps in pique, they made him wait for two hours. Belden took the opportunity to walk up and down outside the huge tent, bigger even than Gen. Slocum's, to work out some of the soreness in his posterior that had accrued from having ridden a horse for the first time in over a month. He even managed to find a Cookie who gave him a tin plate of what he called jambalaya.

He kept standing to eat and considered Pope's troops. They were polyglot, of many different races and religions. Cookie was what was politely referred to as a "high yaller" Negro. One of Pope's aides had a thick Germanic accent, another seemed to be a Frenchie who kept making the sign of the Cross, so he must have been Catholic. How would this strange mixture of men stack up against a foe that was white, mostly Anglo-Saxon and Protestant, all speaking their strange version of English?

So far, not very well. At the first major battle of the War, right across Bull Run there, General Jackson had stood like a stone wall and turned the Union attack, which then deteriorated into a chaotic retreat. Since then Stonewall had run circles around whatever Union adversaries tried to pin him down in the Shenandoah Valley. Lee, by far the best general on either side (a fact no man contested, North or South) had completely stymied McClelland's Peninsular campaign and made "Little Mac" pay dearly for his feeble feints.

The South had the better generals and they were a relatively homogenous army fighting on their own ground, in mostly defensive battles. These were tremendous advantages.

But the North was fighting on the side of the angels, Belden knew, for the preservation of the Union and for the freedom of all men. How could they lose?

*** * * ***

When Gen. Pope finally consented to see him, Belden found him to be a handsome man with long brown curls and a full beard. He took the letter that Belden placed in his hand and asked Belden to wait while he read it. His eyebrows raised in surprise.

"Did you know this missive is from the hand of Secretary Stanton?" he asked.

"No, sir," Belden said, thinking, I was right, then.

"He says here that you are a bright young man with sharp eyes and sound judgment, and that I am to use you to reconnoiter that portion of the battlefield where I suspect there may be counterfeit cannon. Do you understand the mission?"

"Yes, sir."

Gen. Pope beckoned for Belden to follow him to a large map table. He selected one of the maps and asked Belden to step closer as he adjusted it.

"I am orienting the map with the territory around us. You see this large 'N' on the map? I am aligning that with magnetic north, which is manifested by this mark on my table. Do you carry a compass? No? We will get you one, but I caution you to remember that the map is not the territory. There will be distinctions. Here is the road you came down today, here is Bull Run where you crossed it at the bridge. We are here."

He thumped the map with a knuckle. He seemed, Belden thought, a confident man. The scuttlebutt was that he had fought well in the West.

"Today, Jackson attacked us across our line of march along the Warrenton Turnpike near Brawner's Farm, here. We drove him back against Stony Ridge, here, where he is now trapped. Tomorrow I plan to smash him against the Ridge. He has no hope of being reinforced before then."

The general went on to give the particulars of where Lee and Longstreet were and how they were tied down by other units. Though Belden found this information interesting, he didn't see how it related to his particular mission. Pope turned to that next:

"I'd like to know how many of these cannon up on Stony Ridge are real, and how many are painted logs. I suggest that you go through the little town of Groveton, here, and then the old peach orchard, here, that was decimated at First Bull Run. No peaches left, I'm afraid. The forest beyond will give you cover and concealment. You have field glasses? Good. I will provide you with a safe conduct pass to Gen. Reynolds, who commands our left flank. It is now getting dark. I'll have one of my aides find you a cot for the night. You will be awakened just before first light on the morrow. Get through the town and orchard before sunrise and maneuver through these woods. You will hear our cannonade beginning on the right at that time. That should distract them from noticing a single spy. Do not get too close to the Rebel lines, and do not get captured. If you do, we can do nothing to save you. The countersign for tomorrow and the day after will be 'Freedom.' We'll send word to Reynolds's pickets not to shoot a man in civilian attire. Are you clear on these orders?"

"I am, sir."

Gen. Pope put a hand on Belden's shoulder and looked him in the eye.

"You are a brave man to endeavor this surveillance, sir. What you discover will be invaluable to us. Report directly to me as soon as you return. I will alert my staff that you are not to be kept waiting. Go outside and orient yourself. It is best that you carry no map."

"Thank you, sir."

Pope shook his hand.

"Henri!" he bellowed, and the Frenchman came bowing into the tent, as if he were a courtier in the Ancien Regime. "Find this man a berth for the night and have Cook put together a packet of rations and a canteen of water in a haversack. Also get him a compass. You are to wake him one hour before first light."

"*Mais oui, mon generale!*" Henri said, snapping a smart salute. Then, turning to Belden, *Monsieur,* will you please to follow me?"

As Belden was about to follow the Frenchman, Gen. Pope said, "The Union thanks you and blesses your mission, sir."

Belden halted, about-faced, and snapped up a salute. Pope returned it. Their eyes met and Belden felt a flood of love for the man. He knew that upon Gen. Pope's shoulders rested the weight of this whole battle. It became clear to him how important his little jaunt in the woods tomorrow might be to the outcome. At the same time, he realized that the general had no idea of his name or rank. He had become a man who did not exist.

* * *

Henri woke him almost tenderly in the dark. He lit a candle.

"It is time, *monsieur,*" he whispered.

"*Merci bien,*" Belden whispered back, rubbing the sleep from his eyes.

"Ah! *Vous parlez francais?*"

"*Une peu.*"

"*Formidable!*"

Henri left the tent. Belden found the basin of warm water and a straight razor he had left for him. He washed his hands, wet his face, and shaved as best he could in the dim light. As he dried his face with a small towel that was soft cotton, he reckoned it must be one of the general's. He pulled on clothing and brogans, then explored the haversack that Henri had left for him. Inside he found a quart tin of water, two plump sandwiches wrapped in old newspaper, a compass, and the pass.

He put the pass in one front pocket, the compass in the other, pulled out one of the sandwiches, slung the field glasses around his neck by their lanyard, and paused, debating for a long moment. He felt naked without a weapon. He went back to where the razor lay on the towel and, closing it in upon itself, slipped it into his brogan. Then he stepped out of the tent. He could see nothing at first. He was seized with a benumbing panic and, for a moment, he was back in the pitch darkness of the cave. As his eyes adjusted he pulled out the compass and looked down at its luminescent pointer. Okay, that was north. He was facing east, looking back toward Bull Run. No lights there.

He turned to face west and could make out the dying fires of the Rebel lines and the dark ridge behind them. To his right and left he could now see the coals of the Union fires. He let out a long, slow breath, unbuttoned his pants, and relieved himself on the grass beside his tent, as soldiers everywhere did.

Okay, he needed to strike a course for the town. Groveton, Pope had called it. Surely there would be a candle or lantern down there to signal his route. But the valley between the two armies was pitch black. Of course. If he'd lived down there he'd have skedaddled himself.

Unwrapping the newsprint, he took a bite from the sandwich. The bread was still warm and moist. It had been baked that morning. There was salt pork and onion with a spread of mustard inside. It was delicious. He ate it in big bites and washed it down with a swig from the water bottle. He'd have to thank Cookie when he got back.

If he got back, he corrected himself.

He made his way in a generally westerly direction, knowing he must intersect the Warrenton Turnpike soon. When he came near to it he barked his shin on a split rail fence. This was ridiculous. He'd have to wait for more light.

He stepped over the low fence and encountered the hard surface of the road. That was better. He took a few tentative steps and found that his feet could guide him if he walked very slowly.

Wait! He could just make out the edge of the Turnpike. He walked faster. Soon he was at the junction with the Groveton road and he turned right onto it.

The town was, as he had surmised, deserted. He moved between the dark and abandoned houses feeling a kind of sadness for their owners. These structures would probably no longer stand by the end of the day.

At the edge of the town he surveyed the ground before him. The top of Stony Ridge was just beginning to catch the first rays of morning, which turned the rock outcroppings a pinkish-red. Below the ridge the orange and yellow Rebel breakfast fires were blazing up. Taking a fix on the fire furthest to his left, Belden took out the compass and eyeballed a reading a little further to the southwest. He could just make out a bit of a notch in the ridge. That's what he'd key on.

He replaced the compass and stepped off the road into the ruined peach orchard. He was now officially in Rebel territory.

6

SECOND MANASSAS

It was midmorning by the time Belden, moving with extreme care, had made his way into the forest and encountered the cut for the unfinished railroad bed. He could see Rebel troops up on the other side of the cut manning at least eight actual cannon. On his right, he could hear Pope's army attacking—there was a lot of artillery firing on both sides. He shuddered thinking of what it must be like to be marching in a tight square into the maw of the cannon, which would be firing shrapnel into the soft bodies of men.

The day was already hot and muggy. Nestling into a deadfall, he brought out his second sandwich and the water bottle. He'd drunk most of the water, even after he'd replenished his supply from the creek that came down from the Ridge. He'd refill the bottle on his way back. He figured he'd wait for the cover of darkness before trying to recross the devastated peach orchard and the open ground around Groveton and the pike.

He thought he might even take a nap until then. The deadfall concealed him well and the heat was making him sleepy. He felt tiny legs crawling on his arm and looked down to see a wood tick, small and brown, making its way up his forearm. A lot more common down here than up at home, but mostly harmless. Even when they dug into you they didn't suck much blood. They did swell up into nasty, grayish balloons a good thirty times their original size before they'd drop off. He preferred to pick them off before they got their hooks into him.

There were also deerflies buzzing him, audible even over the cannonades. He disliked them more than the occasional mosquito that whined about his ears. The bite of a deerfly hurt—and then itched like crazy for a coon's age, as they said down here. He knocked one off his cheek. Maybe a nap wasn't going to be such a good idea.

That's when he heard the crisp command of a voice accustomed to directing soldiers on a noisy battlefield—on his left. He turned to look in that direction and saw, coming up from the southwest along the Warrenton Turnpike toward Groveton, a mass of men in nutbrown homespun, long squirrel rifles carried anywhichway, moving up on Pope's left flank.

Using the field glasses, being careful to shield the lenses with one hand to protect against a telltale flash that might pinpoint his position, he saw an enormous mass of men pouring up the pike and deploying within the concealing trees of the orchard near the Brawner farm. He could make out the guidons for the 1st, 4th, and 5th Texas Regiments, which meant Hood was here, and if Hood was here, Longstreet must be right behind. How in blazes had they gotten here so fast? Pope had been certain that Longstreet and Lee were out of this fight.

If he remembered aright, Longstreet commanded something like 28,000 men. If they launched a flanking attack on Pope's left while he was concentrating on attacking Jackson on his right, Hood and Longstreet could roll up his army with devastating losses. Belden knew then that he'd have to get back to Pope as soon as he could to warn him of this threat, whatever the danger to himself. He finished off the water, tucked the empty bottle and the greasy newsprint from his sandwich into the haversack, and studied the terrain he'd traversed that morning, most of it then in the dark.

He'd descend to the bottom of the ridge in the orchard, now on his left, hoping to avoid detection by the Rebel soldiers dug in above the railroad cut. At the creek he'd refill his water bottle, then skirt the top of the ruined peach orchard, in which he'd be too visible, and aim to go past the Groveton school house to reach the Union lines there. What was the countersign again? Oh, yeah: "Freedom."

In theory, it was a good plan. What Belden didn't know was that Jackson had just ordered Gen. Lawton, who commanded the troops above Belden's planned route, to mount an attack over the very path he intended to take.

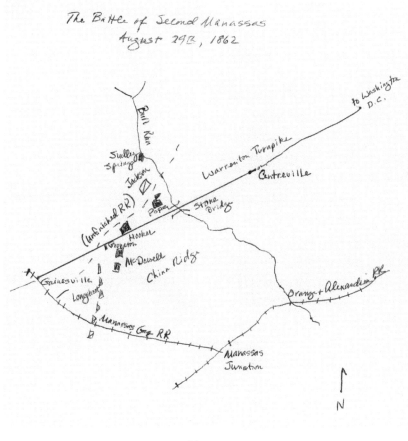

Manassas

He heard them coming as he began to retrace his steps. First the stentorian commands sending Lawton's division forward, then the tramping of thousands of boots. It sounded like what he imagined a herd of Great Plains' buffaloes must be like. There was no longer a way to follow his careful plan and he broke into run.

Belden ran as he had never run before. He had always been a strong runner, having in fact won the race from Bradford to Hammondsport and back for the last two years, besting even Will Van Auken and Jack Knickerbocker, both prior champions, and now in Companies D and K in his regiment. Yet Cinder Silvernail could have outrun them all. But, because she was a woman, no one imagined she could even enter the race. If he ever got back, he'd encourage her to do so. Why shouldn't she take the laurels?

Funny, he thought, what comes to mind when you're in mortal danger.

With musket balls whirring like angry bees around him, he fled back over the ground he had covered in the early morning darkness, down the ridge and back through the mostly abandoned town of Groveton. In the town he saw a boy of eight or nine playing mumble-peg with a jackknife.

"Get inside, boy!" he yelled as he ran by. The boy looked up at him with a face as serene as that of a saint and went back to his game. Belden kept running.

As he came up Chinn ridge toward the Union army, he saw that Pope's left flank was nakedly exposed to the Texas regiments. His breath was coming harder now as he tried to maintain his pace uphill. In trying to crush Jackson against the Stony Ridge across the railway cut, Pope had left his flank unprotected and vulnerable. Belden had to warn him or the entire army could be lost.

As he came through the lines he had to stop to give the counter-sign, at threat of being shot by the sentries, and then at the general's headquarters he was made to wait for nearly half an hour, despite his entreaties that he had information of an emergency nature. So this, he thought, is how great battles are lost. He tried to remember the old poem about how for want of a shoe, a horse is lost.... But he could get no further.

When he was finally admitted to see Gen. Pope, the commanding general had a manic look in his eye.

"We'll teach Stoney to try to run around us and then burn our supplies!" he almost shouted at Belden. "What's the news of the batteries, Private?"

This total change of character startled Belden. Where was the calm man of yesternight?

"The eight batteries I saw on your left appear to be real, sir," Belden said, "but there is a far more important and unwelcome danger. Lee's army has come up on your left flank, sir, along the Gainesville road. Hood's 1st, 4th, and 5th Texas regiments are already in place, and more must be en route. I beg you to call off your attack, general, or you shall be struck with a terrible flanking blow."

"Are you certain of this, Private?" Pope asked. "They were 56 miles away at last report."

"Absolutely certain, sir. I saw them with my own eyes."

At that moment an aide brought the general a written message.

"Ha!" shouted Pope. "Jackson's out of ammo! His troops are throwing rocks at ours. Throw in the reserves! All out attack!"

"But, sir..." Belden protested.

"Henri!" Pope added. "Get a message to McDowell. Tell him to move to protect the left flank across the Gainesville road."

He turned back to Belden.

"Happy now? Get yourself a horse and get back to Slocum or Stanton or whoever sent you to spy on me. Go!"

A reply rushed to Belden's lips but he had the sense to bite it back. He saluted, but the general was busy issuing more orders. He turned on his heel and strode out of the tent. As he came into the sunlight, he blinked, then brought the field glasses to his eyes. Sure enough, the Rebs were already swarming in onto Pope's left flank. He thought it might be Hooker down there trying to defend but he couldn't make out the colors.

For a minute or two he watched in horror, fascinated as he saw the men in nutbrown bowling the men in blue like tenpins down the road.

Then he figured he'd better follow the general's order and went to find his horse.

* * *

As he rode away from the battle, the noise of it seemed to grow like an inferno behind him. Of course they hadn't returned his former horse to him but substituted a bony nag he wasn't sure would last a mile. One part of him wanted to be on an Arabian that could gallop like the wind away from the horror of the sounds of the battle: masses of musket fire, screeching shot, jolting explosions. How could anyone stand in such a Hell? Yet another part of him wanted to do just that, to turn back and try to assist his fellow soldiers.

The nag picked up his conflicting emotions and came to a dead stop. Belden kicked her with both heels and she actually trotted for a few paces before resuming her gimpy walk. What he wanted didn't matter: He was a soldier who had to follow the orders he was given, or he could be shot for insubordination. He'd learned that much during Drill. It had shocked him that he had to follow an order even if it was stupid or immoral or put him or others in grave danger. But, as Sergeant O'Malley explained, "If every damn time I order you to march up the hill you argue with me that the damn hill ain't worth the takin', ain't nothin' gonna git done, is it now? So when we say Jump you Jump!"

"May we ask how high? To jump?" Jack Knickerbocker had asked —and found himself peeling potatoes on K.P.—Kitchen Police. The Army turned everything into initials.

Good old Jack, always the smart mouth.

Well, it would be good to see the lads again, he thought, though he couldn't shake the feeling that in leaving the battle, even under orders, he was doing something dishonorable.

* * *

As he urged his nag back along the Warrenton Pike it dawned on him that he was shocked that a general could be so blind to the realities of the battlefield. Although all Pope had to do was step out of his tent for one second to see the tide of Texas regiments sweeping in from the left, he preferred to rely upon the messages handed to him rather than his own eyes. Was this why the Union generals made so many grievous errors? Or, like McClelland, were so afraid of making one that they did nothing? How was it that the South had all the best generals?

A Reb, Belden knew, would say that it was because the Confederacy had God on their side or because one Confederate soldier was worth ten Yanks. Neither of these propositions was persuasive to Belden. Having grown up in an abolitionist family, he was more than convinced of what had seemed obvious to him since childhood: Slavery was evil, an abomination. And while he was willing to grant that men fighting on their own ground and believing that they were repelling a foreign invasion would fight more fiercely than the "invaders," he doubted that any Reb could equal two Belden Cranes, much less ten.

Nope. It was because the Rebs had better generals.

He knew, as did most Yankee soldiers, that Robert E. Lee had been offered the job of commanding U.S. general but had turned it down, saying that he could not raise his hand against his native Virginia. The rumor was that Lee didn't even cotton to slavery but wished to see it gradually removed from all the States. He just wished Lee had chosen the Government side rather than to turn Rebel. Lee, he imagined, would have listened to him rather than throw in his reserves against Jackson.

Such were his thoughts as he made his way east through the brutal summer heat of late August, through Fairfax and Falls Church and Arlington. By the time he reached the latter he was exhausted by his long day, but he pushed on across the bridge into the District of Columbia.

Though it was late in the day, with the sun setting behind him and the heat like an oven in the still raw city, he found his way to Seward's office in the dark old Treasury building near the White House. The Secretary's aides told him Mr. Seward was gone for the day, but Belden knew they were lying: They wouldn't still be here if their boss had gone. He started shouting. Three of them grabbed him. Seward himself came out when he heard Belden's raised voice.

"Let him go, gentlemen!" he called. "Come in, Belden, come in."

Belden glared at the men who had lied to him and then dared lay hands upon him, re-straightened his dusty clothing, and went to take Secretary Seward's outstretched hand. Seward led him into a large room that was dominated by a desk as big as a lifeboat. He pointed Belden to a chair, into which Belden lowered himself gingerly.

"You must be tuckered out, son. What would you like to drink? How about a sandwich?"

"A glass of water would be much appreciated, sir, and I wouldn't say no to a morsel of food."

Seward stuck his head back out his door and requested both items. Belden was amazed at how fast they appeared. They must have had a stash of sandwiches on hand for all those working late. But it was the water that tasted like something gods drank on Olympus. He'd run out back in Arlington and wasn't about to dip more from the Potomac. This water was cool and wet, two qualities that he relished. And the sandwich—fresh roast beef with horseradish on white bread—was delicious.

Ensconcing himself behind his fortress of a desk, Seward waited patiently for Belden to finish, as though he had nothing else to do.

Belden wiped his lips and smiled.

"Thank you for that, sir," he said.

"You're welcome, son. Tell me what you discovered."

Belden did, starting with the number of actual batteries he had counted and moving on to the discovery of the arrival of Hood's regiments.

"And General Pope reacted how when you informed him of this imminent threat?"

"He sent Gen. McDowell's troops down to attempt to meet it."

"While simultaneously throwing the bulk of his reserves at Jackson, across the railway cut?"

"Yes, sir."

"And when you were leaving you saw Hood's men rolling up Pope's left flank?"

"Yes, sir. Gen. Pope had said the prior evening that his last intelligence was that Lee's army was 56 miles away."

"Thank you, Belden. Would you be so kind as to write out your report for me? I'm going to find you a bed and a bath in a nearby hotel where they will have foolscap and pen and ink on hand. They will provide a breakfast for you as well. Afterward, if you would be so kind as to drop off your report with my aide Alfred tomorrow morning, I would be most appreciative."

He rang a small bell and an aide burst in, as if prepared to save the Secretary from the ruffian who'd stormed the office.

"Alfred," he said, "please usher my dear friend Mr. Crane over to our room in the Willard and see that his horse is cared for at the stable. Give him two dollars from petty cash for his supper."

Alfred, who was about Belden's age and wore a very high starched white collar, agreed he would attend to everything. He had a bit of a stammer.

Two dollars! Belden was thinking. He could eat like a king.

He did, beginning with Puree of Fowl, a la Royal, then Tenderloin of Beefsteak, aux rich gravy, mashed potatoes, fried parsnips, and a huge piece of hot apple pie.

7

ANTIETAM CREEK

After breakfast at the Willard the following morning, which featured one of the richest cups of coffee Belden had ever put to his lips, he handed over his written report to Alfred and received from him a sealed letter for his commanding officer, Col. Van Valkenburgh. He saddled his horse, unfortunately the same one, and rode the few blocks past the White House and over to the Mall, where the Armory Square Hospital had erected eleven long white pavilions aligned with military precision. Belden gave a low whistle. He couldn't imagine the number of wounded men that it could serve. He checked at the admitting office but was disappointed to learn that Ira wasn't on duty there. He guessed Ira was still in Maryland. Well, it had been worth a try.

As he remounted, his eyes rose up to a redbrick Gothic castle, complete with crenellated battlements and fluttering pennants—the famous United States National Museum, also called the Smithsonian, which housed a variety of inventions and artifacts illustrating much of the history of the Republic. He found himself being the country bumpkin, staring up at it open-mouthed as if he'd never seen a castle before, which he hadn't. He debated with himself whether to stop for a brief tour or to be a good little soldier and proceed directly back to his regiment.

He could imagine the wrestling match between his Better Angel and the Devil as they competed for his soul, like one of those banal morality plays which he had been dragooned into acting in by the good Reverend Atwill back home. When he remembered playing the part of Everyman in one such entertainment, he was surprised to feel a wave of homesickness sweep through him with such force that tears leapt into his eyes, blurring the outlines of the red castle. In this blurred vision the fluttering pennants seemed to be the guidons of K Company.

It was a clear sign, he felt, that he should push on to Ft. Lyon, where he had been informed that the 107th was now billeted.

He rode down the Mall past the half-completed monument to Gen. Washington, which he had heard was to rise to a total of 555 feet into the air. The ribald joke among the cruder members of his regiment was that Lincoln was going to construct a second monument, this one to honor Martha Washington: a 555 foot hole in the ground. Belden was still working out why this seemed hilarious to so many of his fellow soldiers. It seemed logical to him that a monument to the Mother of their country would be deep in the Earth, the common Mother of all humanity. He could easily imagine a stone stairway leading deep into the Earth, revealing the underlying strata of the various levels of the geological history of the planet. He supposed that the real joke was that any nation would obscenely honor its Father by erecting a giant phallus.

Still, it was already an impressive structure—and useful, too. He understood that the Army used it as a watchtower, able to oversee a substantial portion of northern Virginia.

He could see scores of black workmen laboring to place the huge cut blocks of stone—good Vermont granite, it looked like—into place. He knew the White House and the Capitol had been built by slaves but hoped that the Negroes constructing the Washington Monument must be free.

He crossed the bridge over the Potomac and was saluted by the green recruits on sentry duty who assumed he must be an officer if he was on horseback heading into Virginia. From the bridge he could see, on the Heights, Robert E. Lee's family mansion, which had been commandeered by the U.S. Army and now flew the Union flag. He wondered how Gen. Lee felt about that. He made his way from Arlington into the streets of Alexandria, which he found to be a charming town reeking of gentility. He had to admit that the South had a very different feel to him than the North, though he couldn't quite put his finger on what comprised that difference.

Other than the number of Negroes, of course. Bradford had only a single Negro, a "teched" old man called Uncle Jim. He remembered Uncle Jim's drunken rages with a trill of fear, even now. He wondered what Uncle Jim thought of this War.

While there was only one Negro in Bradford, nearly half the people on the streets of Alexandria were black. True, they were mostly "servants," as the Southerners liked to call them, and mostly dressed in hand-downs or homespun, but their clothes seemed clean and worn with a certain style: a bright red kerchief here, colorful patches on a pair of pants there. They also seemed to bear out the Rebel myth, which he had read in several tracts, that their "servants" were happy with their lot: They laughed readily, they greeted one another with good cheer, and they stopped to chat as if they had all the time in the world—which, in a sense, they did. Was this the state of mind of people who trusted that all of their material wants were assured? That they would be fed and cared for in sickness and in health? Or was this *joi de vivre* a feature of the Negro race?

He found himself staring as if at exotic beasts.

He saw that the color of their skins ranged from coal black to an almost Oriental yellow, and their facial features from a very broad nose and thick lips to those that mirrored most Caucasians. And, while two of the older women were portly, this selection of Negroes appeared to be excellent physical specimens, lean and strong. Most of them exuded a dignified calm and moved with a subtle grace, as if they were actors upon a stage or as if they knew the whites were watching them with mixed feelings.

When Belden dismounted at a cart where a huge Negro was selling slices of watermelon and handed over a penny for a juicy red piece, he was stunned by the odor that came off the man. He wondered for a moment if this man had had the misfortune of being sprayed by a skunk. It was an odor he had never smelled on a Caucasian. It was so radically different that he had trouble controlling his involuntary response, which was to step back and pinch his nostrils closed. If the watermelon seller noticed Belden's reaction, he didn't let on.

Belden was ashamed to find that he felt a sense of revulsion. He looked down at the slice of melon in his hand, red and green, clean and shiny, and he found himself afraid to put it to his own lips. He shuddered, and bit deeply into it, a little nervous that he might gag. He was deeply ashamed at this unforeseen reaction.

All of his life he had heard his parents and their abolitionist friends speak highly of the Negro as an abstraction, and he was fully convinced that the Southern argument that Negroes were not fully human was poppycock. He himself had sat beside a slaveholding preacher from Georgia on the train from New York to Washington after enlistment and found himself in heated discussion with him.

"The Nigra is more animal than human," this man had said. "They are the descendants of Ham and cursed of God to be our servants. They have nappy hair just like that on a sheep. They are between humans and animals."

"You and I have straight hair like that on a horse's tail," Belden had retorted, "so I reckon we're animals, too."

The preacher, a tall, elegant man with a soft voice and genteel manner, chuckled.

"Oh, I see you are skilled in the Sophist arts," he said. "But you do not know the actual Nigra. You have not lived among them as we in the South have. Had you done so, you would find that they lack intelligence, and with their thick lips have great troubled pronouncing the English language."

"For any slave stolen from his home in Africa," Belden said, "English is not his native language. Of course he won't speak it like an Englishman."

"Oh, come now, suh. You know that since 1808 the Act Prohibiting the Importation of Slaves has largely prevented slaves being brought from Africa."

"And you know full well, sir, that slavers still sail into many a port."

"True, to some extent, I grant you. Highever, most of our present slaves were born on this soil and have been speaking English since childhood. How is it, then, that they yet cannot speak like you or me? Is it not their lips, and lack of intelligence?"

"Sir! Are they not prevented from attending schools where they might improve their diction?"

"Oh, fie! I nevah went to school a day in my life. My daddy did saddle me with one miserable old tutor for a year or two, but all he tried to do was teach me Latin. Latin! And I can't hardly speak a word of that dead old language. But I learnt to read the Good Book, suh, and it has given me all the education I ever needed. It is the word of God, suh, and it speaks clearly of the existence of slavery and of the inferiority of the sons of Ham."

The argument had continued for the duration of the trip, but neither man had changed the other's mind. What Belden had learned was that the Georgian *believed* his "truth" that blacks were born to be slaves and were happiest to be slaves, a doctrine that was anathema to him.

When he rode on, having somehow eaten most of the sweet melon, he turned over that conversation in his mind. How could anyone live with a man who smelled like that? Maybe no one did. He was clearly a freeman, for he was an entrepreneur with his own pushcart and business. He must also farm enough acreage to grow watermelons. How was that possible in a slave economy?

Belden found that his thoughts troubled him. There was much, he realized, that he did not know about the South.

Asking his way, he found Ft. Lyon and, within it, his regiment, where he reported to his commanding officer, Col. Robert Van Valkenburg. The colonel was a plump Dutchman with a merry red face and the worried paternalistic air of a non-military man who had been thrust into a position for which his prior occupation had ill-prepared him. He even had difficulty returning Belden's salute. He took from Belden the letter from Secretary Seward and, reading, began nodding his massive head.

"Goot, goot, you haf done vell, Private Crane. I am to promote you to Corporal Crane! Hah! A zecret mission, eh? Helping to turn ze tide of ze battle? Vell! Dis is zomthing, yah?"

He turned to the executive officer of the 107th regiment, Lt. Col. Alexander Diven, and asked him to see to it that Corporal Crane got another stripe.

The X-O accompanied Belden to the tent of the K company commander, Capt. Allen Sill, and repeated the news. Sill looked at Belden blankly, as if he'd never seen him before, and then scribbled a note for Belden to hand to his squad commander.

At least I'm getting to know the chain of command, Belden thought. Although as one of our congressmen, Diven was well known, and in fact, along with the Reverend Thomas Beecher, got me fired up to enlist. Al Sill I've known most of my life and I voted for him to be our company commander. A good man, even with half of his right forefinger lost in that tree-felling accident when he was a lad. How does he pull a trigger? And now Sarge, whom I'd know a lot better if I frequented the salons. They say the man could drink the ocean dry.

The Quartermaster supplied two stripes, one for each arm, along with a needle and thread. Belden did his best to align them with the existing ones and sew them on, a task he wished he could have turned over to Ma or Helen, who both had nimble fingers. His felt thick.

He imagined that Cinder would also have made quick work of the job. Remembering her slender fingers and how cunningly she touched him with them produced a tumescence in his trousers. He realized that he missed her. He thought about writing her a letter but decided against it. She had been clear: If he was going to go off to war she was going to forget him. He wondered if she'd taken up with Jesse Munsen and how that could possibly be going. Personally, he'd rather take up with a den of rattlers. While he knew she'd threatened it just to hurt him back, he feared she was ornery enough to do it to spite him.

While he was still sewing and thinking of Cinder, cousin Ezra Crane came into the tent, his captain's silver railroad tracks shining on his shoulders, Belden was embarrassed about standing up and saluting. If Ezra noticed the tilt in his kilt he didn't mention it. In addition to being the regimental chaplain Ezra had been elected the commander of A Company. He was a hearty man in his middle thirties, clean-shaven and blue-eyed, like many of the Cranes.

"Congratulations on your new stripe, Belden!" he said. He had the sonorous voice and the bonhomie of a preacher. "I heard you went on a secret mission for Secretary Seward."

Belden laughed, relieved that his trousers were no longer quite so tight.

"Hardly a secret, if everyone seems to know about it," he said.

The two men shook hands warmly. Belden had known Ezra since he could remember. He looked up to him as a model of manliness and human decency. He was also a heck of a baseball player. For Belden and Ira as boys, Ezra had taken on the numinosity of an Arthurian knight.

"Then you can tell me all about it," Ezra said.

Belden shrugged.

"Nothing much to tell. The Secretary wanted me to scout for logs painted black to resemble cannon, as they'd done at the first battle there. I didn't find any, but I did spot Hood's Texas regiments massing on Pope's left flank. I reported it, but Gen. Pope was all agog about having pinned Jackson down finally."

"We heard that Hood crushed Pope's flank and forced him to pull back. It was yet another Reb victory."

Belden shook his head.

"Why don't we have a general like Lee or Jackson?"

"As a man of God, I'd have to say that He works in mysterious ways," Ezra said. "But as a soldier, I'd have to admit that the cavalier tradition of the South produces some damned fine soldiers. I do hear that Lincoln sacked Pope after the battle and McClellan is now our commanding general. The orders just came in for us to march into Maryland to counter Lee's Army of Northern Virginia crossing the Potomac up near Harper's Ferry. I wanted to wish you luck before we broke camp."

"What?! Lee is in Maryland?"

"Either that or nearly there. You're not going to have much time to get refreshed and ready to fall in, Bel."

* * *

In actuality, Belden had almost two weeks to drill and sleep and eat Army rations before the order came to leave Ft. Lyon. He enjoyed the march back through the Capital and into the rolling hills of the Maryland countryside, which was showing the first hints of autumn in some of the hardwoods. There was much arable land with cleared pastures and croplands ready for the harvest. The weather was warm with a hint of chill at night. The troops were in high spirits, singing on the march and laughing around the campfires at night as if they were going on a holiday.

There was a rumor that two Illinois soldiers had found Lee's tactical plans wrapped around three cigars and that from those plans Little Mac knew exactly what the Rebel leader had in mind in taking the unprecedented step of splitting his army into four units. The men had great confidence in Little Mac, who no doubt had a good reason to wait for the four units—which might have been destroyed piecemeal-- to reunite near the town of Sharpsburg on Antietam Creek, with the broad Potomac at their rear. The orders had doubtless been left on purpose to confabulate the Union general. The men cheered Little

Mac whenever they caught a glimpse of him and were certain that they were about to crush Lee's army.

The artillery barrages began at dawn on September 17th.

* * *

The 107th was held in reserve at first but heard heavy artillery screaming overhead. As he listened to cannonballs howling like banshees, Belden felt a terror more profound than any he had ever before, even when he'd been fleeing the Rebel counterattack at Manassas or when he'd been lost in the cave. He could picture what it must be like to have one of those huge chunks of iron tear into your body. He was afraid that he would panic and flee and be known forever as a coward. His teeth chattered, his hands were cold and clammy, his knees shook so that he had no choice but to sit down on the stubble of the field. The solidity of the ground beneath him and the pricks of the stubble coming through his pants seemed calming.

As the barrage continued and he was not blown to bits, a curious thing happened. Gradually, the fear began to ebb out of him and he experienced a strange sense of invulnerability. He laughed out loud at the absurdity of it, and several others laughed with him.

"Them Rebs couldn't hit us if they was fifty feet away!" one man shouted. "They must all be drunk as a skunk."

Belden did wonder how often skunks got drunk.

By the time the order came to advance, Belden was back in control of his limbs. The 107th marched in good order toward the left, where they set up a perimeter in support of a battery that was firing hot and heavy. As the cannon boomed, Belden found himself feeling an almost giddy exhilaration. He *hoped* that they would be attacked so he could shoot some real Rebs. This unnerving switch from terror to bloodlust might have disturbed him more had he not been so overwhelmed by the latter. He had heard how Viking berserkers would strip naked and plunge into battle with a ferocity that bordered on madness. Was that what he was experiencing? It was a feeling far beyond joy, filling his entire body with red energy.

"Come on, you goddam Rebs!" he heard himself yelling.

When a flock of Rebels finally came up at them, the 107th fired synchronized volleys into their ranks. Belden looked for near targets and fired his Enfield at the center of mass. After firing he took one of the 40 paper-wrapped minie balls from his ammo pouch, bit off the end, poured the powder down the barrel, and rammed the mine home. He was then careful to place a cap below the hammer: He'd heard tell of soldiers who, in a panic, forgot the cap and never fired their weapon but kept ramming home additional charges. He wasn't going to be one of those. With Rebs dropping in front of them right and left, he couldn't tell for sure if he was hitting anyone. At home he was acknowledged to be a good shot, and he'd taken his fair share of wild game, but he'd never shot at a man before. It was a strange sensation. It made a tightness in his belly and a weakening in his limbs. He realized that there was a part of him that didn't want to kill another human being, even a Reb. He was jerking his shots off rather than gradually squeezing the trigger. The bloodlust was fading.

A minie ball sang past his head like a demented wasp. Well, the Rebs were sure trying to kill him.

He reloaded, knelt on one knee, and put his sights on the chest of a man brandishing a saber, right at the point where his crossed shoulder belts met. Must be an officer. Yup, he was screaming orders. At least that's what it looked like. Couldn't hear him in the din.

Belden took a deep breath, slowly releasing it while gently squeezing the trigger. The Enfield lurched against his shoulder, the officer went down, and Belden felt the exhilaration of the good shot and the horror that he had just killed a man. Probably. Most likely.

Don't think about that. Reload. Musket barrel was getting hot. Gotta slow my rate of fire. Keep breathing.

The external world seemed to recede. He could still see clearly, but the cacophony of musket and artillery fire, the screams of men, the neighing of horses—all that seemed to be taking place at a great distance. He had a feeling of warmth and relaxation. Both his fear and the bloodlust were gone, as though they had never been.

Then one of the cannons on his right fired a round of grapeshot into the Confederate ranks at point-blank range. It seemed that the gray-brown uniforms melted away.

"They're runnin'!" somebody yelled. "Let's get 'em!"

"Hold!" Captain Sill said. "They'll be back. Reload and fix bayonets."

But he was wrong. The Rebs were retreating.

* * *

That night and the next day they lay on their arms in the field, getting what sleep they could and nibbling hardtack and jerked beef. Belden was so relieved to be alive that he felt like a kid on a camping trip, though he did wonder why they weren't trying to smash Lee during his retreat. Finally, on the 19th McClellan ordered them to pursue Lee, but the wily old general had given them the slip, pulling the entire Army of Northern Virginia back across the Potomac with an efficiency that even the rank and file had to admire.

In the single day of fighting at Antietam, more men died in battle than ever before or after on American soil, but the North needed a victory, so they called it one. After all, they had driven Lee from Union territory, made him retreat for once. On September 22nd, Lincoln issued the preliminary Emancipation Proclamation, which stated that on January 1, 1863, all of the slaves in those states still in arms against the authority of the federal government would be forever free. From now on, they weren't just fighting for the Union. They were officially fighting to end slavery in America.

8

IRA

To Ira's great delight and greater relief he had been transferred from the infantry to the medical corps. He had known that he would have great difficulty in killing a man, which, he also knew, was the primary job of a good soldier. He was much better suited to helping men heal. While he thanked the Good Lord for this outcome at the time, it was only later that he came to realize how uncommon it was in the Army for anyone to be placed in a position that best suited him. In fact, he came to know many lads who'd never before ridden a horse that had been sent to the cavalry and at least one superb horseman who sat out his service issuing wadding to the artillery.

Ira began his training as a male nurse at Jarvis U. S. General Hospital in Baltimore. This hospital had been created at the beginning of the War on the grounds of the former Steuart estate. The Steuarts, father and son, were wealthy Maryland slaveholders and military men who had resigned their commissions in the U.S. Army and moved south to join the Confederacy. Now their former mansion was full of hospital beds.

The wounded poured into Jarvis from both the fighting and widespread illness. Ira was shocked at the number of men who arrived lacking a limb. It seemed to him that the field surgeons' procedure of primary choice must be amputation. Well, it did minimize the risk of gangrene, which was a horrible way to die.

Ira's job was to change the dressings on the men's wounds while keeping a sharp eye out for gangrenous flesh, which had not only a greenish glint but a significant putrid smell. He marveled that anyone could miss it.

As had the doctor on rounds Ira's very first morning in the ward. When Ira unwrapped the bandages from around what remained of a boy's thigh—he couldn't have been more than sixteen—and the telltale odor assaulted his nostrils. The boy smelled it, too. His eyes grew big in his face.

"What's that smell?" he asked, terrified.

Ira could see the discoloration in the flesh and a nasty dark red line moving up the thigh.

"Let's get the doc to give us his opinion," Ira said, forcing a smile and patting the lad's shoulder.

The doctor blanched when he saw the gangrene and immediately brought forth his leeches to chew away the rotten flesh. Ira was stunned that modern medicine still employed this primitive technology, but had to admit that the leeches were efficient, eating only the dead flesh.

* * *

When he had the time, he explored downtown Baltimore and bought himself a novel and writing supplies. One of his first letters was to his brother:

Dear Bel,

I am well-suited to being a male nurse, as we are called here. After training I will probably be assigned to one of the big military hospitals in Washington. In the meantime, I am getting to know this charming old city, with its mix of races and types, its shops and pocket parks. I am struck by how much warmer it is, just this much closer to the Equator.

Found a lovely old bookstore today, where I purchased this paper and ink, as well as a novel about this war called *The Cruise of the Rattlesnake*, based upon the true tale of a Rebel cruiser fitted in Boston and then preying upon us. I discovered that this ship captured and burned a merchantman named the *Harvey Birch*. You will doubtless remember that the actual Harvey Birch was a famous relative of ours who was one of Geo. Washington's spies on the British during the Revolutionary War. James Fenimore Cooper adulated him in *The Spy*, making him out to be a great patriot, whereas our family legend has always been that he was a double agent who sold secrets to the British as well.

In this bookstore I was delighted to find many books of poetry, which I spent hours perusing. I find it fascinating that someone can write verse, at which I know you are quite adept. I might even try my hand at it someday.

You will be amazed—I have learned to smoke tobacco! I bought a corncob and like to take a bowl when I play chequers with one of the other lads. I find it most mollifying. We must save the Union if only to keep the price of tobacco down! In counterbalance to this new vice, and ever mindful of the precarious nature of perdition, I do attend church every Sunday and have begun singing with the choir.

Had a letter from home—everyone is well, though missing us. Pa says it was hard to get in the harvest without us but that Eugene is showing promise of filling the void. Emily says that Charlie Ide has asked her to marry him but that she will wait till we are both safely home so we can enjoy the party afterward. I suppose you've already heard that Cinder married Jesse Jr. and that Uncle Jim died in a fire. Ma sends her love.

As you know I hold you close in my heart. May the Good Lord watch over you and protect you.

Your loving brother,

Ira

* * *

Ira was delighted to find that the local paper often published a poem or two. When he came upon a poem he liked he would cut it out of the paper and paste it in his diary. One such read:

"The Volunteer's Return"

I have come back to you, Mother
Weary, wasted and worn,
With locks matted over my forehead,
And clothes blood-stained and torn.
It's no wonder you shrieked when you saw me,
As if I had struck you a blow;--
I am not looking much like the fellow
You parted with a long year ago!

For that one was stalwart and handsome,
Eager and fierce for the strife,
While this one is weary and wasted,
Scarred, and a cripple for life!
Mother, God knows for the Union
I'd fight till my very last breath;
But just twenty-one, and a cripple—
For you it had better been death.

Not for you, darling mother, you only—
For another there was when I left,
With eyes that were bluer than heaven,
And lips like the ripe cherry cleft!
My Maggie she was—may God bless her!—
I meant to have made her my wife;--
She had promised; but how can I ask her
To mate with a cripple for life?

There, Mother, don't weep; it was cruel
To utter one word of regret;
'T was all I could give, and I gave it—
My right arm is left to me yet;
With that and my pension, dear Mother,
We'll keep off the wolf from the door,
And if you are contented and happy,
God will help me to ask for no more.

But hark! Who is that I heard sobbing
Just then, in the chamber close by?
Oh! Maggie, my love and my darling,
Kiss me once ere you bid me good-bye!
What's this—you will never forsake me?
My loss only makes me more dear?
God bless you, dear Maggie, you've given
New life to your poor Volunteer!

You will work for us both—are you saying?
Nay, dear, though I can't drive the plow,
There are trades that my one arm can master,
And I've courage for anything now.
With your love and Mother's to bless me,
I've no room in my bosom for fears,--
And may God send as bright a home-coming
To all of our brave Volunteers!

For reasons he only partially understood, this poem brought tears to his eyes, again and again. How wonderful, he thought. If only I could write something that would bring up such feelings in another, my life would have been worthwhile.

Putting pen to paper, he began:

The sun glows red as it sets in the West,

All the children of God are going to rest.
We soldiers protect them in their beds...

He paused, chewing on his lip. Where would he go from here? What rhymed with "beds"? "Heads?" "Where they lay down their heads"? Nah. Too corny.

9

THE LONG MARCH

The 107th New York Volunteers marched to Maryland Heights and went into camp on September 23rd, decimated by fever. It seemed that just about everyone had taken ill. Belden had never felt worse that he could remember. At least he didn't itch, as he had with the chickenpox as a boy. When President Lincoln reviewed them on October 2nd, fewer than 300 men of the regiment were able to dress and stand at attention. Belden dragged himself from his blankets to see the great man, though he had to lean on Lew's arm to make it to the parade ground. It was worth it. Here was Honest Abe, in the flesh, the man he'd heard so much about since he'd been a boy. He was struck by how tall Lincoln stood, especially with the top hat, and what deep sadness he carried in his face. He looked as though he carried the weight of all those deaths in battle as deeply as if they'd been his own sons. At that moment Belden decided to do whatever needed to be done to help this man bring about his vision of a free and united country.

The next day Corporal John Couse, of H Company, died of the fever, the first of many. He was buried in a rough box made of old fence boards by his sergeant, Abram White. Still very weak, Belden was unable to stand for the entire funeral service and had to be lowered to the ground. As he sat there, embarrassed by his weakness, he had to admit that the ground felt good beneath his buttocks and legs. It seemed to drain away his illness.

A week later, just as he was recuperating, he got a letter from Helen telling him that Cinder had married Jesse Munsen. She gave no details. He sat with the letter in his hand for a long time, benumbed. Then he dropped the letter into the campfire. The next day he fell sick again. In his fever he dreamed that Jesse was killing Cinder with a paring knife, over and over.

On the tenth of December the 107th marched into Virginia, passing through Harper's Ferry, where John Brown had ignited this war, and down the Leesburg Valley to Fairfax Station. Though he was much recovered, Belden found the long march arduous in the wetter, colder weather. Though there were a few snow flurries, the snowfalls were nothing compared with those he was accustomed to coming off Lake Erie.

While Belden had taken it for granted that he'd be able to keep up with any man on a long march, he was gaining humility as the days progressed. Despite the colder weather, sweat was running in streams down his neck and into his armpits. The uniform he'd been issued was stiff as cardboard and made of a kind of shoddy that seemed to trap body heat and sweat as a hog pen corrals pigs. He reckoned it was a Munsen uniform and cursed the whole clan. The straps of his pack were cutting deep into the fronts of his shoulders and benumbing his arms. He could gain some relief by working a free thumb between strap and shoulder to lift the strap a bit and allow some blood flow, then switch his musket to the other shoulder to alternate the lifting procedure on the other strap.

The worst was the chafing of his new brogans against his feet. He had blisters on both heels, on the tops of his toes, even on the balls of his feet. The soldiers had an ongoing debate about whether it was better to lance the blisters with a pin (sterilized by holding the tip in the flame of a burning match for a few seconds) or to let them be. Lew punctured his blisters; Belden let his be, reasoning that the human body knew what it was doing in creating them in the first place. It seemed to make little difference. Both men complained that their feet were killing them, but then so did everyone else in the company.

They marched for fifty minutes, then had a ten minute break, during which some of them collapsed onto the ground while others rolled smokes. Those ten minutes flew by while the fifty marching minutes seemed interminable. Belden wondered who had come up with this plan. Why not march for an hour and take a fifteen minute break? Or two hours and a twenty? As a non-smoker, he would set down his musket, take off his pack, and try to find a dry spot where he could lie prone with his smarting feet elevated onto the pack. He imagined that this position rebalanced the blood supply in his body.

But when the call "Fall in!" sounded, it was painful to get up, shrug into his pack, and pick up his heavy musket. Sometimes, if there was a nearby stone wall, he could just back up to it and rest the weight of the pack atop it.

He observed that soldiers, himself included, spent much of their time trying to figure out how to make life a bit easier, in tiny ways. He had developed, for instance, what he called the Rest Step, in which he would focus his attention upon the foot that was in the air, resting. It gave him at least the illusion of a moment of serenity. He observed that in normal marching he tended to focus on the efforting leg, not the resting one, and that the efforting leg was usually the one in the most pain. Pain drew attention. If, however, he focused instead on the leg and foot dangling in midair, his mind would relax and feel calm. That, he thought, was a useful trick.

He remembered how Charlie Ide passed on his father Julius's wisdom in a single axiom: "There's a trick to everything." Meaning you can either do it the hard way or find the easy way, and there's always an easier way. Julius was a blacksmith, so he should know, after years of shaping metal, which was among the most difficult of tasks. He remembered Julius Ide taking a regular nail and bending it around on itself to form a ring. He told the story that many pioneers had wed their wives with just such a ring in the days when a store-bought ring was an anomaly. He'd made such a ring for Belden when he was a whippersnapper. Belden still kept Julius' ring in his box of souvenirs at home in his bedroom, even though his fingers where now too large for it. He wondered if maybe Cinder could wear it. Stop that, he told himself. She went and married that fool. Drive her out of your mind.

The thought of the people at home nearly drove him to his knees. A wave of homesickness passed through him and he felt tears start at the corners of his eyes. He sure had taken the people he loved for granted. Now he knew different. The smell and taste of one of Ma's molasses cookies came to mind. Just being able to pull a molasses cookie or two from the blue ceramic cookie jar on the kitchen counter...something he'd done a hundred times without thought...was no longer an option. He reminded himself that he needed to write home and tell Ma how much he missed her cookies. And her.

Ma. More than anyone, he'd assumed she'd always be there, as though she were a force of Nature like summertime or a good soaking rain. She was always present, always steady, creating three squares a day for everyone as if by magic. She always kept herself presentable, with her hair braided and pinned up like a crown atop her head, her hands and nails clean, her dress ironed. She kept the house spotless and organized. If he ever needed something—a lost sock, his mud boots —she could tell him where to look. She had nursed them all through illnesses, brewing up pots of chicken soup and herbal concoctions such as rose hips tea, placing her cool hands on his fevered forehead and seeming to draw all the pain out with her touch. How he remembered her best was sitting in the rocker between his or Ira's bed (they usually caught one another's "bugs," as she like to call them), reading from the tales of King Arthur or one of Walter Scott's novels.

He felt water on his face and looked up to see that it wasn't raining for a change before he realized that he'd been crying.

* * *

At the end of a day's march, he and Lew were usually so tired they simply fell out where they had been standing, throwing off their packs and lying on whatever surface happened to be there.

Experience soon taught them to be a bit more perspicacious. After twenty minutes or so it behooved them to push themselves back up onto their aching feet and look around for a suitable site to pitch their tent. The tents worked on the buddy system. Each "buddy" carried one half of the shelter, which was a simple sheet of canvas with buttons along the ridge for connection and grommets along the sides through which hand-whittled wooden pegs could be inserted into the ground. Two tent poles upheld the ridge.

Belden wondered what genius had ever imagined that a ridge of buttons could possibly keep out rain or snow, and it didn't. So he and Lew had taken to covering the ridgeline with one of their rubberized ponchos secured in place with ties to the tent poles and grommets. The second poncho they attached to one end, the end where their heads were to be, to keep some of the slanting precipitation and a few of the bugs off.

It amazed them both that there could be bugs in December, but this was Virginia.

A suitable site had to be relatively level, lest they slide right out of the tent during the night, but not *too* level, or precipitation would pool. Optimally, they found a grassy or mossy spot with about a five percent gradient. This area they first cleared of any debris, keeping a sharp eye out for insect colonies. After one night atop an ant colony they had learned that lesson. They pitched the tent with the covered end uphill and side-to-side levelness. They collected pine needles or dry leaves or cut cedar boughs to make mattresses. They stowed their packs beneath the poncho-covered end of the tent and used them as pillows. Their muskets they kept at their sides, unless they had been given the order to stack them in elegant pyramids. Then, employing their trenching tool, they would surround the tent with a shallow moat designed to carry water away from their little home. Each of them had two wool blankets which they folded into two intersecting U-shapes before bedding down, although on warm nights they slept atop them.

When it rained, at first it was rather pleasant. The sound of the drops spattering on the taut canvas was almost musical. Belden loved the smell of the newly-watered earth, rich and musty, that came with rainfall.

But when the rainfall turned into a downpour, things changed. Water began to drip from the ridgeline. They moved away from this central drip but had to be careful lest they touch the canvas sides and create seepage there. If their moat got overwhelmed by a prodigious drenching, the resultant flood under the tent walls turned blankets sodden. Belden discovered that one of the virtues of wool was that it retained the capacity to hold some heat even when wet, though sodden blankets were never a happy prospect.

Belden had never liked wool much. It itched him something terrible. He much preferred cotton or linen clothing to wool. But he had to admit that wet wool was warmer than wet cotton. Like most soldiers, he slept in his clothes, which minimized the degree of contact with his blanket. However, his uniform itched like the dickens. He was thankful that he'd brought his cotton long johns to wear underneath the uniform, and he'd already written home begging a second set. A long march and 24-hour wear suffused his small clothes with a stench even Lew complained about, but Belden seldom had the time to rinse them out. If he had a second set, he reasoned, he could wash the set he'd worn that day each evening and don the other pair, which would have had a 24-hour period to hopefully dry and be refreshed.

He remembered how offended he'd been by the Negro watermelon-seller in Alexandria. Perhaps he had only a single set of small clothes and no access to bathing facilities.

Lew didn't mind wool at all. It was something Belden hated about him. That, and Lew's ease with beautiful women. He could just walk up to one and begin a conversation on just about anything, and the beautiful woman would just smile and laugh, and within minutes they were getting on like old friends.

The more beautiful the woman, the more tongue-tied Belden got. He felt like an idiot walking over and saying, "Nice day, isn't it?" the way Lew could. Lew had coached him to be direct and honest: "Just say, 'I think you're very attractive and I'd like to get to know you better,'" he suggested, but saying that made Belden feel like a lame man trying to run the hundred-yard dash hopping in a gunnysack.

Awkward, to say the least.

Lew said he was easy with women because he had three sisters and had learned early how to talk to girls. Belden wondered at this, since he had a sister and a mother who didn't talk any differently than his father or brother did. He'd never had a problem talking to *them*. But the more attracted he felt, the harder it was to make himself approach a woman. With Cinder it had been easy, having known each other from childhood.

"Faint heart never won fair maid," Lew pointed out, needlessly.

"That doesn't help," Belden said.

"Practice on old women and plain women," Lew suggested. "Skip the beauties until you get more relaxed with women in general."

Belden had always liked much older women. They were so receptive. Most even seemed grateful that a strapping young man would take the time to notice them. He took Lew's advice to heart and made a conscious effort to chat women up on the rare occasions they encountered one—and Lew hadn't already launched himself on her. When that happened Belden felt like a third wheel, standing there watching the two of them gushing. He often just wandered away. It was best when they ran into two young women and Lew had snagged the beauty. Then Belden could then push himself a bit to have a go at the also-ran.

He did notice that most beauties seldom had beautiful friends. He wondered if they picked a plain friend so there wasn't any competition. There was only one Queen in any beehive.

* * *

They halted outside Fairfax and began cutting trees to build cabins for winter camp. Belden and Lew used their tent over slating pole rafters for a roof and chinked the walls and chimney with moss and mud. Unlike that of some of the other boys, their cabin didn't burn down when they built their first fire in the fireplace, which they had the good sense to line with stones. The tiny cabin was soon so hot they had to open the door. They sat in their skivvies and dried their uniforms and brogans, warm through for the first time in weeks. They "borrowed" one of Cookie's pots and a bar of soap and heated water for a delicious sponge bath. They felt like kings, and clean kings at that.

But their comfort was short-lived, for it was here that they got news of Burnsides' defeat at Fredericksburg, where the plucky general had attempted to move the Army of the Potomac across the Rappahannock on pontoon bridges in the face of Lee's entrenched Army of Northern Virginia. Lee hadn't contested the river crossing, but when the Union troops were on the south shore, he'd slaughtered them wholesale in a withering fire. Burnsides had lost close to 13,000 Union soldiers and had been forced to flee back across the river.

"At least he took the battle to the Rebs," Lew said. "Unlike chicken-hearted McClelland."

"Yeah, but he led a lot of good men into harm's way," Belden said. "I heard that the Union bodies were stacked up so high on the field that the next wave used them like a wall. Can you imagine?"

They both felt pretty sober when they thought about it. The Union couldn't seem to find a general who could beat Lee.

* * *

On the morning of January 19th in the year of Our Lord 1863, the 107th broke camp and marched south to Stafford Court House through the worst storm imaginable. A slushy rain alternated with stinging sleet driven by ferocious winds. Belden could hardly see the man marching before him in line. The wet turned the roads into bogs and the mud collected on their brogans, weighing down each step. They forded cold, rushing creeks, which wet them through but at least drove the mud off their brogans for a brief time.

All his young life Belden had dealt with such weather by staying inside as much as possible. The Cranes had always stacked sufficient stores of dry, split wood on the back porch to see them through the longest storm, and they kept their stoves and fireplace crackling. The walk to tend to the animals in the barn was short and their winter chores brief. They were soon back inside a warm house tight enough to keep out the winds that hurtled down from Canada across the Great Lakes. The temperatures in Virginia might not have been quite so low as in New York, but the continual exposure to the bitterest elements was grueling. The entire regiment was coughing so hard upon rising mornings that they sounded like a sanatorium full of consumptives. Many fell ill and had to be sent back to hospitals. Belden wondered how many of them got to be cared for by his brother.

Those that managed to continue grew tougher, inured to the harshest weathers, able to march twenty miles a day in mud and sleet. They began to imagine themselves the equals or betters of Jackson's "Foot Cavalry." Someday, they told themselves, they'd show old Stoney a thing or two.

* * *

A pleasant surprise awaited them at Stafford Court House: They received their pay for the first time. No matter that there was almost nowhere in the tiny town to spend it. The roll of greenbacks in a front pocket made a man feel frisky, putting him in mind of the finer things in life, like a glass of good whiskey or a woman's soft touch.

A week later they marched to Hope Landing, on Aquia Creek, where they began erecting winter quarters for the fourth time. Belden and Lew had become efficient at it. They had a snug, chinked cabin within the week. They also got a look at their new commander, Major General Joe Hooker, of whom Belden wrote home "Hooker is a very pretty man." Nor was Belden the only one who made this observation.

Noah Brooks, who wrote for the newspapers, described Hooker as "by all odds the handsomest soldier I ever laid my eyes upon....tall, shapely, well dressed, though not natty in appearance; his fair red and white complexion glowing with health, his bright blue eyes sparkling with intelligence and animation, and his auburn hair tossed back upon his well-shaped head." Despite the fact that Hooker had preached that what the country needed was a dictator, Lincoln, desperate for a fighting general, had sent him to replace Ambrose Burnside, stating, "What I want of you is military success, and I will risk the dictatorship."

Hooker's fame preceded him, on two counts: That he was a fighter and that he took care of his troops. On the rumor telegraph, Belden and Lew heard that their new general had brought with him a hundred "clean women" to provide his men with feminine favors, for a small price. These women became known as "hookers," in tribute to the general's thoughtfulness.

While most of the rank and file was pleased to be rid of Burnside and proud to be in an army led by a general the newspapers dubbed "Fighting Joe," Hooker could not fight off the scourge of sickness in the winter camp. Illnesses swept through the ranks like Mongol assassins. On February 13th only some 400 men of the 107th were left for duty out of a regiment that had originally numbered 1019 six months ago. The remainder were either dead, wounded, or absent-sick.

Belden was sick for a week, then well, then sick again.

"Lew," he groaned, "there is no difference between people, North or South, rich or poor, black or white, greater than that between the sick and the well."

In mid-March they got word that John Singleton Mosby and two dozen of his Partisan Rangers had infiltrated the Union cavalry cordon around Fairfax Court House that had been sent to capture him and instead, turning the tables, captured Brigadier General Edwin Stoughton, two captains, thirty privates, and about 58 horses—all without firing a shot.

The story was that when the Rangers knocked on Stoughton's

door in the Truro Church Rectory, which he had commandeered for his headquarters, the startled general, suddenly awake and staring into the light of the lantern, asked, "Have you got Mosby?" and Mosby had replied, in his soft Virginian drawl, "No, suh. Mosby's got you."

It was rumored that when Lincoln heard of this contretemps he said: "I can make a much better Brigadier in five minutes, but the horses cost a hundred and twenty-five dollars apiece."

* * *

That was the bad news. The good news was that Union packets docked regularly at Hope Landing, off-loading not only better quality food and drink but **the hookers** who seemed to be dedi-cated to raising the morale of the troops to the best of their abilities, in exchange for a portion of that roll of greenbacks that kept growing heavy in your pocket over the months.

One balmy spring day, when the trees were budding and the wild roses were blooming in profusion, Lew said he was bored with both drill and sitting around camp whittling chess pieces.

"Ma always said, 'Only boring people are bored,'" Belden replied, setting up the pips for the next game of checkers. "I guess she wanted us to find something to do other than expect her to do a song and dance."

"Let's go down to L'Etoile for a drink of whiskey and some of their fish-head soup," Lew said. "I have a craving for fish-head soup and good whiskey."

Belden looked at his hut mate sideways. He added:

"Not to mention feminine companionship."

Like most of his fellow soldiers, Belden had been brought up in a good Christian home that looked askance at "harlots" or "scarlet women." While it might be the world's oldest profession, prostitution was not held in high esteem in the Bible or by the womenfolk at home, even though Jesus had befriended prostitutes and other scorned classes. Helen said that he'd made the prostitute Mary Magdalene his wife and had fathered a child with her.

Belden felt mortified when he remembered mocking her for this belief.

Lew rubbed his chin.

"I confess I wouldn't be adverse to a little feminine companionship. It would serve as an antidote to bunking with you all these long months. I mean, you are as fine a bunkmate as a soldier can have, but you lack feminine charms."

"I confess I am glad to hear it. That I lack feminine charms, as you put it so delicately. Okay, partner, grab your greenbacks and let's live like Frenchmen. *Viva L'Etoile! On y va!*"

L'Etoile had been named by an optimist. Far from being a star, it squatted more like a toad on the muddy banks of the river. It did have a deck built out over the water, and to this somewhat wobbly structure Lew and Belden were directed by a small, squinty man with a pencil-thin moustache who attempted a French accent. When Belden addressed him in French, he blushed while pretending that he understood. Their subsequent conversation went like this:

"*Comment sa va, le pain ici, monsieur?*"

"But yes, monsieur, the view is breathtaking, is it not?"

"*Non, monsieur, le repast, si'l vous plait.*"

"But yes, the ladies will join us a bit later."

And so it went. Belden gave it up and they ordered whiskey straight and bouillabaisse. The whiskey had probably cured for more than a week and the "fish-head soup," as Lew insisted on calling it, was chockablock with the bounty of the Chesapeake Bay—mussels, clams, filets of whitefish, and bits of what their waiter assured them was lobster but was more than likely crawdads. There was also a half loaf of sourdough bread with real butter. After months of hardtack and salt beef it was all delicious. Belden found his spirits rising with each bite.

"I do believe," he said, "that I've died in battle and gone to Valhalla. I've never eaten anything so good."

"We are probably missing the fried chicken and fresh kale back at camp," Lew joked. Cookie had never prepared either of these delicacies for the troops. In fact, the only chicken or fresh vegetables they ever ate had been purchased or purloined from local farmers.

"Do you remember that tough old rooster you arrested as a Rebel spy?" Lew went on. "And asked us to form a jury to give him a proper trial? I thought I'd die laughing when you banged your 'gavel'—what was it you used?"

"My pistol. I wisely unloaded it first."

"You banged the butt on a stump and declaimed, 'I hereby sentence this spy to immediate execution for treacherous spying activities. And if he is then cooked and eaten, such a fate is only fair and just.'"

"We cooked him up pretty tasty in that clay," Belden acknowledged, laughing. He loved the warmth and ease he felt in his body brought on by the whiskey and good food.

At that point two attractive young women were seated at the table next to theirs. They ordered beer and the bouillabaisse.

"Howdy-do!" Lew said. "Beautiful evening, isn't it?"

"Yeah," replied the shorter of the two, who had blonde hair and a red dress. "It shore is."

"Do I detect a Manhattan accent?" Lew asked. "We're from upstate ourselves."

"Brooklyn," she said. "Good guess. I'm Sadie. This is Maggie."

Lew reached over to shake hands and Belden followed suit, though he never would have been so bold on his own. Ma said that a gentleman didn't shake hands unless the lady offered her hand first. Ma was particular on points of etiquette.

At that moment he was very glad that Lew was his friend.

Maggie's hand was soft in his and she looked into his eyes. Hers were a dark brown, verging on black. She had smooth olive skin. Belden felt a ridiculous impulse to kiss the back of her hand like some European courtier but restrained himself.

Soon Lew and Sadie were joking and laughing together like old chums. Sadie was a firecracker with a sharp wit and tongue. Maggie was the quiet type, who sat very still and smiled like the Mona Lisa. She had full lips which Belden loved to watch smile. He could feel his heart beating as if it would jump from his chest. Was he really going to do this? Well, why not? He would probably be dead in a month. Why not have a bit of life before then?

Lew ordered another glass of whiskey all around and Belden found himself a bit giddy with the feminine company. He couldn't remember the last time he'd felt so good.

He found himself walking arm-in-arm with Maggie to her "boarding house" room. There was a large man in the lobby that took his greenbacks and no doubt kept order in the house. That gave him a moment's pause, but then Maggie was pulling him into her room and pouring him a glass of plum wine.

Although he'd always imagined that a "working girl" didn't enjoy her work, he wasn't sure why he thought that. In Maggie's case it wasn't true. She really enjoyed her work. Or else she was a consummate actress. It occurred to Belden that, in a society where a woman's choice was either marriage or spinsterhood, wouldn't prostitution be a possible option for a woman of passionate sexuality? Maggie wanted them both to be naked as the day they were born and she wanted to touch him all over, and vice versa, before anything else. This beautiful woman, who had seemed so demure, was quite capable of letting him know what she wanted, in a manner that was invitational rather than commanding. And he found that what she wanted was what he wanted as well.

His prior sexual experiences—all with Cinder—had been constrained by clothing and the fear of being discovered. To be naked with a woman who seemed to relish the act thrilled him beyond anything he had ever imagined. When he ejaculated quickly she was undeterred. Like a sorceress she enchanted a second erection. And a third. In between they laughed and talked quietly together. Their tryst was ended only when the large man (it must have been his ham-sized fist banging the door) shouted that he had ten minutes to get back to camp for Bed Check.

Dressing hurriedly, he promised her that he would come back as soon as he could. She kissed him deeply and said she would count the hours.

She would have many to count, because the next morning, April 27th, his regiment, now under the command of Fighting Joe Hooker, marched south and west.

10

THE RAPPAHANNOCK

April 1863

I t was a glorious morning. It seemed as if all the birds in the world were singing them off: Robins, cardinals, and bluejays produced a cacophonous symphony in the early light that animated the brilliant greens of the forest. Oaks and sycamores, maples and flowering dogwoods waved at them from overhead, while legions of dandelions turned bright yellow faces up toward them. Ahead, the colors of the Twelfth Army Corps fluttered like a tethered shooting star.

"I feel like a convict escaping from jail," Lew said. Lew was in fine fettle that morning. If he was missing Sadie he didn't let on.

As Belden marched beside Lew, he tried to sort out his own feelings. He had fallen in love with a prostitute—though to him she seemed just a regular girl. It amazed him how powerful was his feeling of connection with Maggie after only a few hours together. When he thought about it, he was even jealous, realizing she would be with other men before he could see her again. While he knew that such a feeling was ridiculous, given her *métier*, he couldn't help it. Well, feelings didn't always make sense. They just came, like springtime or winter. He wished he could master them better but knew that was a lost cause in his case, though he judged himself weak that he was so damned emotional.

That was a good reason not to participate in lovemaking with someone he knew from the get-go wasn't a good bet for the longer term. Well, why not have a longer-term relationship with someone who'd made her career choice one of making many men happy? Nah. He knew his jealousy wouldn't permit that. Could he rise above jealousy? Probably not. The green-eyed monster that had savaged Othello would make mincemeat of him.

He had to acknowledge to himself that his heart followed wherever his loins led him. He had heard other men talk as if their bodily parts didn't communicate.

Lew, for instance: "It's just like playing baseball, Bel. We play baseball with guys we don't fall in love with, right? Sex is just adult playtime. Think of it that way."

Belden shook his head. For him, that analogy was a real stretcher. And, in fact, he loved to play the game that was spreading everywhere with the soldiers. Someday, people might even play it in a field in Ohio. He laughed out loud at that preposterous thought.

"What's so funny?" Lew asked.

"Can you imagine men playing baseball in a cornfield in Ohio?" Belden asked, laughing all over again.

"Not hardly," Lew said. "It's just popular with the troops. If we weren't so goldanged bored we'd have better things to do. When this war is over, it'll follow in the footsteps of the dinosaurs, you mark my words."

"Wouldn't you rather be sharing a bed with Sadie tonight than a tent with me?"

"Hell, yes! But that's just a half hour of the day! What am I supposed to do for the other twenty-three and a half? Drill? Play baseball or checkers? We're off to see the Elephant, Bel!"

"And not just us, Lew. Even the Munsens will have to join us, now that Lincoln has proclaimed a draft for all healthy men between twenty and forty-five."

Lew laughed. "They won't serve, Bel. They'll just hire substitutes."

Belden had to admit that Lew was probably right.

* * *

They soon heard, by way of the Soldiers' Telegraph, that they were heading to Fredericksburg, which had been built on a hillside just to the south of a wide river known as the Rappahannock. General Lee had dug in along the heights a mile behind the town and supported his infantry with many artillery units whose guns had long since been calibrated on the south shore of the river. These heights were part of a chain of hills reaching from Banks' Ford three and a half miles to the west to Port Royal eighteen miles to the east, where the river became a broad estuary too wide to bridge. The town itself still bore the scars of Burnsides' misbegotten attempts to cross the river and take it. Surely Hooker wasn't fool enough to do the same, but there was much muttering among the common soldiers that he might be. He was, after all, a Union general.

Lee had chosen his line of defense well. Since repulsing Burnside, he had constructed redoubts for his artillery atop each of the higher hills between the ford and the port along a line of twenty-five miles. At the base of each hill he had ditches dug five feet wide and two and a half feet deep, throwing the excavated dirt up in front of the ditch to form a parapet which enabled a soldier to stand in the ditch and reveal only his head and shoulders to those approaching him. There were, of course, many more such hills in the twenty-five mile line than he could garrison. But, operating on interior lines, he could readily move troops and guns to whatever point the Union troops chose to attack. So secure did Lee feel behind such defenses that he sent away Longstreet with 20,000 men to protect Richmond.

Hooker, however, had no intention of making a frontal assault.

Belden and Lew knew this because William Van Auken of D Company was now his staff amanuensis, keeping the written record and passing on those discussions to his dear Bradford friends despite severe injunctions to the contrary. Hooker's plan was to flank Lee to the west, above Banks' Ford, with a strong force, while leaving sufficient strength across from Fredericksburg to deceive the enemy of his intentions and thereby hold Lee's Army of Northern Virginia in place. This flanking movement was to be made in absolute silence and out of sight of Southern eyes. That Hooker could imagine that he could march thousands of men, horses, and artillery around one of Lee's flanks in his home state of Virginia without the wily old general being aware of what was happening was breathtaking; that he might actually be able to pull off this maneuver was nothing short of mind-boggling.

To the rank and file soldier a flanking attack was the obvious strategy. Because the Rappahannock was only 150 yards wide at Fredericksburg, the pickets from both sides often bantered across the relatively peaceful waters

"Hey, Yank, when is youal comin on over? We cordially extend an open invitation."

"You can leave off throwing up so much dirt over yonder, Reb. No way we're coming across here again. But I reckon you better watch your back."

Since the first battle of Fredericksburg, the pickets had instituted an unofficial truce, which was still in place all these months later. There was no gunfire across the river.

There was even a free trade policy. Each side made ships out of wooden boxes fitted with sails to cross the river, carrying tobacco one way and coffee and tea the other. Newspapers were also a popular item of exchange. It was as if, Belden thought, the common soldiers on both sides held no ill will for one another, but realized they were caught up in a drama far larger than themselves.

* * *

The 107th had made camp well back from the river. But Lew and Belden often strolled down to its banks to see what they could see of the Rebel defenses, and, hopefully, to catch sight of a fair Southern lass. One mild afternoon a Union regimental band marched down to the river and began serenading Yankees and Rebels alike with Northern tunes, including "Yankee Doodle Dandy." Hearing the music, Lew and Belden sauntered over to listen. There they found the riverbank almost blue with Union soldiers sitting on the grass. Across the Rappahannock they saw a mass of the gray uniforms of the Confederates. It occurred to Belden that the artillery batteries of either army could open up and slaughter a passel of their opponents, but both sides respected the truce. It was like everyone had laid down their weapons and was attending a concert together. It was a beautiful spring day and the balmy atmosphere was perfect for a concert.

During a brief break, one rebel soldier called out from across the river: "How 'bout playin' some a ourn?"

The bandmaster conferred with his musicians, tapped his baton on his leg, and the band swung into "Maryland, My Maryland." The cheers and applause from the other side was so loud that it was as if the Confederates were sitting in the same concert hall with the Yankees. When that song was over, they shouted out more requests, and the band played "The Bonnie Blue Flag." The cheering was now almost deafening, despite the expanse of water. When the band struck up "Dixie," the Rebels stood up and cheered their lungs out. Belden felt himself tearing up and hoped no one noticed.

* * *

Belden was impressed by the sheer number of Union troops encamped along the northern bank of the Rappahannock, with some units as far to the rear as Aquia Landing, where Maggie plied her trade. He wished he could be there yet. Maybe he could get a day pass. If not, maybe he could slip away for a night with nobody but Lew knowing.

The 107th New York was in the Third Brigade of the First Division of Major General Henry Slocum's Twelfth Corps, which was one of seven regular corps in Hooker's Army of the Potomac. There was also an eighth all-cavalry corps commanded by Brigadier General George Stoneman. This was an innovation Hooker had devised. He called them his "Dragoon force." Instead of attaching separate cavalry units to each division, he had amalgamated the bulk of his cavalry in a separate corps. This reorganization was to have a momentous impact upon the upcoming battle.

According to Van Auken, Hooker had entrusted Gen. Dan Butterfield, his chief of staff and the man who had written "Taps," the lovely mournful melody the bugler played at sunset, to convey his plans to Lincoln, and to Lincoln alone. Such was Hooker's concern with security. On Sunday, April 12th, Butterfield walked into the White House, told Secretary of War Stanton that he was sorry but had orders to disclose the plan of battle only to the President, which left the Secretary, Butterfield reported, looking "black as a thundercloud." Only when he was closeted alone with Lincoln did Butterfield unveil Hooker's plan.

Hooker was going to send Stoneman's cavalry corps of almost 10,000 horsemen far west to the Rappahannock Ford to flank Lee's Army of Northern Virginia. Their mission was to swing in behind Lee, brush aside any resistance, and cut the railroad from Richmond that was the main Rebel supply line. Without supplies, and with a strong Union force in his rear, Lee would have to fall back from his strong position at Fredericksburg to protect Richmond. Hooker would then cross the river with his infantry and catch Lee between hammer and anvil.

Lincoln was impressed. It was by far the most innovative plan that any of his generals had thus far created. He wished them all Godspeed.

* * *

That same day Hooker gave Stoneman his orders. They were clear and explicit. "I worded my instructions so strongly," Hooker later wrote, "I thought that they would wake up a dead man to his true condition." The orders themselves said "your cavalry corps is the initiative in the forward movement of this grand army. Upon you must depend to a great measure the extent and brilliancy of our success. Bear in mind that celerity, audacity, and resolution are everything in war....Let your watchword be fight, and let all your orders be fight, fight, fight...."

Stoneman was instructed to take rations for eight days and to make at least a daily report. He was to begin the march upriver at dawn the next day.

To mislead about his objective, Stoneman was told to drop the word that he was bound for the Shenandoah Valley to pursue Grumble Jones' Rebels there. Then, or so Will reported it, Dan Butterfield had a true inspiration. Remembering that Col. Sharpe, their intelligence officer, had divulged that both sides had broken the other's signal flag codes, he created a ruse.

On the afternoon of April 13th, just back from his conference with the President, Butterfield concocted a deceiving message for signal officer Samuel Cushing to flag from his station right across the river from Fredericksburg:

> *Our cavalry is going to give Jones & guerillas in the Shenandoah a smash. They may give Fitz Lee a brush for cover. Keep watch of any movement of infantry that way that might cut them off & post Cap. C.*

The next day Butterfield was delighted to hear that a Federal signal station had intercepted (and decoded) a Confederate flag message that began "Dispatch received from Yankee signal flag," followed by his ruse message. He reckoned that this message would be passed up to Lee.

Lee took the bait. He telegraphed Grumble Jones on April 14[th:]

I learn that enemy's cavalry are moving against you in the Shenandoah Valley; will attack Fitz Lee in passing. General Stuart, with two brigades, will attend them. Collect your forces and be on guard.

"Can you believe it?" Will asked them as they sat around the evening fire smoking Rebel tobacco, which they all agreed was the best product of the South. "Butterfield's a genius. He suckered them good. Now we've gotta hope Stoneman has some stones."

Stoneman's cavalry corps was already on the march. The 13th was clear and dry, with solid footing on the roads. By nightfall he was twenty miles upstream with the largest cavalry force the war had yet seen.

At the same time Hooker ordered each soldier to draw eight day's rations and 60 rounds of ammunition, with more rations and another 80 rounds per man to go on pack animals. Rumors flew, but no one was certain what was happening, other than something big.

"We're off to see the Elephant," Jack Knickerbocker said. "Write out your will and testament."

"I've got nothing to leave to anyone," Belden replied. "But I am writing a letter home. So much for a trip to see Maggie."

"You po', brokenhearted boy," Jack sang, then added: "I heard the postmaster's been told to hold all mail for two days, so the Rebs can't intercept any revealing letters."

"As if we know anything. Old Joe's good at keeping a secret."

"Except for Will's loose lips."

Later, in their tent, Lew said to Belden, "Do you think what Will tells us is on the level?"

"Sure. Why would you doubt him? He's always been a straight shooter."

"You do know that he likes to dress in women's clothing, don't you?"

"What?! Pshaw, Lew, how in the dickens do you know that?"

Belden could feel Lew shrug in the dark.

"I thought everyone in Bradford knew it. Says he has a 'feminine soul' that he must express."

Belden was quiet for a time. At last he said:

"Well, so what. Doesn't make him a liar. Just the opposite. If he's that open about something that embarrassing."

* * *

The good weather held on the 14th, but, according to Will's report, Stoneman spent the day creating a complex scheme for crossing the Rappahannock at four widely separated fords that involved a lot of noise at two other ones. Though none of the fords was guarded by more than a token force of pickets, Stoneman seemed reluctant to cross. It was clear that Hooker's admonition that "celerity, audacity, and resolution are everything in war" had gone unnoticed by the Dragoon's commander. Night came with Stoneman still meandering on the northern bank.

At 2:00 a.m. on the 15th the skies opened and the rains came in buckets, and it pelted down for twenty-four hours. By the end of the day the river had risen seven feet at the Rappahannock Bridge. Stoneman pulled back the one unit that had crossed the river, several of them drowning when they did so.

Hooker, meanwhile, was assuring Lincoln that the campaign was starting well. "If Stoneman can succeed in getting all his cavalry across the Rappahannock, the storm and mud will not damage our prospects. In another 48 hours they should be astride the railroad to Lee's rear."

But far from sitting astride the crucial railroad, Stoneman couldn't even cross the river.

* * *

Storm after storm came down from the Blue Ridge, battering the roads. Will reported Hooker was furious, but there was nothing to be done. Stoneman's timidity had lost him the best chance. He began to amend his original plan. His spies told him that because of Butterfield's ruse, Jeb Stuart and Fitz Lee had repositioned themselves far to the west, to thwart the supposed attack on Grumble Jones in the Valley. This left a twenty mile wide gap on Lee's left. Hooker decided to throw 40,000 infantry into that gap as soon as was practicable. Although it was a gamble, Hooker put his odds of success at "eighty out of one hundred."

Secrecy was once more of the greatest importance, so Lee would not have prior knowledge of the plan. Only Hooker and Lincoln knew the details. When Hooker called his commanders together at HQ, with Will present to take notes, he disclosed only that the divisions encamped along the river were to remain in place and make plenty of noise, while three corps—the Fifth, Eleventh, and Twelfth—under the commands of Meade, Howard, and Slocum—were to march out as silently as possible at first light on Monday the 27th. They were instructed not to burn their trash when leaving camp, as was customary, and there were to be no bugle calls, no drums, and no cheering by the men.

Howard's "Dutchmen"—Americans of German descent—were in the lead. The order of march had been dictated by where the three corps were encamped, and Howard's Eleventh was nearest the crossings. The largely German regiments had been under Siegel's command (they had liked to say, "I fights mit Siegel!"), but Siegel had been replaced with Howard. With a non-German in command, no one knew how the heretofore timid units, who had a reputation for bolting, might fight under him, but they were now the point of the spear.

Howard's corps was the smallest of the three; Meade's, with 23,600 men, was the largest, nearly the size of Howard's and Slocum's together. All three fell into line of march and kept as quiet as possible. Because the roads were still damp from the prior storms, they raised no dust and their footfalls were muted.

Hooker took the further precaution of ordering each household to be secured as the Union forces came to it, garrisoning each with soldiers who prevented the occupants from leaving their homes or signaling across the river.

* * *

The first day's march went smoothly enough over wide roads to the Harwood Church, where they bivouacked for the night, keeping their cooking fires small and concealed behind hills. Before they could sup, however, Lt. Goodrich ordered Belden's squad from K Company to secure the rectory and the minister's family.

"Just make sure no messages or messengers go out, including any attempt to put a candle or a lantern in a south-facing window. Keep the curtains drawn. Above all, be civil. I want to hear of no behavior unbecoming of a gentleman. Take your own supper and breakfast rations with you."

"And here I thought I might get a good night's sleep," grumbled Simon McGee, a man who Belden and Lew did their best to pretend wasn't in the squad. They hadn't liked him since school days; he had been a bully henchman of Jesse Munsen.

"You have something to say, Private McGee?"

"Nothing, sir."

"Good. Belden, I'm promoting you provisionally to Sergeant. You'll be in charge of these rapscallions. Catch up with us at daybreak."

"Yes, sir."

* * *

At the rectory door, Belden knocked politely. A girl of perhaps twelve or thirteen opened the door. She had a mass of blonde curls and bright blue eyes.

"Damn!" McGee whispered. "They sure do grow 'em good-lookin' down South."

Lew gave him an elbow in the ribs.

"Please forgive us for intruding," Belden said, doffing his cap. "Might I have a word with your father, the minister?"

The girl smiled. It was the widest smile Belden had ever seen. It seemed to stretch from ear to ear.

"Of course, suh. I shall go fetch him."

When she walked back into the house, she left the door open.

McGee was muttering something about "risin' beauties." Lew gave him another elbow, harder this time. Belden heard him grunt.

"Hell, boys," McGee said, "if she's old enough to bleed she's old enough to butcher."

Belden turned on him a face white with fury.

"Take your caps off when you go inside," he said. "Simon, you keep your big mouth shut, or Lew will shut it for you."

When the minister came to the door, Belden had to wonder whether he was the pretty girl's father, for he was one of the ugliest men Belden had ever laid eyes upon. Short and skinny, he had a deformity in his back that caused his body to contort and for him to move sideways, like a crab. His mismatched eyes—one gray and one green—stared off in opposite directions behind thick spectacles. Belden looked at first one, then the other, unsure which might be focused on him. At last, he chose the one on the right.

"Good evening to you, suhs," the minister said, in a high voice that might have come from a woman.

"Good evening, sir," Belden said, saluting. "Please excuse us. We come from Gen. Hooker and convey his compliments. He has ordered that all households this side of the river are to have a guard of Union soldiers to prevent anyone from leaving the house or from signaling across the river."

"Well, suhs, then by all means I must invite you in. Will you sup with us this evening?"

"We appreciate your hospitality, sir, but wouldn't dream of imposing upon you in that manner. We have our own rations. Perhaps we could prevail upon your kindness to allow us to heat them at your fire."

"Even better, suh. We have been blessed by the Good Lord

through the agency of our congregation with a cookstove. Please come in, and welcome to our humble home."

The other seven soldiers, even Simon, took off their caps and crowded through the doorway into a spacious hall that ran all the way through the house to a back door that was open to the air. Belden set one guard by the front door and another at the back.

"No one in, no one out," he cautioned them.

The minister looked taken aback at this but said nothing. He led them into a large kitchen, in which stood a small cookstove with a large pot bubbling on top, smelling delicious. At the kitchen table sat a still-handsome woman in her forties and two small children, probably six or seven. The older girl stood behind the woman who was clearly her mother and from whom she had inherited her beauty. The two younger children were both rather homely. Belden deduced that the mother had been married before and widowed, then bore the two smaller children to the minister.

"Please let me introduce my family," the minister said. "My wife, Betty, my elder girl, Sophie, my younger girl, Liz, and my son, Robert. Oh, and I am the Reverend Johnnie Jones."

Belden bowed, as his mother had taught him, and introduced himself and the other men present by rank and name. He went on to explain what they had been ordered to do and once more apologized for the intrusion.

He sent two men upstairs to draw the curtains and keep watch. After asking permission of Mrs. Jones, he set Simon and Lew to heating up their rations on the stove. He caught Lew's eye and Lew nodded in understanding: He'd keep close tabs on McGee. Sophie ran to fetch a pot from the pantry large enough to heat all eight rations at once. Belden noticed that Simon was watching her the way a cat studies a mouse.

"We'd be happy to share our humble repast with you gentlemen," Mrs. Jones said. "We have more than enough. It is a simple rabbit stew, full of vegetables from the spring garden."

In the end, the soldiers shared their rations with the Jones family and accepted healthy portions of rabbit stew in their tin cups. The Rev. Jones said grace while they all stood around the supper table holding hands. Belden found the moment touching. Young Robert took his hand with no hesitation and smiled up at him. It had been a long while since Belden had been in the bosom of a family and it came to him how much he missed it.

They chatted around the supper table as though they were old friends and then sang some hymns together. They were the same hymns that the Union soldiers had sung at their churches at home. They sang one of Belden's favorites, "The Son of God Goes Forth to War," and once again Belden marveled at the fact that men who prayed to the same God and sang the same hymns fostering the same martial spirit could be trying their best to kill one another.

It was, he thought, a crazy war.

As the Jones family prepared to go to their beds for the night, Belden changed the guards. He sent Lew upstairs to monitor the second floor and put Jim Fuller on the back door, while he himself took the front. The other men stretched out on the kitchen and parlor floors for forty winks. Belden told them he'd wake them for their shift halfway through the night and sat down on the stairway facing the door with his Enfield leaning against a newel post. The riser behind him had just the right spacing for him to lean back on the step on his elbows. He never thought he'd have found sitting on a stairs so comfortable.

What seemed a moment later he was swimming upward out of his recurring dream of being lost in the cave. He was mortified that he had fallen asleep. The acting sergeant. Dereliction of duty. He could be shot for it. Hell, he should probably order his own men to shoot him. At sunrise.

Then he heard again the sound that must have wakened him. As if it were an echo. A whimper. Pushing himself to his feet, aware of the stiffness in his arms and shoulders, he moved back in the house toward where he thought the sound must have originated. It must have come from Rev. Jones' study, the cluttered room that they had left closed. No room to sleep in there, with all of it stacks of books and papers.

Belden slowly pushed the door open. It was pitch black within. He felt a small touch of panic, as if a moth's wing had touched his belly, and he almost shut the door.

There it was again.

Reaching into his breast pocket, Belden extracted one of his prized possessions: a loco foco match, against which he flicked a thumbnail.

As the match burst into flame he saw first the face of the boy, Robert, white with terror, then the back of the head of a man kneeling beside him holding a hand over the boy's mouth.

Belden extracted his revolver from his holster with his free hand, still holding the sparkling match, and pressed it against the man's head.

"Let him go," he said.

Releasing the boy, Simon McGee turned, squinting into the light, saying "I was just trying to keep him from signallin'!"

At the same time the boy screamed and grabbed onto Belden's leg as if it were a life preserver. He pressed his face into Belden's thigh, sobbing.

Belden dropped the match and the room went dark. McGee slapped away his hand holding the revolver and bolted from the room.

"Bring a light!" Belden called.

A door wrenching open on stiff hinges, voices in the kitchen, then the metallic sound of a lantern's chimney being raised to allow the match in. A minute later, footsteps thundering down the stairs, and light coming toward the study.

"Catch McGee!" Belden ordered. "He went out the front door!"

Then Betty Jones was in the study in her robe and Robert ran to her arms. Belden said, "I think he's all right, but please check!" to her and went past them into the hallway with its lanternlight. The hall was full of men with muskets following the lantern out into the front yard.

There was no sign of McGee. It was as if he had been a ghost who had evaporated into the cool night air. There was nothing to see but hosts of stars peeking through the gathering clouds.

* * *

They slept little until the sun rose. After a breakfast of grits and eggs with the Joneses, who couldn't seem to thank them enough, they followed a path through the woods that the Rev Jones pointed out to them and intercepted the Warrenton Post Road ahead of their unit.

The problem for the entire Twelfth Corp as well as the Fifth was being behind Howard's Eleventh. Will had confided that Howard failed to follow Hooker's orders to travel light and had burdened himself with a mile-long pack train of mules carrying far in excess of the standard amount of baggage and ammunition. For every two hours the Eleventh dawdled forward, the other two corps had to wait another hour for the Dutchmen.

Hooker had ordered his troops to move out at four a.m. but when Belden and his squad, minus one, reached the Warrenton Road it was still full of the mules and wagons of the baggage train of the Eleventh.

"It's because the Dutchmen need to have their kegs of beer," Lew joked, "to provide liquid courage. That's why they need so many goddam mules."

It was widely held that the Germans had been recruited with the promise of free beer in any campaign.

"Wish I could have a beer right now," Belden said. "Even though"—and here he squinted up at the sun— "it's not yet ten in the morning."

At midday Hooker came riding up, his face red with fury, to berate Howard for holding up the entire right flank of the army. Despite the orders to the contrary, his men cheered him as he rode past, his staff, including Will, in tow. After all, they were well away from observation by the Confederates. Hooker doffed his hat and kept riding. Howard later said that the subsequent tongue-lashing he endured from Hooker was "my first mortification of the campaign." It was not to be the last.

Not long after, Belden's squad was proud to see the bright colors of the guidons of the Twelfth Corps swing into view. They fell in with the 107th and Belden made his report to Lt. Goodrich.

"He ran off, you say?"

"Yessir."

"I'll list him as a deserter."

"I hope you bring charges against him for what he did."

"Of course. Fall in, sergeant."

Belden hesitated. It was clear that Lt. Goodrich had more pressing concerns than one soldier's sexual predilections. Then, saluting, he said:

"Yessir." Thinking: *when I run into McGee again, I'll cut off his balls.*

* * *

That day they made a twelve-hour march. The Eleventh camped near Mt. Holly Church, just behind Kelly's Ford. Slocum's Twelfth and Meade's Fifth fell out along the road past Crittenden's Mill, still cursing the "Dutchmen" and longing for their kegs of beer. They all knew they would be assaulting the ford in the morning.

Meanwhile, Will told them at supper, Hooker had ordered Reynolds' First Corps and Sedgwick's Sixth, on his far left flank, to move quietly up behind the hills right in front of the river with their pontoon bridges. They were to camp without fires and stay off of the ridgelines, waiting in readiness to cross the Rappahannock below Fredericksburg when Lee pulled his troops out to meet the flanking movement from the other side.

Though Belden liked knowing what was going on, he also felt uncomfortable: If Will was blabbing like this, how could Lee not know what was coming?

* * *

Though they saw less of Will now that he was required at HQ so much of the time, he told them an amusing tale that night as they did without any fires and ate cold rations:

Two weeks earlier, when Stoneman had set off on his now much-delayed flanking movement, Col. Adolphus Bushbeck's brigade from the Eleventh Corps had taken position opposite Kelly's Ford to facilitate Stoneman's crossing. When Stoneman failed to cross the Rappahannock, Bushbeck's brigade stayed in place and arranged an unofficial truce with Rooney Lee's pickets on the south bank. As the days passed and the Federals set up their camps and made no threatening moves, the Rebel pickets began to relax.

But at 6:00 p.m. on the 28th, when the Rebs were cooking dinner, out of Marsh Run, 500 yards south of the ford, came a flotilla of canvas pontoon boats, each manned by fourteen paddlers, splashing straight across the river. At the same instant the sharpshooters from the 73rd Pennsylvania set up a withering covering fire. The Rebels got off one wild volley and scattered away on their horses, leaving dinner behind.

The engineers soon had the pontoons tethered and then planked. The 17th Pennsylvania Cavalry were the first to cross, watched with satisfaction by Hooker himself. His revised plan, he thought, was working. By the light of torches, Carl Schurz's division followed. The Union army was on what had been till then Confederate ground.

* * *

The Confederate pickets, cut off from any chance of warning the others downstream, fled west to Rooney Lee's headquarters at Brandy Station. Some of Jeb Stuart's cavalry did pick up a Captain Jules Schenofsky, a Belgian soldier of fortune who was on Schurz's staff. Capt. Shenofsky enjoyed the Rebels' hospitality so much that he soon told them that the entire Eleventh Corps was now on this side of the river, adding that it contained 14,000 men and six batteries of artillery. Apparently, he had forgotten that he must divulge only name, rank, and serial number under interrogation.

Jeb himself had received this intelligence by 9:00 p.m. at his HQ at Culpepper Court House. Stuart communicated with Lee by way of a roundabout telegraph system, but at least one of the stations had shut down for the night, and Lee didn't receive the news of the Kelly's Ford crossing for almost twelve hours.

At daybreak Stonewall Jackson, whose men were on Lee's right flank, got word that Reynold's First Corps and Sedgwick's Sixth were crossing the river on pontoon bridges *below* Fredericksburg. He sent an aide with this information to Lee, who was still asleep. Upon waking and hearing that the enemy was across the river on Confederate soil, Lee said with good cheer, "Well, I thought I heard firing, and was beginning to think it was time some of you young fellows were coming to tell me what it was all about."

Soon the bells of the Episcopal Church in the town were ringing to awaken his army. Hooker knew it had never been Lee's intention to attempt to meet the Federals at the river, where their superior artillery could decimate his troops. He would allow them to cross and make his stand in the strong defensive positions in the heights, as he had done in December when he had watched the Union soldiers' bodies stack up like cordwood and had said, "It is well that war is so terrible, or we should grow too fond of it." He had complete faith that no Union forces would dislodge Jackson's Second Corps of 38,000 infantry.

A Rebel deserter revealed that Lee had finally received Stuart's telegraph message informing him that at least one corps and probably several had crossed the Rappahannock at Kelly's Ford and were marching downriver. Lee now saw Hooker's plan: To catch him in a vise squeezing him on two fronts simultaneously. Fighting Joe was living up to his reputation. The advantage Lee had was one of interior lines: Unless Hooker could strike him on both flanks simultaneously, Lee could shift his forces to meet the attacks as they developed.

* * *

After their long day all Belden wanted to do was fall onto his blanket. In addition to his lack of sleep the night before, he found himself weary of leadership. He hadn't realized how much extra it took out of him to be in charge and responsible. Now, as he listened to Will's stories, he felt a sense of compassion for General Hooker and the pressures he must be dealing with. He yawned and felt a great lassitude in his limbs.

Lew didn't seem tired at all.

"I propose a night mission," he said. "Let's sneak up on those Dutchies and separate them from some of their beer."

"Great idea!" laughed Will.

"I'm in," said Jack Knickerbocker.

"Not me," Belden said. "I can hardly stand, much less sneak."

"Aw, come on, Bel," Jack said. "We deserve a little bit of payback from those louts."

"I can tell you right where the beer wagons are," Will added. "Not a mile up the road."

Belden stretched.

"I might be able to walk a mile for a taste of Dutch beer," he said. "Just as long as you lads promise to carry me back."

Laughing together, they left muskets stacked and haversacks tossed aside and began sauntering up the road as if they owned it.

They hadn't far to go before they were challenged by the rear guard of the Eleventh Corps.

"*Wo gehst-du?*" said a fat man who was perspiring like a hard-ridden horse. He held up one huge hand. The fingers on it were like sausages.

Will stepped up to the front of the merry group, who had stopped laughing at the wonder of a man wearing Union blue speaking a foreign language.

Will spoke loud and distinct, as if he were addressing a deaf child.

"WE...GO...HOWARD."

The fat sentry looked at him without comprehension.

"GEN-ER-AL HOWARD!" Will elucidated. "MACH SCNELL!"

Looking flustered, the fat man saluted. Will returned the salute and they pushed past the sentry, walking abreast up the road. On both sides of the road the rear guard's tents were lined up in neat rows with uniform stacks of muskets between them at precise intervals.

"What did you say to him to get us through?" Lew asked.

"I told him to make it snappy," Will said. "But it wasn't what I said but how I said it. Hooker pointed this out to us on his staff: Germans only understand hierarchy. They'll bully you unless you bully them bigger."

"Wait a minute," Jack said. "The Dutchies ain't even Dutch? They're German?"

"Yup."

"Well, they sure give the Dutchies a bad name."

Fireflies were appearing in the gathering dusk, blinking their greenish lights. Will pulled out a pint bottle. It held a couple fingers of amber whiskey.

He took a swig and passed the bottle around.

"Empty it," he said. "Don't leave a single drop."

His friends happily obliged.

As they did so, Will captured a firefly in his cupped hands. When the bottle was returned, he held it upside down and eased the firefly up inside.

"Everyone," he said, "catch two or three and bring 'em here to me."

"Great idea!" Belden said, already capturing one. He noticed it had a dry, musty odor. It crawled calmly within his hands.

"What the...?" Lew asked, puzzled.

"He's gonna make us a lantern," Belden said.

When the bottle was pulsating with the insects' natural light, Will held his makeshift lantern aloft, one finger partially over the spout to prevent the odd firefly from escaping while still letting in air for them to breathe.

"Brilliant!" laughed Lew.

"On to the saloon," Will said.

* * *

The 'saloon' came a half mile later in the form of several kegs resting on scalloped sawhorses. The pranksters joined a queue of soldiers speaking German who were filling battered pewter mugs from the flow out of the taps, which was continuous and splashing onto the ground when some drinker didn't position his mug soon enough after the last. The boys of the 107th pulled out their canteens, emptying them of water, and filled them with beer by the light of their green lantern. The German-American soldiers pointed to it and laughed, shouting at them in German in a friendly manner.

"*Ja, ja,*" Will said, nodding his head and grinning. "*Das ist goot!*"

And then, after receiving many hearty slaps on their backs, following the greenish pulsating glow, they started back to their bivouac.

"Jesus God and Mary," Will said, after a swig from his canteen. "Not only do they have kegs and kegs of beer, good beer I might add, if a bit warm, they even carry scalloped sawhorses on which to erect them."

"Will," said Lew, "you seem to have erections on your mind."

Will laughed as hard as the rest of them.

"Not just on my mind," he said, eliciting another laugh.

Belden stopped to take a long drink, sighed, and said:

"Yesterday we were cursing the Dutchies or Germans or whoever they are for plodding. This evening I would like to propose a toast to them for hauling this ambrosia into the wilderness and sharing it so freely with us."

"Hear, hear," said Lew.

"Beer is also proof that God loves us and wants us to be happy," Jack added.

"And," said Will, "predisposes us to the belief in a beneficent Deity."

"Praise God," Belden said, "from whom all blessing flow."

"With the emphasis on *flow*," Will said.

By the time they reach the sentry for their own regiment, they were singing the same hymns they'd sung the previous night with the Joneses.

* * *

At Kelly's Ford at dawn on Wednesday, April 29th, Hooker put Gen. Slocum in command of his right flank, issued his orders, and returned with Will in tow to his headquarters on the south bank. His plan was for the flanking movement to divide in a tripartite spear: Meade's corps was to head straight southeast paralleling the Rappahannock toward Ely's Ford on the Rapidan River, while Slocum's, followed by Howard's, was to march four miles farther south to Madden's Tavern, then turn southeast to strike the Rapidan at Germanna Ford.

Behind them, George Stoneman's much-delayed cavalry corps finally made it across the Rappahannock and set off to harass the enemy in his rear, if harass is not too strong a word. He dithered about, burning a few supplies, and seemed to be avoiding conflict.

Slocum carefully selected the seasoned brigade of Thomas Ruger —3rd Wisconsin, 27th Indiana, 2nd Massachusetts, 13th New Jersey, and the 107th New York—as his lead brigade. Belden and Lew, among several others, were named to be skirmishers.

Being a skirmisher meant that you were fifty or a hundred yards out in front or on the flanks of the main body, a good ten yards from your nearest fellow, your musket—with bayonet fixed—at the ready, all your senses alert for danger. The lucky ones got to be on the main road. Belden and Lew were out in a cow pasture on the left, trying to avoid stepping in fresh patties.

It was beautiful country, with gently rolling hillsides of lush forage and fertile crops, well-kept farmhouses, and verdant stands of hardwoods. At one farm gate smiling Negro slaves met them with buckets of cold water and tin dippers.

These, thought Belden, as he gratefully accepted a drink, *are the people we are fighting for.*

"Yassuh," one man said to him, "yo drinks all you wants. Jes keep yo eyes on that stand a timbah back yonda. It be full a Rebs."

Trying to be casual about it, Belden glanced over the black man's shoulder to the copse two hundred yards distant. Lush oaks, sycamores, and maples, seeming almost park-like. He could see no movement within the sturdy trunks of the trees.

"Thank you, sir," he said.

The man grinned, showing well-spaced teeth big as pearls.

"Ain't nobody nevah called me suh, befo', suh," he said.

"They will be, from now on," Belden said, and then felt embarrassed that he sounded so arrogant. "With God's help," he added.

"A-men to that," the man said, chuckling now. "Luther, you hear that? He done called me suh!"

Belden did his imitation of a hawk whistle and Lew turned to look at him. Belden pointed to the copse and made what they called the Injun' sign language for two-leggeds: waggling fore and middle fingers with the palm facing down, as if walking on air. Lew nodded and began surveying the trees.

A puff of smoke blossomed from near an oak, then came the sound of the shot and the ball whistling past his left ear like a demented wasp. Belden dropped to his stomach. He thought he could see movement in among the trees now. Though he had no solid target, he fired his musket so the main body would hustle up a company or two to drive the assailants off.

Behind him he could hear the slaves running, and for a moment as he reloaded he suspicioned that the Rebs had ordered them to set up the water stop to collect the Yankees for a bunched target. No, they wouldn't risk shooting down their own "property," as they liked to think of their slaves.

Belden glanced over to where Lew had found minimal cover behind a split rail fence and was now firing off another ball. He saw the musket recoil, the puff of white smoke, and then Lew lying down on his left side to reload. There was so much powder smoke in the copse that it looked like a fog seeping out from among the trees. This was a good-sized delaying force, not just a few pickets.

After reloading, Belden rolled over onto his belly and pulled off another shot. Behind him he heard a bugler sound the charge and, turning to look back over one shoulder, he saw a blue line moving toward him at the double quick. From the copse he heard a single command, and the firing coming from it halted. The Rebels were retreating.

The blue line went past him and into the copse, firing as they went, bayonets fixed. Belden reckoned that by the time they got there, there wouldn't be a Reb left to capture. He had to give it to them: The Rebs were too smart to make a hopeless fight. They could disappear like melting snow on ground they knew well, leaving their adversaries perplexed and frustrated.

The blue line entered the copse and the firing stopped. For all those Union soldiers knew, the skirmishers had been shooting at will o' the wisps.

Regimental commander Col. Alexander Diven came up to Belden on his horse.

"How many Rebs do you reckon were in that copse?" he asked.

Belden got to his feet, saluted, and said: "No way to tell, sir. I couldn't tell the Rebs from the trees."

Diven chuckled.

"Well, maybe that's a good thing. No matter. They're on the run now. Our boys showed them some spine. Good work, Corporal Crane."

Belden felt himself flush with pride that the colonel remembered his name. He saluted again, but Col. Diven was already trotting away.

Lew came over and gave him a thump on the back.

"We showed 'em!" he shouted. "We taught 'em some manners, didn't we Bel? Goddam, I wann kill me some Rebs!"

Belden saw a strange and frightening look in Lew's eye.

"You okay, Lew?"

"Okay? Okay? I'm colossal, I am! I could take on the whole Reb army!"

"Lew, I'm worried about you. Just breathe deep for a minute."

Lt. John Goodrich came up to them. He looked at Lew with some alarm.

"Are you well, Private?"

Lew saluted.

"Never better, sir!"

"You did well in the van, gentlemen," Goodrich said. "Fall back in with the company now. I suggest you chew some rations before we push on."

"Yes, sir!" Lew shouted. He and Belden saluted, and their lieutenant returned the salute and walked on.

Belden took Lew's arm, noticing as he did so that it was trembling like the leg on a nervous colt.

"Easy, Lew," Belden said. "Let's fall back and take some succor."

"I'm not hungry," Lew said. "I want to fight."

"Oh, I'm sure we'll get a chance for some fighting yet. Com'n, Lew."

* * *

After chewing some salt pork and hardtack, Belden and Lew fell in with K Company and began marching south and east. Soon they reached the bridge at Germanna Ford on the Rapidan River. Or what was left of it. Only the tall stone piers stood in the riverbed. The bridge itself had been burned.

The Rebs on the south bank decided to make a fight of it. Belden watched as Gen. Ruger sent the 3rd Wisconsin to the left and the 2nd Massachusetts to the right, flanking the Confederates and exposing them to enfilading fire. They soon raised the white flag.

Gen. Slocum ordered his corps to wade the river, powder pouches held high on the bayonets of their rifles. "Never mind your pocketbooks, boys, but keep your powder dry!" he called out. The river was running fast and came up to their armpits. Two boys were washed under. The bulk of regiments got across safely.

On the south bank the engineers discovered a treasure trove: a sawmill with pre-cut stringers and planks to repair the bridge. But, rather than effecting a full reconstruction, the imaginative engineers secured the stringers against the stone piers at water level and nailed the planks to them there. Both corps, their artillery, and a smattering of cavalry was soon across the Rapidan and in the rear of Lee's left flank.

Gen. Meade, meanwhile, had crossed the Rapidan at Ely's Ford. Hearing that Slocum and Howard had achieved the crossing, he ordered his men to wade the three-foot deep ford. Cavalrymen downstream laid down a thick rope across the river to catch those who lost footing. The small Rebel defense force trotted away without firing a shot.

Hooker had accomplished a masterful pincers movement, almost encircling Lee. A British military historian present at the battle compared it to Hannibal's attack on Rome through the Swiss Alps. Perhaps even more honoring were the words of Lee's artillery commander, Porter Alexander, in his *Personal Recollections*: "On the whole I think this plan was decidedly the best strategy conceived in any of the campaigns ever set on foot against us."

Belden Crane and Lew Whitehead, in Company K of the 107th New York, in General Tom Ruger's brigade, were at the very point of the spear aimed at Lee's flank. Between the two armies lay a miserable tangle of dwarf pines, fallen trees, wild blackberries, and honeysuckle overgrowths locals called The Wilderness.

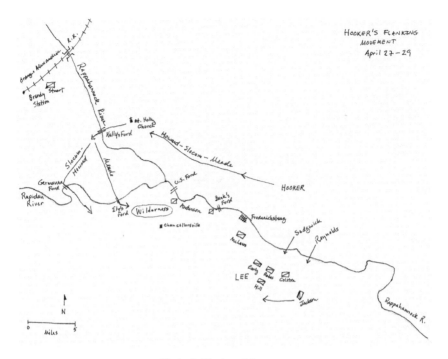

Hooker's Flanking Movement

11

CHANCELLORSVILLE

April 30-May 5

The next morning the 107th marched forward over the Germanna Plank Road, which was in poor condition, full of potholes and, in places, covered with mud. But Company K was elated to be on Rebel ground and on Lee's flank, facing minimal opposition.

"We're on our way to Richmond!" Lew shouted.

A Rebel cavalry unit was shadowing them, and from time to time they had to form a line and sweep them out of the way.

"Cavalry is no match for infantry!" Lt. Goodrich yelled. "Give 'em hell, boys!"

By midafternoon they had joined up with Meade's corps at a road crossing dominated by a redbrick mansion house. In it lived Fannie Pound Chancellor, widow of the brother of the builder, and her seven children, one boy and six attractive unmarried girls, the youngest of whom, Sue, was fourteen. These young women had been the belles of the ball when the Confederates had been present, and Sue was in love with Jeb Stuart. The Yankees seemed to lack gentility, pushing them all into a single room and commandeering the mansion for their head-quarters.

When Slocum came up, Meade was ecstatic, a profound change from his usual dour demeanor.

"The road is open, Henry! Let's push on and hit Lee's flank before he knows we're here!"

Gen. Slocum pointed out that, as the commanding general of the flanking column, he would follow Hooker's plan and wait till ordered forward, but he could certainly see how tempting it was to fall upon Lee's exposed flank. Slocum ordered the troops to set up a defensive perimeter and fell trees to form an abatis.

When Hooker finally arrived, he acknowledged that, had he been present, he might well have ordered the advance. He brought Slocum and Meade up on developments:

"Couch and Sickles are coming to our support here with both their corps, across the U.S. Ford, which we have secured. We are laying telegraph wire across that ford that will connect us here with HQ on the north bank. Reynolds and Sedgwick are across just below Fredericksburg, ready to assault Lee when he shifts troops to face us. Stoneman's Dragoons—Stoneman has been a great disappointment. He seems to have trouble crossing rivers. He was to have cut the railroad from Richmond that supplies Lee—and could bring up Longstreet. But he dithers about in the west. The railroad line is still open and running."

Slocum and Meade shook their heads gravely. They knew the problems that arose when subordinates failed to do their jobs. And they felt quite smug that they had done theirs very well thus far.

When Belden caught a glimpse of Sue Chancellor, he felt his heart beat like a wild bird in his chest. He couldn't believe she was only fourteen. She was one of those rare girls who seem to blossom into full womanhood at puberty. She seemed all soft curves and long hair. Her smile was radiant. She seemed to glow with an inner incandescence. When he said he was going to go give Hooker a piece of his mind about kicking the whole Chancellor family down into one shabby room, Lew had to restrain him.

"Bel! Get hold of yourself! The man's got a battle to fight! You give him trouble he'll have you shot!"

"Oh, pshaw!" Belden replied, but he gave up a quest even he knew was quixotic.

* * *

That evening they ate the fourth of their eight day's rations.

"Our packs are gonna be light from here on out," Lew said.

"Especially mine," Belden said. "I'm eating day five's as well. You know, eat, drink and be merry..."

"Don't say it," Lew interjected. "It's bad luck."

"Since when did you become superstitious?"

"Since the day that bullet passed through our coffeepot that was hanging off the back of my pack."

"Was that the day you wet your pants?"

"Slander, sir! Slander, I say!"

"How 'bout some coffee after dinner? Brewed in a patched pot."

"Good idea. Lighten the packs as much as we can."

"Moon's almost full tonight. Look how big it is!"

* * *

A thick fog covered the ground of The Wilderness the next morning. Belden could hardly make out his hand in front of his face. They breakfasted well and were ready to march by 6 a.m. but stood around till eleven before the order to Fall In came. By then the fog had burned off and the day was turning into a perfect May Day. Belden wondered if, back home, the children would still be twirling around the May pole holding ribbons. Would Cinder be one of them, or would she now be a stately matron watching from the outside? He pushed the thought of her from his mind.

Meade's corps had already gone ahead, marching northerly toward

Banks' Ford, and Howard's set out down the Orange Turnpike. Slocum's corps, with the 107th still in the lead, angled southerly down the Orange Plank Road. Within half an hour each column had lost sight of the other two as The Wilderness closed in like a curtain being pulled across a stage.

They hadn't marched far before they ran into Confederate skirmishers. They were ordered to halt and then to deploy on either side of the road.

"Slocum must believe there's big old bunch of the Rebs up ahead," Lew said. Belden could tell he was getting excited.

"I just wish we had something to deploy in other than interlaced dwarf pine," he added. Belden had to agree.

After a bit of a firefight, they were ordered to countermarch back the way they had come. That was the most discouraging thing that had happened to them in the last five days. There was a lot of grumbling from the soldiers in Company K.

"I hate going backwards," Belden said. "You can't win a war going backwards."

"I'll bet you a cigar Lee sent Jackson around our flank," Lew said, "and it's retreat or be enfiladed."

"Well, hell," Belden said. "Then why not face us due south and take it to him?"

"At least we might be able to see Sue again," Lew laughed.

* * *

They were not granted a vision of Sue Chancellor that day. Instead, they spent most of the rest of the day and night, while the nearly full moon gave them light, with ax and spade, strengthening their defensive position. Fightin' Joe had lured Lee out from the Fredericksburg lines and now had a chance to fight from behind earthen breastworks and abatis, a tremendous advantage in any battle.

By first light both Lew and Belden were exhausted and filthy.

There was dirt on their faces and down around their collars. Their hands were blistered and throbbing.

"Hard to believe," Belden said, "that a couple farm boys like us can't throw up a bit of a wall without getting blisters."

"We've grown soft soldierin'," Lew said. "God, I wish we could go jump in the river for two minutes."

"Let's go over to the well," Belden said, "and splash one another down."

"And maybe see Sue," Lew chuckled. "Be sure to strip off your shirt and skivvies so she can admire your noble physique."

"I'll get the lieutenant's permission," Belden said, grinning.

The water from the Chancellor's well was cold and refreshing. They felt renewed sufficiently to cobble together a breakfast of moldy biscuits and green bacon.

"A feast," Lew said, "fit for a king."

"Yeah, if we were trying to poison him," Belden replied. "I believe the word is regicide."

Lew was about to make a retort when the Rebel batteries opened up and they dove for cover.

* * *

Dan Sickles' boys, led by Berdan's Sharpshooters with their Sharps breechloaders, came through and made an attack around noon up the road at Catharine's Furnace. They returned with 296 Rebel prisoners, mostly from the 23rd Georgia.

"Hey, boys," Lew yelled at them as they trudge past, "hope you didn't surrender so you could eat some Yankee rations, cuz you'll be surely disappointed."

"Just you wait, Yank," one of them yelled back, "for Old Jack to get around your right. You'll catch hell tonight."

Belden fell into step with one of the Sharpshooters.

"Any sign of Stonewall Jackson out there?" he asked.

"We saw the end of a column of artillery, but they were heading south," the man replied. "I do believe they're retreating."

"Stoneman's Dragoons must have cut the railroad," Belden said.

"I doubt it. One of the Rebs had today's Richmond paper on him. The morning train got through, at the very least."

"What the hell is Stoneman doing then?"

"God knows, cuz no one else seems to."

When Belden and Lew got back together they traded information. Several men from the 107th listened in. After Will Van Auken, the Soldiers' Telegraph was the most reliable source of information about the larger picture they had. Each scrap of news was subjected to critical analysis and gnawed at like dogs with a bone.

"I don't see how Jackson could be doing one of his flanking movements without being seen," Jack Knickerbocker said. "We've got observation balloons up. They'd spot that many troops for sure."

"It's pretty breezy today," Bill Graves from A company put in. "Maybe the balloons are twirling so fast the professors with the spyglasses can't do much for tossing their hardtack."

"Good thing they're not right over us then," Lew joked. He got a good laugh. Belden had come to expect that soldiers would laugh a lot at the silliest comments when the danger was the greatest.

"Well," Jack said, "we know Stoney is the master of the flank attack. He's done it time and again with his foot cavalry."

"They march at two miles per hour," Graves said, "but they can keep it up for sixteen hours. They don't have much to carry."

"And a lot of them are barefoot," Lew added. "Did you notice that half those Georgians didn't have shoes?"

"Once your feet are toughened up," Belden said, "you don't need shoes. Remember when we were kids? We'd start going barefooted as soon as the ground thawed and in two weeks you could step on a bumblebee in the clover and not feel the sting."

Lt. John Goodrich appeared as if from out of the ground.

"Fetch your muskets, strap on your packs and fall in, boys!" he called out. "We're gonna go help Sickles win this battle."

By the time they were marching forward in a column of fours, the

Soldiers' Telegraph began reporting that Jackson had turned the right flank and that Howard's "Dutchmen" were fleeing, leaving behind even their muskets. The rumor gave Belden a peculiar feeling in the back of his neck.

12

CAPTURE

After marching east to attempt to shore up Hooker's center, the 107th was countermarched back west again to try to stem Jackson's attack and the subsequent panicked rout of the "Flying Dutchmen," as they were coming to be known. The Flying Dutchmen and their huge baggage train of mules and lager kegs kept coming through their line all evening, impervious to the officers who tried to halt the flood by, in many cases, shooting them down. They had dropped their muskets (or never picked them up) and were fleeing through the Wilderness for the fords. One Confederate noted that the Wilderness acted as a skein, letting the skinny ones slip through and holding the fat ones to be captured.

Captain Allen Sill addressed K Company when they were at rest in view of the Chancellor's mansion. They were getting tired of marching in loops.

"Gentlemen, we have had a long and trying day. I dislike countermarching as much as do you. It is up to us to thwart the Rebels flank attack that has overwhelmed Gen. Howard's Eleventh Corps. We must hold the high ground up yonder at Fairview to prevent them bringing in their artillery and subjecting the entire army to a deadly enfilading fire. K Company will be acting as a picket line out in front of the defenses. You may fire at anyone coming from the west. Jackson will continue to press the attack until we stop him, despite the fall of night. It is up to us to stop him. Leave your bedrolls here. Carry only one ration and water. Proceed one hundred yards beyond our breast-works, staying at least five yards apart, and try to find cover and concealment. Absolutely no one is to smoke or even light a match. Fire at any sound to the west of you. If the Rebs attack in force, the bugle will sound Retreat. You may re-enter our lines at that juncture. The password for tonight will be 'Fortitude.' God bless you all, and God bless the Union."

* * *

Belden and Lew shucked off their knapsacks and set aside tent, blankets, extra clothing and rations. They took 60 rounds of ammunition apiece, full canteens of water, and a single hearty ration of salt beef and hardtack. Belden also took the pistol he had purchased but had yet to fire, though now fully loaded. Then they went out through the Union line and began creeping to the west.

The moon, one night before full, lit their way, creating an eerie penumbra over the land. They made their way from rock to tree to bush, every sense alert. They were aware that not far out in front of them were Jackson's men, known by all to be the fiercest fighters in the Rebel army. Belden could feel his heart beating the way Charlie Ide would smash hot iron on the anvil with a hammer in each hand. He could see Lew off to his right, pausing now behind a split-rail fence that hadn't yet been used for the campfires. When Belden came to it he stepped over and kept moving. He thought he heard the click of hooves on stone ahead. Of course the Rebs would have a screen of cavalry out in front. He went down on one knee as they had been trained to do when fighting cavalry, raising his musket to his shoulder. He wished he could get one of those Sharps breechloaders. He tried to keep his breathing steady and listened carefully. There it was again. A horse. More than one.

He glanced over to where Lew had also sunk to a knee behind a rock. He'd heard it, too.

Then came the click of bridle and a low whicker. Belden squeezed the trigger and fired at the sound, aiming low to compensate for the declining slope before him. Lew's musket cracked a moment later.

The sounds of shouted voices and galloping hooves. Yup, it had been Reb cavalry. He hoped he'd hit one.

Still kneeling, he began the steps to reload: taking out the ramrod, attaching a cleaning patch, ramming it down the barrel, pulling out, and remembering to replace the cap. He could now reload in under a minute, and he was proud of his skill in doing so.

He rose to his feet and continued forward.

The dark forest erupted in flame and then came the staccato explosions of many muskets. Belden dropped to the ground.

OmyGod! That must have been our cavalry! And I drove them right into the Rebel lines!

But then he heard a man crying out, "Cease fire! This is General Jackson's staff! Cease fire!" And another voice saying, "It's a trick, boys! Keep firing!" And the fusillade re-commenced.

Belden rose and trotted a dozen yards to a small copse. He saw Lew following him in. Should be good cover in here.

It was much darker in the trees. As he waited for his eyes to adjust, Belden felt more than heard it—a movement close by—and then the cold steel of a musket pressed into his neck.

"Don't move or make a sound, Yank!" a whispered voice hissed. "Less'n you want to be crow meat. Set down your piece real slow-like."

Belden laid his Enfield on the ground and raised his hands up in the traditional gesture of surrender. He saw from the corner of his eye that Lew was doing the same. With another hiss his captor prodded him forward down the slope.

* * *

Within fifty yards they heard a voice from out in the dark of the thick forest say "Liberty." The countersign was "Or Death." Belden reckoned he could have come up with that one all on his own. Every schoolchild in the nation knew Patrick Henry's stirring declaration in support of the Revolution.

They passed through what seemed to Belden to be hundreds or thousands of men, dressed in a motley collection of clothing, many of them barefooted. But he could see the pride flashing in their eyes in the moonlight. These were Jackson's Foot Cavalry, and many of them had more than once covered upwards of twenty miles a day without shoes.

He was escorted to the rear under the guard of two men whose parents appeared to have been half human and half weasel. While they were delighted to be heading away from the battle, these two pretended to be disappointed that they were missing it and took out their manufactured frustration on Belden, prodding him with their musket barrels and cursing him in accents fermented in the Deep South. They also relieved him of his rations, his pistol, the few greenbacks he had on him, and his brogans.

They entered a clearing where a macabre tableau was lit by two lanterns. Several men were attempting to hoist a man in a resplendent uniform onto a litter. One arm was bound up in a sling. He groaned in pain when they moved him.

One of his guards boxed him on the ear.

"Don't be lookin thataway, you Yankee scum!" he hissed.

Belden averted his eyes as the litter was borne away into the darkness, following one of the lanterns.

He was pushed over into the light of the second lantern where a captain in gray examined the insignia on his uniform and spoke in a soft, cultured voice.

"I see, Corporal, that you are in the 107th New York Volunteers."

"Yes, sir," Belden said. Might as well be polite.

"That would be part of Ruger's brigade in Slocum's corps, would it not?"

"That is correct, sir."

"Is the entire corps in front of us?"

"I believe so."

"Any others?"

"I'm not sure, sir."

"Thank you for your honesty, Corporal. Take him away."

His guards prodded him once again and Belden, walking gingerly on tender feet, began picking his way through the forest. He seemed to step on every pine cone and blackberry. His feet were starting to hurt like the dickens but he tried to keep himself from crying out.

"Hold up a minute," he heard the Confederate captain say. His guards turned him to face his interrogator.

"How come you have no shoes, Corporal?"

Belden kept his eyes on the captain and off the guards.

"They were taken from me, sir."

"Lonnie, give the man his shoes back," the captain said, and the weasellier of the two guards sat on the ground and pulled off the brogans he'd just deprived Belden of.

"Thank you, sir," Belden said, slipping them back on. He felt a wave of gratitude for the captain that stunned him in its enormity. And he was grateful to himself for stowing his razor inside his sock, where it had stayed.

When they reached the rear of the Rebel lines, Lonnie spat on the ground at his feet and then turned him over to the sergeant of the prisoners' guard. Belden was roped up with a long string of bluecoats, who looked beaten and dispirited. He didn't see Lew among them. When Belden asked the sergeant where they were going, he got himself smacked on the same ear for his troubles. He wondered if he'd be deaf in that ear for life.

No sooner had he suspected deafness when the high ground to the east erupted in flame and thunder and grapeshot whistled through the air. Men, mules, and horses began screaming all around them. As he dove for the ground, pulling those tied to him with him, Belden thought, *This must be what the Apocalypse is like.*

Once the Union cannonade had abated, they were moved further toward the rear.

That night they got no dinner, just a single tin cup of brackish water. They were roped so closely together that they had to lie down or stand up as one man, which made sleep near impossible. Every time a Union captive had to relieve himself the whole line had to stand up.

Right then Belden decided that if he ever got out of this alive, he'd never again watch another man urinate or defecate in front of him. He'd had enough of that for a lifetime.

* * *

He must have gotten a couple catnaps, however, for he startled when his captors rousted them up and gave them a square of weevil-infested cornbread. He glanced down at his feet to see if he still had his brogans. Yes. Relief flooded him.

Still tied in line, they were marched south and west, then north and west. They stumbled along for most of the day, then, as the sun was going down, herded into a fenced corral that put Belden in mind of a sheep pen. Here they were unroped and fed some ham-flavored beans on a tin plate. That night they slept on bare ground. Fortunately, it was almost balmy.

The following day they were herded onto boxcars on a train and confined in darkness. It seemed to Belden that the train was heading north rather than south, which made no sense to him.

The next morning the train lurched to a stop, they were kicked awake, made to relieve themselves in an open-trenched latrine beside the tracks, and marched down a dirt road. A thick deciduous forest lined both sides of the road. After they had marched a couple of hours, the forest gave way to a clear-cut gash in the trees in which stood a wooden stockade.

There were fresh stumps everywhere, like a pox upon the ground. They were herded through a gate into the stockade. Several dirty men, thin as rails, stared at them without comment. Through the center of the stockade ran a trickle of brown water. Iron bars driven into the creekbed secured both the entry and the exit of the water flowing beneath the stockade wall. There was one section of the stockade where there was a break in the logs perhaps ten feet wide. Here there were strands of barbed wire about six inches apart which seemed to be nailed to the exterior of the stockade. Immediately to one side of this opening there was a log guard tower with several boys in butternut brown, each with a musket or rifle, no doubt hoping that one of the prisoners would be stupid enough to attempt to climb the barbed wire.

The barbed wire fascinated Belden. He had read of it being used in the Argentine and in the American West but had never seen it before. The barbs were sharp and could snag a man trying to climb up and possibly flay his flesh to hamburger. He wanted to touch a barb to assess its sharpness, but even as he had the thought one of the boy guards, who was no more than fourteen, pointed an old Revolutionary War musket at him.

"Git away from that thar fence, you Yankee ijit!" he yelled, in a voice that still had cracks in it. Belden backed away, hands up to placate the lad.

On the other side of the tower was a second gate. This now opened with a loud creak and a dandy of a man in a Napoleonic hat with a feather and a spotless gray uniform replete with a chest full of gaudy ribbons minced in, accompanied by four simian-like guards carrying hefty oaken clubs. One of them barked out, "Ten-shun, prisoners!"

The stiff and tired Yankees attempted to stand up straight. The dandy stepped forward.

"At ease, gentlemen," he said, in a voice that would have made Vermont maple syrup envious. They relaxed a little, going to Parade Rest, hands clasped behind them.

"I am Colonel Wolfe, commandant of this here holdin' area, where you will remain incarcerated until exchanges can be accomplished. We hope that those exchanges will not be long in coming. Until that time, you will enjoy our hospitality, and you will behave yourselves as gentlemen, mindful of your status as guests in our country. We expect that you will cause no ruckus and make no attempts to escape—if you violate our expectations you will be severely punished. If you attempt to leave the stockade, you will be shot. Though our sharpshooters in the tower behind me may be young, they have been firing their weapons most of their lives and are remarkably accurate in their targeting. You would be astute if you do not approach within ten feet of the walls, for in that space they are at liberty to shoot you. For our part, as your hosts, we will do our best to feed you as well as we ourselves eat, which, since the illegal and scurrilous Yankee blockade of our shipping, has not been up to our customary standards. As to shelter, you see that we have erected a few canvas tents. More are on the way. We leave it to you to arrange sleeping shifts."

He cleared his throat and smoothed his thin moustache with one finger before continuing.

"Finally, I wish to make you aware of the generosity of the belles of the South, who, with naught but charity in their hearts, sometimes visit during the afternoons between four and five. They often bring delicacies to supplement your meager diet and are willing to act as an amanuensis to write letters home for you. You may converse with them through the barbed wire, remembering the ten foot rule. Guards will be on hand to pass their delicacies to you—and to occasionally exact a carrying fee. We offer this privilege to you out of our sense of Southern hospitality, and we have no doubt that your sisters are offering Confederate captives in the Northern prison camps the same."

He said this last as if everyone was aware that the Union lasses would be doing no such thing and that the South was, in every way, a superior civilization. Still, Belden found himself enheartened by the idea, and, as he glanced at the faces of some of the other prisoners, saw many of them smiling. Being able to converse with a woman, after not having even seen one since Sue Chancellor, was a pleasant thought.

"Are there any questions?" the Commandant asked.

"Yessir," a new prisoner said. "What in tarnation is an amanu— whatever you said?"

"A secretary," Commandant Wolfe said. "Whatever do they teach you in those Yankee schools?"

Belden held up a hand, as if he were still a schoolboy.

"Please identify yourself, suh," Colonel Wolfe said,

"Belden Crane, Corporal, 107th New York Volunteers," he said.

"You have a query, Corporal?"

"Yessir. I'm wondering how long we might be quartered here before an exchange can be effected."

"Ah. I see you are a man of careful diction, Corporal Crane. The exchanges seem to take place in fits and starts, as the politicians use them as pawns in a chess game, which we men of action abhor. However, you should expect to enjoy our hospitality for approximately six to eight weeks. My aide-de-camp, Captain Martin, will be along presently to transcribe your names, ranks, and units of origin. The sooner we get that information to the proper authorities in the North, the sooner the process may begin. Through that process your families will be apprised that you are still alive and that they may reasonably expect to be reunited with you in the near future."

There were a few more questions, which the Commandant answered in his genteel and syrupy tones, and then he left them to their thoughts. Soon after, Captain Martin appeared with two privates carrying a table and a chair. Martin was a porcine man with a moon face and a sloppy look. He ensconced himself at the table in the chair and waved them forward.

"New prisoners only," he said. "Youal form a line. Name, rank, and unit designation only. Let's get through this as quick as we can. The ladies will be visiting us soon and I have no doubt that you wish to beautify."

Belden hadn't thought of that. He stepped out of the long line of new prisoners and made his way to the trickle of water that they had called a "crick." More like a seepage, he thought. He squatted beside it and reached for the water when he felt a powerful blow strike the side of his head. First he saw stars. Then a huge man who towered above him, blotting out the sun and seeming all dark shadow.

"Downstream for wash-up, you ijit!" the shadow said, in the accent that meant he was from New York City. "This is where we drink!"

"Sorry," Belden managed. "You didn't have to wallop me."

"That'll help you remember the Rule," the New Yorker said, laughing raucously and turning away.

Belden sat and rubbed the left side of his head. It was the same side that had absorbed the previous blows. It was becoming quite tender.

"Hey!" he called after the huge man. "What's your name?"

"Puddin' Tame. Ask me again and I'll say the same."

"Thanks for the lesson, Mr. Tame," Belden said.

Still walking away, the big man shot Belden the middle finger of his right hand over his shoulder. Yup, definitely a New Yorker.

Standing and walking down along the trickling water, Belden found several men reaching into the seep to bathe hands and faces. He joined them. The water smelt of roots and earth, but it was cool and refreshing.

"We noticed you met Tony Spaghetti," one of his fellow bathers said, not looking at him.

"That isn't really his name," Belden said. "He has a funny way of introducing himself."

"He won't tell us his real name," another man said. "But we know he's a wop so we made up a suitable moniker. Don't get on his bad side. He's head of a gang of wops in here that run the camp."

"What are wops?" Belden asked.

"Damn Eye-talians," a second man put in. "Come over here and think they can take over our country. Goddam mackerel-snappers. They're not even Christians, they're goddam Roman Catholics." He spat to one side to show his contempt.

"Well, he better not mess with me again," Belden said. And he pulled his straight razor from his sock and flipped it open. The blade flashed like a semaphore. The three men moved closer to him to obscure the view of the razor from outside.

"How in God's name did you smuggle that in here?" one asked in a whisper.

Belden shrugged.

"I didn't realize it was contraband," he said, grinning. Then, using the murky surface of the water as a mirror, he began to shave.

As he did so, he tried to bat away the cloud of gnats with his free hand. He couldn't remember if the pesky creatures had existed in Bradford. Black flies, yes, but not gnats, at least in this number. They swarmed around the eyes, trying to dip in for a drink. Then they'd often get stuck in his eye. If he held still and stopped himself from blinking, he had found, they would usually escape. Otherwise, he'd have to fish a gnat carcass out of his eye. Which wasn't easy, without a good mirror.

He could understand why God had created this War, but not why he'd created gnats. Or mosquitoes. Two creatures Noah should have left off the Ark.

PART III

PRISONS

13

WALT WHITMAN

After his training at the Steaurt mansion was complete, Ira was assigned to a hospital in Washington, D.C. At first he was consumed with learning his duties and attending to the many patients put under his care. It was some time before he wrote a letter home describing it and the poet he met there:

Dear Family,

I am now in Washington, D.C., stationed at the Armory Square Hospital, which is on Seventh Street just across from the grounds of the Smithsonian Institute and just beyond the old City Canal. While the Smithsonian is a grand redbrick building that resembles a castle, the Canal is a fetid moat filled with dead cats and reeking with pestilential odors. I avoid the latter and look forward to exploring the former, which I understand to be filled with remarkable objects from the history of our nation, including George Washington's sword.

The Hospital itself comprises eleven long pavilions placed side by side. Each is 149' long and 25' wide and 13' high at the gable peak. The one in the center is the administrative center, contains the officers' quarters, and boasts both a mess hall and a laundry. The remaining ten each hold 50 beds, which are usually full of patients. At the end of each such pavilion are the mess halls and lodgings for the nurses, many of whom are maternal females. Dorothea Dix, the Superintendent of Nurses, requires that they all be over 30 years of age and quite plain in face and dress. I hope that the same standard was not applied to me, though perhaps I appear older than my years. Our quarters are of course segregated by gender. When will the Abolitionists rail against this unfair separation? I have already written a letter of protest to the Director of the Hospital, an intelligent and fair-looking man named William Hammond, whom I hope will share my sense of humor.

From my numbers you can compute that we serve 500 wounded and sick. In the whole of this city I understand that there are 20,000 such invalids and therefore probably another 39 such hospitals. While there are many who lost limbs on the battlefields, the great bulk of them are stricken with dysentery, influenza, typhus, or typhoid. The degree of suffering is overwhelming. Had it not been my good fortune to meet a truly wonderful volunteer by the name of Walk Whitman, I am not certain that I could face each day. Walt is a poet and a Great Soul. He is a good man of Quaker background who follows the Inner Light. He shows by his example that what is truly healing is a compassionate ear, that is to say, the ability to really listen to a man in pain and to receive him as he is, rather than to attempt to "fix" him. Many of our patients are beyond fixing. He has a better bedside manner than do most of the doctors, who seem consumed by trying to imagine which nostrum to prescribe. As I follow Walt through the ward, I am amazed by how the men thrive when he attends them. I am attempting to learn his methods so that I, too, can bring a mitigation of suffering to the sick and wounded.

Walt is also, as I mentioned, a poet. He gave me a copy of his book of poetry, entitled *Leaves of Grass*, which I assume is meant to be a pun. At first I was shocked, for he eschews the use of conventional rhyme and meter, but instead sets up a kind of surging rhythm, through which, he says, he hopes to "capture the music of the ocean waves playing upon the sandy shore." He seems to speak in poetry. Many would say that he writes mere doggerel, and I am quite certain he will never achieve fame or even widespread popularity, but I must confess that the more I read his *Leaves* the more impressed I am by his originality. It is as if he has exploded the traditional bounds of poetry and is creating a new form.

I shall conclude now, as I wish to make the post. With this letter I send you each my love. I have had no epistles from Belden and wonder whether you have any news of him.

Ira

After Ira posted this letter he walked down the Mall toward the Capitol. He was seized with a moment of whimsy in which he saw the unfinished Capitol as a trope for the Nation. Would it not, he thought, be a sign if, when the Capitol was completed with the statue of "Freedom" atop its tholos, the Nation would be One again.

He had learned from Walt that this colossal statue was being sculpted by a Negro slave named Philip Reid. He could see, as he approached the immense building, that the vast majority of the workers up on the scaffolding were black men. Was it not a bitter irony that the very center of the Nation was being built by men who were still slaves?

At that moment he made himself a solemn oath: "I am willing to die for the Cause of Freedom, and I will fight against the evil of slavery until my last breath!" He thought that if, in part by his efforts, the curse of slavery could be eradicated from his country, his life would have been worthwhile in the eyes of God. He hummed the melody to himself:

As He died to make men holy,
Let us die to make men free.

If Christ could make the sacrifice for all of us upon the Cross, so he, Ira Crane, could make the sacrifice to rid this Nation of slavery.

* * *

Ira wrote his next letter to the unit where he'd last heard from his brother:

Dear Bel,

I have met a fascinating human being by the name of Walt Whitman. He is a scholar and a poet, quite familiar with the works of Mr. Emerson, but capable of thinking far past that good gentleman's ideas. For instance, the issue of the belief that the Soul is separate from the Body, an unchallenged doctrine coming down to us from our Puritan forbearers. Emerson believes that each of our souls coalesces in the Oversoul, which seems to me yet another name for God. So, when we die, our soul rejoins the Oversoul as a drop of seawater that has splashed up against the hull of a ship, having had a brief moment of separation, will fall back into the ocean and rejoin it. Here we can see the Oriental influence upon Emerson. Walt, however, believes that the Body and the Soul are one! That there is no Body without a Soul and no Soul without a body!

I do seem to remember from when we were in confirmation class with Rev. Atwill that the Christian, or at least the Episcopalian, belief is that when we go to Heaven we are reunited with our best bodies. The Apostles' Creed contains the statement of this belief in "the Resurrection of the Body," does it not? (Do we get to choose which body? Or are we assigned one? Can we put on a different one each day as if it were a suit of clothes? That might be amusing. Might we not have access to, even, say, a feminine form? I have always thought that if a man could live within a woman's body for but a brief time, his compassion for the fair sex would deepen. And vice versa.)

Please forgive my flights of fancy. I fear that working among so many of the sick and dying turns my thoughts to final things. I do not mean to complain that these thoughts are necessarily dark and somber. In fact, just yesterday a young man from Ohio was brought in whom we believed to be quite dead. But he awoke with a strangled cry and began breathing again. His face—I fear I cannot do this part justice—contained a shining light and his eyes held a serenity one seldom sees in quotidian life. He said that he had been apart from his body for some time. That is to say, he could look down as if from the peak of the pavilion and see his own body lying apparently dead upon the cot. Then he went up through the canvas and hurtled into the vast darkness of space, toward a bright light that, he said, filled him with perfect peace. From the light emanated a voice, a beautiful, calm voice, which seemed both male and female at once, informing him that his work on Earth was not yet done and that he must return to complete it. He said that he wanted more than anything to stay in the presence of that Being, whom he called Jesus Christ, but that he accepted His command and came back to his body.

Now, I ask you, dear brother, had this young man in fact "died," gone toward Heaven, encountered our Lord and Savior, and then returned to his bodily existence? Certainly those of us who had examined him upon admittance could find no sign of life in his body, neither breath nor pulse. We were ready to consign him to burial. I am heartened by his experience, for it seems to validate our beliefs. Shakespeare somewhere speaks of Death as that "country from which no traveler has returned," but did this young Ohioan not do just that? And does this case not seem to suggest a radical separation of Body and Soul? Walt's answer was that perhaps we leave behind our shattered body and gain a pristine one at the Resurrection.

Do I bore you with such theological speculations? Perhaps I am suited to becoming a man of the cloth? Shall I, after this damnable war is over, attend Harvard and dress in black with a high white collar? Believe me, I shall lecture you long and hard about your sinful ways, dear brother.

I hope this epistle finds you well and happy.

Yr loving brother,

Ira

P.S.

I cannot resist appending a portion of the Preface to Mr. Whitman's aforementioned tome. I find it quite profound and hope you will also:

"This is what you shall do; Love the earth and sun and the animals, despise riches, give alms to everyone that asks, stand up for the stupid and crazy, devote your income and labor to others, hate tyrants, argue not concerning God, have patience and indulgence toward the people, take off your hat to nothing known or unknown or to any man or number of men, go freely with powerful uneducated persons and with the young and with the mothers of families, read these leaves in the open air every season of every year of your life, re-examine all you have been told at school or church or in any book, dismiss whatever insults your own soul, and your very flesh shall be a great poem and have the richest fluency not only in its words but in the silent lines of its lips and face and between the lashes of your eyes and in every motion and joint of your body."

* * *

When Walt invited him to walk out for a beer after their shift, Ira was...he wasn't sure how to describe his feelings. "Ecstatic" was too strong, while "honored" seemed stiff and pedantic. What he said to Walt was, "I'd be happy to," which was pretty close.

It was one of the warm and muggy days of early summer, with the golden light of the setting sun illuminating the Capitol like a huge gold orb. Well, an unfinished orb.

"Now that," Whitman said, pointing with his beard, "is sublime."

"I have never quite understood the precise meaning of that word," Ira replied.

"That's because it has no precise meaning but rather is an amalgam word with myriad meanings brought together imprecisely," Walt said. "A year ago I would have told you that in that one word, 'sublime,' coalesced the larger meaning of our age, which some are calling the Age of Romance. I see a certain sublimity in our landscape painters as well as the essays of Mr. Emerson and the poetry of Mr. Bryant. I would have said, grandly, that we live in the Age of the Sublime. By which I would have meant that as a nation we were experiencing adumbrations of the Divine, such that the hairs on the forearms and the back of the neck erect. The sublime is marvelous, that is to say full of marvels, and at the same time awe-some, by which I mean provoking some feeling of awe. It is what you feel when you are in untrammeled wilderness and you are overwhelmed by its beauty and its terror at the same time. In that feeling you experience the Divine, which is also magnificent and awe-some. I trust I make myself perfectly obscure."

Ira laughed, then said: "It is, you must admit, an ineffable concept. And yet I think I know a bit of what you mean. It is more a warm bodily sensation than a cold idea, and therefore it escapes hard definition. I have felt it when, hiking through virgin timber, I come out upon a prospect over one of our Finger Lakes, blue as a gem set in the green breast of the forest, with the distant mountains floating like clouds beyond. Or sometimes I have it in church, when the music of the organ swells my heart with some familiar hymn and I look up above the flames of the candles to the heavenly light streaming in through the stained glass and feel unbidden tears wet my face. I have always assumed that it is a bodily experience of the Creator's presence."

Whitman was nodding, his hat flopping on his head.

"You've got it, Ira, you've grasped it! God, but I wish I had a hundred like you to read my *Leaves*. I'd be the most exalted poet in these States!"

Ira felt himself blushing with pleasure, a feeling he warded off by re-directing the conversation:

"You said that you felt this a year ago. But not now? What has changed?"

"This war has changed everything, Ira. You are no longer in your forest at home, coming out upon a prospect that lifts your heart, as you have just so eloquently described. What you see around you is not sublime but terrible: men maimed by the machines of war, men sick unto death. And this putrid canal, reeking with effluvia."

He pointed to the Old City Canal nearby, looking like a disgusting pudding, its miasmic odor stinging their nostrils.

"These experiences are the opposite of the sublime. They even call into question the very existence of the sublime, which is, as you say, ineffable. This odor, the smell of gangrene, the sight of a newly amputated arm—this is our new reality. It overwhelms the senses, it blots out the sublime. It makes the sublime seem unreal, even. Yet we both know that that is not the case, for we have felt it. How then do we equilibrate these two very different realities, what we might call the Sublime and the Sordid? No! That alliteration is but a cheap rhetorical trick. But what is the right word? If we call it the Real it makes the Sublime seem to be the Unreal. Yet this new Reality has taken over our senses as well as our perceptions and when we look at the new grass upon the graves of our brethren we think of the rotting bodies beneath rather than the green coat our Mother puts on in renewal. I fear we shall lose all connection to that portion of the Real that is also invisible, so flooded are our senses with what is so painfully visible. But enough of my barbaric yawp! Let us turn in here at Ma Maples's establishment and sample her brew! She produces a singular beer within one week. Amazing. Yet be not tempted by her foodstuffs, lest you perish of ptomaine poisoning! In fact, in my great experience, I have come to the conclusion that one should never eat at a place called 'Ma's.' That is the first rule of the good life, my son. The second is 'Never play cards with a man named Doc.' You shall meet many men of that name in this establishment. I suggest that you steer clear."

Ira laughed.

"Have you any other such rules of life, Walt?"

"Several, but to learn them you'll have to buy me at least one mug of grog."

They wedged their way in through the mass of men, most of them red-faced with drink, and ordered two pints from Ma, who was like no mother Ira had ever met—sour of face and disposition, with gray, untidy hair and hands like claws that were adept at snatching up their greenbacks.

Ira judged the beer to be bitter, warm, and flat, but he hesitated to mention this finding to Walt, who seemed to be enjoying both it and the surrounding company of men.

14

SOUTHERN BELLE

After Belden had shaved, he washed face and hands and plastered down his unruly dark brown hair. He brushed off his clothing with his hands as best he could, but he still reckoned he looked a fright, as Ma would have put it. He felt a stab of homesickness and a longing for Ma's unfailing kindness. He gave his information to Captain Martin, who was one of those genial, plump men who abhor work and who are skilled at finding shortcuts around what had to be done. Belden squinted up at the sun. It must be getting on to four. Like most people who didn't carry watches, he'd long since become adept at telling the time from the sun and the stars. The heavenly timepieces weren't all that different down here in Virginia from how they were in New York. He was looking forward to the visit from the ladies.

He heard them before he saw them, chattering and laughing together like happy magpies. When they came into view he saw that they wore the plumage of the males of the avian species: long dresses in mauves and greens, pink and pastel parasols, and hats—goodness gracious, he'd never seen such hats, some of them laden with feathers and some with imitation fruits and flowers. It was a startling contrast to the butchered clearing with its ugly stumps. It was a bit overwhelming to see so many young women after so many days of hardly seeing one.

With them came their servants, black women and men, most of them grey-haired, walking a few paces behind, carrying baskets. From these they produced fried chicken, biscuits, apples, and jugs of apple cider. Belden couldn't believe his eyes. It was like a panorama out of a children's book.

Then he saw her. Or rather, he saw her eyes, staring out at him like two oval emeralds from under a broad-brimmed straw hat. He had never seen eyes so green, liquid, and unblinking. They captivated him. He felt like a butterfly being pinned to the specimen case. His breath caught in his throat.

Her skin was an alabaster white. She must have been careful to avoid the sun. Her lips were full and very red, as if she had been sucking on ripe strawberries just that morning. He immediately wanted to kiss those lips. He took a step toward her, then felt himself tremble as she took off her hat and a cascade of redgold hair fell down around her neck and shoulders.

Her hair shone in the sunlight and for some reason he thought of the fairy tale of the girl imprisoned in the tower, having to spin straw into gold. He had never seen or even imagined hair of that color.

She was staring at him through the barbed wire and across the ten or twelve feet that separated them as if she knew him and was trying to place him in her memory. Their eyes locked and he felt as if he had been struck by lightning. His entire body was shaking now. His vision narrowed to the point that the wire, the stockade, the other people around them disappeared.

Though Belden had read of such experiences, he had never had one before. So this is love, he thought. It *does* happen at first sight.

She found her voice first, and a lovely voice it was, low and cultured, with only a hint of the famous Virginian accent.

"Suh, might I offer you a piece of my fried chicken? Would you prefer a leg or a breast?"

Belden smiled.

"Either would be manna from Heaven, my lady," he said. "*Merci*."

The fact that he had fallen into French surprised him as much, apparently, as her.

"*Parlez-vous francais, monsieur?*" she responded.

"*Mais oui, mademoiselle. A ma maison, il y a un homme avec le nom de Eugene de la ville de Mon'real, avec qui je parles francais tout les jours.*"

"Why, suh, you are fluent! You overwhelm me! I am struggling to learn the tongue at Miss Beatrice's School, but I must confess that I am a very poor student at it. My lips don't seem to want to work right."

Here she blushed prettily, the warm pink rising up from the sides of her neck to her cheeks, and looked down with genuine modesty, or so it seemed to Belden.

"I would be honored to assist you in whatever way I can to adapt your lips to the language, *mademoiselle*," Belden said, with a small bow.

"Why, suh, you are too kind! I would be more than happy to write letters home for you as a small token of reciprocity. I am a great believer in the principle of reciprocity."

"Then we share that belief, my lady. I believe Mr. Emerson penned some wisdom on the subject."

"You are a student of Mr. Emerson as well! Suh, you are full of surprises! What do you think of his concept of the Oversoul? Oh, excuse me. I think I must give you both a leg and a breast, with a biscuit to leaven the taste. Guard, would you be so kind as to pass this to Mr.—suh, I have yet to learn your name. Mine is Hadley Winfield."

"Belden Crane, Miss Winfield. It is a pleasure to make your acquaintance."

"Please call me Hadley, suh."

"If you will call me Belden, ma'am."

She smiled. Her teeth were perfect. Everything about her, he thought, is perfect.

"I would be glad to call you by your Christian name, Belden. You see how easily we have come to our very first agreement? I hope there will be many more achieved with as little strife."

"I don't see why there should be any strife between us," he said. "Would you consent to taking down a letter to my parents and sister?"

"I would be delighted."

She set down her basket and drew forth a flat piece of beautifully polished wood, foolscap, a quill, and a bottle of ink. Her manservant held the piece of wood in both hands while she laid out her tools.

Belden had to admire the steadiness of his grip, which enabled her to dip her quill into the ink with perfect confidence. But there it was, he thought, the turning of a human being into a thing, the pedestal for a desk. He realized with a start that she wasn't going to introduce him. Later, he asked himself: If the circumstances had been reversed, would he have introduced Eugene? Well, hadn't he already?

But at the moment he was overwhelmed by her presence and by trying not to observe her body too closely. He knew from Helen how uncomfortable young women were made by such bold attentions. Nevertheless, he was aware of the remarkable slimness of her waist below the fullness of her bosom. She had the classic hourglass figure. That curve, from waist to hip....In an attempt to distract his mind, he focused his attention on the fried chicken.

"Hadley, this is delicious."

"It's an old recipe my Mammy taught me," she said. And there it was: an acknowledgement of the differences in their households. She had been raised—perhaps even been suckled by—a Negro slave. The image of her full red lips on a black breast leapt unbidden to his mind. He quickly banished the thought, but not before he realized that it had excited him.

"Please tell her from me that her recipe wins first place in any cooking competition," he said.

Was that a trace of a smile on the lips of the black man holding her writing board? When Belden looked more closely it had disappeared.

"I shall be happy to convey your enthusiasm. Now, how should the address read?"

"To: Mr. and Mrs. William Crane and Helen Crane, the Crane Farm, Bradford, New York, U.S.A."

As he said the address out loud, particularly the last initials, he was aware of another great difference between them: They were, for all intents and purposes, citizens of two different nations. Her home address would be in the C.S.A. The fact that these two countries had not existed a little over two years ago did not obviate the painful fact of this distinction.

But who knew what lay ahead? Perhaps we will be one nation once again, Belden thought. Isn't that what this war is about?

As he thought this it came to him that the entire war was a great silliness. Here were good people who wanted to carve out their own country, as the colonies had from Great Britain when it became evident that a separation was necessary. Weren't the Confederate States of America just taking that process one step further? They had a very different economy from that of the North. Was it fair that we insisted that they conform to our idea of how that economy should be administered? Her voice brought him out of this reverie.

"Body of the letter: Do you wish to begin with...what sort of salutation?"

"Dear Ma and Pa and sister Helen."

She wrote that down, then dipped her pen into the ink bottle, looking at him expectantly. She was, he saw, a very bright young woman. He wondered what her thoughts might be about this great split in what had once been their common nation. Too soon to ask. He cleared his throat and continued:

"I am blessed with the good fortune of having an angel from Heaven pen these words for me."

Hadley blushed again. He loved to watch how the pinkness rose up in her throat and then her face, as if in a direct flowing from her heart.

"Suh, you are too extravagant!"

"I am merely stating fact, ma'am. This is to be, after all, my letter, in my words."

She looked across the barrier of wires at him. Again their eyes met and again he felt as if he might lose consciousness as his scope of vision narrowed to her face, her lips.

"I stand corrected, suh. It shall be as you command."

That did it. He felt himself in a male state. He sat down on the ground to hide this embarrassing development as best he could.

After that, his letter became more prosaic. He told how he had been captured but treated fairly and was even now enjoying a nutritious meal of fried chicken and biscuits. He had every hope of being exchanged in the near future. He hoped they wouldn't worry about him, that he was in excellent health. Please convey my happiness to brother Ira and to all my good friends and relatives in Bradford.

"Please sign it, 'With much love, Belden,'" he concluded.

"I deduce," she said, blotting the letter dry with an instrument designed for that purpose, "that you come from a warm and loving family."

"Your capacity for deduction is superb, ma'am."

"I hope that you will be soon reunited."

"I do, too," he said, "though I must say that having met you, I feel a certain reluctance to have that be too soon. I pray that I might see you again soon, Hadley."

"I shall visit you every day but Sunday, when I teach the children of the congregation their catechism and the life of Our Savior."

"Might I ask which denomination?"

"I am a member of the Episcopal Church."

"I am also Episcopalian. We have much in common, you and I."

"More than you may even hypothesize, suh."

From the corner of his eye he saw a guard coming toward him and guessed that his time for fraternizing was about to end.

"I shall look forward to discovering whatever those commonalities might be, Hadley."

"Step back from the wire!" the guard snapped.

"*Jusque la prochaine fois,*" Belden said to Hadley.

"*A bientot!*" she replied. "*Demain.*"

The guard looked from one to the other as though he suspected them of passing secrets. Belden smiled. In a way, they had been. But the arrival of the guard had resolved his problem with being upright. He got to his feet and smiled at her. When she smiled back he felt his heart leap.

Her manservant seemed to ignore them, as he replaced her writing materials in the basket that had borne them.

* * *

In the days that followed, she came, as promised, every day but Sunday. Some days she brought her dog, a bluetick hound named Sam, with her. He seemed to approve of Belden, coming right up to the barbed wire with his tongue lolling. The weather went from pleasant springtime to hot and humid summer. During the days the camp air was full of gnats that pestered the eyes and nasal passages, seeking moisture. When dark came on, the gnats retired and the mosquitoes abounded. Their whine in the ears was constant.

The one period of relief was when Hadley visited. She wrote letters home and to Ira for him. He helped her practice speaking French. He was impressed by how quickly she picked up his French-Canadian pronunciation.

Nor did they hesitate to discuss politics, which both surprised and delighted Belden. At first he feared that the guards might take umbrage at such discussions through the barbed wire, but if anything they seemed to enjoy them. Hadley likened the separation of the South to a divorce in a marriage that had been initiated upon agreements now unilaterally abrogated.

"When the various States consented to form an imperfect union," she said, "it was with the clear understanding that the 'peculiar institution,' as it is disparagingly called, was a part of that compact. As you know, the Constitution of the United States recognizes slaves in counting them as three-fifths of a vote. It's as if you and I were to marry—"

Here Belden found himself blushing.

"—and we both recognized that I was bringing with me into the marital union a slave. Actually, we Winfields don't own slaves, having freed them ourselves some time before this contretemps, which we call 'The War of Northern Aggression,'—

"Hold on!" Belden spluttered. "You call this the War of the *Northern* Aggression? Who was it opened fire on Ft. Sumter?"

"I suggest we postpone that discussion for another time. I wish to stick to one argument at a time, suh!"

"That makes sense. You are a very sensible young woman, Hadley."

"Why, thank you, suh. May I continue? If, when we married, we both agreed that I would keep my slave in our household but then after some eighty-five years—my goodness, that would make us as old as Methuselah!--you decided without my consent that I could no longer do so, would that not violate our original compact? And if such a union is violated by one party, is it not the right of the other party to withdraw from it?"

"I reckon so, since you put it that way," Belden said, "but what about the part in the marriage ceremony where the two people agree that their union is 'till death do us part'? Doesn't that imply that you *must* arrive at a workable compromise and that divorce isn't an option?"

"Do I gather that you are opposed to a woman's right to leave an unhappy marriage?"

"Golly, Hadley, I've never really considered that. Where I come from, nobody gets divorced. Murdered, yes, but not divorced. When John Knickerbocker was catting around on her, Mrs. Knickerbocker waited up for him and shot him dead with his own scattergun when he tried to sneak in the back door. She claimed at the trial that she mistook him for a vagrant come to rape and murder her, but everyone knew why she did it. The jury let her off."

"Are you saying that murder is the only way out of such a painful situation?"

"I truly hope not. Now that you bring it to my attention, I must admit that there are circumstances that should warrant terminating a union, be it a marital or a political one."

"I am encouraged to hear you say so."

He smiled at her and nibbled at the piece of deep-fried catfish she had brought for him that day.

"You will remember," she continued, "that our original country was formed through a Revolution against the British Empire. That set the precedent for divorce. Our Declaration of Independence states quite clearly that when two peoples are incompatible it is the right of the aggrieved party to separate. Isn't that self-evident?"

"I suppose it is. But wasn't the primary cause of the Revolution taxation without representation?"

"That is my understanding as well," Hadley said, smiling—with those lips!—in such a way that Belden lost track of the path of the discussion. "And there is a clear parallel with the Abominable Tariff that was foisted upon us. Such tariffs protect Northern manufacturing but only raise prices for us in the South. Highever, with its greater population giving it control of the House of Representatives, the North could dictate to the South the taxes it had to pay. That was just plain unfair."

"I hadn't thought of that," Belden admitted. "So you're saying that the southern states saw themselves as unfairly taxed and rebelled because of that? Not because of the peculiar institution?"

She nodded.

"Yes, suh, I do believe both issues were a part of our discontent. And, over and above those causes was one even more powerful, if more nebulous. And that was the very fact that one section of the country—the North—could stand upon some moral high ground of their manufacture and tell us how we should live, without having any understanding of how we were already working to mitigate the institution of slavery and how unfair it was to tax us to the detriment of our economy...."

Belden felt a bit lightheaded. She sure knew a lot of big words, some of which he didn't know the meanings of, though he wasn't going to let her know that. But there was no doubt that she was good with words and more logical than about anyone he'd ever met. Except maybe Ira. She had, he thought, a perfect mind to match her perfect exterior. He had to admit it, he was falling in love with her. Or, he should say, more in love with her. He reminded himself that he'd felt the cannonblast of that potent emotion when he'd first seen her, at a distance, as if thousands of pieces of sweet hot shrapnel had penetrated his body. Like Romeo and Juliet at the masked ball, falling in love across a room crowded with revelers.

Love at first sight. Well, Ma had said that she had fallen in love with each of her babies when she first saw them—wasn't that the same thing? And if, as Jesus said, Love was the most important quality, was it not a Divine experience? Sure felt like it.

It also made sense that he wouldn't have that kind of experience in Bradford. He'd known every girl in town since he could remember. His first sight of them had been back when they were children. He remembered, now he thought on it, that he'd had tender feelings for Cinder back when they were both in first grade—and for Mrs. Atwill when he was in her Sunday School class at St. Andrews. But those feelings had been sweet and tender, whereas this was, well, more like a cannonblast. He'd always have a tender spot in his heart for Cinder, and for Mrs. Atwill, but what he felt now was the difference between the lightning and the lightning bug.

He was thinking these, for him, deep thoughts as he walked back to his tent, still chewing the catfish. Though the guards seemed to allow him more time than other prisoners with one of the belles, whenever the Commandant appeared they sent him on his way, and then Col. Wolfe would spend a few minutes chatting with Hadley.

His reverie was interrupted by the man who'd introduced himself as Puddin' Tame.

"I'll bet you a plugged nickel you could use a piece of that redhaired gal," he sniggered. "I know I'd like to make her squeal like a hog."

Belden grabbed the larger man's shirt, twisting it up against his throat.

"You keep your filthy mouth off of her!" he shouted into his face.

The big man pushed Belden back with a strong thrust of his two ham-sized hands.

"Or whatcha gonna do about it, Pretty Boy?"

Belden controlled himself.

"Just show some manners," he said.

"Or what? You'll spank me?"

The big man threw back his head and guffawed, adding, "I'd like to see you try. Pretty Boy."

Belden looked him in the eye with what he hoped was a stern gaze, then went to the tent he was sharing with a dozen prisoners.

There was going to be a reckoning with Mr. Tame. He could feel it coming.

* * *

On subsequent visits Hadley told him, in broken French, of her family, how she'd lost her mother to consumption when she was five but how her father had raised her with a gentle and loving hand, how she lived in the nearby town in a three-story white house right beside the store and across from the church, and how as a girl she'd come to love the whistle of the locomotive when it approached the crossing near the station. She spoke of her older brother Fax, who rode with Mosby's Rangers, which gave him time to be home to give her father help with the crops.

She told him how Lee had extricated his army from Hooker's trap, though they had lost General Jackson, which had plunged the whole South into mourning. He had been, in her estimation, their greatest general.

Belden shivered, as if with a chill, though it was a warm June day. It was as if, in being captured, he'd stepped through a portal into another world. The battle he'd been fighting in had been completed, and once again Lee had performed magic and whipped superior numbers. Lew and he were separated. He missed Lew. He hoped he was still alive.

Now, Hadley said, Lee was marching through Harper's Ferry into Maryland and the Union army had fled back north of the Potomac.

"My father, Judge Winfield, says that Maryland may well rise up in rebellion against the Union, being a slave state that Lincoln had manhandled into compliance only by suspending habeas corpus and tossing half the Maryland legislature in jail. You will no doubt remember that back then Chief Justice Taney of the Supreme Court ruled that that Lincoln was violating the Constitution. And when he did so Lincoln tried to have Taney arrested, too. He is a tyrant."

"I must have missed the news about that," Belden said. He felt a bit ashamed to hear his hero called a tyrant without rebutting the aspersion. Had Abe really tried to arrest the Chief Justice?

"If we but win another victory," she said, "I have no doubt that Lincoln will call an end to this terrible war. And then there shall be peace and you shall go free."

"When that happens," he said, "I shall make haste to your home and ask your father for your hand."

She blushed a deep pink, the color streaking up her neck into her cheeks and then her temples. He felt his heart flip over in his chest.

15

BRADFORD

May 1863

While Belden had promised to write once a week, his letters seldom came weekly. There might be a whole month with no word and then they'd receive a packet of several. When they hadn't gotten one in over ten days, Helen would start to fret. Ma did, too, but she hid her feelings better. Pa assured them both that Belden was too ornery to get killed.

For two weeks after the battle of Chancellorsville, they heard nothing from him. They knew from other soldiers' letters home, Will Van Auken's among them, that the 107th had been in the thick of things and had suffered the loss of one-quarter of the regiment, dead, wounded, or missing. Then they got a terse notification from the Department of War stating that Belden was Absent With Out Leave, AWOL, as of May 6th.

"What in God's name does that mean!" Ma asked, now having trouble disguising her true feelings.

Pa wrote to Seward for clarification, and the Secretary replied that it meant that Belden had gone missing during the battle and there was every hope that he was still alive. The AWOL designation meant only that he wasn't with his unit and had not been granted a furlough. No doubt he would show up on the Confederate prisoner-of-war rolls.

The not-knowing was horrible. Helen felt like she had a large ugly crab in her belly, gnawing at her innards with dull claws.

Charlie Ide held her while she wept.

"I can't stand this!" she told him. "Is he still alive? How can we know? I want to take the stage and go south to find him!"

"I'm sure you do," Charlie said, stroking her hair. "And if anyone could find him it would be you. Give it a bit more time and maybe you'll get news."

"I hate feeling so helpless!"

"That's a bad feeling," Charlie agreed. "Would a marriage cheer you up?"

"Oh, Charlie, you know I won't marry you till my brothers can attend, if they're still alive."

"Of course they're alive, and they wouldn't miss your wedding for all the tea in China."

"I pray every night for God to keep them alive," she said. "I hope He hears me."

"What's He say about it?"

She shook her head.

"He doesn't say a word. I sometimes wonder if He's really there, Charlie. I'm afraid I'm becoming a heathen."

"Well, those we call 'heathens' have their own beliefs. All the Red Indians hereabouts, at least what's left of them, believe in a Divine Creator who has agency in our lives. Whoever that may be, He's got a lot to do these days. Let's both keep praying."

Helen believed their prayers had worked when the next day official word came by telegram from Seward: Belden had been captured at Chancellorsville and was being held in a Confederate prison camp, awaiting exchange.

Helen and Ma wept together in relief.

"How long till he's exchanged, Pa?" Helen asked.

"That's problematic," Pa said, shaking his head. "Seward tells me Lincoln has halted the exchanges for now, in protest of the way the Rebels have been mistreating our boys. At an exchange, our boys come in half-starved and unfit for duty, while we return their boys well-fed and ready to go right back to the front."

"We have to send Belden food, then!" Helen said.

"Even that's a problem," Pa sighed. "I hear that most of the food boxes we send down are shanghaied by the Rebs. Because of the blockade, they're having trouble getting enough to eat themselves. So when we say, 'Feed your prisoners proper, as we do!' they come back with, 'Lift the blockade so we can trade our cotton and tobacco for food!'"

"I hate war!" Helen said.

"Can all this be worth it?" Ma asked. "Why don't we just let them have their own slave country and be damned!"

Pa stared at her in shock. Then he took a deep breath. And another.

"For two reasons," he said. "First, because slavery is a great wrong which must be erased from this nation and this Earth. By acceding to it in our Constitution, however covertly, we are responsible and must rectify that error. We are paying for this error with our blood and treasure. Second, because if anytime some minority in the Nation doesn't get their way they secede, you'd soon have a hundred new countries."

"I'd rather a hundred countries than one of my boys dead," Ma said.

"And when we were reduced to the Country of the Lake District," Pa said, "do you think we'd stand a chance if, say, Canada or Britain decided they wanted to take us over? Together we are a strong country. Divided, weak. As the Bible says, 'A house divided cannot stand.'"

"That's a good point, Pa," Helen said. "Maybe you should write to Mr. Lincoln and let him use that in one of his speeches."

"Thank you, Helen. Maybe I will."

Eugene Gascone, who was bringing in a load of freshly-split wood for the cookstove, made a mental note to inform his superiors that the Lake District was preparing for a Canadian invasion.

"I'm just happy we know Belden's alive," Helen said. "I'll visit Cinder Munsen and let her know."

"Why would that hussy care?" Ma asked.

"Oh, she cares, all right," Helen said. "She cares a lot more than she lets on. And don't call her such names, Ma. Yes, she went and married Jesse Junior out of spite. But Belden really hurt her by going off to war."

"She's not the only one," Ma said, and began to pound the bread dough on the counter.

* * *

Although it meant that her tasks in the mansion were few, Cinder wasn't sure she liked having servants. Cinder had grown up being the mistress of her father's house, in charge of the cooking and most of the housework. Not just accustomed to hard work, she relished it. For the first month or so of having a cook who prepared all the meals and a maid who did most of the housework, she had enjoyed the vacation. Soon, however, she found herself making her own bed and asking Cook to show her how to prepare the more esoteric dishes that Jesse liked, such as sauerbraten, roasted pheasant, and kippered herring. Cook would allow her in the kitchen only on the pretext of finding a way to her husband's heart through his stomach. Though they never spoke of it, Cook knew full well how Jesse treated her.

She thought it significant that Cook wouldn't divulge her name, even when asked directly.

"Cook I've been and Cook I'll always be," was her retort. "Now, let's find some of the rosemary in the herb garden. Rosemary's for memory. It sharpens the mind almost as well as the real brain food."

"What's the real brain food?"

"Fish, my dear, fish! How is it that you're not knowing such a fact? And why did you think menfolk are so preoccupied with catching the poor things? They intuit that fish will postpone their dotage, which will come soon enough, believe me, despite their best efforts. My husband, God rest his soul, would wander about the house for hours, searching for his spectacles. Half the time they were perched on his head like a thin bird."

Over time Cinder decided she liked Cook despite, or perhaps because of, her prickly personality. You knew where you stood with Cook. And, from her, Cinder learned much about the culinary arts. Cook introduced her to a world of herbs beyond the use of garlic, which Cinder had relied upon as her primary flavoring after salt. Her father touted garlic as not only flavoring but as panacea for all the ills that beset the human body. He'd wanted her to wear a wreath of garlic bulbs around her neck to school but Cinder had flatly refused.

"No one would want to play with me!" she'd shouted.

That was a wonderful capacity Baba had, Cinder realized. Unlike Jesse, he listened to her wishes and often acceded to them. Jesse was one of those men who believed that it was the wife's duty to obey her husband and his to rule with an iron hand. She was getting sick and tired of that attitude as well as being backhanded for whatever Jesse considered an offense against his dominance.

One duty she had retained was putting away the ironed laundry. Jesse wanted his starched shirts folded just so in the middle drawer of his wardrobe. His handkerchiefs, embossed with his initials, were to be placed in the right-hand top drawer, the left-hand one holding his socks. Small clothes and long johns went in the bottom drawer. God help her if she got things in the wrong drawer.

It was as she was placing Jesse's handkerchiefs in their drawer one morning that the idea came to her. It was like a flash of lightning. It took her breath away.

Then, for the first time in months, she laughed out loud.

* * *

When Helen arrived at the Munsen mansion, she had to admit that it was ostentatious. She'd passed it many a time but never really noticed the columns, the filigree, the golden cock weathervane. But when Cinder opened the door to admit her, she forgot about all that.

"Why, Cinder, you're pregnant!"

Cinder smiled.

"Helen," she said, "you have remarkable powers of deduction. I'm about to pop. Speaking of deduction, how's that investigation into Uncle Jim's murder coming? Any progress? Come in and let me make you a cup of tea."

Helen blushed, then grinned. This was the Cinder she knew. The feisty girl with the razor-sharp wit.

She followed Cinder through a palatial parlor thick with Persian carpets and then an elegant dining room with polished oak flooring into a kitchen that took her breath away. It was as large as her father's entire house. There was a bank of windows facing south to gather in the winter sun. Beneath them were boxes full of several different kinds of herbs: rosemary, sage, thyme, lavender, coriander, oregano, fennel. Ma would have been envious. But what really took the cake was the stove, a behemoth as big as a wagon, black with silver trimmings and a huge pipe that went out through a stone wall designed to retain the heat in winter. The kitchen was very warm even on a cool summer's morning, with all the windows open to admit a breeze through the screens. Screens! How in the world had the Munsens managed to import such a luxury?

Helen decided to divert the conversation from such extravagance.

"Well heavens to Betsy, Cinder!" Helen said. "How do you even keep this monster in wood?"

Cinder laughed.

"I don't. Jesse has a man who splits the wood and brings it in to feed this dragon—and the others around the house. There's one in pretty much every room, 'ceptin' the parlor, which has the fireplace. He also tends the grounds. Then he has a woman in to cook most of the meals, and a butler to serve them. Good thing today is the servants' day off. It's wonderful to see you, Helen. What news of Belden. And Ira?"

Helen's head whirled. Servants! This was the first time in her life she'd been in a household that employed servants. She wondered what Cinder did with her time all day. Right now she was pouring heated water from a blue cook pot into a silver teapot. At least she could make a cup of tea on her own.

"That's what I came to tell you about. He's alive and well. He fought at the Battle of Chancellorsville, where he was made a prisoner of war. The Confederates are holding him until there is another exchange."

Cinder had her back to Helen, fiddling with the tea. Did her shoulders seem to relax as she absorbed this news? After a long pause she asked:

"And what news of Ira? Is he well?"

"He seems very happy being a male nurse," Helen said.

"Well, I'm glad to hear they're alive," Cinder said. "Thank you for coming to convey that news to me. Shall we sit in the parlor or at the dining room table?"

As Cinder turned with the tea tray, Helen noticed it for the first time: a nasty bruise on her left cheek and temple that had hitherto been hidden beneath an artfully arranged lock of hair. Helen gasped and Cinder saw where she was staring.

"Oh, it's nothing, Helen. I fell and hit it on the corner of the table."

"You must be more careful, in your condition."

"Thank you for your concern. Lead on, MacDuff!"

Cinder often made obscure allusions that passed over Helen's head. This one she guessed probably came from Cinder's voracious reading of the fat English novels she fancied. As she led the way into the parlor, she came to a decision.

Once Cinder had deposited the tea tray and had begun to pour, Helen said: "I don't believe that you fell against the table, Cinder. I think Jesse smacked you."

Cinder sighed.

"You *are* a detective, Helen. I can hide nothing from you. Yes, I fear he has become dissatisfied with me. In truth, I am not a good wife to him."

She had lowered her eyes.

"You mean...?"

"Yes, I shun the marital bed. He disgusts me."

"But you are to have a child together!"

Cinder shrugged.

"It's not his child. At least, I'm pretty sure it's not."

Helen almost dropped her teacup. She managed to set it down.

"Is it...?"

"I think so. I tried, Helen, but I cannot stop loving him."

"Why don't you leave?"

Cinder laughed bitterly.

"And go where? How would I support myself, much less a child? I am trapped by my own folly."

Helen reached across the low table to take Cinder's hands.

"Come and live with us!"

Cinder smiled, shaking her head.

"You are very kind, Helen. You know your father would never allow that."

"But if we told him the truth..."

"Helen, I cannot swear upon the Bible as to what is the exact truth. I only know what my body tells me."

"But that is your truth!"

"Yes, and it is not a truth a man would give credence to."

Helen released Cinder's hands and stared down into her teacup, as if seeking guidance in the floating tea leaves.

"What are you going to do, Cinder?"

Cinder smiled. It was a very sad smile.

"I must put my faith in Providence," she said. "Meanwhile, not a word to Belden, or to anyone. I have told you this in the strictest confidence."

Helen nodded, and tears ran down her cheeks.

* * *

Two days later Cinder gave birth to a baby girl she named Abigail.

"It's not eight months since the wedding," Ma said.

"Now, Emily," Pa said, "where's your Christian charity?"

"He's beating her," Helen said. "We need to stop him."

"Everyone in town knows he's beating her," Ma said, "but she's not asking us for help, is she? She's been lying about it, covering it over. She hasn't decided what to do yet."

"If I had a husband who treated me that way, I'd give him one chance to mend his ways. If he did it again, I'd take the butcher knife to him. If he was a lot stronger than me, I'd wait till he was asleep to stick him."

"I see you've been thinking about this quite a bit," Pa said. "That's you, not Cinder. You have a family that would take you in and protect you. If it went to trial, you'd have a chance of winning. Cinder wouldn't. Her mother is long dead and her father is the only Jew in town. She's on her own."

Helen stamped her foot.

"It makes me so mad! The powerless have no rights! Those with power can burn Uncle Jim in his house or beat the daughter of the Jew and get away with it. It's not right!"

"No, it's not," her mother said softly.

William Crane cleared his throat, as he usually did before he made a pronouncement.

"One can judge the quality of any society by how it treats the powerless," he said. "A great nation is one that protects and cares for those without power—whether it be the slaves, women, children, or those who aren't Protestant Christians. That is really what your brothers are fighting for—the right to protect those without power from those that hold it. Once we free the Negro we must free women to be able to vote and thus wield political power. Women like Cinder need to be able to divorce and be provided for. If they are facing penury, what good is the legal right to divorce? In addition to raising her children, how is she to earn enough money to provide for herself and her child, or children? Right now, Cinder must feel that she's got one leg caught in a beartrap. But she'll figure a way out, you wait and see. She's a smart girl."

Helen sighed.

"But, Pa, couldn't we let her know that if she wanted to leave Jesse we'd take her in?"

"Possibly. We have to consider how that might be for Belden, coming home. And Ira."

"Because they're men?"

"Don't be silly. Because they're members of this family, wherein we don't impose any decision upon anyone of age, but discuss it together until we reach a consensus that feels good to everyone. You know this, Helen."

"And am I an equal member, or must I wait until I achieve my majority?"

"Oh, I think you're close enough. But we'll have to see what the men say."

Helen made as if to punch her father.

"None of that!" Pa laughed. "You know that in this household people are not for hitting."

* * *

Cinder was having trouble getting Jesse Jr. to adhere to that rule in their house. She had gone from shock to outrage to reasoning, then to pleading, and finally to a cold silence. At first he had been repentant and said he would amend, but amend he did not, and soon he gave up even the pretense of trying. When Abby was wailing with the colic one night, he flew into such a rage that Cinder feared he would hurt her baby in ways that jolted her imagination. To forestall such horror, she bundled Abby up and took her out into the cool night air. The starlit sky seemed to settle the child. She gazed up at the stars with wide eyes.

It came to her that night that if Jesse hurt Abby, she would hurt him much worse. She knew she'd probably have to kill him lest he kill her.

He sensed her resolve, and one night crept into her bedroom and, while she was fast asleep on her tummy, secured both wrists to the headboard and both ankles to the footboard with leather thongs he had fashioned into slipknots. She didn't wake until he was stretching her body taut. Feeling herself tied down on her belly, spread-eagled, she jerked against the restraints as a paralyzing panic began to weaken her limbs.

"What do you think you're doing?! Let me go!"

Without replying, he opened one of the doors on the dark lantern he'd set on her dresser and then pulled her nightgown up to expose her underclothes. She felt a terrifying vulnerability.

"Jesse Munsen! You stop this right now! Let me go. Please."

He chuckled.

"I like the 'please,'" he said. His voice was hoarse, his breathing ragged and quick. "You need to be taught to mind your manners, missy."

He ran the cold steel of a knifeblade down her white back, slipped it under the hem of her drawers, and began cutting them off.

"Stop it! You're crazy!"

"Crazy with love for you."

"If you love me, stop doing this!"

He pulled her severed drawers from beneath her and began caressing the soft moons of her buttocks with the knifeblade, pricking her from time to time.

She couldn't help herself, she was sobbing with fear and despair now.

"Jesse, please stop this..."

He withdrew the knife and she heard him setting it on her dresser.

The relief she felt was almost overwhelming.

"Jesse, what is it that you want?"

"I want you to resume your marital duties. You have no right to withhold your body from your husband. To deny me my pleasures. To leave my bed cold and empty. To treat me with scorn. You don't love me. You don't even like me. You just used me to get back at Belden for leaving you. Well, now I'm going to use you back, you harlot!"

She heard a whistling sound. She guessed it was his horsewhip. He was swinging it in the dark above her.

"Don't you dare!" she hissed, trying to lift her head off the sheet. Her helpless immobility infuriated her.

When the whip slashed across her buttocks she saw a flash of lightning. Had it been inside her head or was a thunderstorm coming? She bit the pillow with her teeth to stop herself from screaming. She would not give him the satisfaction, she would not scare Abby. Again the whip slashed, and again. She could feel the skin of her buttocks rending, the warm blood flowing. He was panting now. When she thought she could take it no more, that she must scream out, she heard the whip clatter on the floor, heard him unbuttoning, and then his weight was on her like a boulder, and the hot shaft of his member was rubbing against her.

She felt his hands prying at her buttocks.

"Open these!" he hissed.

Somehow she knew what he intended, though she had never heard of it, or even imagined it. She clamped her cheeks tight together. His hands grabbed her hair, pulling her head up till she thought her neck would break, but she kept herself closed to him. He rubbed faster and faster on her blood-slicked buttocks and then she felt his ejaculate as he released her hair and collapsed upon her back, panting.

Somehow Abby, sleeping in her bassinet beside the bed, had not awakened.

By the grace of God, Cinder thought.

Jesse rolled off of her, stood, and began wiping the ejaculate and blood from her with a corner of the sheet, so tenderly that she had to hold onto herself hard to prevent herself from sobbing. Then he gently pulled down her nightgown to cover her.

When his voice came, it was as if from someone she didn't know.

"I'm going to cut you loose now, if you promise to be good."

She nodded into the sheet. She didn't trust herself to speak.

"You ever raise a hand to me," he told her, cutting the leather restraints from her wrists, "I will kill you, and no one in this town will blame me for it."

He released her ankles as well. She rolled over, wincing with pain, and got to her feet. She felt dirty, besmirched, humiliated. She hated him. Her voice came back to her.

"Belden and Ira will."

"Belden and Ira are dead, or will be. You'll never see them again. You'd best mind your manners. Remember what happened to the town nigger. That could happen to you."

"Are you telling me that was your handiwork?"

He smiled. It was not a nice smile.

"Just remember. A wife cannot testify against her husband."

And what, she thought, if I'm no longer your wife?

* * *

Alone, benumbed, Cinder berated herself for her stupidity.

I hate him, and I also hate myself. He's right. I seduced him, got him to marry me, because I was furious with Belden for abandoning me.

Now that I know who Jesse really is, I must face the fact that I made an awful mistake. That's not easy for me to do. It was stupid to bind myself to a man who is so twisted inside. He cannot admit error. He rationalizes that whatever he does is right. He pretends to be the big businessman when inside he is a frightened little boy who believes he will never be loved, and he must punish me for that. He lacks all capacity to know how other people feel, or to care how they feel, as long as he can bend them to his uses. He seeks power over others because he is so scared inside. But he won't admit to feeling fear.

A divorce is impossible. The court will not grant one for physical damage to one's "property." Even if I could leave him, just run off, where could I go? My father has little money or capacity to support us, and he would just say I must obey my husband. I might go to a city and find work in one of the mills, but who would care for Abby while I'm working? It's impossible for a woman to work and raise her children.

I have stuck my head into a noose that draws tighter every day. I can see no escape from this doom, other than death. Mine, or his. His. I must survive to tend to Abby. Henceforth, I will take a sharp knife to bed with me, and prop a chair against the handle of the door. If he tries to do that again, I will kill him.

* * *

Jesse surprised her. He let her sleep in peace, and he treated her with great civility for two days.

On the third day, over dinner, he surprised her even more.

"Would you like to play that game again?" he asked.

She couldn't believe what she was hearing. Did he mean....?

He smiled at her. They were having Cook's pot roast, a juicy cut of sirloin smothered in a red wine sauce with chanterelles, new potatoes, and fingerling carrots. The beeswax candles glowed in the tall scalloped-base candlesticks, creating points of light in the Waterford crystal wine glasses.

Cinder had to admit that she enjoyed eating well, off fine British porcelain, using heavy Sterling silver. As a girl, she had sometimes gone hungry, and used a pewter spoon and a wooden bowl.

She shifted in her chair. Her backside still smarted.

"Exactly," he said. "I liked playing with your beautiful arse. And I know that a part of you enjoyed it."

"Don't be absurd! If you think I enjoyed that violation at all you are mad."

Jesse smiled once again and reached into the pocket of his jacket. He pulled out a slim volume.

"I want you to read this, my dear. It is the work of a brilliant French nobleman, the Marquise de Sade. You read French, do you not? I think you will find it revolutionary. Let's discuss it next week. I believe marriage should include intellectual stimulation, don't you? As well as unabashed carnality?"

16

THE WINFIELDS

Late Summer, 1863

"Had-leee! Hadley! Get your lazy backside out of that bed, girl! We got us some bakin' to do!"

Hadley groaned and rolled over, pulling the covers over her head. Jemima poked her shoulder with one long black finger.

"Don't you be goin' back to sleep on me, honeypie! You want to learn to cook, you gotta get up with the rooster! Come on, now!"

"Mammy, I have come to the conclusion that I am not a morning person," Hadley grumbled, while extricating herself from the featherbed. She wore a white nightgown. Jemima handed her a green silk robe and reached beneath the bed for the chamberpot, which was decorated with blue flowers.

"I am so grateful that you still take care of that for me, sweet Mammy. Whatever will I do when I marry?"

"Don't you worry your pretty head 'bout that, chile," Jemima said. "You know I'll go with you whosomever you marry yourself to. Now, you wash your face and meet me down in the kitchen."

Hadley Winfield brushed out her long reddish-gold hair with a silver brush and tied it back with a blue ribbon. She splashed water from her basin onto her strikingly beautiful face—arched brows, green eyes, high cheekbones, and Cupid's bow lips—and patted it with a cotton towel. She slid her plump high-arched feet—the one feature that caused her some embarrassment—into lambswool slippers and went to the top of the stairs.

Though both Jemima and her father had forbidden her to continue what they assured her was a "dangerous" practice, Hadley threw one leg over the banister, hooking her instep up on it, mounting it as she would a horse facing uphill, and slid down to the balustrade at the bottom. Giggling with delight, she dismounted and stepped onto the well-joined oak floorboards of the hallway. Her father, whom everyone, including Hadley, addressed as "Judge Winfield," had employed a crew of nine free Negro craftsmen to build the house more than a decade ago. He had purchased the best materials available and even felled and then cured some of the tall oaks on his property to use for the crossbeams and support structures that underlay the entire subfloor. He said that he wanted to build a house that his progeny could live in for centuries, like the old manor houses of England. He had overseen every step of the construction, from picking the site above the hundred-year flood plain of the creek to the thick stone foundation to the copper roofing, which he said that he had learned of from a visit to Mr. Thomas Jefferson's Monticello.

"If it was good enough for Mr. Jefferson, it's good enough for me," he said.

It was a well-built and beautiful dwelling. He had it painted white and the window shutters forest green to match the gradually greening roof.

By the time Hadley skipped into the kitchen—a spacious room with a big black wood-burning cookstove—Jemima had the hoe cakes on the griddle.

"For a not-mornin' person," Jemima said, "you get perky pretty quick. Here, take that big knife and cut us some ham steaks off'n the ham that's hangin' in the pantry. Throw away the green mold. Fry 'em on the slow heat at the back of the stove."

"Can I at least have my coffee first?" Hadley protested, taking a blue mug off the shelf and pouring from the big black pot on the stove. "When you gonna teach me how to make coffee, anyway?"

"One step at a time, girl. You always was an impatient thing. When we rush, we trips up."

Hadley took a small pail of milk from the icebox and added some to her coffee. The milk, thick with clots of cream, came from the family dairy cow, Esmeralda, who produced at least one calf per year. When the calf was a month or so old, it would be slaughtered for veal. Hadley couldn't bear to watch the calf being killed. She didn't feel the same way about the big ol' ugly hogs that had the bad manners to snort and rut, but the calves had such beautiful eyes that stared at her so imploringly. She usually refused to eat the veal. At first, anyway.

She whittled slabs from the hanging haunch, discarding any bits with signs of discoloration, and set four pieces on the back of the stove. The odor was tantalizing. And, sure enough, she could hear the menfolk's footsteps overhead. Ham or bacon usually brought them like flies to sugar.

Fax was the first to appear, his hair plastered down with water. He always ducked his head in the bucket to tame his wild mane, which was a duller red than Hadley's. He also had the green eyes and fine features that seemed to run in the family. He, however, had not escaped freckles, to his everlasting mortification.

Hadley took down a red mug and poured him coffee. Well, they called it coffee, though it was mostly chick'ry root since the blockade had begun. Fax drank his black.

A minute later Judge Winfield came in. He was a man of medium height, imperially slim, with the family green eyes and a shock of white hair and a neatly-trimmed white beard. He was, as always, immaculately dressed, today in his riding kit, including an ascot and boots to the knee.

"Do I smell ham steaks?" he asked. "And who, might I inquire, is the chef today?"

"I am, of the steaks at least," Hadley said, flipping them over with a spatula.

"I am delighted that you want to learn the culinary arts," he said. "As we free our servants, we shall be cooking more and more for ourselves. Isn't that right, Jemima?"

"Yes, suh, if you say so," Jemima said, handing him his customary cup of English tea. Judge Winfield was a great admirer of all things British, tea foremost among them. He paid outrageous sums to procure it from a blockade runner.

They loaded up their plates and carried plates and mugs into the dining room, which was already set with Birmingham silver beside gleaming white cloth napkins rolled into silver holders, each with a family member's name engraved upon it. Jemima remained in the kitchen. Some things didn't change.

They sat and bowed their heads. Judge Winfield said the blessing:

"For these and all Thy gifts, we humbly thank Thee, in Christ's name. Amen."

They dug in and ate in silence for a minute or two. Then the Judge, after wiping his lips with his napkin said:

"For today's topic of discussion I would like to propose the issue, 'Are our actions preordained, or do we have free will?' Fax, would you be so kind as to offer your thoughts first?"

Fax shrugged his shoulders and finished chewing a piece of ham.

"Everything is predetermined. God is omniscient, which means he knows everything and that means he knows what's gonna happen. If He knows what's gonna happen, it must already be predetermined. Q.E.D."

He grinned and took a drink of coffee.

Her father turned to Hadley.

"Daughter, what are your thoughts on this weighty matter? If I know you aright, they will be the opposite of your brother's."

"Why, suh, are you insinuating that I am contrary?"

"On occasion. Today, I am hazarding the wild guess that your views will differ from Fax's."

"How prescient of you, suh. Fax has spoken from the perspective of the Almighty, to which I am not privy. I will speak from the human viewpoint. We are not omniscient. We agonize over our choices, trying to choose the right path. We therefore have the illusion of free will, even if God knows how we will ultimately choose. I would use Occam's razor to split the matter thus: God knows, Man is in doubt, and therefore has free will."

"While I am not sure that is the correct application of Occam's razor," Judge Winfield said, "I give you high marks for a subtle distinction. Now, let us apply your theories to the story of the Fall of Man. God tells Adam and Eve not to eat of the fruit of the Tree of Knowledge—"

"The apple," Fax interrupted, not looking up from the hoe cake he was buttering, his face a parody of the know-it-all.

"Ah," said Judge Winfield, "as so many artists have imagined it, including the one you have seen in the Truro rectory. Yet in fact there is no such specification of it in the Book of Genesis, if you will but take the time to review the text. The mysterious tree is described as the Tree of the Knowledge of the difference between Good and Evil. When the Serpent tempts them, they eat of it and realize that they are naked. Up to that moment they were unashamed, in a state of ignorant bliss."

"Don't forget," Fax said, "that it was Eve who the Serpent seduced, and then she went and got Adam to eat it with her."

"You never fail to underline any point that you can find to disparage women," Hadley said, eyes flashing.

"It's God's word, not mine," Fax said around the hoe cake.

"Please stick to today's topic," Judge Winfield said, holding up his hands, palms toward them in supplication. "The issue as I see it is this: Why would God give them freedom to eat or not eat of the Tree if He already knew what they would do? Is that not ascribing a certain level of perverse cruelty to Him?"

"Your logic is, as always, ineluctable," Hadley said. "Further, when God goes on to banish Adam and Eve from the Garden, He says He must do so lest they eat of the Tree of Eternal Life. He speaks in the conditional, not knowing whether they would do so. *Ergo*, He doesn't have certain foreknowledge of their choices."

"Then you are heretical," Fax said, "for you assert that God is not omniscient, and for that heresy you shall be burnt at the stake for a witch."

"You don't frighten me, Fax Winfield. We are long past the days of witch hunts, thank the Lord."

"Children, children, can we not discuss an idea for its intrinsic merit without descending into this internecine warfare? Enough for today. What plans has each of you? Fax?"

"I'm gonna take Shadow and go for a ride with Col. Mosby, suh. I might not be back for supper, or for a day or two."

"I see. And you, my dear?"

"After we bake our bread, Jemima and I are going to plant greens in the garden, Father."

"Excellent. You know **how** good our greens are for our health. I myself am going to ride into Alexandria and fetch us some more tea. Our supply is getting low. Is there anything either of you require from our dear blockade runner?"

"Hairpins," Hadley said. "I'm running out. I swear, you'd think they run off on those little legs of theirs."

"Pins for you," Judge Winfield said. "Fax?"

"A repeating rifle, if you can find one."

"That sounds like a tall order."

"If one should appear at a reasonable price."

"The concept of 'reasonable price' flew out the window at the inception of this conflict," Judge Winfield said. "Well, let's carry our dishes and utensils into the kitchen to spare Jemima's 'rheumats,' as she puts it. For our next breakfast seminar, I'd like you to re-read the two quite different stories of the Creation in Genesis I and II and we'll consider the implications of those differences. If, as our minister proclaims, the Bible is the unassailable word of God, why are there two such disparate tales of the Creation included therein and what conclusions does that imply? Meanwhile, remember, 'This is a day which the Lord hath made. Let us rejoice and be glad in it.'"

* * *

While the men saddled their horses for their respective journeys, Jemima washed and Hadley dried the breakfast dishes and then began the baking. They were still working out the terms of their changed relationship since Judge Winfield had freed Jemima from service. Although Jemima seemed content to maintain her former work load, Hadley was aware that the older woman could not, in actuality, keep up with the chores she had performed in her younger days, when, in addition to nursing Hadley after the death of her mother, she had minded Fax, tended the vegetable garden, fed the chickens, hogs, and cow, cleaned the house, washed and ironed and mended the clothing and bedclothes, planned and cooked all the meals and cleaned up after them. She was the first up in the morning, building a fire in the cookstove in the kitchen and grinding the coffee beans and chicory root in the hand grinder before the rest of the household stirred. Even the man she called her "husband," Ezra, was usually slugabed, unless she needed him to split some pine kindling for the stove that day. Not being an early riser, he made a practice of stock-piling kindling in the evenings.

Ezra, who was at least a decade older than she, had fewer duties. He felled the dead trees on the estate, trimmed them with an ax and bucked them up with a one-man saw and split the logs into sizable pieces for the cookstove and fireplaces, which he kept supplied from the woodshed where he seasoned the wood in an order of his own devising. The family had taken over starting the fires in their own rooms on cold mornings, which was a sacrifice: It had been very molli-fying to stay warm in bed beneath a goose-down quilt while someone else started the morning fire in a cold room. Ezra still filled the wash basins and emptied the men's chamberpots. He took the trash out, burning the paper and composting the garbage. He cut the grass of the lawns and raked the leaves in the fall, hauling both to the compost pile. He cared for the two horses, black bays named Shadow and Sunset, mucking out their stalls, making sure they had enough hay and, when he could get them, oats and carrots, and currying them with comb and brush daily. He also kept all their tack in high polish, working saddle soap into the leather with his bare fingers. He was the repairman who fixed whatever broke—be it a hinge on a door or the seat in the outhouse—as well as the chief ratcatcher and spiderkiller. For all her courage, spiders where one thing Jemima could not abide.

The way Hadley saw it, manumission had little inconvenienced her father or brother, who did little more than when Ezra and Jemima had been slaves, except for the cold morning fires. Whereas she, out of both a sense of fairness and a feeling of compassion for Jemima's aging body, tried to ease her surrogate mother's labors wherever she could. She managed to do so mostly by stratagem, such as pretending that she wanted to learn how to cook or how to mend her future husband's riding breeches. Jemima was one of those people who was determined that she could do as much at sixty as she had done at twenty, a questionable belief that weighed on her much more than any sense that she needed to continue to do all those duties she had as a slave. Over time, Hadley had been able to somewhat lighten Jemima's load. She had been successful in so doing by abandoning the direct approach and relying upon subterfuge, which, if Jemima suspected, she allowed to proceed.

This subtlety of approach she had learned from the tales of the wily Bre'r Rabbit that Jemima had regaled her with since childhood. Bre'r Fox might be stronger and more ruthless, but Bre'r Rabbit survived by his wits.

* * *

For a piece of paper which neither Jemima nor Ezra could read that legally gave them freedom and a Confederate dollar or two every week, the pair had been removed from slavery—but not, or at least not very much, from the multitude of duties they performed in keeping the Winfield estate running and what passed for prosperous during a war that included a crushing blockade.

For Hadley, however, the change in Jemima's status was monumental. She had always considered Jemima her mother, which, for all intents and purposes she was. Their bond was close and familiar. The removal of the status of "slave" made Hadley feel much better and allowed her to take on a portion of Jemima's work. It hurt Hadley to see the growing stiffness in Jemima's once fluid body and a big part of her wanted to take even more of the load off this precious woman's shoulders. Jemima had given her breast milk and changed her diapers, sung her to sleep and told her stories. She had guided her through childhood frustrations and into her young womanhood, being able to talk with her about bodily matters that, Hadley knew, most white girls never heard from their white mothers. She felt blessed to have had Jemima as her mother and she loved her deeply.

She would always remember Jemima's frank answer to her question, "What's it like to make love?"

Jemima fixed her with a squinted eye.

"Girl, why you be wantin' to know sech things?"

"Well, I'm going to have to deal with it sooner or later, less'n I die an old maid."

Jemima sighed.

"T'ain't likely," she said. "Well, I'll tell you true, it'll hurt like the dickens the first time, when you get opened up. After that, it get *good*. Your man'll be puttin' that thing in you—"

"His penis," Hadley said.

"Girl, where you be learnin' all them big words? He be puttin' it in and Lord have mercy it'll be the best feelin' you ever had. Unh-huh! You be feelin' all trembly and you hear sounds comin' out you mout make you wonder who dat be. Don' even pay dat no mind. Hollar all you wants. Den yo' body commence to shake like a leaf on a tree in de wind and you fly up to the moon and de stars and don' even know where you be at. But den you comes right back. Den you hafta wait fo' yo' man to catch up. Sooner or later he give a grunt and you feels him shudder and de next ting you know he be snorin' atop you and you cain't hardly breathe. When yo cain't abide the weight no mo', just push him off."

Jemima giggled like a girl at some memory.

"Yes'm, you just push his big ol' weight right off a you."

To Hadley, this sounded like an experience she could wait to have, and she was intimidated by the pain of losing her hymen. She had studied her father's medical book when he was gone, feeling a bit like a spy collecting illicit information, and learning a lot of big words that seemed to be Latin.

Now Jemima was kneading and punching the dough with hands that seemed a bit more clawlike every day. She bore the pains in her aging body as she did all suffering and as had her forebearers on the slave ships—with a stoic silence. The complainers, she knew from oral history, had been thrown overboard. She trusted in the Lord and accepted both the good and bad in life as gifts from Him, as blessings to cheer us and tests to help us grow larger in Spirit. Hadley knew that she had borne suffering beyond her own imaginings, things Jemima would not speak of—being sold away from her parents as a small child, the loss of her own children to illness, and severe abuse at the hands of her former owner. A life that would have embittered most people, Jemima had endured with a deep faith, a faith she attempted to pass along to Hadley.

"When you bake bread, chile, always think on our Savior, how He break bread with his sweet hands at the Last Supper and say to his disciples, 'Eat this in remembrance of me.' Think on how He say, 'Give us this day our daily bread' in prayer for us. This here ain't just flour, water, and yeast, honeychile, this be Holy. When you make bread you be serving the Lord. You got to keep the big picture in yo' head. In the big picture even this here war don't make no matter. Men always be killin' each other, since time begin. What matter is that we be makin' daily bread and feedin' the chilluns, in His name."

Hadley had long since become accustomed to what she thought of as Jemima's Little Sermons. Sometimes they seemed trite. Sometimes profound. But the faith that undergirded them never failed to move her.

"Mammy," she said, once the menfolk were all in the stable, "I do believe I am falling in love with that Yankee prisoner."

"Mr. Belden, you mean? Ezra say he be one pretty man, fo' sho'. I understands, honeychile, I sho'ly do. The heart do things that don't make no kind a sense to the haid."

"Oh, Mammy, whatever will I do?" Hadley said, running into Jemima's arms and burying her face in her warm neck.

"There, there, honeychile," Jemima said, as Hadley burst into tears. "Yo' know this too will pass."

"It won't!" Hadley said fiercely. "I'll love him forever!"

"Mebbe you will, and mebbe you won't, honeychile. That's the thing 'bout what you call 'love.'" One day you be ready an' willin' to die fo' some man, and the next you be wonderin' what ever made you so crazy. That kinda love don't stick, honeychile. It run off 'bout as quick as it come on."

"You're right about one thing. I feel like I'd do anything for him. It just tears me apart to see him kept caged behind that wire like some animal!"

"Course it do, honey, course it do," Jemima said, stroking Hadley's hair.

"He wants to marry me!"

"Course he do. What man in his right mind, wouldn't?"

"Don't make fun of me, Mammy!"

"I ain't makin' no fun on you, baby. It be a fact. You the prettiest thing in North Virginia."

"That's kind of you to say, Mammy, but what am I going to *do*? How will I get him out of there?"

"You cain't, and that's God's truth, girl. But sooner or later he'll be getting' ex-changed. They'll send him back to Yankeeland and he'll fo'git all 'bout you."

"He will not! He'll come for me!"

"An' say he do. How yo' pappy and yo' brother be feelin' 'bout that? You reckon they be all happy an' ready to throw you a church weddin'? An' even if they was, which you know ain't never gonna happen, what you and him gonna do? You gonna leave us all and go up north and live with his fambly, that you don't even know from Adam? Or mebbe you think he be movin' into yo' room in this here house and takin' over the fambly farm? Girl, you gotta think practical!"

Hadley began sobbing again and Jemima held her, stroking her hair and making the soothing sounds that mothers for eons have made to their beloved children.

17

SHOWDOWN

S ummer began to inch toward autumn. The days grew shorter and the leaves of the deciduous trees surrounding the camp began to change into brilliant reds and yellows. The gnats and mosquitoes began thinning out, thank God. As far as Belden could tell, not a single prisoner was exchanged. Several died, from sickness or malnutrition or at the hands of what the other prisoners called the Brute Squad. They seemed to be able to kill and terrorize with impunity.

Belden began observing their leader, Puddin' Tame, whose real name turned out to be Tony Accetta. The big apelike man had thick black hair descending low on a Neanderthal brow, very dark eyes peering out from beneath the brow, and powerful arms that hung to his knees. Belden thought that if in fact Charles Darwin was correct, and men and apes shared a common ancestor, then Accetta was the missing link.

Accetta had organized a gang of his fellow Italians, all of them dark and swarthy men who seemed to relish physical violence. They had appropriated the tent on the best ground, high and dry, and from this lair they descended like a pack of hyenas on the camp, intimidating the prisoners and separating them from their possessions. Since Belden's sole valuable was his hidden straight razor, which was seldom far from his right brogan, he had so far been spared a shakedown by this gang of thugs, and he took precautions not to be seen with it. His clean-shaven face was not a clear tell, since many soldiers, Union and Confederate, had yet to sprout whiskers.

In fact, Belden thought, the rank and file of both armies are mostly beardless boys, full of ideals and short on common sense.

He was amazed by how many of the prisoners of war had arrived with valuables or received packages of treats from home. Accetta's gang sniffed out these items or foodstuffs with a precision that made Belden suspect that they must have an informant among the guards. Today he watched as they surrounded a boy who couldn't have been of military age yet who had just received a small box from home. Before he could open it, two of them grabbed his arms and held him back. When he attempted to put up resistance, they laughed and pummeled and kicked him until he lay still. Then they ripped open the box, took a small tin of cookies, and ripped up the packet of letters, which, Belden judged, was just mean.

His eyes went to the guards, who were in the process of turning their backs, as if they had never seen the incident. At first he was angry. But when he thought about it, he came to the conclusion that this gang of thugs made the guards' job easier, for their rule of terror kept the regular prisoners in check while they themselves posed no threat to the guards. They were in fact an extension of the repressive confinement who did the guards' dirty work for them. All the guards had to do was to turn a blind eye. The Brute Squad kept order so they didn't have to.

Belden decided at that moment not to allow them to intimidate him, if at all possible. He knew from the schoolyard back in Bradford that bullies are cowards—they will terrorize you if they can but, if you stand up to them, they usually just wet their pants. That was Jesse Munsen for certain. However, this gang had numbers. He'd have to enlist a few good men in a gang of his own, to meet numbers with numbers.

He began with a tough Irishman named Billy Keogh. Keogh called himself a "black Irishman," by which he meant not that he was Negroid but that he had the jetblack hair and jade eyes of that subset of Irish who are more purely Celt. He was a bit nearsighted, having lost his spectacles, and would stand quite close to those he talked to so he could "read the face," as he put it. Though he wasn't a big man, Keogh could throw a punch. In fact, he'd been a professional boxer in his hometown of Roxbury, in Massachusetts. He talked with the strange accent that dropped the r's and broadened the a's, as in "caaht" for "cart" and "Haavaad" for the college he bragged he had attended—until dismissed for public drunkenness.

While Belden thought it unlikely that Harvard College had accepted an Irish Catholic roughneck within its ivy-covered brick walls, he went along with Billy's story. After all, why brag that you'd been expelled? Sometimes Billy added that he'd been found drunk in bed with the Dean's wife and had then thrashed the Dean into the bargain. He'd avoided the penalties, other than dismissal, by volunteering for the Army.

"That, and the fact that the Dean didn't want the story getting out," Keogh said.

Belden had heard of the famous Irish gift of gab and he suspected that Billy had a fertile imagination. However, he found Keogh amusing and thought he'd be an asset in a fight.

Together they persuaded a giant of a man, a farmer from Indiana or Iowa or another of those Midwestern states with Indian names, to join them. He said his name was Schweitzer and that he grew corn to fatten hogs and was sure that his farm was going to hell with his wife and six children trying to run it without him. He also complained about the minimal quantities of food he was getting in the camp.

"They give us all the same sized portions here," he said. "One size for a bull and a chicken is injustice. A big man needs to eat more just to sustain the body. Here I am wasting away to a shadow of my former self. I'll probably be no help to you at all."

Keogh dubbed them the Three Musketeers, which proved that he was at least literate, and suggested that they immediately attack Accetta and his gang of goons.

"No," Belden said. "We don't start the fight, we finish it."

Keogh shrugged.

"We Irish are not constrained by such delusions of honor as the Marquis of Queensbury," he said. "We like to hit first and hit hardest. Unlike these fancy men like Pope and McClellan. If I was general of this Army, the Rebs would be on the run."

* * *

While Keogh and Schweitzer prepared enthusiastically for the show-down with Accetta's gang, the former honing a sharp point on a tin spoon, the latter adapting a piece of firewood into a short club, Belden was more interested in the four o'clock visitation. Hadley came every day but Sunday, as promised, even when it rained. On rainy days her "servant" held a protective umbrella over her.

"I notice," Belden said one sunny day, when Ezra, the black man who always accompanied her but who, on fair days, stood apart from her to lend her privacy, "that no one in the South has slaves. You always refer to them as 'servants.'"

"For the Winfields that is in fact the appropriate term," Hadley replied. "As I believe I explained, my father freed all our help a decade ago, because he felt it was the right thing to do. Two emigrated to Pennsylvania. Ezra and Jemima stayed with us. Now we pay them what we can. In addition to providing food, shelter, clothing, and medical care, I should add. They know they will be cared for as long as they live—unlike your wage slaves in the North, who are discarded if they are sick or old. I ask you: Which system is more humane?"

Belden thought about it for a minute.

"Well, I'm not much on economics," he said, "but you make a good point. We Northerners lack a system for providing for the sick or old, other than the family, the church, or, I suppose, the poor house. I'm not sure what happens in the big cities, though I do hear horrific stories. But in our little town we have one example—Mrs. Morse, who is so old she can't remember her own age. She won't accept charity from any of the churches, so we, the townsfolk, leave her food and clothing on her porch. And the town council passed a resolution to forgive her any taxes on her property. So she manages."

"Human beings have always provided for people they know. That is why it is so difficult for the faceless masses in the cities of the North."

"I agree. But back to my original point—many Southerners have slaves but I never hear that word down here."

"Well, suh, first of all, the proportion of Southerners who own slaves is actually quite small. That is why we are mystified when you Yankees say this war is about slavery. The vast majority of our Confederate troops never owned a slave. They will tell you that they are fighting for their freedom, to prevent you Yankees from imposing upon us a political and economic system that favors you over us. Like most folks, we don't like being told what to do."

Belden nodded.

"That makes sense to me, but the fact remains that if there were no slaves, we wouldn't be fighting each other."

"I don't believe that to be true, suh. The South was ready to secede back in '48, over economic issues—taxation without adequate representation, as you will remember. The basic difference is economic: Yours is an industrial economy, while ours is agrarian. Our entire way of life grows out of the land, with the cotton and tobacco and corn."

Belden nodded again, then said:

"Having grown up on a farm, I know something about how a way of life grows out of the land. You do know, do you not, that most of the Northern economy comes out of small farms. The rise of industry is relatively new for us and is mostly the great spinning and weaving mills that transform your Southern cotton into articles of clothing. Seems to me we're interdependent."

For some reason that he couldn't understand she blushed at that. Or perhaps it was the arrival of the Commandant, Colonel Wolfe, who swept off his plumed hat and made her a bow worthy of an actor on a stage.

"Delighted to find you here, Miss Hadley. I hope this Yankee is showing you the proper respect?"

"Why, Col. Wolfe, how kind of you to inquire after my welfare. Mr. Crane is being a perfect gentleman. We were just discussing the philosophical differences between our two countries."

"Far be it for me to intrude upon a weighty philosophical discussion, Miss Hadley. I shall look forward to seeing you this evening when I come to dinner."

Hadley seemed surprised.

"Ah didn't realize that we would have the honor of your attendance at our evening repast, suh."

"Fax invited me over. I hope that is not an imposition?"

"Of course not, suh. We always enjoy your visits."

"Till this evening, then. May I remind you that the camp visiting hour is over in five minutes."

The Commandant bowed again and strode away. Hadley seemed flustered.

"Ah have no idea why Fax keeps asking him to dinner," she said.

"Who's Fax?"

"Fairfax Winfield is my brother."

"Maybe he's trying to set you up with the colonel."

Hadley blushed. Uh-oh, thought Belden.

"Ridiculous, suh! He's old enough to be my father!"

That reassured Belden. He grinned.

"I'm happy to hear you feel that way," he said.

Hadley looked into his eyes. He felt a thrill pass through his entire body.

"What do you mean, suh?" she asked.

"Hadley, *tu sais. Je t'aime, ma cherie.*"

This time her blush went all the way up to the roots of her hair. Her eyes never left his.

"*Moi aussi, monsieur,*" she whispered, and, turning, almost ran back to where her servant awaited her.

Belden felt as if he were ten feet tall. She loved him, too! And she'd remembered to add the sibilant between the two vowels.

* * *

After Hadley had gone, the Commandant sought him out.

"Step to the side, so I may confer with you."

Uh-oh, thought Belden, he's going to try to shoo me away from her. But he was surprised.

"Corporal Crane," Col Wolfe began formally, "it has come to my attention that you are planning to deal with the criminal element here in the camp."

"By 'criminal element' you mean..."

"Accetta and his band of apes."

"I have no intention of starting a fight, sir."

"Suh, let us not split hairs. We are not lawyers but men of action. I have come to you to tell you that if Accetta or any of his band were to meet with an, ah, accident, I would be the last to be troubled by such an occurrence. Do I make myself clear?"

"I believe so."

"In fact, I would be in your debt. Perhaps I could find a way to make your confinement, ah, less arduous."

He looked at Belden and raised one eyebrow. Then the Commandant turned on his heel and strode away.

Belden felt both excited and afraid. What was Wolfe playing at, he wondered.

* * *

As soon as he could find them he told Keogh and Schweitzer of the Commandant's words.

"He wants us to do his dirty work for him," Keogh said.

"Why doesn't he just do it himself?" Belden asked. "He's the sole authority here. He could have them shot and say they were trying to escape."

"There are some guards who are on the take," Keogh said. "The ones who turn a blind eye to Accetta's shenanigans. They get a cut. If the Commandant ordered the Brute Squad shot, the purloiners might tattle on him up the chain of command."

Belden nodded. That made sense.

"What's 'purloiners' mean?"Schweitzer said. "Oh, them. Let's just bust them now,"

"No, I still want a pretext," Belden said. "But carry your weapons. It won't be long."

* * *

At visiting hour the next day Hadley spoke again, in her terrible French, of her home. Her vocabulary was expanding. She said they had five acres on which they grew a variety of vegetables and also raised chickens, hogs, and a milk cow. While he knew much of this, it delighted him to hear it in that lovely language from her beautiful lips. They had a big barn for the cow and their two riding horses. Her family—this part interested Belden particularly—consisted of her father, her brother, and their two freed slaves, Ezra and Jemima. He found it fascinating that she included Ezra and Jemima as family members. He had not done the same with Eugene. When he spoke of his own family—Ma and Pa, Ira and Helen—tears came to his eyes.

"*Je suis desole, monsieur! Je vous bouleverse!*" she said. I'm sorry, I upset you.

"*Non, non, mademoiselle, ca va.*"

He smiled at her. Though she had written and presumably sent a letter home for him every week, he had yet to have a response from home or Ira.

"Your family sounds lovely," she said, switching to English. "I would love to meet them. After this conflict, of course."

Belden stared at her, his mouth open. He felt like an idiot. He realized that he had been seeing Hadley as an unreachable woman, far beyond him. In her possibly naïve but nonetheless simple clarity she saw this "conflict" as a temporary aberration, after which normality would resume. When peace had broken out, why wouldn't they be able to court, to get to know each other's families, to marry? Why had he assumed that they had between them a gap much larger than the one through the barbed wire fence?

She misinterpreted his look. She drew herself up.

"You don't think I am worthy of your family?" she said.

"Of course I do!" he almost shouted. "They would adore you as much as I do. It's just...that you've made me see how this conflict is but a transient bump in our path that has not the power to come between us. I had made a mountain of a molehill."

She softened, smiled. He thought he could never see enough of her smile.

"When this conflict is over, Hadley," he said, "I will come for you."

* * *

It didn't take long for the pretext Belden wanted to occur. At dinnertime the next evening two of Accetta's goons moved in on a skinny boy who had just received his plate of mystery food.

"We take that offa your hands," one of them said.

"Looks a-like too heavy for you to carry," said the other.

The first goon grabbed the plate and began stuffing his mouth, the second tripped the boy to the ground and began kicking him.

Accetta stood by, laughing. That made Belden angrier than if he'd been one of the overt bullies.

Keogh stuck the man now holding the plate with the shiv with one hand and saved the food with the other. Schweitzer clubbed the other man across the back of the head. Both men toppled to the ground, one quiet, the second groaning.

With a roar of rage, Accetta leapt at them, a stiletto that seemed to have appeared from his belly in his hand. Belden stooped to pull the razor from his brogan, flicked it open, and grabbed Accetta by the hair as he went for Keogh. With one quick slashing motion, one he had done with a sharp knife to dozens of chickens that were ready for the pot, he severed Accetta's carotid artery. Breaking loose and turning on him, spewing a geyser of blood before him, Accetta lunged at Belden with the stiletto. Belden jumped back and to the side, but not before getting showered. Accetta's eyes took on a look of disbelief and his knees buckled. He went down in a heap.

Several guards grabbed them and disarmed them. When Keogh tried to hand the plate to the thin man, the guards knocked it from his hand. The stew, if that's what it was, lay in the trampled grass like vomit. The three of them were thrust into manacles.

My God, thought Belden, I just killed a man. All I feel is a sense of exhilaration. And a sense of repulsion that his blood is on me. What am I becoming?

One of the guards came back with Col. Wolfe.

"I do declare," he said, "what do we have heah?"

The head guard gave his version. It was accurate enough.

"Take the bodies to the cemetery," "Wolfe said, "and have the medic have a look at that stab wound. Confine these three in the Cage."

Belden, Keogh, and Schweitzer were deprived of their brogans and put into the "Cage," a roofless, iron-barred structure in one corner of the camp. They did not get dinner. That night it rained. At least it washed Accetta's blood off.

* * *

At first light, two guards came to the Cage and led Belden outside the stockade. He was certain that they were going to execute him. He was so wet and cold that he decided it might be a relief. As he stood shivering outside the log wall and barbed wire, Col. Wolfe, neat and tidy as always, came up to him smiling. He was carrying a nondescript bag.

"These men," he said, pointing to the guards, "are going to escort you into the forest and fire their rifles into a tree. As far as anyone inside knows, you will have been executed for murder. Highever, they will then escort you to the train station and accompany you to Richmond, where I have arranged for you to be incarcerated in the luxurious officers' prison there, the Libby Lifeboat. You'll have a solid roof over your head, wood stoves for heat in the coming winter, and running water. It is my way of saying thank you for ridding me of the leader of the troublemakers. And—"

With a dramatic flourish, he pulled a pair of officer's boots from the bag.

"You'll need these to pass for an officer, to which rank I now promote you, Loo-tenant Crane."

Belden sat down and began pulling on the boots. The leather was smooth and soft. There was one for his right foot and one for his left foot.

"Not only them there boots, " the colonel said, "I brought you another little goodbye present."

Belden paused from pulling on his new boots to look up at this little man, for whom he was beginning to feel something like affection.

He paused to open his hand like a magician to show Belden his razor.

"—I believe that this is yours. You'll need it to shave in Libby. Don't be one a them hirsute officers."

Belden took the razor and slipped it into his right boot. After the brogans and being barefoot, the boots felt luxurious.

"Today is Sunday," he said.

Wolfe looked at him with raised eyebrows.

"Miss Hadley won't be coming to visit," Belden said. "But tomorrow she'll wonder where I am."

Wolfe smiled. Belden noticed that his teeth were yellow and crooked in his mouth.

"I shall convey your regrets."

"Tell her I'll come back for her."

"Of course, of course. Now, don't miss your train."

The two guards discharged their rifles into the stump, freshened the charges, saluted Col. Wolfe in a desultory manner, and led Belden away from the prison camp.

18

LIBBY PRISON

Belden's first sight of the new prison lifted his mood somewhat from the melancholy he had fallen into since being sent away from Hadley. Even being called "Loo-ten-ant" and treated with more courtesy than he had so far experienced at the hands of the Confederate soldiers did little to buoy his spirits. The infamous prison appeared to be a sturdily-built three-story structure of brickwork and tall chimneys, with large windows on all floors, the bottom ones barred. The bottom floors—a first and a partial basement—had been whitewashed. A huge sign with black letters on a white backing read "LIBBY PRISON." It looked like a palace compared to the tents and barbed wire of Commandant Wolfe's Resort.

The two privates who had been his escorts handed him over to the Libby prison guards, about-faced, and slouched off. His new guards slammed the thick door behind him and expertly patted him down.

"I reckon them there other boys done fleeced this here pretty little lambkins already," one of them drawled to the other, and Belden realized they were more interested in money or other valuables than that he might be smuggling in concealed weapons. Taking his elbows with an almost gentlemanly touch, they steered him into a side room were a young clerk saluted him and then took his papers from the larger guard. A second clerk sat at a table with a fat ledger open before him.

"Welcome to Libby, sir," the first clerk said. "I am Erasmus Ross, the Chief Clerk here. I see you are, hmm, Lt. Belden Crane of the 107th New York. Take him to the second floor, if you would be so kind. I hope your stay will be brief and pleasant, sir."

Belden could hardly believe his ears. RHIP was a truism, then: "Rank Hath Its Privilege." He had to admit he was enjoying the better treatment he'd been getting ever since Wolfe had promoted him. On paper, anyway.

As his guards turned him toward the door, he heard Erasmus Ross say to the clerk at the ledger, "I'll take care of the entry, Joe. Would you go fetch me a small bundle of leaf from the tobacconist?"

The guards steered him up a stairwell and then unlocked his handcuffs before pushing him through a door leading into a large room nearly filled with men, many of whom were wearing partial Union uniforms. They turned to see who was coming in and shouted as one, "Fresh fish!"

They clustered around him, asking who he was, from what unit, and what was the latest news.

After introducing himself, only partially stumbling over his new rank, Belden said: "I'm sorry to say I don't know the latest news, as I was captured during the battle of Chancellorsville and then held in a stockade somewhere in north Virginia since. I assume you all are aware that Stonewall Jackson died from his wounds at that battle."

A very large man with a dark, bushy beard but with his upper lip clean-shaven stepped forward and offered a huge hand. Belden found him a bit intimidating.

"Colonel Abel Streight, 51st Indiana," he said. Belden wondered if he shouldn't salute a superior officer, but Col. Streight was holding his right hand.

"No saluting here," the big man said with a broad smile. "We're all just prisoners of war. We had heard of General Jackson's demise. He was a brave soldier, and a thorn in the side of the Union armies. Three, in fact, that he kept tied up in the Shenandoah so they couldn't reinforce the attacks on Richmond. A loss for the Rebs, a gain for us. We now have a greater hope of being liberated. If Abe can find a general who's not afraid to fight. Last year McClelland sat on his arse for months a few miles from here when he had at least a three-to-one superiority in numbers. Then Burnside got his arse royally kicked at Fredericksburg. Then Hooker at C-ville. But Meade turned back Lee at Gettysburg. Maybe he can get us out of here."

"Wait. Where is Gettysburg? What happened?"

Col. Streight was joined by several others who told Belden how Lee had invaded Pennsylvania and thrown his divisions against entrenched infantry on higher ground well-supported by cannon. His army had been shredded. Pickett had lost his whole division. However, Lee had retreated back across the Potomac before Meade could crush the rest of his army.

"How'd you come to get captured?" asked a fully bearded man with an intelligent eye. One of his feet was bandaged up. "Colonel Tom Rose, 77th Pennsylvania. We got flanked by the Texans at Chickamauga."

Belden grinned. He immediately felt a kinship with this man.

"My company, K, was ordered forward as skirmishers against Jackson," he said. "I guess I got a bit too far out front."

"I love any man who goes forward," Rose said. "You're fortunate that the Rebs didn't shoot you. They got pretty hot after they went and killed their own best general. Took him and his staff for Union cavalry and shot them up."

"Thank God for large favors," Belden said. "You here seem to have pretty good information. What about being exchanged? I've heard that there aren't any more exchanges now."

"You heard right," said a third man, slim and hatchet-faced with a trimmed goatee, thrusting out a hand. "Major A.G. Hamilton, 12th Kentucky Cavalry. Call me Andy. We Unionists feed and house our prisoners well, while they starve and abuse us in all manner of ways, as you no doubt know. Our days go by here like scarcely moving tears."

Tom Rose chuckled and said, "Andy considers himself a bit of a poet. You'll get used to it in time."

"So," Andy continued, as if there had been no interruption, "when we make an exchange, their men are immediately ready to go back to battle, while ours take months to recuperate, if ever they can. Abe ordered the exchanges halted sometime over the summer. There have been no exchanges since May. We're on our own, unless our boys can take Richmond and liberate us."

There was a weighty silence as the men considered the chances of that happening.

"Where do you sleep?" Belden asked at last. "I see no cots."

The three men laughed as if he'd told a very funny joke.

"Welcome to the Lower Chickamauga Room," Rose said. "Many of us here were captured at that battle. We each get a six-by-two space on the floor, and we have to spoon if we don't want to freeze. I'll see if I can't find you a berth."

As Tom Rose limped off, Abel Streight said, "That man escaped from the prison train in Tennessee. Busted his ankle jumping off the train and still eluded capture for the better part of a day. He's a man with escape on his mind."

"Then he's a man after my own heart," Belden said.

Colonel Streight looked at him intently, then nodded.

"All we need is a plan," he said. "We're going to have to manage it on our own."

"I noticed that this building has a partial basement of some sort," Belden said. "What's down there?"

"Rats," said Abel Streight. "Thousands of them."

And then he shivered. Belden didn't think it was in jest.

"Directly below us," Andy Hamilton said, "is the kitchen where we cook the offal they call food. The middle section is a civilian carpenters' workshop and the dungeon, for those in solitary confinement. The western section is the Negro prison. It has had no new prisoners since Lincoln announced the Emancipation Proclamation."

It took Belden only a moment to figure out why.

* * *

Tom Rose found Belden a "berth" next to Chaplain Louis Beaudry.

Beaudry was an energetic man with a firm handshake.

"5th New York Cavalry," he said, "and here Sunday chaplain and Friday editor of the *Libby Chronicle*, our weekly tabloid, which I read aloud from scraps of official newspapers to the assembled hordes. From me you will also find who is giving which classes that week at what times: For example, today I seem to remember that there are classes being offered on mesmerism, which is very popular, Pitman shorthand, French, Latin, rhetoric, and geometry. There is also to be a debate by the Lyceum, or, as we call it, the Lice-I-see-um, a pun on the prevalence of our little friends, don't you see, on the topic 'Resolved: That intemperance is a greater evil than war.' I'm sure that will be most entertaining. You see, young man, the whole secret of making our time here endurable is to have something to do, at regular hours, so that one forgets for a brief spell where he is. I therefore encourage you to enter into our University of Libby with enthusiasm, for you will find the days pass more quickly."

"Thank you, Chaplain," Belden said, "but I believe I'll have plenty to do just finding a way to get out of here."

"As to that," the chaplain-editor said, glancing around nervously, "be careful to whom you confide such information. There are amongst us little birds who sing to our captors for small favors. Speaking of birds, we also have a bird-watching society, which has an element of danger, for the Rebs have sharpshooters posted around this building with orders to shoot anyone who gets too close to the windows. I assume you've been informed of this peculiar excitement?"

"No, sir," Belden said. "And I am grateful that you are alerting me."

"Oh, no one's 'sir' in here," Beaudry said. "We eschew hierarchy. We simply work together to make life bearable. I will be delighted to share my sleeping berth with you, Belden."

"Thank you, s..., uh, Chaplin," Belden responded. "For now, I think I'll look around a bit."

"Just don't get too close to the windows."

Belden said he'd try to remember and headed for the nearest one.

Standing well back, he saw through the south-facing window a canal of flowing water a stone's throw away. Beyond the canal there was a river with a tall schooner docked in it. Not a promising avenue of escape, and there were workmen both within and without fitting heavy iron bars into the window frames. The ones outside were standing on a wooden scaffolding that had been erected against the brick of the building. He wondered how much time he had before all the windows at Libby were barred.

As he crossed the large room of the former warehouse he came upon a circle of men watching a chess game. The "board" had been roughly marked out on the wooden floor with charcoal and the pieces were bits of carved wood and bone. Though two men sat cross-legged facing one another on opposite sides of the board, one of them was looking over his shoulder up to a third man standing with his back to the board who was speaking out the moves. The man on the floor directly behind him was making the actual moves for him and then identifying those of his opponent.

"Knight to Queen's Bishop five," the standing man said and the sitting man behind him moved a bit of soup bone.

The other sitting man straightened up as if in surprise, rubbed his jaw, then hunched forward to ponder the board. When he finally moved a pebble, the other player said, turning to speak to the standing man, "Pawn to King four."

Belden caught the eye of a short man standing next to him.

"What's going on?" Belden asked.

The short man had a very deep voice.

"You must be a new fish," he said.

"'Fraid so," Belden replied.

"That man with his back to the board is Captain Wilson," the short man said. "There's nobody here that has beat him at chess yet, with him not even looking at the board. You wanna give it a try?"

"Not me," Belden said. "My little sister can beat me at any board game ever invented."

"She write you letters?"

"I reckon she will, once she gets my address."

"You write to her and give it. Just don't be trying to write secrets in lemon juice. The Rebs figured that one out, and now they heat all the letters in the stove before they'll send them on."

"How'd they figure that out?"

"Some fool told his wife, in the letter, to bake it for five minutes. So the Rebs did, and sure enough, the lemon juice cooked enough to spell out a secret message. If I get any lemon juice, I drink it down. Good for the health."

And, laughing to himself, the short man moved off.

Belden thought about that for a minute or two. He was beginning to believe that there were more stupid people in the world than he'd ever imagined.

Another man, barefoot and dressed in rags, accosted him. He had, Belden thought, a wild gleam in his eye.

"Fresh fish," he said, "you got any maple candy with you? I do love a bit of maple candy."

"I'm sorry I don't," Belden said.

Moving like a snake's strike, the man grabbed Belden's shirt and twisted it in both hands.

"I want your maple candy!" he screamed, spittle flying from his lips.

When Belden drew back a fist to hit the man, Tom Rose held his arm.

"Let him be, Belden," Tom said. "He's a bit teched. Let go of Belden's shirt now, Saul. No one has any candy today."

"Bread, beans, and soup," said Saul in singsong. "I'm sick of eating poop. Soup beans and bread, I wants maple candy instead."

With that, he scurried off into the crowd of people watching the chess game.

"What happened to him?" Belden asked.

"About what's happened to any of us here," Tom said. "Some get pushed over the line. We care for them as best we can. The Rebs just mistreat them."

"How vile!"

"Yes, and you were just about to hit him. Their impulse is the same."

"I didn't know..."

"Of course not. And they don't really know either. There is massive ignorance about and fear of the insane. Always has been. We understand so little of our own minds."

Belden looked more closely at Tom Rose and saw the sadness and gentleness in his eyes.

"You are a kind and wise man," he said. "What did you do before the war?"

Tom Rose laughed.

"I am a simple schoolteacher," he said, "who's always been curious why things are the way they are."

Belden grinned.

"I did some schoolteaching myself," he said, "when my brother Ira needed a substitute, anyway."

"We have that in common, then," said Tom, "as well as a penchant for escape."

"How are we going to get out of here?" Belden asked.

"Look around and tell me what you think," Tom said. "Just don't get too close to the windows."

"So I heard. Thanks for securing me the berth with the chaplain."

"He'll talk your ear off if you let him," Tom laughed. "I hope you can get some sleep."

Belden watched as Tom limped off. There, he thought, goes a good man.

* * *

Belden crossed the room, skirting the chess game, to see what lay to the north. The windows, he noticed, lacked glass and were open to the elements. Below, there was a street and then a vacant lot. Down the street from the vacant lot was what looked like a warehouse with a Rebel sentinel in a gray uniform standing in front of the large doors. Another sentinel, his musket resting on his shoulder, paced up the street from him, did a wobbly about-face, and came pacing back. Atop the warehouse Belden saw a third graycoat lying prone on the roof drawing a bead on him with a long-barreled squirrel rifle.

Belden stepped back quickly. So it was true that there were sharp-shooters surrounding the prison and plinking at anyone who got too close to the windows. How in the devil did the Libby birders association manage?

He walked west through a doorway to cross another large room and saw another street, another vacant lot, another sentry pacing. Turning back, he went down a wooden stairway and walked east until he came to the upper "kitchen": Two stoves whose outlet pipes entered a brick chimney going full blast heating iron pots of a thin soup. Between them was a fireplace full of stacked kindling for the stoves. The "chefs" were Union officers doing their best to transform a few ounces of blue-black meat and a handful of beans per inmate into an edible meal. This area was many degrees warmer than the rest of the prison and the chefs were red-faced and perspiring.

Belden pushed through a doorway into the easternmost room. It was full of sick men on cots. He hesitated a moment, fearful of catching one of their maladies. Then he crossed the room. Not getting too close to the window he saw yet another vacant lot perhaps fifty feet wide with yet another pacing sentry. On the other side of the lot was a wall and then a building of some sort.

Aha, he thought.

"What's that building used for?" he asked a man who was attempting to darn a much-patched sock.

The man didn't even look up from his work.

"That's the Goodie Shack," he said. "When your mother or wife sends you a package of goodies from home, it gets ransacked in there by the Rebs. They say it's to prevent weapons being smuggled in, but it's really so they can have first crack at the goodies. We only get what they don't want."

"How do they enter it?"

"There's a south-facing door onto the street, Canal Street they call it."

"Thanks," Belden said.

"When you get your first package, give me something out of it, will you? I could sure use a new pair of socks."

The sock-darner looked up at him. He had only one eye. The lid was mostly down over the vacant socket where the other had been.

"If I ever get one, count on it."

An elderly man wearing a white coat came in. He had a deep southern drawl.

"Ah youal sick, boy? Whatcha doin' heah?"

"Just visiting a friend," Belden said, retreating the way he had come.

He was mildly depressed by his reconnaissance. The prison was buffered by streets or vacant lots on all sides, and all were patrolled by sentries. The best bet, he reckoned, was to tunnel to the east and get beyond the wall, maybe even into the Goodie Shack.

* * *

Before they ate dinner that evening, Chaplain Beaudry offered up a prayer. Everyone bowed their heads.

"Almighty Father, Creator of all things," he began. "Help us to bear our misfortunes with the grace of our Lord Jesus Christ when He carried the Cross up Calvary. Let us be mindful of our blessings—that we are alive, that we have this food to eat and these good companions to eat it with, that we have the hope that we shall one day be freed.

Give us the moral fortitude to persevere until that day of freedom. We ask it in Christ's name. Amen."

Belden heard the man standing next to him mumble, "Brevity's the soul of wit," then scamper toward the food line. Belden followed. He watched what the Shakespeare scholar in front of him did and like him picked up a tin cup and a spoon from a wooden table. A chef with a ladle filled his cup with the bean-and-meat soup and another handed him a chunk of bread so stale he could see the fungus on it.

He sat with his back to the wall on the floor next to the Shakespearean and began rubbing the fungus off.

"Don't waste that!" the man said, "That's the best part! I've noticed that those who eat the growth get ill less than those who don't —and sometimes get intoxicated and do St. Vitus's dance."

"I'm not sure I want to indulge in that experience," Belden replied.

"Oh, you will," the man said. "You will. It's a lovely vacation from this hellhole. A brief vacation, I should add. No more than a day."

And he bit deeply into his own stale crust, grinning from ear to ear.

It had been a long time since he'd last eaten. Though Belden was ravenous, the sight of the grayish-white growth on bread hard as a baseball and the greasy, semi-putrid odor of the soup turned his stomach. However, he knew that he'd have to eat if he wished to have the strength to escape. Pinching his nostrils shut with one hand, he forced down some of the soup. It didn't taste as bad as it looked. It took some doing to break his hunk of bread into two smaller pieces. He dunked one of them into the cup of soup and let it soak. As he did so he noticed that several weevils were swimming in his soup. His stomach heaved.

It's just more protein, he told himself. Don't be squeamish. Build your strength any way you can. He wanted to vomit.

Jesus, please help me.

* * *

No sooner had he fallen asleep than the flash of lightning and almost simultaneous crack of thunder startled him to wakefulness. Extricating himself from the arm that the chaplain had thrown over him, Belden rose and picked his way around and over the sleeping prisoners, whose combined snoring made the room sound like a hog pen.

Outside, the lightning flashed again. This time he was able to count "One one-thousand, two one-thousand," prior to the thunder-clap. The storm was beginning to move on.

He had to pause to allow his eyes to readjust after the brightness of the jagged bolt. He was now at the south-facing windows, some of which had already been barred. But some had not.

Climbing out through one of the yet unbarred windows, he lowered his feet to the wooden scaffold. It was slick and the rain pelted his head and body. Though it was a very cold rain, the freshness of it seemed to cleanse him. He turned his face up and let the fierce drops wash it. He opened his mouth and let the fresh water sprinkle in, as he had so often as a boy.

Feeling his way carefully in the pitch blackness, he found the ladder that enabled the workmen to ascend the scaffolding. And, he presumed, would enable him to reach the ground—and freedom. He wasn't too worried about sentries—he knew that most soldiers liked to stay dry and warm if they had the option at all. They'd duck under the eaves or into the guard room while the worst of the storm passed.

Then he felt a cold hand upon his own.

In the flash of the lightning, he saw a bearded, wild-eyed man staring at him in the same state of terror that he himself was feeling, and he raised his fist to strike him. The man's hand reached across the ladder to hold his arm. He knew that hand. He glanced down at the dirty whiteness on one of the man's feet.

"Tom Rose?!" he croaked.

"Quiet, or we die!" Tom whispered.

"Let's get down!" Belden whispered back.

"No! They pulled down the last ladder. You have to jump the last ten feet."

"I'll risk it!"

"I can't, with this foot," Tom said. "And if you escape, they'll tighten the security. Let's find a way that most of us can get out. Not just one."

Pictures of faces flitted through Belden's mind. Hadley. Ma. Pa. Helen. Cinder. Hadley.

The lightning flashed again, then the thunder shook the scaffold. In the light of the flash Belden saw two things: Tom's honest face beseeching him. And the head of a guard poking out of the guard room.

"All right," he whispered.

They crept back toward the window. Another bolt of lightning froze them in place. When they could see again, they crept along the scaffolding and back into Libby prison through the open window.

It was one of the hardest decisions Belden had ever made.

The next day, the workmen disassembled the scaffolding and carried it away.

19

FINDING A WAY OUT

That morning at 6 a.m. Belden awoke to a thunder of drums. This reveille was loud and lively, the drummers clearly relishing their task. Men rose stiffly from the floor upon which they had been sleeping, or trying to sleep, and stumbled toward the faucet that piped in cold, yellowish water from the James River for a quick wash of hands and faces. A lucky few employed their toothbrushes before replacing them in a buttonhole for security. Others used a forefinger to massage their gums. The overflow ran down a trough into which the men further down were urinating, then out through a pipe in the wall.

At first Belden was disoriented. He'd incorporated the drums into a dream of marching into battle at Chancellorsville with his company in tight formation, muskets at port arms, fixed bayonets sparkling in the sun. It seemed he'd been shot in his left arm. He was shocked to find himself lying on an aching left side with the arm of the chaplain over his side and the back of another man spooned up against him.

Quickly sitting up, he realized that both hips were painfully stiff from having been on the wooden floor for almost seven hours. He remembered now the commands to "Change sides!" every couple of hours all night, when the entire mass of prisoners would rotate. He also had a crick in his neck.

The chaplain arose, stretched, and said, "Good morning, Belden. Follow me. I'll show you the drill."

"Who's drumming?"

"Oh, that's the Negro Drum Band from down in the west wing of the basement. They start off the day with reveille."

They joined a line of sleepy-eyed men shuffling toward a long line.

Down on the street they heard a basso profundo voice calling, "Get your papers here! All the latest news! Only twenty-five cent! Bragg done whip Rosecrans at Murfreesboro!"

Belden looked quizzically at the chaplain.

"That's Old Ben," he said, "the newsboy. The men downstairs will buy a couple copies, read them, and send them up to us for resale. They'll be handed around until you can't read the print, it's so smudged. I usually get hold of a pretty good copy and read it out to our room after breakfast."

"Is breakfast next?"

"Head count first, then breakfast. Let's get in line."

Belden could see the lines forming up in the front of the room. He heard someone say, "Dress right, dress!" and each man in line stuck his right arm out akimbo, where the next man moved up against it with his side. Then came the command, "Ten-shun!" and the right arms dropped. The prisoners were in fairly straight lines and columns after this exercise. Belden saw the Chief Clerk, Erasmus Ross, counting heads down the rows.

Then he heard the chaplain chuckle as two men from the already counted first row peeled off and disappeared through the door into the next room.

"Watch the back door," the chaplain whispered.

Turning his head Belden saw the rows of grinning men behind him and then, slipping in through the back door, the two men who'd peeled off merging into the last row.

He watched as Erasmus Ross studied the notebook where he was adding up the head count and stamped a foot in frustration.

"Damn!" he said to the other clerk. "We've got two too many! We'll have to count all over again! Let's start back here."

All of the Union prisoners were grinning and Belden heard a few poorly-suppressed laughs.

"Don't youal get me angry now!" Erasmus shouted, and the twittering stopped.

"It's another way we have a bit of fun," Chaplain Beaudry whispered. "We call it 'repeating.' It drives Erasmus crazy."

"It may come in useful," Belden whispered back.

* * *

Belden found Tom Rose in the breakfast line and said, "I've got some thoughts I'd like to discuss with you."

"Not now," Tom said. "Later."

He pushed his chin toward the door.

"There's The General."

Belden expected to see an actual Union general. Instead, he saw a huge black man swinging a fumigator from which poured clouds of dark gray smoke reeking of tar.

"Here come your nice smoke!" The General sang out. "At no charge and no price."

"That's supposed to kill the bugs," Tom said, "but I believe it's only hastening our mummification. Most of us are full of lice. They even rain down on us through the floorboards. You'll see, after breakfast."

Again the tin cup and spoon, this time a square of bacon richly discolored and another hunk of the stale, weevily bread.

"Masticate thoroughly to maximize caloric benefit," Tom advised. "Pinch your nostrils if you must." He led Belden a bit apart from the throng. "What are your thoughts?"

Belden swallowed with difficulty.

"We tunnel out," he said.

Tom smiled.

"Step over this way toward the south-facing window," he said. "But, as you know, not too close to it. What do you notice?"

"They're taking down the scaffolding," Belden said. "There goes our main chance."

"Further out," Tom said.

Belden looked out onto Canal Street. Confederate workmen were entering and leaving a large hole that had been dug along a portion of the street twenty feet from where he and Tom stood. Some were carrying out and emptying buckets. Even at the distance, the stench hit him so hard he almost gagged. It was like nothing he'd ever smelled, even the manure pile behind the barn at home. It smelled like rotting corpses.

"It's a sewer," he said.

"Yes," said Tom, "a big sewer. Big enough for those workmen to stand in."

"So, if we could tunnel under the cobblestones from the basement to the sewer..."

"We could walk east to the Kanawah Canal..."

"And be free as birds. Smelling a bit ripe, though."

"Let's go down and take a look in the lower kitchen," Tom said, leading the way.

After returning their cups and spoons to the wash basin, they went down a narrow stairway into the room called Rat Hell. A different stench surrounded them: grease, filth, rotten food, mold. Squealing rats ran over the straw-covered floor in waves. It looked like a rat army. In one corner cooks were sweating over a huge cauldron. The ceiling was low, the room nearly dark despite the bar-covered windows to the south. The gloom was oppressive.

"I see why they call it Hell," Belden said.

Tom led him to an especially dark recess in the wall behind a groin supporting the upper story. The groin created a shadow over the wall.

"We can dig here," Tom said. "At night. We can hide the hole with straw during the day."

"Dig with what?"

"That's our next task. Let's confer with Andy Hamilton."

For a moment, Belden allowed himself to see Hadley in his mind's eye: her long redgold hair, her porcelain skin without a single freckle, the sunshine of her smile. He would get back to her.

* * *

As Belden and Tom climbed back up the stairs, Belden felt as if he were ascending from a miasmic swamp into the air. A strange pantomime greeted them in the Lower Chickamauga Room: Most of the prisoners had disrobed, at least to their waists, and were examining themselves and one another closely, particularly in the hair of the head, then rubbing together forefinger and thumb.

They found Andy and approached him.

"Welcome to Monkey Scratch," Andy said to Belden. "We're attempting to keep the parasite population down to a minimum. Howdy, Tom."

Andy showed them a dark smear on his thumb that Belden guessed had formerly been a sucking parasite.

"Doesn't look like the fumigation works very well," Belden said.

"Oh, it doesn't kill them," Andy said, "but it does get them moving so we can find them more readily."

Belden shuddered.

"I hate fleas," he said. "They love me. They'll jump off a dog to bite me."

"Those aren't fleas," Andy said. "These are louses."

"When you've completed the extermination," Tom said, "we'd like to have a word."

"I've dispatched sufficient unto the day," Andy said, pulling his grayish shirt back over his head. "What's on your mind?"

"Belden's in on the tunnel to the sewer."

Andy grabbed Belden's hand and shook it.

"Welcome," he said.

"What about digging implements?" Tom asked.

"I've come up with a case knife, dull of course, and the blade of a broken shovel."

"Where are they now? No, don't tell me. Fetch them and re-hide them down in the southeast corner of Rat Hell, where that support groin casts a dark shadow. If the Rebs discover them, we don't want them to be able to link them to anyone."

Andy grinned.

"They're already there," he said, "and you didn't see them, did you?"

* * *

They began work on the Canal Street tunnel that night two hours after lights out. That gave the guards time to go below and either start drinking or climb into their beds. One at a time, Belden, Tom, and Andy rose and picked routes through the sleeping prisoners to the stairway leading down to Rat Hell. They didn't attract undue attention because, at any given time, somebody or other was making his way to the water closet to relieve himself. Given the quality of their grub, the percentage of men with dysentery was high. It seemed to be the norm to have someone stumbling to and fro toward the W.C. all night.

At night Rat Hell was full of Stygian darkness as well as squealing rats. They proceeded mostly by feel. Rats ran over their feet, apparently fearless. Andy showed them where he'd hidden their digging tools and took the first turn digging. They set up a simple rotation: While the digger widened the breech in the wall, pulling out dirt with hands and the shovel blade, a second man loaded the spittoon they'd lugged over from the kitchen area. When it was full he'd haul it away to dump, covering the fresh dirt with straw. The third man kept watch. They called him The Rat, because if he heard a guard approaching he would imitate a rat's squeal. When the digger tired, they'd change places, the digger becoming The Rat, the former watcher taking over the dirt-hauling, and the hauler moving into the tunnel.

Tom pointed out that when the tunnel got a bit longer, they'd need to include another man to fan air into the tunnel.

"You know something of this craft," Belden said.

"I'm from Pittsburgh," Tom replied. "We have coal mines everywhere. I went down the mines now and then as a lad."

They fell into a rhythm of starting work around 11 p.m. and knocking off around 4 a.m. They'd check that the newly dug dirt was covered with the plenty of straw, conceal the tunnel entrance, and hide the tools. Belden suggested they hide the knife in one spot, the shovel blade in another.

"That'll halve the chances of losing them both to discovery," he said.

They'd then cross Rat Hell, creep up the stairs, and go to the W.C. to wash off as much of the filth as possible in the cold water before getting a couple of hours of sleep. At best, they were sleeping only four hours at night, though they tried to nap during the day. Although there wasn't much required of them during the day once Head Count was completed, napping while hundreds of men were talking and moving about wasn't easy to do. Nonetheless, they were usually tired enough to fall into a semblance of sleep in a series of cat naps. Belden found he lacked the energy to enter any of the Libby U classes, though he was drawn to the one on mesmerism.

The tunnel had breached the prison wall and was descending to get below street level when everything changed. All of the chaplains and surgeons were moved out of the prison and sent to Danville. With the smaller population in Libby, there was no longer a need for two kitchens and the stairway to Rat Hell was sealed.

The day it happened Belden had been napping after a long night of tunneling when the pounding of hammers jerked him awake. At first he thought they must have come under cannon fire. Still half asleep, he had a brief hope that Yellow McClelland had broken through the Confederate lines and was coming to free them. In that moment he forgot his antipathy toward Li'l Mac and felt a wave of gratitude rush through his aching body. When he went to investigate and saw Rebel carpenters driving sixteen-penny nails into the thick boards now sealing off Rat Hell, the gratitude changed to a nausea so profound he thought he would vomit. He felt a firm hand on his arm and saw Tom, pale with frustration, standing beside him.

"We'll find another way," Tom said.

* * *

That night Belden, Tom, and Andy met in what was now the only kitchen area remaining. The heat of the stoves lingered around them. A kerosene lantern hanging from a spike in the brick chimney cast a wavering light. Tom went to the pine kindling stacked in the fireplace and selected a slim piece. Sitting on an upturned box—the only chairs available to them in Libby—he drew out the clasp knife and began whittling. Belden felt his mouth drop open.

"How…"

Tom smiled. The corners of his eyes crinkled.

"Something made me want to bring it up this morning when we knocked off," he said.

"God inspired you," Andy said.

"Something like that," Tom said. "We know Rat Hell is now sealed off. The east cellar is the colored prison, with the guards' quarters immediately above it, so that's out. That leaves the middle cellar room with the jail cells for men in solitary and the carpenter shop. I'm thinking we might just take a gander at it."

He held up the former piece of kindling, which he had whittled into a wedge. Forcing this wedge into the crack between the floorboards, which were almost two feet wide, he began levering one of them up. It yielded with surprising ease.

"Them Rebs don't like to waste too much iron," Andy said. "There's only two nails in that entire twelve-foot plank."

They worked the plank loose from the stringers and peered down into the dark below. They could neither see nor hear anything. Belden and Andy pulled the plank up past the stringers and then carefully lowered it. The plank touched the cellar floor with almost a foot protruding from the kitchen floor.

"Hopefully," Tom said, "I'll be back soon. Keep watch and replace the plank if anyone comes"

Grasping the plank with both hands, he placed his feet on it and began lowering himself backwards between the floorboards. His legs disappeared, then his hands, then his head. He had to turn sideways to ease his shoulders through the gap.

He soon realized that the room he was lowering himself into wasn't completely dark. He saw that there was a doorless entry onto Canal Street that let in some of the light from the streetlamps. By this illumination he could see the stacked lumber in the room, the carpenters' benches, and the jail cells, fortunately empty.

Creeping across to the doorless entryway, Tom stood up against the wall and peered out into the street. He could hear the sentry before he saw him and pulled back as the soldier walked past the entry so close Tom could have touched him. He held his breath and counted silently until the sentry had paced down to the corner of the building, made his turn, and paced back. Picturing the layout of the building in his mind's eye, he calculated time and distances. Maybe, just maybe, they would have time to slip out of the entry while the sentry had his back to them and be out of the lighted area before he made his turn.

When the sentry passed the doorway a second time, Tom counted till be reckoned the guard was farthest away, then backed away to the carpenters' workbench, feeling along it until his right hand touched the cold steel of a chisel. He slipped the tool into his boot, then returned to the angled plank and shimmied up it. After Belden and Andy replaced the plank, Tom told them, in an excited whisper, about the sentry and his timing.

"Why don't we just hare out right now," Belden asked.

Tom shook his head slowly.

"Let's gather more intelligence first," he said. "We're not sure where the Union lines are now. We'll also need to begin collecting an escape kit: warm clothes, money, food, a canteen of some kind, a compass if we can get one. Let's also get one of the men who was in the Peninsular campaign to draw us a map."

"Have you someone in mind?" Andy said. "We'll probably have to include him."

"I do," Tom replied. "Now, let's catch up on our sleep."

* * *

Belden slept hard the rest of the night and yawned through Head Count and breakfast. He realized that he had been badly sleep deprived. He watched Tom and Andy working the room, trading greenbacks for the items they would need in the escape. How they had managed to hold onto any greenbacks he couldn't imagine: The Rebs loved them while openly scorning their own shoddy currency. One of the guards had said that Confederate counterfeits were easy to spot because they were usually better made than the legal specie. Ironically, at the same time they were trying to throw off the Union, the Rebels were dependent upon its economic system.

When they gathered in the kitchen at eleven, Belden was impressed with what Tom and Andy had gathered in one day: two knapsacks, 4 sweaters, 4 knitted caps, a rough map of the Peninsula, and—most amazing of all—a 100-foot length of rope that had been braided from the shorter pieces that Colonel Harry White had collected off the bales of clothing he had distributed to the enlisted Union prisoners on Belle Isle out in the James River. From some of Libby's windows one could see the enlisted men's tents. Col. White told grim tales of their desperate conditions:

"Many prisoners there have no shelter and no shoes. On cold nights several freeze to death. The filth is unimaginable. Their rations are even worse than ours, believe it or not. Some of them are walking skeletons. It is a terrible place."

Belden thought, *Maybe Commandant Wolfe did me a better service than I knew*. He felt a flash of gratitude for the wily hypocrite.

They quickly loosened the floorboard, lowered it at an angle into the carpenters' shop below, tied the rope around a nearby post supporting the ceiling, and went down into the middle cellar.

Belden could hardly believe his eyes when he saw the open entry. Though Tom had told them of it, he couldn't quite imagine the top security prison in the Confederacy would have so obvious an escape route. As his eyes adjusted to the scant light coming in from the street-lights, Belden saw that the solitary cells were still empty and that worktables ran along both walls. He could smell the sweet clean odor of fresh wood shavings. The normality of that familiar odor brought memories of home and tears to his eyes. He joined Tom and Andy at the entry and heard the sentry's footfalls on the cobblestones.

As he pressed his body against the brick wall beside the entry he had to fight the urge to bolt out into the street. Freedom seemed so close. Then the sentry paced past no more than a yard from him. He could see the cloud of the sentry's exhaled breath hang for a moment in the cold night air. A burning sensation suffused his chest and arms. He could barely restrain himself from leaping upon the sentry's back, snapping his neck, snatching his rifle and fleeing toward the one thing he really wanted: Freedom.

In the prison above him, he knew, was protection from the elements and a certain level of warmth, two meals a day, and a dry place to sleep. Out there it was very cold and very wet as winter approached. Out there he would be hunted with hounds and shot at by militia. Yet the pull was palpable on his body.

Tom reached out to touch Belden's shoulder and whispered, "We'll go when the time is right."

They stayed for another half hour or so, counting and recounting the sentry's steps from the entry of the carpenters' shop to his turn at the far corners of the building. Then they retreated back up the plank, pulling themselves up with the rope.

Hadley, Belden said to himself, I'm coming. Wait for me.

* * *

A week later they decided the time had come. They had collected enough food for a week and extra clothing to keep them warmer than their usual rags. Tom had found a nearly new pair of boots for himself. His foot was much healed and could fit into them.

At midnight they collected their equipment from various hidey-holes and made their way along with Abel Streight to the kitchen. They levered loose and then lowered the floorboard. Belden tied a bowline around the column and they went down the plank backward holding onto the rope. Col. Streight stayed in the kitchen to untie and re-hide the rope once they were well away. The hope was that others could use the escape route on subsequent nights.

Belden, Tom, and Andy crept across the carpentry shop. At the entry they heard the sentry pace past. Their hearts were hammering. Tom waited till the sentry was fifteen paces away and slipped out the entry and into the shadows.

A shout came from the opposite end of the building.

"Prisoner loose! Corporal of the Guard, prisoner loose!"

In the room above and to the west Belden and Andy could hear the guards putting on their boots. Their blood seemed to freeze. Then they saw Tom running back toward them. They ran to the plank, grabbed the rope, and started up. Belden, waiting to go up last, thought he saw movement in the back of the carpenters' shop. He went up as fast as he could, Tom and Andy pulled up the plank, and Abel untied the rope from the post. As quickly as they could, they hid their rope and knapsacks and lay down in their sleeping places. Minutes later, they could hear a babble of voices down in the carpenters' shop. Sadly disappointed, they did their best to get some sleep.

The following day they heard on the grapevine what had happened. The newly activated second sentry had seen a man come out of the entry to the shop and, assuming it was a prisoner trying to escape, raised the alarm. But that night there had been, unusually, a few carpenters sleeping on bedrolls in the shop. When the guards charged in and found sleepy and confused carpenters rubbing their eyes, they reckoned that it must have been one of them going out to urinate. After all, it was obvious that there was no way a prisoner could get down into the shop as there were no connecting stairs.

Belden, Tom, and Andy each breathed a sigh of relief.

"We need to recruit more men," Belden said, "so we can over-power the guards if need be. We'll also need a lookout near an upstairs window to whistle like a whip-poor-will if he sees trouble brewing."

Tom and Andy agreed and began to bring in a few more men, pledging them to secrecy. They took turns taking their new recruits down into the cellar to familiarize them with the layout and the plan. They made sure each man could scramble back up the plank quickly. That turned out to be a wise precaution.

* * *

It was a week since they had aborted the last escape attempt. The nights were growing steadily colder, with frost on the ground mornings.

Tonight was once again the big night. Belden lay in his place on the floor of the Chickamauga room unable to contain his excitement. He was feeling an almost desperate sense of urgency to be free. He longed to see Hadley again and wondered whether the Commandant was pressing his suit with her—and, worse, whether she might be responding. He tried to put what he couldn't control out of his mind, but he knew he had to escape and get back to Hadley before too much more time went by. She was an impulsive girl. He wondered whether she might have already forgotten about him.

That fear made him pause. He realized that he knew, absolutely, that Cinder would never put him out of her mind. Even if she was already married to Jesse Munsen, he knew he would always have a place in her heart.

Why, then, did he imagine that Hadley might forget him and take up with the Commandant, or anyone else? Well, she was a very different person, for one, and they had never even been able to touch each other, for another, much less make love. Third, they hadn't known each other very long. He'd known Cinder all his life, and hers.

He only knew that it was Hadley he was crazy in love with and it was to Hadley he must return. Even if that might mean risking recapture. Yes, it was a form of insanity, but a blissful insanity. Whenever he thought of her he felt first warm and happy, then cold and terrified that she wouldn't wait for him. He went back and forth between these two states, unable to keep himself in the happier one for very long. He tried to imagine making love with her but couldn't get much past the kissing part, because he had no idea what her body looked like. In clothing, she had a pleasing shapeliness, so he guessed she had firm breasts and taut buttocks with a slim waist between, but was her skin the same creamy white of her face? Did she have any freckles or moles to set off that creamy whiteness? And was the color of her hair between her legs the same as the redgold of her tresses?

He was surprised to notice that he was growing within his trousers. Erections were not common on a diet such as Libby's, in a prison without females. He'd better watch out or he'd have trouble getting between the floorboards. The picture that came unbidden to his mind made him almost laugh out loud. He had to clasp one hand over his mouth to restrain himself.

Enough of this. Have to focus on the plan. I'll be the last man out, therefore in the greatest danger of being detected. Wait till both sentries are halfway down their route, then break for the shadows across Canal Street where there are hogsheads to hide among. Then eastward ho.

He felt in his pocket for his copy of the rough map of the Peninsula and was relieved to find that his tumescence had subsided.

Got to keep a clear head. Escape first, get to Hadley second.

And make love with her...Stop that!

He saw Tom rise to pick his way across the sleeping prisoners.

Here we go!

* * *

When Belden got to the kitchen the floorboard was up and the rope tied off at the post with an easily releasable clove hitch. Streight was on hand to take charge of the rope. Another man had positioned himself near one of the windows to keep a lookout. He nodded an all clear and Tom Rose lowered himself into the carpenters' shop. Hopefully there were no carpenters sleeping down there tonight. Andy Hamilton went second, and the other ten men followed as quickly as they could. Belden went last and found himself trembling with excitement.

By the time his feet touched the earthen floor of the shop, he could see that Tom and Andy had already left the room, and the second pair were about to break from the entry. At that moment, they heard the whip-poor-will alarm from the lookout overhead. Belden wanted to weep with disappointment. The escapees turned and began hauling themselves back up the plank. A few giggled in panic.

Going to the entry, hoping he might join Tom and Andy, Belden was shocked to see them running back toward him.

"Militia guards are coming!" Andy whispered. "Someone gave us away!"

Belden followed Tom and Andy to the plank, where they stood together at the end of the line of men scrambling to get back up the plank.

"Hurry!" Andy whispered, although clearly the men were doing their best.

Belden looked back at the entryway, expecting to see armed militiamen charging in with fixed bayonets. Then the rope was in his hands and he scurried up the plank.

No sooner was he up than Tom and Andy pulled up and repositioned the floorboard. Steight had already untied the rope and was carrying it off to hide. Below them they heard the shouts of the militiamen in the carpenters' shop. Belden tucked his knapsack in behind the split kindling. Andy grabbed his arm and led him up the stairs.

"What about Tom?" Belden whispered.

"He'll cover for us," Andy whispered back. "Quickstep!"

They could hear the prison guards running into the kitchen below them.

* * *

While stowing his knapsack, Tom drew out his pipe and matches. He sat down on a box by the stove, struck a match on it, and lit up his pipe, then picked up a blurry copy of that day's news sheet. When the prison guards ran in a moment later, he looked up from the sheet and blew a cloud of smoke into the air. They hardly glanced at him as they ran past to get to the stairs up to the Chickamauga room. Taking a lingering draw on his corncob, Tom let the leaf settle his nerves.

That had been a close one.

* * *

When the guards came clattering into the room swinging their lanterns, they found all the prisoners apparently sound asleep on the floor. A few poked up startled faces and held up hands against the bright lights intruding into their eyes. The guards did a cursory count, then tramped up the stairs to check the room above.

Lying in his berth on the chilly floor, Belden kept his eyes closed and tried to still the wild beating of his heart by breathing slowly, and longer on the outbreath than the inbreath as his father had taught him. He listened to the guards' boots against the floor overhead, then going back down the stairs. He let out a sigh of relief and fought against the urge to laugh hysterically. His whole body felt energized, fully alive, and was pervaded with a warm sense of well-being. In fact, he could hardly remember ever feeling so good.

Well, there had been that one time when he had been swimming in the lake and was lying beneath a beautiful sycamore, watching the interplay of light on the fluttering leaves. He had been suffused with a quiet joy for a whole minute, but as soon as he began calculating how to hold onto the feeling, it dissipated. Yes, that had been another such time, though that was a moment of serenity and this was quite the opposite.

He marveled at that. Here he was, lying on a plank floor, cheek to jowl with smelly, lice-ridden prisoners, half-starved from the terrible diet, over-exerted from his anxious retreat back up the plank and stairs, and he could recall only one other instance in his entire life when he'd felt so vividly alive. He lay there in the dark, wondering at this phenomenon, until he fell into a dreamless sleep.

20

NEWS OF BELDEN'S DEATH

The harvest, smaller this year with only Eugene and Ma and Helen to help, was in, and they had had a sprinkling of snow already. Pa reckoned that it was going to be a cold winter as he watched the squirrels gathering a larger supply of acorns than usual. The *Farmer's Almanac* supported his observation.

Then there arrived a terrible letter from a man who claimed to have been a fellow prisoner of Belden's.

From the heights of joy at the prior information that he was alive, they were plunged into the Slough of Despond. They were familiar with the Slough of Despond from their reading of John Bunyan's book *Pilgrim's Progress.*

The letter had a military frank upon it and was postmarked "Fort Lyon, Virginia," wherever that was. Within was a single sheet of foolscap. Pa put on his spectacles to read it:

29 September 1863
Roxbury, Massachusetts
The Crane Family
Bradford, New York

Dear Cranes,

I apologize for not being able to salute you by your Christian names as well, for, though Belden spoke of you often and with much affection, I didn't record them. Fortunately, I did remember your address.

Belden and I spent some weeks together in a prison camp somewhere in Virginia. I am not allowed to say where, but I can tell you I myself come from a small town near Boston.

In this prison there was what Belden called a "Brute Squad" of rapacious Italians who spread terror in order to take whatever they wanted from their fellow prisoners. We decided to stand up against this reign of terror and recruited a stalwart fellow named Schweitzer from Ohio to assist us. When the Brute Squad attacked a poor helpless wretch to steal his food, we intervened. There was a quick fight, leaving two of their number dead and one wounded.

We were put into a Cage within the prison that night. The next morning Belden was taken from it and outside of the prison camp. We heard shots, and Belden did not return. Though we fear he might have been executed, we have every hope that he escaped.

I wish I could be the bearer of more lucid and cheerful news, but I have written because if I were in your situation I would appreciate hearing something of him.

Myself, I was lucky to be exchanged for a Rebel major.

I knew Belden only for a short time, but I can say without reservation that he was one of the finest men I ever met: brave, true, and honest. I pray that you will be reunited in the near future.

Your humble servant,

Private Wm. Keogh

As Ma, Pa, and Helen looked at one another, each of them had an awful feeling. It sounded very much as if Belden had been shot for his part in killing the Italians.

"How will we find out whether he's still alive?" Ma asked.

"I'll write Henry," Pa said.

Helen ran from the room. She got her diary from its drawer, and, dipping her pen nub in India ink wrote:

Can it be true? Is Belden really dead? I cannot believe it. I will not believe it!

Yet my soul feels a terrible aching. O God, why don't you end this war!

21

THE FIREPLACE

Belden awakened to an excited buzz of voices. Groups of men surrounded Tom and Andy. Belden guessed what they were saying before he actually heard it: They all wanted to be part of the next escape attempt. Requiring them to lay the right hand on a Bible, Tom and Andy were swearing them to secrecy.

Later that day, when Belden got a chance to talk to them alone in the kitchen, he asked: "How many?"

"Four hundred and twenty," Tom said.

Belden gave a low whistle.

"How can we possibly keep any escape plan secret? Clearly there's at least one informant among us who leaked last night's attempt to the Rebs. That's the only explanation for the fact that the militia was on its way. And how will we uncloak the stool pigeon?"

"Keep an eye out for who gets any special privileges," Andy said.

"We won't let most of them know until the last minute," Tom said. "We'll keep our plans to the minimal number of diggers until then."

"Diggers?" Belden asked. "We're giving up on the carpenters' shop?"

He felt a huge wave of disappointment. Freedom had been so close.

"They've put a contingent of guards in the shop now," Andy said. "They've shut it down as an escape route. We've got to go back to Rat Hell."

"But how do we get down there now, with the stairway sealed? Through the hospital next door?"

Tom sucked on his pipe, then shook his head. Belden wondered how he came by his tobacco. For one terrible moment he wondered if Tom was the stoolie.

"Can't," Tom said. "There's always somebody in there. Patients, nurses, the doc. We have to think of another way in."

The three of them were sitting on boxes in front of the fireplace. As usual, it was packed with kindling for the stoves. Belden suddenly stood, pointing at it.

"We can go down through there!"

Tom looked at him as if he'd lost his mind.

"We break through the back wall of the fireplace," Belden continued, "into the flue from the chimney that comes up from Rat Hell."

Tom looked at Andy.

"You built houses," he said. "Is it possible?"

Andy thought for a minute, then slowly nodded.

"It might be," he said. "We'd have to remove the bricks from the back wall and then enlarge the flue, being careful not to break through into the hospital. We dig back beneath this fireplace's floor a bit and descend far enough to clear the floor of the hospital and ceiling of Rat Hell, then curve back and punch out into that room. The passageway will look, from the side, like an inverted S, which should give it enough strength to stand. We can use our rope to lower ourselves down through it."

"But surely," Tom said, "the Rebs will spot the hole in the back of the fireplace—and where will we hide the missing bricks?"

"We can replace the bricks each time we've completed that night's work," Andy said, "and cover the missing mortar with soot."

"We get hold of one of those rubber blankets," Belden said, "and collect the soot and ashes from the fireplace onto it. After we replace the bricks, we smear that mixture over the bricks, shake the remainder back into the fireplace, and stick the kindling back in. I don't think anyone could spot the loose bricks, unless one of the wood carriers jams a stick of kindling in too hard."

"I'll talk to the carriers," Tom said, "and encourage them against forcefulness. The current carriers are already a part of our group."

"The big problem," Andy said, "will be working the mortar loose with our knife blades. They might well shatter. What we need is a chisel."

Chuckling, Tom reached into his boot and, with a showman's flourish, pulled out—a chisel.

"Where in the dickens did you get that?" Andy asked.

"From the carpenters' shop. They had lots of them, so I didn't expect them to begrudge us one."

"Of course," Andy said. "They were lying all over their worktables, like the lilies of the field. How prescient of you, Tom!"

"I figured it might come in useful. Andy, can you find us someone willing to lend us his rubber blanket? Probably someone who isn't currently sleeping beneath a leak. And best if he's already taken the pledge."

"I do believe I can," Andy said.

"Excellent. All right, gentlemen, let's assemble here when the guard sings out eleven o'clock."

* * *

When Belden got back to the kitchen after the eleven o'clock "All's well," the two stoves and the kindling had been pulled from the fireplace and a black rubber blanket was laid out beside it. As always, he was impressed by Andy' capacity to forage successfully.

Belden kneeled before the fireplace and began moving handfuls of the ash and soot from it onto the blanket. When he'd finished, Tom handed Andy the chisel and soon there was a pile of mortar in the fireplace.

"What do we do with that?" Tom asked.

"Once we break through," Andy said, "we can just toss it down the flue. It'll collect at the bottom of the flue down in Rat Hell where no one can see it. The flue most likely goes all the way down to the ground, so there should be plenty of space for chunks of mortar and the bricks from the interior of the chimney."

He grunted as he loosened the first brick and handed it out to Belden.

"Lay the bricks out on the floor in the same order they've been laid within this wall," Andy said.

"What if a guard comes in?" Belden asked

"You can throw a brick at him," Tom chuckled. "We'd be sunk anyway."

Andy's low laugh was magnified by the small amplifier he was working within. He handed out a second brick.

* * *

Belden was impressed by how efficiently Andy worked. He'd already freed some seventy bricks and had pitched the loose mortar from the floor of the fireplace down the flue. When it crinkled at the bottom they all froze, hardly breathing, wondering if anyone in the hospital had heard. After a minute or two, they inhaled deeply.

"Okay," Andy said, "I'm going into the flue headfirst. If I start kicking, pull me out."

He plunged into the opening like a mole into his burrow and they heard the clink-clink of the chisel as he dug his way back and down. Then came a louder sound as a brick tumbled down the flue. Again, they all froze and listened.

The building creaked as it moved in the cold wind, which also moaned in the chimney. But there were no human sounds, other than the snores of the men sleeping nearby.

"Clear," Tom said, and Andy began working the chisel into mortar again.

* * *

When the sentry outside sang out "Four o'clock and all's well!" they helped Andy extract himself from the chimney, refitted the bricks in the back of the fireplace, smearing them with the soot and ash from the rubber blanket, and replaced the kindling. Finally, they moved the two cookstoves back into their places and reattached their tin pipes to the holes in the chimney through which they vented.

Hurrying to the water tap, they cleaned the rubber blanket and then themselves, scrubbing off the soot that made them all, but especially Andy, look like chimneysweeps.

"Damn water's as cold as a well-digger's belt buckle," Andy said, his teeth chattering. He'd needed as much washing as the other two combined.

Belden had to admit that Andy had quite a vocabulary.

They shook hands all around and headed off to their berths to try to get in two hours of sleep prior to reveille.

* * *

They continued the same routine for ten more nights. On the eleventh, Andy broke through into the east cellar.

When he came back up to report this success, his blackened face was luminous with triumph.

"Half the battle is won!" he chortled.

"We ought to have champagne!" Belden said

"We do still have a tunnel yet to dig," Tom reminded them, grinning ear to ear.

* * *

Tom wanted to go down the passageway. Though Andy warned him that it was narrow and tricky, he insisted. He decided to back in on hands and knees, going feet first, though Andy had always gone in headfirst. All was well until, at the sharp descent after the gently sloping access, he lost purchase, rattled down the passage, and found himself stuck with his arms pinned to the sides of his head. When he struggled to free himself, he found that he only was more profoundly stuck. He was having trouble breathing, and panic began to grip him.

"Help!" he said with barely enough air to make a sound.

"Tie the rope around my ankles!" Andy told Belden, preparing to enter the passage.

Belden threw a bowline around Andy's ankles as he began descending. Andy grabbed Tom's hands in his own and said "Pull!" Leaning back, Belden began a steady pull on the rope. Nothing happened.

"Harder!"

Belden turned, put the rope over his right shoulder, bent his knees so most of his body weight centered at the point where the rope crossed his shoulder, and started walking away from the chimney. For a moment he feared that the rope might break. Then he felt a loosening and, as he moved steadily away, he felt the two men coming back up the passage.

He continued pulling until Andy told him to stop. Dropping his end of the rope, he ran back to where Andy was kneeling over Tom's trembling body, pushing on his chest.

"In your mind's eye," Andy was whispering to Tom, "see your valley in the Alleghenies, the way the green hills rise up and up into the taller peaks covered with snow."

Tom took a deep, gasping breath, like a man pulled up from under a heavy sea, and sat up.

"That," he said, "was terrifying. I'm afraid I'll have to change my drawers."

Belden shuddered at just the thought of having to navigate the passageway down the chimney.

"Enough for tonight," he said. "Let's close up and clean up."

"I cannot agree more," Tom said. His face was still pale.

* * *

On the following night, Andy worked to widen the passageway. If Tom had gotten stuck, Belden was sure to. And what of Col. Streight, who was three inches taller and probably forty pounds heavier than Belden? He was especially enthusiastic about escape, given that he was the prisoner most hated by the Rebels, both for his rapacious cavalry raids into their homelands and for his many letters of protest that he managed to smuggle out to the Union newspapers, which cast the Confederates in a very unflattering light.

Once the passage through the chimney was widened, Tom and Belden joined Andy in sliding down the inverted-S shape into Rat Hell.

Though he had long feared the tightness of the descent, Belden was pleased to find that he made it without soiling his drawers. In fact, it was kind of fun. Rat Hell, however, was a different story.

In the weeks since it had been sealed off, the population of rats in the dank, reeking basement room had multiplied several times over. The rats gave off a nasty odor all their own that mingled with those of rancid lard, wet clay, and sewage that permeated the former kitchen. During high water in the James, this cursed room, lit only by what light from the lamps on Canal Street managed to eke in through the one barred window, frequently flooded. When it flooded, bringing in copious amounts of filth from the sewers, the rats would attempt to flee between the iron bars on the one window. If this happened during the daylight hours, the prisoners upstairs vastly enjoyed the spectacle and would cheer the rats on, making bets of tobacco or hardtack on how many rats would come out in one hour's time and which one would go the farthest. Even the Rebs seemed to enjoy the show, allowing the prisoners to crowd the windows without shooting at them.

The multitudes of rats were a terrible nuisance. They scurried over their feet when the men were standing and over hands and legs when they knelt to dig. In time, the men grew almost inured to them, batting them away with hand, foot, or broken shovel blade absent-mindedly. Similarly, though the reek of the place made them gag whenever they first entered the cellar from the hole in the chimney, within a few minutes they could hardly smell it. They were amazed by how a human being could accommodate to just about anything.

Their plan was to dig down and under the east wall, then turn south toward the six-foot high sewer fewer than twenty feet away. Once in the sewer, they could walk to where it emptied into the Lynchburg Canal and freedom.

The first two new digging attempts ended quickly when the thin soil collapsed. The third attempt was from the southeast corner, where the soil was better compacted.

Tom Rose showed himself to be part mole. He was a tireless excavator. Working with knife, chisel, and shovel blade, he dug a hole two feet in diameter, putting the dirt into the spittoon. When the spittoon was full, he'd tug on the clothesline tied to it and Belden would pull it from the tunnel, scattering the dirt around the cellar floor and covering it at night's end with the two feet of straw the Rebs had thrown in from the relief boxes and the mattresses in the hospital. Belden wondered what kinds of bugs might have been thriving in those mattresses. His first task each night was pulling some of the straw aside to use later for the concealing cover over that night's dirt. While Tom dug, Andy kept up a steady fanning with his hat to drive air into the tunnel while at the same time keeping alert for any sounds of approaching guards—other than the ones marching back and forth a few feet away out on Canal Street.

At first Tom worked by candlelight, but as the tunnel progressed there wasn't enough air in it even to keep a candle lit. Yet he burrowed on, in total darkness and a claustrophobic tightness that neither Belden nor Andy could tolerate. Several times partial cave-ins threatened to bury him. He had tied the rope around one ankle so they could hopefully pull him out from under a cave-in or if he fainted from lack of air. Despite the difficulty breathing, the tight walls around him, the pitch darkness, and the rats scampering all over his body, Tom labored on like a machine. When he could stand it no more, he would back out of the tunnel and, for a few minutes, breathe the relatively fresh air of the fetid cellar. Then he'd dive back in.

But after several brutal nights of this effort and another cave in that left him spitting sewage-contaminated dirt, Tom sat on the straw looking grim. When a rat ran into his lap, he hit it so hard with the shovel blade that the squealing rodent was catapulted through the air across the cellar and into the stone foundation wall. After smacking into the wall with a hair-raising squeal, the rat ran off as if unhurt.

"Damn things are indestructible," Andy said. "What's up, Tom?"

"We need more men," Tom said, "to help dig."

Both Belden and Andy looked down. They knew they were no good at it.

"I want us to come up with a total of fifteen, including us," Tom went on, with no tone of judgment in his voice. "I figure three teams of five: one digger, one fanner, one spittoon emptier, one relief fanner/spittoon emptier, and one lookout. They can exchange jobs as they wish. Each team will work one night and have two nights off, with some second-floor lookout duty to signal if guards or militia are stirring."

"Sounds good," Belden said. "But since only six of us even know about the passage in the chimney, how do we recruit nine more men who we know to be trustworthy?"

They paused to consider this point.

"Well," Andy said, "we know who the toadies are. They're obvious, bowing and scraping to the guards in hopes of an extra piece of hardtack. It's the spies that worry me."

"Spies?" Belden asked.

"The Rebs plant spies in the prison to act as informants," Andy said. "We can often tell who they are, because they're the ones shouting 'Let's plan an escape!' in a hillbilly accent. But one or two might be more circumspect. At least one's in the 420 pledges. May I remind you that someone tipped off the guards to the carpenters' shop attempt."

"And we'll have to smoke him out before the escape," Tom said. "I have nine more candidates in mind, mostly men who fought beside me. I would trust them with my life. In fact, I have done. Three of them used to be miners. We just need more hands on the job."

"Of course you're right," Andy said. "You talk to them and we'll pledge them into our fraternity of moles."

"Good," said Tom. "Let's knock off for tonight. Belden, will you hide the tools?"

"Yessir," Belden said, gathering up knife, chisel, and shovel blade.

"And remember, never call me sir."

"Never, sir," Belden said, saluting with the shovel blade.

* * *

On the following night nine new men pledged themselves to secrecy on a Bible and witnessed the fireplace transform into a passageway. Belden was delighted by their astonishment at what had so far been accomplished. After Tom and five new men disappeared down the Rabbit Hole, as they had taken to calling it, he stayed with Andy and the other nine men in the kitchen, discussing the plan. He liked all the new men and was basking in the friendly camaraderie until he realized that, inspired by Andy's poetic pronouncements, they were creating quite the hubbub.

"Gentlemen," Belden said, "let's not awaken the guards. I'll remain on lookout here with one other while the rest of you take to your berths."

The man who stayed on watch with him was Col. Abel Streight. Standing next to him, Belden wondered how in the dickens Col. Streight would be able to squeeze down through the Rabbit Hole and then out a tunnel with a two-foot diameter. He was what they call a mountain of a man.

"I know what you're thinking," the big man said, holding one forefinger up beside his prominent nose.

"Do you?" Belden asked, barely restraining himself from adding "sir."

"Of course. You are amazed that I have survived this long in this prison. You know the Rebs hate me and you know that I do not hide my light under a bushel. No, I speak up and castigate them for their many failures to provide adequate living conditions for us."

Belden smiled. He was amused that this strapping man had very little awareness of how big he actually was. He'd noticed that was often the case with big men.

"Further," Abel Streight continued, "they know that I will not only write directly to their authorities on this matter but smuggle my little jeremiads out to be printed by the international press. Why, even the *London Times* has reproduced my works, none of which conduce to presenting the Confederacy in a manner that they are proud of. No, I speak truth and the truth shall make us free."

While Belden was impressed by the big man's courage and rectitude, he did wonder why the Rebs didn't simply arrange for him to take a neck-breaking tumble down the stairs. Was Col. Streight of such a stature that his death or disappearance would reflect more harshly upon them than his barrage of complaints? Or was continued existence evidence that the Rebs were in fact men of honor who would not stoop to such barbarity?

Col. Wolfe hadn't hesitated to send Belden away from Hadley, but at least he hadn't arranged for an unfortunate accident for him while being transported. Nothing easier than to shoot him in the back and say he'd been trying to run.

For the rest of the long night Belden listened to Col. Steight talk, mostly about what a hero he was. Maybe, he thought, the Rebs don't like him because he's such a self-important windbag.

He was glad when the tunnelers came up through the fireplace, the bricks were put back in their places, and he finally got some peace.

* * *

With three teams of five working most of the nights, the tunnel progressed yards at a time. The "moles" who dug with hands and chisel or knives were a minority of the fifteen, for most of the men couldn't endure being in the tight dark tunnel for long while rats ran across their faces. Belden understood; he couldn't stand being confined like that for more than a few minutes before panic set in. Of all the moles, Tom Rose was the acknowledged champion, working, as one man put it, "like a beaver." On any given night Tom was likely to tunnel twice as far as anyone else could.

After a night tunneling, however, Tom and the other moles came up filthy, reeking, bruised, and battered. They washed as best they could in the cold water from the single faucet and then plunged into sleep like men seeking oblivion. Most of them had a second set of clothing that they changed into in Rat Hell before entering the tunnel. The odor of these clothes was indescribable.

Andy invented a larger device to fan the air into the lengthening tunnel. Procuring a second rubber blanket, he stretched it over a wooden frame, which enabled the fanner to pump in a much larger quantity of air.

Then early one night Tom gave a double tug on the rope around his ankle, signaling that he wished to be pulled out. He came out gasping, as usual, and when he had regained his breath reported the new obstacle: He had run into an oaken timber in the foundation of the east warehouse that resisted even the chisel.

"We need a saw," he said. "I've encountered a massive timber."

There was a long silence. No one wanted to attempt to steal something else from the carpenters' shop.

"How about we take a couple of the knives," Belden said, "and serrate the blades. You can use them like a saw."

"Great idea," Tom said. "Can you do that for me?"

Glad that he'd learned a bit of metalwork from Charlie Ide, Belden used the chisel to notch one of the knife blades and handed it to Tom. Tom re-entered the tunnel. Just watching his feet disappear, Belden shuddered.

* * *

The serrated knives worked. After what seemed like thousands of cuts, the oaken timber gave way, and they were in red clay again. The sewer was only a few yards away.

Two nights later, Tom Rose was beavering at his usual frantic pace when water began trickling into the tunnel. A few minutes later a wave of it hit him full in the face. He jerked his ankle twice, then twice again, sure that he was drowning.

On the other end of the rope, Belden could feel Tom's desperation in the abruptness of the jerks in his hands. He pulled for all he was worth, steadily but powerfully. When Tom came out, a river of water following him, he was choking and coughing. Water poured from his mouth.

"Seal the tunnel!" he finally croaked. "We must have gone beneath the Kanawha Canal!"

Quickly, men leapt to the task, shoveling dirt into the tunnel as fast as they could.

If they were disappointed to be once more thwarted within inches of their freedom, they didn't show it.

* * *

It was now November and the cold winter winds howled around Libby Prison. Belden began having second thoughts about running through the snow and sleeping in the sleet once they got outside.

Meanwhile, Col. Abel Streight was churning a much grander plan.

"What we need is an uprising of all 13.000 Union prisoners in Richmond," he said. "It'll begin in Libby, of course. We'll overpower the guards and seize their arms, then free all the men on Belle Isle. One group, under me, will take Jeff Davis and his cabinet captive, while the second group, under Captain Reed here, will destroy the Confederate arsenal, burning the Tredegar Iron Works and the other arms factories. Then we'll march down the Peninsula to the Union lines at Williamsburg and present Abe with the whole damn shebang of rebels for a Christmas present."

Belden found himself growing dizzy at the prospect of this audacious plan. Though he couldn't imagine that it had a snowball's chance of succeeding, he liked the boldness of the idea.

Streight called himself the Commander in Chief of the enterprise and appointed Tom Rose, Bill Ely, and Will Powell his "brigade commanders." Libby's black prisoners had contacts in the Richmond servant community who provided information about where and when Davis's cabinet would meet, the Rebel troop locations, the security protocols at the arsenals, and the current positions of the Union army. There was evidently a certain well-connected Richmond lady, a Union sympathizer, whose servants passed this valuable intelligence into Libby when they came to the prison to deliver food, newspapers, and clothing to the Negro prisoners. Then, when the drummers beat reveille mornings as they marched through the prison, one of them would pass on the info to Abel or Tom.

Belden was fairly sure that, because virtually all the Union prisoners were in on the plot, that some spy would squeal on it.

He was proved correct. As the appointed hour neared, Confederate artillery hove into sight outside Libby, their ugly muzzles trained on the prison windows. The prison guard was doubled, and General George Pickett's reconstituted division came marching up Canal Street.

Reluctantly, Col. Streight issued the order to stand down. He was certain that the spy was none other than Col. James Sanderson, the former Army of the Potomac commissary chief, who had been in charge of the rations at Libby and thus worked closely with the Rebs. Streight and Sanderson had tangled before, over the paucity of the rations, which Streight, as a big man, had complained were insufficient to keep soul and body together. He and his brigade commanders met with Sanderson and persuaded him to resign as culinary director, after which Sanderson spent a week in the hospital with contusions.

Streight and Reed had a back-up plan afoot. For a bribe of $100 U.S. greenbacks and two watches, guards assured them they could make their escape. Tom and Belden held the rope at a window on the second floor after dark. Reed slipped down like a squirrel. But Streight seemed to have second thoughts. Or perhaps vertigo.

"You've got to go now, sir, or not at all," Tom whispered.

Finally, Streight went down. Tom hauled up the rope and Belden started off to hide it when they heard voices raised and then shots.

They feared for the worst. But the next day they got word from the Band member that Reed and Streight were confined in the dungeon on hardtack and water. Streight had already written and smuggled out a letter protesting the meager provisions.

Once again they had been betrayed. This time they knew it couldn't have been Sanderson, who was still in the hospital and had been kept out of the loop. There was an unknown spy among them.

* * *

Tom and Belden began surveying their options the next day. Belden pointed out the Goodie Shack in the east.

"There's a sewer line to the east in that vacant lot," Tom said. "We can tunnel to it, staying a bit higher this time, and then use it to access the big sewer and thence to the canal bank. Or we can go into the Goodie Shack."

"And freedom," Belden added. "Please move back from the window, Tom. I don't want to lose you. See the kid with the squirrel rifle atop that building? He's got a twitchy trigger finger."

Several Confederate carpenters entered the room, carrying their wooden toolboxes and a sheaf of iron bars. They began to cut the wooden bars from the windows.

Andy joined Tom and Belden.

"So they suspect some kind of escape plan is afoot," he said.

Tom looked at them with a small smile.

"They're going to replace the wooden bars with iron ones," he said. "To prevent us from escaping."

"How many of their tools will we be able to purloin?" Belden asked. "In attempting to prevent our escape, they actually assist it."

"I would say 'How ironic' if that were not a terrible pun," Andy added.

"A verbal sleight of hand worthy of Cicero," Tom said.

Before the day was over, they'd deprived the carpenters of a hatchet, an iron bar, and an auger. That night they began the new tunnel. It was New Year's Eve. Above them they could hear their fellow prisoners singing "Auld Lange Syne." It was 1864. Belden tried to compute how long it had been since he had last seen Hadley. Her image was fading in his mind, no matter how fiercely he attempted to make it stay. Strange that he could still remember Cinder and his family, though he hadn't seen them for a much longer time.

It must be a wonderful thing, he told himself, to understand the mysteries of the human mind. There must be somewhere, at some college no doubt, men of learning who study it and understand it. He'd like to be one of them one day.

* * *

As the new year came in the thermometer plummeted. It snowed on successive days. During the days the prisoners could see skaters sailing past on the frozen James River, their scarves trailing them like flags. At night the diggers began a new tunnel from the southeast corner. Fortunately, the freeze did not penetrate that deeply into the ground and they made good progress. As they neared the small sewer, however, the reek was awful. Then the tunnel caved in.

Belden pulled Tom out once more, spluttering and gagging with a mouth full of dirt and sewage. The next day they looked out of the east windows and saw the problem. They'd dug directly beneath a massive brick furnace. When the east cellar had been used as a kitchen, the furnace had heated the area. Once this section was no longer in use, the large furnace had been carried out to the vacant lot and left unused. Its weight had crushed the tunnel—and almost Tom Rose as well.

A group of Rebel officers surrounded the furnace, examining the cave-in and talking. Belden edged as near the window as he dared to eavesdrop. He heard the word "rats" several times and relaxed. The Rebs thought that the cave-in had been caused by the tunneling rats. They couldn't imagine that humans could get into Rat Hell, much less tunnel out of it.

When he reported his finding to Tom and Andy, Tom was unconvinced.

"They may well stake out Rat Hell tonight," he said. "I'll go down alone to find out. Better that they get only one of us than all."

"I'll do it, Tom," Belden said. "You're too valuable as a beaver."

Tom shook his head.

"Thanks, Belden," he said, "but it's got to be me."

When Belden stared to protest, Tom just shook his head.

That night Belden and Andy watched as Tom went down through the fireplace. They stood close to the Rabbit Hole, listening to his descent. There was silence for a long time. They guessed Tom was carefully checking out Rat Hell from the hole in the chimney below. Then Tom's weight went off the rope for a good half hour.

"He's closing the tunnel so they don't find it," Andy guessed.

He was right. When Tom at last reappeared, filthy as usual, he told them the good news was that there had been no Rebs waiting for him.

The bad news was that they'd have to find another place to dig.

* * *

Many of the men were demoralized and ready to give up tunneling. Belden, Tom, and Andy had to do some cheerleading to reignite the desire to escape. Tom told them it was their duty to continually work at escaping. Belden asked them to tell him about their hometowns and who they wanted to return to. Andy waxed poetic. Between their three different approaches, they managed to re-inspire the teams.

"We've got to get the teams working in the day as well," Tom said. 'By speeding up our progress, we'll keep them enthusiastic."

"But what about head count?" Andy asked.

"We use the Repeating Game," Belden said. Tom nodded.

The objective of this third tunnel was also the small sewer, avoiding the brick furnace. Before the night shift stumbled back to their berths at four in the mornings, they woke the day shift, who slipped down the Rabbit Hole to take their places in Rat Hell. When Erasmus Ross called "Head count!" everyone dutifully lined up. Once he'd counted the first three lines, five men from the first, hunching low on the opposite side of the room, ran back to the last line. Sure enough, the count came out.

Belden watched this "game" with amusement at first, then grew suspicious.

"He can't be that dumb," he said. "He's letting it go on purpose."

"Oh, I reckon he's just about that dumb," Andy laughed.

The next day two other prisoners from the first rank decided to tag along with the designated five, not realizing how serious this maneuver was. When Erasmus's count came up two over, the diggers held their breaths.

Then a prisoner in the back row joked that there must be Confederates bribing the guards to let them in to get out of the cold. When the whole roomful of prisoners broke up into thunderous laughter, the guards couldn't keep their faces straight and joined in. Finally even Erasmus Ross, blushing red, had to laugh. It was a rare moment when they were all just men who were joined by circumstance, without all the differences of geography and politics and enmity.

Laughter did that, Belden marveled. It bridged the gap. It brought even disparate people together. What if the politicians in Congress would start each session with ten minutes of laughter? Would it bring an end to this conflict?

Then he remembered the words of Jesus, how he said "Nation shall rise up against nation until the world is at an end."

You couldn't be any clearer than that. War would always be with us.

* * *

Belden took Tom and Andy aside that afternoon.

"I think Ross is on our side," he said.

"What makes you think so?" Tom asked.

"Just watch him closely," Belden said.

"Fine," Andy said, "but who's the spy?"

* * *

What happened the next day made Belden even more suspicious of Ross's allegiance.

During Head Count, Ross called out the man Belden suspected of being the spy for some minor transgression—Belden never heard what it was—and punched him viciously in the stomach. The prisoner fell to the ground, clutching his abdomen and gasping.

"You two guards!" Ross shouted, seemingly furious. "Take this insubordinate pig to my office for further admonishment!"

The two guards hauled the barely conscious prisoner out like a rag doll, his feet dragging along the floorboards.

When the punched prisoner didn't return, many men assumed he'd been murdered, or confined to the dungeon. Belden just smiled. He'd seen the same man, dressed in a Confederate officer's uniform complete with a saber, striding away from the prison. Either he was a Reb who'd been planted to spy on the prisoners or, and Belden thought this more likely, he was a Yank who Ross was helping escape.

Belden was convinced that Erasmus Ross was a Union sympathizer who was dumb like a fox and was making the errors in counting on purpose.

* * *

With two shifts working every day, the tunnel progressed rapidly, but when they reached the small sewer they were disappointed to discover that it was too small for even the smallest man. Discouraged, they sat around in Rat Hell, oblivious of the rats, to whom they had come to pay little mind. When one crawled up onto Belden's lap, he said, "I'll bet we could make pets of these little fellas."

No one would take the bet.

"How about we remove the wooden liner of the small sewer," he continued. "Then we can enlarge the tunnel. It's only a few feet to the big sewer."

"Let's try it," Tom said.

Removing the planks that comprised the small sewer and dragging them back into Rat Hell, where they had to be hidden from discovery beneath the straw was not easy work. But then nothing had been easy.

As usual, it was Tom who was the lead digger when the planking of the large sewer was reached.

"It's going to be a challenge," he told the team when he backed out of the tunnel, filthy and reeking horribly. "It's made of seasoned oaken planks that are, as best I can ascertain, three inches in thickness. We'll have to saw our way in."

The long-buried oak was hard as rock. The chisel barely dented it. The saws broke. And, when they finally breached the liner in one spot, the overwhelming odor of the raw sewage that squirted through made the digger faint. He had to be dragged out, limp as a rag doll.

"Good Christ spare me," he said upon regaining consciousness, "from ever going back in there again."

Others, including Tom, tried it and had to concur that they were thwarted by the toughness of the oak and the stench of the sewage.

They took a vote. It was unanimous. With much regret, they sealed the third tunnel.

Captain I. N. Johnston wrote in his diary the next day: "All the labor had been in vain. The feelings of that little band, who can describe! From hopes almost as bright as reality, they were suddenly plunged into the depths of despair."

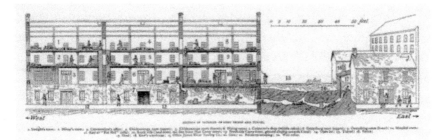

Libby Prison with Tunnel

22

THE STARVING WINTER

The prisoners were starving. There had been no meat at all since Christmas. The hardtack was alive with weevils. Few prisoners had the heart to celebrate the coming of 1864.

One frigid morning the warden of the prison, Major Thomas Turner, began kicking a man who wasn't standing for Head Count until he realized why.

"My God," exclaimed Turner, "I've been kicking a dead man."

A few days later Belden watched a young blonde lieutenant of about his own age who was lying in what seemed to be his own liquefied feces feebly raise a scrap of hardtack to his mouth and die before he could bite off a piece. A one-legged prisoner hopped across the floor to where he lay and snatched the hardtack from him, gnawing at it as he sat next to the body.

The corpses were piled like lumber in the west cellar with the Negro prisoners. A rickety cart pulled by mules was backed to the door and the black men loaded it with the white bodies, stiff with rigor and cold.

Libby's adjutant, Lt. John Latouche, told the prisoners: "I wish I were rid of you, because I cannot feed you."

It wasn't just the captives. All of Richmond, it seemed, was hungry. Ragamuffin bands of stick-thin children clutching shreds of clothing around them, would beg outside Libby's windows. When the prisoners would throw out a rock-like piece of hardtack or a greenish soup bone, they would fight like dogs over the offal.

"I am afraid," Capt. Robert Cornwall wrote to his wife, "that the Confederacy will rot down over our heads."

Letters were now restricted to six lines, once a month. Even many of those never got through. The letters Belden had been getting from Helen and Ira at least once a week now came through only sporadically, with references in them to past letters he had never received. He did learn that Ira was now a nurse in a large hospital in the District where he had made the acquaintance of a full-bearded poet named Walt, also a nurse. Emily's letters spoke of the weather and the crops and, increasingly, of Charlie Ide, who had so far been dissuaded from enlisting.

Belden wrote back that he hoped Charlie would not enlist, a sentiment he was fairly sure the Rebel censors would not redact.

There had been no letters from Hadley. Were they being intercepted? Or was she not writing to him? She'd probably forgotten him. No! She'd never forget him! Were his letters to her getting through?

The winter had grown colder than anything Belden had experienced in upstate New York, where the winds off Lake Erie had penetrated the mountain valleys like frozen spears. A captive from Minnesota said it was as cold as it ever was in the Midwest.

One night at Lights Out, Belden heard a sad Irish tenor singing an old lament:

> *Backward, turn backward, O Time, in your flight.*
> *Make me a child again for just to-night.*

To which another Irish prisoner responded: "Yis, and a girrul child at that!"

The general laughter showed that everyone had been awake and listening.

Though many Yankees were prejudiced against the Irish and put signs on their establishments stating, "No Irish," Belden found them a warm and friendly race, given to song, story, and the poetic turn of phrase. He wondered whether Andy might be part Irish himself. He thought back to his companion in the first prison camp, Billy Keogh, the Black Irishman, and wondered if he was still alive.

* * *

General Neal Dow, a white-headed sexagenarian, assembled all the officers who wished to warm up in the kitchen in columns of four and led them in what he called a "healthy double-quick" march in place to warm them. Often their stamping feet triggered an influx of guards who were certain a breakout was happening.

Then one cold day they got a diverting visitation. Major Turner brought in two famous Confederate generals to view his captives, as if, one prisoner wrote, "We were animals in a zoo." Gen. A. P. Hill had commanded Rebel troops on every major Eastern battlefield—and never retreated, or so his legend told. He was a wiry little man with a bushy beard covering most of his face and a fierce eye. With him was his brother-in-law Gen. John Morgan, who had been perhaps the most famous Rebel in Yankee captivity. Called "the Thunderbolt of the Confederacy," he had led terrifying raids deep into Ohio, reaching the highwater mark of the Rebel push north, capturing thousands of Union soldiers on the way. He had been captured and interred in a Federal prison, from which he had escaped with six companions, leaving behind a thoughtful note for the warden explaining how they had done it.

He was a tall, handsome man with a crisp goatee and an easy smile. He shook Col. Abel Streight's hand, for Streight was his counterpart, as much despised by Confederates as Morgan was by Unionists, though Abel had not yet escaped.

Like many Southerners, Morgan had been opposed to secession and had hoped that Lincoln would make a good president, but had finally decided, as had so many others, that he couldn't fight against his family and his native land.

He then searched the crowd for Gen. Dow, with whom he had initially been slated to be exchanged, before the exchanges had been stopped. When he found him, he proffered his hand.

"General Dow," he said, "I am happy to see you. Or, rather, I should say, since you are here, I am very happy to see you looking so well."

Dow shook the proffered hand warmly.

"General Morgan, I congratulate you on your escape. I cannot say that I am glad you did escape, but, since you did, I am pleased to see you here."

"General," Morgan replied, "I am surprised and saddened to see Union officers in such conditions and promise to speak to the authorities about remediation, if that be possible."

"My thanks to you, sir. Whatever part you might play in such an endeavor would be greatly appreciated by us all."

Belden watched this exchange with something like awe that these two great generals could be so gentlemanly in such conditions. He knew that many of the officers on both sides had attended West Point together, had fought together in the Mexican and Seminole Wars, and were often friends. Friends bitterly divided by a war over principle.

With a wry smile, Belden remembered the arguments he'd had with Hadley over just such principles. What wouldn't he give to be having one with her right now.

Hadley. He could still remember her redgold hair, her flawless skin, and those piercing green eyes. God, he wished he could be with her.

Now he'd come down to a simple truth, one that he'd heard many a soldier articulate:

"It's a rich man's war and a poor man's fight."

When he got out of Libby, he was done with it. He'd made a separate peace. He could even see himself marrying Hadley and living in Virginia and raising their children for the rest of his days. At least the Virginia of the summer and fall. In winter, he'd go back to the warmer climate of upstate New York.

Lord, but it was cold. And it was into that cold they were trying to escape.

* * *

They began the fourth tunnel in late January. After much discussion, they agreed to Belden's proposal to abandon their attempts to reach the sewer through the wet red clay to the south and to construct a new tunnel from the northeast corner of Rat Hell aiming at the fence and the storehouse about 50 feet distant: the Goodie Shack. The ground there was drier and they wouldn't have to contend with sewage. On the other hand, one sentry would be pacing directly over the tunnel and another would be making his turn within view of the storehouse's door onto Canal Street.

"We dig deep enough that the sentry's tread won't collapse the tunnel," Belden said. "And when we come up inside the storehouse, we do so in the middle of the night, when they're not delivering parcels. As to the Canal Street sentry, we leave by twos and threes when he's made his turn and has his back to the storehouse."

It seemed the best they could do.

Tom was given the honor of starting the project. Selecting a spot in the shadow of one of the fenders supporting the wall, he bored in with the auger about six inches above the floor, eventually creating a hole about sixteen inches high and twenty wide. This they would conceal as best they could with straw during the random inspections the guards mounted from time to time. They put faith in the fact that the guards hated Rat Hell even more than they did and were unlikely to cross it into this far corner.

Once he breeched the brick wall, Tom discovered that the dirt was gray and dry.

"We're above the flood plain," Andy pointed out. "This is excellent."

Tom said nothing. He was back to beavering.

* * *

Tom was able to persuade most of the men on the prior three crews to return to work on the new tunnel. Although a few were too discouraged, he was able to recruit new hands to fill their places. Once again, one crew worked a day shift and another the night shift, while the third crew got a day off to catch up on sleep. The day crew had to be in Rat Hell before reveille and couldn't return until well after lights out. At Head Count, five men would have to repeat and be counted twice to cover for them. When Belden witnessed how easily Erasmus Ross seemed to be duped by this stratagem, he was more certain than ever that the little man was a part of the Richmond Unionists' spy network.

They knew from the Negro prisoners who had got it from the Negro servants in Richmond who came down to the prison that such a network existed. The ringleader was purported to be a grand lady of a prominent Richmond family who sent and received encrypted messages with General Butler, who was at Fortress Monroe. The rumor was that Gen. Butler had attempted to mount a raid with 6000 troops to liberate the prisoners in Richmond but had been thwarted by a Union convict who was being held on murder charges. This man had escaped to Rebel lines and, to show his good faith, had spilled the beans about the intended raid. What puzzled Belden was how he could have known the details of the raid while being held prisoner.

The Rebs had burned the bridge that Butler had planned to cross and met him with such an array of artillery that he had had to retreat.

That was the rumor. What amazed Belden was that a surprising number of the rumors that floated around Libby turned out to be true. Maybe this one was, too. It didn't really matter. They hadn't been freed. They'd have to effect that themselves.

He had to get back to Hadley.

* * *

The tunnel was progressing rapidly through the dry earth. But then a tragedy occurred. At Head Count, Major Turner and Lt. Latouche came in flanking Ross, who had no choice but to come up with an accurate count in front of his superiors. Only two men of one of the crews, I. N. Johnston and B. B. McDonald, were still down in Rat Hell, but there was no way to disguise the fact that they were missing —and who they were. The guards commenced a search immediately.

When they couldn't find either man they assumed they must have escaped.

After lights out, Tom and Belden went down the chimney chute and found Johnston and McDonald, hungry and shivering, in Rat Hell.

Belden handed over two pieces of hardtack that had been saved from dinner. The two men seized them and began gnawing, ignoring the weevils. Belden had also brought a canteen of water, which they took with many thanks.

"It seems to me that you have only two options," Tom said. "One is to return with a cock-and-bull story about why you weren't counted. Two, stay down here till the escape. We can bring you food and water and maybe blankets."

There was a profound silence, disturbed only by the crunching of hardtack and then the squeal of rats seeking crumbs and slithering over foot. Belden noted that none of the diggers seemed to pay rats the slightest mind anymore.

"I'll stay down here in this lovely accommodation," Johnston finally said.

Tom nodded.

"We'll bring down what we can. You won't starve."

McDonald sighed.

"I won't be able to tolerate Hell for that long," he said. "I'll have to trust my Scottish gift for storytelling."

* * *

Erasmus Ross was shocked to find Major McDonald present for Head Count the next morning and sent a guard to bring in Major Turner. Like most of the men in the room, Belden tried to edge closer to hear what B.B. had to say.

"I was on my way, sir, to report to the hospital yesterday when the count was happening and was in the upper west room, which had already been counted," he said.

Turner didn't believe him. He scowled and almost rolled his eyes.

"We counted each room twice. You couldn't have been missed."

McDonald looked down with apparent remorse.

"I was afraid of being found out of my quarters, sir, and so I climbed up onto a plank that ran across the rafters and hid there during the count. I'm sorry, sir, it was a foolish thing to do."

The whole room seemed to hold its breath while Turner thought about this.

"Well, son," he finally said, "I believe an open confession is good for the soul. Just don't let it happen again."

"No, sir," McDonald said, looking at the tops of his muddy shoes.

Belden was stunned. He couldn't believe that Turner had fallen for such a tall tale.

* * *

The prisoners covered for Johnston by concocting a story about how he'd bribed a guard who had since left to bring him a Confederate uniform, had whittled a sword out of wood, and thus attired had simply walked out of the prison and was no doubt by now in Williamsburg eating fresh oysters and drinking beer. However preposterous, this story was believed.

Johnston, meanwhile, was truly in Hell. A farmer's son from the Blue Grass state, he was accustomed to being out all day in the open air. Libby itself had been torture enough, but Rat Hell was ten times worse. Even in daytime, only a wan light filtered through the iron bars of the door. He was alone all day, the squealing rats his only companions, for Tom had suspended the daylight crews since Turner had instituted a second Head Count each day, at unpredictable hours. It was just too risky.

When the night crew came down the chute, they brought him food and water, and he would sometimes climb up to the relative warmth of the upper floors to sleep for a few hours.

He had scooped out a depression that he called "my shallow grave" from the dirt floor of Rat Hell. He lined this with straw and then pulled more straw over him, trying to stay warm and sleep away the days. When the guards poked their heads in through the doorway to the carpenters' shop, they seldom bothered to even set foot in Rat Hell.

But then one day several guards came in with a terrier to have a go at the rats, who scurried away under the straw, many fleeing into the tunnel. The guards came into the cellar, kicking at the straw, and passed within a yard of the tunnel opening without seeing it. Johnston watched them through a lattice of straw, expecting to be found out at any moment and clapped into irons. The straw was tickling his nose and he felt a sneeze arising. He couldn't stop it, despite pressing firmly on his upper lip, a remedy his mother had taught him. When he finally sneezed it sounded like a cannon blast inside his head. But the guards just went on talking in low voices. Somehow, they hadn't heard.

"Then that damn dog came right up to me and sniffed and barked," Johnston told the digging crew that night. "I thought I was a goner. All I could do was play possum. A rat ran right across my face and off toward the south and that terrier went zippety-skip after it. After that, he let me be. I guess he figured out I wasn't a rat."

The other men had a good laugh over that. Johnston didn't join in. He was, they noticed, beginning to look a bit peaked.

"Boys," said Tom Rose, "they know we're using Rat Hell as a staging area. We've got to finish this tunnel as fast as ever we can. We need to get a precise measurement on how far it is to that fence."

* * *

Captain John Gallagher volunteered to find out. He was a cheerful Irishman with a lovely singing voice who was quite popular with the guards. They clapped and cheered when he sang:

> *Oh you take the high road and I'll take the low road,*
> *And I'll be in Dublin afore ye.*

"I'm due a package from home, don't ye know," he told them. "Canna ye let me take a look in yon storehouse. It's in my mind that there might be some of my sister Molly's ginger cookies there that I'd love to share with ye."

To the amazement of Belden, Tom, and a few other men who watched this compelling performance, the guards agreed to march him across to the storehouse. They peeked out the east windows as John, walking very stiffly with a precise gait, made the trip. Sadly, he found no package addressed to himself, but he did come back with a number.

The distance to the fence was 52 or 53 feet.

* * *

The tunnel was progressing at almost five feet per night and was, by Sunday, February 5th, to the point that Tom and Andy, conferring, decided that it had passed under the fence. Tom told Captain Randall, who was the Chiseler that night, to dig up to the surface. As Randall squirmed into the tunnel, Tom, Andy, and Belden waited with bated breath for him to return with a report from outside Libby's walls.

As Randall was beavering upward, the soil falling in his face and half-choking him, he felt a sudden flow of clean air descend upon him. Looking up, he could see stars in the nightsky. However, as he pushed further up, his excitement transmogrified into horror. He was on the Libby side of the fence, in plain sight of the prison and the sentries.

Even worse, there was a sentry within a few feet of him who had heard a large stone dislodge and was coming to investigate.

Randall froze. The sentry's clodhoppers were right beside the hole Randall had made, but he was looking not down at it but over the fence, where Randall had hoped to be. The sentry stood there for a good minute, while Randall tried to breathe silently. He was certain the sentry could hear his frantic heartbeat.

"The events of my life seemed to flit before me," he said later.

Then the sentry walked away, not having seen Randall's pale face, covered with cold sweat, staring up at him.

Randall wormed backward through the tunnel. When Andy and Belden helped pull him out into Rat Hell, he blurted:

"All is lost!"

Tom went into the tunnel to inspect the damage. He found that the hole to the surface had been made about five feet from the fence on a downslope that hid it somewhat from the Libby side and the sentries. He plugged the hole as best he could.

* * *

"We're within five feet of the fence," Tom said. "With two more nights of digging we'll be past it. We've got to dig as fast as we can. It's only a matter of time until the Rebs find the tunnel."

After that, he refused to turn over the chisel to anyone else. Because it was Sunday, he didn't expect the guards to be vigilant. He, along with Belden and I. N., whom Belden had taken to calling "Innie" since he would only give his initials, stayed down in Rat Hell, with the repeaters covering for them. Belden fanned while Tom dug and Johnston kept watch. On the upstairs floors, lookouts moved as close to the windows as they dared, monitoring the pacing of the sentry directly over the tunnel.

Tom dug all that day and long into the night. When he at last came out into Rat Hell, he was exhausted. Belden felt ill from so long in the reeking cellar and wondered how Innie stood it, as they left him to his "shallow grave" and ascended the rope. They washed off as best they could and slept until dawn awakened them.

* * *

Before Reveille they reopened the fireplace and went down into Rat Hell once again. Their co-conspirators closed the fireplace behind them and repeated for them at Head Count. Tom, Belden, and Innie worked tirelessly all day. The preternatural silence of the cellar was broken only by the scraping of the cuspidor as it slid out of the tunnel to be emptied in Rat Hell. And, of course, the constant squealing of the rats. Belden and Innie took turns fanning, but little of the air was any longer reaching to where Tom labored like a man possessed with the chisel and his hands.

By midnight he was slick with sweat and clay, his entire body betraying him with sudden tremors and cramps. But on he burrowed. He got a second wind as he hit and then dug around a fence post. He was under the fence. Angling gradually upward toward the surface, on the verge of passing out for lack of air, Tom turned onto his back and kept going. With a final effort he struck upward with both hands and punched through the crust. Dirt spilled over his face, choking him.

And then he felt fresh cold air on face and hands. He gulped it in like a man who had almost drowned. He lay on his back looking up at what he hoped was the roof of the Goodie Shack, thinking, *I am free!* He was overcome with emotions he couldn't name. He fell into a kind of trance.

He was startled from it by the cry of the sentry a few feet away, just on the other side of the fence: "Half past one, and all's well!"

You have no idea how well! Tom thought. Taking care to be quiet, he crawled out of the hole he had punched to the surface.

He saw that he was inside the storehouse, shielded from the prison and the sentries by both the fence and the walls of the dirt-floored structure. He was surrounded by stacks of packages from the North, many of them gaping open, looted.

He felt his way to the massive double doors of the storehouse, which were secured by an iron rod that was opened from the outside by a simple latch. From the inside it would be easy to dislodge the rod, assuming there was no external padlock. Slowly, he pushed it up. As one door eased open, he peered through the crack and saw that the Canal Street sentry was marching away from him. He stepped out into the street.

He was free from Libby Prison. It was as though a drug coursed through his veins. He could run for it right now.

No, of course he could do no such thing.

But he could scout a bit.

He walked east on Canal Street, turned up past Pemberton Prison, avoiding the patrols there, back west on Carey Street, then south on 20th. On Canal again, he silently followed the sentry pacing east, hid in the carpenters' shop while the half-asleep young Confederate ambled back west, and slipped back into the door to the storehouse, securing it behind him.

A sense of wild exhilaration passed through him.

This was going to work.

He re-entered the tunnel, pulling a large package over it behind him to conceal it from sight, and wriggled the 55 feet back to Rat Hell.

When he had caught his breath, he told Belden and I. N. Johnston what he had just done. They both shook his hand, and then Innie began dancing like a child around the straw-covered floor where he had endured so many days and nights.

* * *

Belden went up the rope in the chimney chute, found Andy and shook him awake.

"Gather the crews in the kitchen," he whispered.

Andy rubbed his eyes and began waking snoring men.

The three digging crews could hardly believe their ears when Tom told them that the tunnel was complete. All wrung his hand. Many danced as wildly as Innie had. Andy cautioned them to keep their voices down.

"What are we waiting for?" one of the captives asked. "Let's skedaddle!"

Tom shook his head.

"It's tempting, I know," he said. "But it's already three a.m. That gives us only three hours this morning till we would be discovered. By waiting till tomorrow night, well, actually today, we can give ourselves almost nine hours before a search is mounted. We'll need the additional six hours to maximize our chances of escape."

Many men were nodding at the wisdom of this plan, but McDonald said: "But what if the Rebs find the tunnel between now and then? What if a spy tips them?"

A long silence followed this bit of frightening possibility. They had come so far for so long. Fifty-three days since they had removed the first bricks from the fireplace. They had visions of a squad of guards greeting them here tomorrow night.

"Well," Tom said, "we've not been ratted out yet, if you will forgive the pun. Speaking for myself, I will need the rest. I'm plumb tuckered out. Let's keep this to us fifteen and one friend each of us trusts fully until after lights out tonight. Meanwhile, accumulate whatever cash, food, and extra clothing you can."

Though nearly bursting with the strain of holding themselves back, the men agreed to Tom's plan. They replaced the bricks in the chimney and went to their berths to get what sleep they could.

Tonight, Hadley, Belden thought. *I'm coming.*

PART IV

THE GREATEST ESCAPE

23

BREAKOUT

Belden couldn't sleep a wink. His entire body trembled with excitement. In a few hours, God willing, he'd be long gone from this prison. If he was fortunate, he could be with Hadley in a couple weeks. He was going to be a free man.

He arose stiffly at Reveille and shuffled through the breakfast line, secreting an extra piece of hardtack in a pocket. He hadn't been able to collect much for the escape: two pieces of hardtack, a canteen, a sweater that was more holes than fabric, and—his prize—a small tin of red pepper.

"What do you want with that?" John Gallagher asked him. John had been Belden's selection to join in the escape. Always good to have an Irish tenor along.

"You'll see," Belden said, grinning.

John had a haversack stuffed with food, matches, an oilskin coat and cap. His cash and map he kept in his shoes.

The daylight hours crept by. Belden tried to rest but he was too excited to sleep more than a few minutes at a time. Each time he awoke with a start, thinking that some spy had betrayed them.

Though he knew well the dangers that awaited him outside the prison—sentries, guards, militia, citizens hoping for glory, rivers and swamps to be crossed, not to mention the bitter cold of midwinter—he could think only of how it would feel to be free and what it might be like to see Hadley again without a fence between them. He could almost taste those full red lips.

* * *

The daylight hours passed with excruciating slowness. He felt a sense of irritation with everything: Head Count had lost its sense of mischief, Lice-See-Um was just a torture, and the new newsman's reading of the stories from the paper was like chalk screeching on the school blackboard back in Bradford.

"The U.S. Congress has passed a conscription act calling for 500,000 men to be drafted for three years or the duration of the War...."

Well, Belden thought, maybe Jesse will have to join the Army after all.

"Lincoln ordered Sec. of War Stanton to send a transport to San Domingo to return Negro colonists disillusioned with trying to set up their own country....The CSA Navy captured the U.S. gunboat *Underwriter* near New Berne, N.C., and burned her to the water-line.... Gen. Sherman is leading a rampaging army ripping up railroads and burning property around Meridian, Mississippi...."

He checked over his gear yet another time and wondered if he could lay hands on anything else. He tried to sleep. When that failed, he joined the Walking Club in their circuits of the prison. Best to get his legs in shape. One of the Walkers told him they'd accomplished 22 miles in a single day last week.

"How did you know how far you'd gone?" Belden asked.

"It was our best guess-timate," the man said, "based upon multi-plying stride length by number of strides. Someday someone will invent a device to measure such peripatetic mileage."

"If someone could invent the watch, they probably could come up with such a thing," Belden replied.

Finally, Belden sat and looked around the room at men he knew he would probably never see again—and to whom he couldn't risk saying farewell. One of them, they knew, was a spy.

When the day began to darken with the early advent of the February night, Belden could feel his heart beating in his breast like a wild bird struggling to free itself from a snare.

* * *

Colonel Harrison Hobart of the 21st Wisconsin was designated as the gatekeeper at the fireplace. Everyone agreed that the Beavers—those that had actually created the escape route—should go first. After the first fifteen went down, he was to rebrick the opening and wait one hour, at which time the second fifteen were to follow. After that, he would reopen the fireplace at regular intervals to allow groups of others who now knew of the escape to descend, beginning with those of the highest rank who wished to go.

Some didn't. Gen. Dow said that he had been so broken down by his incarceration that he feared he would only hold up the operation.

Col. Hobart was to keep a running total of how many escapees went down the chute so those remaining could conceal their absence at Head Count the next morning. The hope was that a second wave of prisoners could escape the following night, then a third, and so on, though to Belden this seemed a tall order.

The first fifteen assembled in the kitchen at seven o'clock that evening. The darkness outside the prison was lit by a wan, two-day new moon. While Col. Hobart removed the bricks, Tom Rose whispered final instructions, shook each man's hand, wished them all "Godspeed and farewell" and entered the chimney first. Andy and then Belden followed on his heels.

When the fifteenth digger descended, Hobart sealed the fireplace, and in came the second fifteen, accompanied by a banjo player who picked out a lively tune while the men danced and sang as if at a hoe-down. A guard stuck his head in, grinned, listened and watched for a while, then went back downstairs.

After a few minutes (rather than the hour planned) the second fifteen went down, John Gallagher among them, and a group of high-ranking officers, including Abel Streight, took their places in the noisy hoe-down.

* * *

As Belden came out of the chimney-hole into Rat Hell, he hardly noticed the rats, the stench, or the gloom. It had become as familiar to him as a second home. He was, however, nervous about the crawl through the tunnel. He knew well that he never liked being in tight confines. While the opening behind the groin had been widened over time to a roomy three feet by two-and-a-half, the tunnel quickly narrowed to about two by two. At one point, he knew from Tom's instructions, it would be a scant sixteen inches. He found himself sweating in the cold.

Innie Johnston begged to go ahead of him. He was filthy from his long stay in Rat Hell. Belden gladly waited the few extra seconds.

He plunged in headfirst, following Innie's heels, and heard the next in line come in close behind him. Using his elbows alternately, he wormed his way forward. He felt a rising panic seizing him, numbing his limbs. The darkness was unlike anything he had ever experienced, even in the cave. The air smelt stale and he was soon gasping wildly.

Slow, deep breaths, he told himself, though his lungs seemed not to heed his counsel and he found himself panting like Ma had, giving birth to Helen.

At the sixteen-inch passage, he felt a degree of terror that threat-ened to overwhelm him. He wanted to scream. The pepper tin pressed into his ribs and he cursed himself for bringing it. He scrabbled and clawed, hunching his body forward. The tunnel began slanting upward, which made the going harder, but it was wider here and he was seized by a sense of power that dispelled the panic. His entire body began undulating and thrusting as if it had become a burrowing machine. He was going to make it! He was getting out!

Then his head popped from the end of the tunnel in the storehouse and Andy helped pull him out, grasping both sides of his head to do so. Belden felt an immense relief. He lay panting on the floor for a moment, then sprang to his feet to help the next man out.

In the dim light he surveyed his surroundings. There must have been 5000 packages in the room, most of them already open. Belden felt an anger at his captors stronger than any he had felt before. How dare they keep these treasures from then!

But he knew that such anger at this time was a luxury he could not afford. He joined Tom at the now-unlocked doors to the Goodie Shack.

They watched as the sentry came marching up to within a few paces of the doors, made a sloppy about-face, and began pacing east. Belden knew from Tom that the sentry would now march west for forty-five steps before returning.

Tom, Andy, and Belden slipped out of the doorway and headed east, trying to walk casually. In a few minutes they were in the shadows. Innie and two other men followed soon behind.

* * *

From the upstairs room, the prisoners' whispers grew louder as they watched the groups of twos and threes exit the storehouse and walk off down Canal Street. There was a moment of strained silence when a sentinel waved to one group—and failed to challenge them.

"He thinks they're Rebs who've been robbing the storehouse!" Hobart whispered.

The second group of fifteen had gone down the chute and now the kitchen was filling with prisoners who wouldn't be denied access to it. Hobart struggled to control them, but they were near-hysterical with the chance to escape. Hobart shrugged and went down the chute himself. Behind him, a long line of men, shoving for position, leapt into the chute one after another.

Someone in the kitchen suddenly cried out "The guards! The guards!" and a melee ensued. Men scrambled over one another to get back to their proper rooms. They knocked into the cook stoves and utensils that had been moved away from the fireplace, and stovepipes crashed down and pots and pans skittered across the floor.

"It made so much noise that one might easily have mistaken it for an earthquake," Captain David Caldwell wrote in his journal.

But it had been a false alarm. No guards appeared, despite the huge cacophony. One at a time, the prisoners crept back into the kitchen. This time, they queued up properly to take their turns dropping down the chute. But no one kept a tally of how many men were leaving.

* * *

In the middle of this mass exodus was Col. Streight, the biggest man in the prison. He got stuck in the sixteen-inch narrows of the tunnel and could neither advance nor retreat. It was a bad moment, not only for him but for all the prisoners waiting to follow him through. After a fitful struggle, he was able to back out. In Rat Hell, he removed his overcoat and vest, and tied them to his legs for a second attempt. He barely squeezed through.

Around half past three in the morning the fireplace was once more bricked up and re-sooted. The cookstoves were moved back into place, the stovepipes reconnected. A strange silence fell over the whole prison. Gen. Dow did his own head count and subtracted that number from the one Erasmus had made that morning.

According to his calculations, 109 of their fellow captives had escaped.

* * *

Belden, Tom, and Andy turned onto Carey Street, going east. After months of little stimulation and poor lighting (or the utter darkness of the tunnel), Carey Street was overwhelming. The gas lamps shone brightly and hundreds of people milled along. The shops were open and filled with patrons. There was no food but a lot of folks seemed to have money for purchases of other kinds.

Belden felt a dreadful self-consciousness invade him, for him a quite unusual feeling. Everyone on the street seemed to be nicely turned out in fashionable clothes, except for the three recent escapees. Tom still wore his blue Union uniform, albeit beneath a bulky topcoat. Belden was in his holey sweater.

Passersby shied away from them, making faces as if they stank. Belden reckoned they did, after so long in Rat Hell. He had to control himself to keep from running. His legs shook with the repressed need to run.

Then their worst fears were realized. A Rebel hospital guard in gray approached them and stopped Tom, inquiring about his Yankee uniform. Andy kept on walking. Belden fought down the urge to stay with Tom and walked away up a side street leading north. Once he was in shadow, Belden waited, watching Tom and the guard. The two talked for a bit, seemingly amicably, then the guard and Tom walked back down Carey together. Uncertain, Belden finally decided to go it alone. For the first time in months, the three were no longer together.

* * *

Andy continued east down Carey Street and was relieved when the bright gas lamps ended and he reached a quiet residential section of Richmond. On the outskirts of town he slipped through the Confederate lines, not a particularly difficult task since the boys in gray were laughing, smoking, and carrying on. The smell of the burning tobacco alone gave away their positions. Using the North Star as his guide, he kept it back over his left shoulder as he headed southeast, heading for the Union lines at Williamsburg.

* * *

The hospital guard led Tom to his headquarters and turned him over to a fat and sleepy major who began the interview by stuffing his bulbous lower lip with an immense chaw of "baccy," as he called it. Dark yellow spittle drooled from one corner of his mouth, dripping down into his stained beard.

"How come you are in Yankee blue, soldier?" he mumbled. "Are you with that there New Kent Cavalry?"

Tom's brain seemed to work like lightning. The New Kent Cavalry must be a Rebel unit that wore Union uniforms to deceive the Yankees. He'd heard of such. This man was not bright enough to attempt to trap him in a lie.

"Yes suh," he said, saluting. After so long in Rebel custody, he could do a pretty fair imitation of the accent.

"May I see your leave papers, soldier?"

"Well, suh, that there's the thang. I done come to town to meet my fian-cee, she was all hot and bothered 'bout our marital plans, and I neglected to get leave papers. I know I was wrong, suh, but it was sudden-like and I only meant to be away for a couple hours when the sergeant was asleep anyways. Might I impose upon you for a small bit of chaw, suh?"

The major's eyes widened.

"Get the hell outa heah, you marryin' fool, and don't let me never see you back heah without them papers!"

Saluting a bit sloppily, as he had witnessed so many Rebel soldiers doing, Tom about-faced and walked free back onto Carey Street.

* * *

Belden felt a terror that turned his limbs to water. Though the relative darkness of the side street comforted him at first, he was disoriented. He was afraid he had been going round in circles. Well, squares. He couldn't find the damn North Star. He'd start down one street, see people coming, and duck into another. Then he almost bumped into a group of four men, one of them huge, coming around a corner. He slowed his pace. His heart went into his throat.

He'd counted on being with Tom and Andy for the entire escape. Now he was on his own, in an unfamiliar city and most of the people he'd encounter would want to put him back into Libby. In irons.

The group of men stopped and seemed to assess him. He wanted to turn around and run, but started to edge away, slow and steady, hoping to be beyond them in a few seconds.

He looked again at the huge man and breathed more easily.

"Well met, Col. Streight," he whispered.

Able Streight stopped, looked at him closely, then chuckled.

"Damn if it isn't that tunnel rat, Belden Crane," he said. "I do wish you'd made that passage a few inches wider in the middle! I could hardly squeeze through. Come along with us, lad."

Relieved, Belden joined them, shaking hands with Streight, Major McDonald, and a Captain Scearce, who he had seen but didn't know. Their guide was a Negro slave named Robert Ford, familiar to Belden as the man who carried messages between Col. Streight and the Richmond underground. Belden proffered his hand. Ford pretended he didn't see it. Belden realized he'd probably never shaken a white man's hand.

"Please hurry, suhs," Ford said, pointing ahead. "You ain't got all night."

Ford led them through the back streets, then turned them over to a black woman who guided them on to the northern suburbs of Richmond to a working-class home belonging to a member of the Unionist resistance. There another Negro woman named Lucy Rice showed them where they could wash up and dress in clean clothes. Belden found himself immediately attracted to Lucy. He thought her beautiful. She smelled good to him, a bit like rosemary. He wondered whether the clothes she had given them had been worn by Negroes. They smelled good to him, as if they had been washed with lye soap and then dried in the sun. He shrugged and pulled them on.

Lucy fed them collards fried up with onions and bits of ham. Belden had never tasted better food in his life. Beautiful, and she could cook. He thought he might be falling in love.

That night he slept clean in a bed with clean white sheets. He couldn't believe how soft they felt against his skin.

* * *

The house, while comfortable, was small. The blinds were always drawn, day and night, to prevent any searcher from looking in. They played cards a lot around the kitchen table, a rickety wooden affair that Belden wished he had the tools to mend. He learned how to play whist and was glad he had no money to lose at it. They played for matchsticks instead.

Except for Lucy's gracious femininity and delicious cooking, and the soft bed, being cooped up in this Unionist safe house wasn't all that different from being in prison.

After six days, they received a visitor.

In preparing the others for her visit, Col. Streight said that she was the head of the Richmond Unionists and an accomplished spy, keeping Gen. Butler apprised of the strength and positions of the Rebel forces protecting the Confederate capital. She communicated with him via a cipher. Because she was from a prominent Richmond family, she had thus far been safe from inquisition.

Her name was Elizabeth Van Lew.

She was an unassuming-looking woman of what Southerners called "a certain age," meaning well into spinsterhood. She had, however, a bright eye that bespoke intelligence and determination. She was fashionably dressed, in hat and gloves, and greeted them graciously:

"Gentlemen, I hope that you are finding this humble house comfortable and that Lucy is feeding you well enough. As you probably know, there is little food in all of Richmond, due mostly to the blockade, which is quite effective. I had hoped to entertain you at my house on the hill, in fact I had a secret room built just for the purpose, but we have been under close scrutiny ever since the escape. One hundred and nine! How marvelous! And Col. Streight himself! I declare, colonel, the papers are beside themselves about you escaping! According to them, you've already made it to Washington! The number of search parties has already been much reduced."

She handed him a copy of the *Daily Richmond Enquirer* dated February 11th. From it Col. Streight read aloud:

"'One of those *extraordinary* escapes of prisoners of war occurred at Libby Prison, the most important escape of Federal prisoners which has occurred during the war. Among the escapees we regret to have to class the notorious Straight...'"

He stopped reading and shook his massive head.

"Why must they always misspell my name?"

He cleared this throat and continued:

"'...who is charged with raising a nergo regiment.' Why can they never capitalize that particular word?"

Here he stopped and handed the newspaper to Major McDonald.

"In point of fact," said Col. Streight, "I never did raise nor command a Negro regiment. However, let it be known that I would have proudly accepted command of Negro troops."

McDonald shook the paper out, chuckling.

"Says here we reached the cellar by boring though the floor of the hospital, after somehow breaking into the hospital from the second floor. No explanation of how we might have done so without the hospital staff's noticing."

Miss Van Lew shook her head.

"There is more recent information, I fear," she said. "According to my sources, a Lt. Melville Smart, formerly of the 51st Maryland, showed Major Turner the passageway down the chimney. Why he would do such a thing one can only speculate."

"Damn! He's the stool pigeon," Col. Streight said. "I always thought so. Please excuse my language, ma'am."

"No apology needed, colonel. I hope he is damned indeed. The prison could have emptied over time otherwise."

"True," Col. Streight replied. Then, after some more speculations among the group about how Smart might have profited by his perfidy, he smiled at Miss Van Lew.

"Ma'am, if I may inquire, in your estimation, what is the real cause of this war?"

The grand dame looked thoughtful for some time. When she at last replied, it was with a single word:

"Slavery."

"Not the protection of the Union then?"

"No, suh, though that be a secondary issue. The fundamental reason that the South seceded was to protect the slave power. That is the original sin of this nation, and we are now engaged in expiating it with the lifeblood of thousands. Until all Negroes are free and equal, we shall never be a truly great nation."

When it was time for her to go, they all stood up at attention and saluted her.

* * *

And as soon as her carriage had pulled away, Col. Streight said, "Well, lads, pack up your worldly possessions, such as they are, and prepare to leave. I have no doubt that she was followed and that this house will be the next place to be searched. She is beyond any doubt a remarkable asset to the Union, but I fear she is a bit naïve. Miss Lucy, where can we go now?"

"Robert will guide you," Lucy said.

"Miss Lucy, we thank you for your kind hospitality, not to mention your bravery. Words cannot express the depth of our gratitude to you."

As Belden watched, he realized that black people blushed almost as obviously as whites.

* * *

Robert Ford took them to another safe house, provided them with haversacks, traveling food, and a few weapons: four knives and a hatchet. He also connected them to a Rebel deserter named Rod, last name unknown, who knew the territory and wished to liberate himself in the North. He was to be their guide from here on.

They left that evening as soon as darkness fell.

* * *

Belden was overjoyed to be heading due north. They had all agreed that any remaining search parties would be in the southeastern area between Richmond and the Union lines at Williamsburg. The expected little harassment once past the Richmond defenses, until they reached the Potomac. There would be, however, several rivers to cross, and the nighttime temperatures were now extremely cold. Belden hoped it would freeze the ice across the rivers.

Their guide Rod proved true until they came to the Chickahominy, which, though full of ice floes crashing into one another, was not yet frozen solid. There was no way they could walk across it. Rod took one look at this spectacle and bade them farewell. Though Belden had come to like Rod on their journey, he was gathering that the other Union men were suspicious of him. He was, after all, a deserter. Regular Army men looked down on deserters, even from the enemy. If they would do it once, they calculated, they'd probably do it again. And here was Rod, leaving them and quite possibly heading to the nearest garrison to report them for the benefits it might leverage him. In Abel Streight's eyes Belden thought he could see the debate over whether or not to kill Rod before he could betray them. In the end, they let him go.

"I cain't swim a lick," he said in parting.

The Yankees could. Stripping naked, they stuffed shoes and clothing into their haversacks and waded into the frigid water.

Belden was very glad of the seven days' rest and regeneration he had just had under Lucy Rice's ministrations. He knew that if he'd just arrived straight from Libby he'd have drowned. Although he'd always considered himself an able swimmer, having learned early in Mud Lake and once crossed Keuka in an afternoon swim, the Chicka-hominy nearly killed him.

The shock of the cold itself was excruciating to every cell in his body, though it gradually went numb and became reluctant to follow his mental commands to move. The force of the current, which several times knocked him off his feet and launched icebergs at his head, was terrifying, swirling around him in eddies whenever he regained his footing on the rocky bottom. While the stones there were mostly rounded by years of water-polishing, they bruised his numb feet. He'd left his woolen socks on, hoping they would provide some cushion. When the water reached his waist as he stepped into a hole, he could feel his privates retreat into his body. He hoped the crossing would become no deeper.

But it did. Now he was up to his armpits and his teeth were clacking together like dice. Then he stepped into a hole with no bottom and went under. He kicked his legs as hard as he could to keep the haversack in his hands above water. As he did so, his right sock that held his precious razor came off and the razor plummeted away from him. For a brief moment he considered attempting to retrieve it, then accepted the futility of that plan. No way was he going under to try to salvage it. He felt a flash of anger at Rod for leading them to this place and telling them it was usually an easy fording spot in the Chicka-hominy. Maybe they should have killed him. Maybe he'd lured them into a death trap.

Then the water became shallower and he was soon stumbling up the opposite bank, his entire body jolting with shivers. The other three joined him, all blue with cold even in the faint light, all shaking violently, none of them apparent males.

"What I wouldn't give for a f-f-f-fire"!" gasped McDonald.

"We're too c-c-c-close to R-R-Rebel lines!" Streight gasped back. "R-R-Rub yourselves down with something dry and g-g-g-get into dry clothing."

Belden found that the extra clothing Miss Van Lew and Robert Ford had provided them with had stayed mostly dry in the haversack. He rubbed himself down with a cotton shirt and pulled on woolen breeches, a canvas shirt, a thick sweater and a thin oilskin, but he was still freezing.

He pulled off the sock from his left foot, rubbed both feet hard with the shirt, and pulled on dry socks and his boots, despite the pain of doing so. He squeezed the water out of the wet sock and attached it to the outside of his haversack with a safety pin.

"Up and A-a-adam, l-l-lads!" Streight commanded. "We keep moving or we turn into icicles! Belden, you've got good eyes and ears. Take the point, if you would be so kind."

Belden shouldered his haversack and began walking north, leading the way. Polaris was like a magnet in the sky, pulling him forward.

Hadley, here I come.

* * *

It took the better part of an hour to stop shivering. At that point he felt a warm lassitude permeate his body and he wondered whether this was that seductive warmth he'd heard one felt just before freezing to death. Then he felt his toes coming back to life, stinging like the dickens. He wished he had gloves. The best he could do was to worm his blue hands into his third pair of socks and then shove them into the pockets of his breeches. Though this strategy warmed his hands, it left him feeling helpless to defend himself if they were set upon by a Rebel patrol.

* * *

Just before dawn they heard the nickering of the horses first, then the metallic rattle of sabers or carbines. With a hand signal, Belden led them off the road and into the forest. At first the trees were large and widely spaced, but he soon found a thicket and crawled in. The others followed. They huddled together in the middle of the thicket. Along the road came Rebel cavalry, talking in low voices. They couldn't make out individual words.

When the patrol had passed, they breathed again.

"Well, it's gonna be light soon," Streight said. "This is as good a hidey-hole as any. Let's get some shut eye till it's dark again. Eat something to help keep you warm. I'll take first watch and I'll kick the first man who snores."

Belden fished a piece of dried venison out of his food bag and began chewing it slowly and thoroughly. He noticed that over his time in prisons his teeth had begun to loosen in their sockets. He was sure he'd lose at least one. The venison was tough until it was well-masticated with saliva. Then it was delicious. He fell asleep before he could get it all down.

24

FOLLOW THE STAR

McDonald woke Belden from a dream of Hadley kissing him. He felt as if he were swimming up to the surface of consciousness. The moon was almost down.

"You're last watch," McDonald said. "Wake us all at sunset."

Belden forced his stiff body to sit up and McDonald took his place beside Streight, pressing up against Belden with his back. Belden found he could lean against McDonald enough to take some of the strain off his own back, gaining warmth at the same time.

We've learned to accept just being puppies in a pile, he thought.

He yawned and stretched his arms above his head. They'd been fortunate that the cushioning of leaves in the thicket had been relatively soft. He realized he'd slept through most of the day and he still had venison in his mouth. He chewed, relishing what remained of the juice, and swallowed.

Breakfast.

It would be something to have a hot cup of coffee to wash it down. He remembered how Lucy had concocted a form of coffee out of chicory. Even that would be more than welcome.

Then he heard the jangle of spurs and bridles, and the plop of horses' shod hooves on the dirt road. No talking. He reckoned it was the same patrol that had gone past them the opposite direction in the morning. They'd been out all night. He could feel the urgency in the horses' steps: They knew they were getting near the stable, and a ration of oats.

Even oats would taste pretty good right now.

As the soft plop of the horses' hooves and the jingling of the bits went past, he yawned. This escaping thing was getting boring already.

He remembered how, back on the farm, when he'd had to leave his warm bed to feed the animals by lantern-light, he'd help himself to a handful of the horses' oats or the chickens' mash to hold him until breakfast. "Always feed your animals before you eat," Pa had dictated. "That way you won't forget to feed them. When you feel hunger pangs, just imagine how hungry they are, and how dependent. Take care of what depends upon you before you take care of yourself."

Then he recalled what Ma would cook up for breakfast: scrambled eggs, bacon, toast with butter and blackberry preserves, hot coffee with the thick cream from their cow—his stomach began to rumble. He reached for his haversack and picked out a piece of hardtack. At least Lucy's didn't have any weevils.

As he watched the western sky turn pink and orange, he pushed himself up to crawl out of the thicket, unbutton his breeches, and relieve the pressure on his bladder. He was glad to see that his member had returned to its normal size and that his stream had some color to it.

As the western sky showed its last colors, mostly purple this evening, he woke his group. They chewed on some kind of food and grumbled about no coffee.

Belden told them how the patrol had gone past not long ago and they speculated that they must be near a garrison town. Streight studied his map.

"We might have made good enough time to be coming up on Ashland, which has a garrison," he said. "We should bear a tad bit easterly to skirt it. Belden, you lead on. You're doing a good job of holding course and are a good point man. When you fatigue, let me know and we'll send up a relief."

"Yes, sir."

"I thought you knew not to 'sir' any fellow prisoner," Streight said.

"Well, colonel, we're not prisoners anymore. Besides, I'm used to it. My pa made us all 'sir' him morning noon and night."

"You were well brought up, Lieutenant."

"Ma and Pa did their best...sir. And I'm actually just a Corporal."

After throwing a quick salute, Belden hitched up his haversack and went out ahead on point.

* * *

They gave Ashland a wide berth with the guidance of Polaris. Belden wondered how many escaping slaves had followed this same path under the same guidance. It was almost, he thought, as if God had placed the star there off the lip of the Big Dipper to steer them to freedom.

Their next major obstacle was the Pamunkey River, which made the Chickahominy look like a creek.

"We're not going to be able to wade this one," Col. Streight said.

"Let's build a raft," Belden suggested.

They quickly agreed. Using their hatchet, they cut several fat saplings and bound them together with pieces of the rope thoughtfully provided by Miss Van Lew.

"That woman has expended all her substance supporting the Union," Streight said. "When we reach Washington I'm going to make damn sure those lousy politicians vote her a hefty reward in recompense."

"Hear, hear," the little band seconded.

They also cut two long poles. They got Abel Streight to sit in the center of the raft with the haversacks with Belden in front and B.B. McDonald poling in the rear. Scearce pushed them off and scrambled aboard, nearly tipping them over. Once they'd rebalanced, they bade him sit and poled themselves across the Pamunkey.

On the other side Streight had them tear the raft apart and scatter the makings in the surrounding brush.

"No sense in giving the Rebs any extra incentive," he said.

* * *

At the Mattaponi they were lucky: They found a boat with oars in it.

"God smiles upon us," Streight said, grinning through his now unruly beard, which had overgrown his upper lip as well. Even Belden had a beard, though his was but peach fuzz compared to the older men's.

They were still traveling at night, sleeping cold in thickets or deadfalls during the day. Each night seemed longer than the prior one, though they knew this couldn't be so, and their bodies were growing fatigued.

Even miles to the south of it, they heard the crashing of huge ice floes in the Rappahannock. At first they thought it might be distant thunder. When they realized what it was, dread filled them.

"This is going to be a big one," McDonald said.

At that moment their world changed.

"Who goes there?!" rang out a Rebel challenge.

All four of them ran. They heard an explosion and a ball whistled just overhead.

"Christ help us," Able panted. "Rebels behind us and the river ahead."

Then they heard the baying of the hounds.

* * *

Abel Streight had a few tricks for putting the pursuit off the scent. He led them splashing up a creek and, when they crossed a road, had them walk across it backwards so their wet footprints made it seem they were going in the opposite direction.

But the hounds were still gaining on them.

"We'll have to go to ground," Streight said, "and pray."

"Well, sir," Belden said, reaching into his pocket. "God helps those who help themselves."

He brought out the tin of cayenne pepper and began sprinkling it over their tracks until they came to yet another thicket to hide in.

It was nearly morning. Peering through the lattice of branches they watched as the pack of hounds—a good dozen of them, piebald curs that the Rebs loved to hunt with—poured into the glen.

Belden had always liked dogs. He'd raised Becky from puppyhood and considered her to be a human sister to him. But seeing the hunting hounds on their trail flow like a colorful wave into the glen stopped his heart.

Then the dogs encountered the cayenne. They halted abruptly, sneezing and snorting, and retreated. As they milled about their handlers, half a dozen civilians in ragged clothing, loped into view behind them.

Into Belden's mind came a line from Shakespeare: "Methinks they hath a lean and hungry look." He held his breath.

The men cursed the dogs and urged them onward, but the dogs would have none of it. The men held a brief powwow and then, shouldering their long rifles, went away to the south.

"That was too close for comfort," McDonald said, expelling a long-held breath. "Belden, we are in your debt. That was perspicacious of you, to bring pepper."

"You don't mind being perspicacious in public, do you?" Bill Scearce joked.

"Gentlemen," said Streight. "We need to get away from this glen, though it is now daylight, and find some better place to hide."

It had dawned gray and foggy. The wisps of fog looked to Belden like ghosts.

Streight consulted his map.

"I believe we are somewhere around here," he said, jabbing a dirty finger at a long neck of land that forced the Rappahannock into a horseshoe bend. "A notation by my scribe indicates that the local slaves at the plantation hereabouts might be helpful. I suggest that we throw ourselves upon their mercy."

Moving as silently as they could, the four fugitives continued north, as best they could approximate it. Within a mile they reached cleared fields. In one of them, black field hands were planting corn. There didn't seem to be an overseer.

"I'll go speak with them," Streight said. "You stay hidden here."

Belden watched as Streight sauntered over to one of the Negroes and, raising his hands to show he was unarmed, greeted them. An older man, the color of heavily creamed coffee, his little remaining hair a salt and pepper mix, walked warily toward the white man in rags.

Belden noticed many of the others looking back over their shoulders as if fearing discovery.

"If you can pray," McDonald whispered, "now would be the time."

In under a minute they had been waved forward and were hastening with the older Negro toward the several buildings of the plantation.

"Don' you worry," the black man said, "Massa don' get hisself outa bed till de sun be in de sky."

"We're being hunted by hounds," Abel said.

"Dawgs!" the older man said scornfully. "We bin 'scaping dawgs since we was chilluns. Don' you worry none 'bout no dawgs!"

They entered what was clearly the slave quarters, two lines of ramshackle wood cabins that looked as if they might blow over in the next wind. They were led into the second from the end, where a huge black woman in a white apron looked at them in horror.

"Union sojers, 'scaping' the dawgs," the man said. "Keep 'em hid till dark."

"What you talkin' bout, George? You know I got to gits up to the Big House to make Massa his grits. You gonna git us all whipped!"

"You do what Ah sez now, Sally! Call in Lizbeth if you want, but git them some vittles. They look plumb starved. I'll go up and see if'n I cain't throw Massa off the trail."

The four fugitives found themselves with steaming bowls of ham-flavored grits and tin cups full of hot chicory behind a partition in the shanty. Against the back wall was a bed with a corn-husk mattress and an ancient "chiffarobe," as Sally called it. She admonished them to "lay low and be mouses" and left them in the care of a young woman who seemed hardly beyond childhood. She said her name was Lizbeth. She stared at them with wide eyes for a long time and then said, "Thank youals for settin' us free."

Col. Streight stood up to bow to her.

"It is our duty and pleasure, ma'am," he replied.

At that Lizbeth giggled and ran from the cabin.

* * *

An hour later they watched through the chinks between the pine logs as "Massa," fat and resplendent in a white suit and broad-brimmed hat, sat a tall gelding and organized his field hands into three parties to aid in the search for the Yankee escapees. Pointing with his riding crop, he led them southwards, away from the slave quarters.

"Our George is a brilliant tactician," Abel Streight said. "He hides us where a damned Rebel would never set foot and then misdirects the search to where we used to be. Brilliant."

They spent the day alternatively napping and keeping watch. Lizbeth brought in a chamberpot so they could relieve themselves without leaving the cabin and later a lunch of chittlin's and greens.

"How do you come by greens at this time of year?" Belden asked her.

"Them greens grows all winter long," Lizbeth said. "When it snow, you can find 'em 'neath the snow."

As dusk approached they witnessed the return of the tired and dejected Massa and his shuffling troops. Unsurprisingly, they had been unsuccessful in their hunt. Massa went off to the Big House to no doubt drown his sorrows in mint juleps or hot toddies and his slaves came into the quarters. As soon as they were sure Massa was in the Big House, they transformed. They stood up straight, they laughed and slapped each other's palms, and one of them even did a spontaneous victory dance. Once again, they had outsmarted Massa, "just like ol' Bre'r Rabbit outsmart Bre'r Fox," as Sally put it. She started to tell him "Bout how when Bre'r Fox catch Bre'r Rabbit in da Tar Baby, Bre'r Rabbit be tellin' him, 'Whatever you do, Bre'r Fox, don't be throwin' me in dat briarpatch.'"

George came in with a wide grin.

"Let's git youal some fixin's," he said, "then I be rowing you 'crost de river."

"Sir," said Col. Steight, "we thank you kindly. We are in your debt. What, may I presume to ask, is your full name?"

"Oh, I be famous," the older man said, laughing. "I be none other than George Washington."

* * *

Belden knew by now that the Southern slaves often dropped their African names and took the surname of the owner of the plantation that had bought them, or on which they had been born. He was also aware that the range of coloration among the slaves varied from midnight to what Belden couldn't distinguish from an Italian or even a darkly-complected Irishman like Keogh. He had learned enough about genetics from reading Mendel and observing what resulted from his father's planned breeding practices on the farm to suspect what the abolitionists had been hinting at for years: The Southern master class was fornicating with their slaves. Miscegenation, it was called. It didn't take a genius to figure out that the slaves probably had little say in the matter. They could be sold off, they could be beaten, they could be murdered—all with impunity. What choice did they have if Massa or his sons called them to bed? Or took them in the stables, like a stallion atop a mare? He felt a revulsion at the image.

He wondered how closely this George Washington might be related to his namesake. That gave a whole new perspective on the great man who was called the "Father of his country."

He remembered hearing something about a smear campaign when Jefferson was running for President, something about his having taken a mistress from among his slaves. While he didn't know for certain that it was true, he suspected that it might be, even though he believed gossip to be a scurrilous crime and tried his best to shun it.

As Ma always said, "If you can't say something good about somebody, don't say anything at all."

The thought of his mother brought a lump to his throat. She'd already heard one time that he was dead. Would the Rebs report him dead rather than escaped? As soon as he got across the Potomac he'd get a message to her. And Pa and Helen.

But first, he had to find Hadley.

* * *

After a satisfying meal of fatback and beans, George Washington made them wait till all the lights in the Big House had been extinguished. He led them past the columned mansion through a park-like deciduous forest and down a wide lawn to the Rappahannock River. A small jetty poked out into the broad waters that seemed choked with icebergs. George stepped into a rowboat that was tied to the jetty. He greased the oarlocks with a bit of fatback that he had carried in a rag, fitted the oars into the oarlocks, and motioned them into the boat. Belden cast them off into the dark and icy waters, leaping aboard once the boat was waterborne.

George rowed deliberately and quietly. The ice floes crashed against the upstream gunnels so that the entire boat shuddered, even though weighted with the bodies of five men. Belden feared they would tear the boat apart, but it proved a sturdy craft. Though the passengers did their best to fend off the floes, many came too swiftly to thwart. The crossing seemed to take an eternity. Several men were praying aloud. George kept saying, "Lord, have mercy!" in a guttural undertone.

They were relieved to feel the keel grating upon the sandy shore of the northern bank.

After thanking and blessing George, they shoved him back into the terrifying hell of ice and watched him row away alone into the darkness. Belden took a deep breath. As far as he knew, this was the last major river until the Potomac.

They hoisted their haversacks onto their shoulders and, keying on the North Star, walked single file into the night.

* * *

After that crossing they made good time and were not harried. When they hit the railroad tracks that headed northeast, they followed the bed, ducking into the woods when they heard a train or a patrol approaching. When they came to the small rivers they might have had to wade or swim, they delighted in using the railroad bridges. They soon reached Manassas, the town near where the Union had lost two devastating conflicts, and where Belden had played at spying. They gave it a wide berth to the east, rejoining the tracks just below Fairfax Station.

Belden's heart began to pound. He'd been here before, and he knew that they were getting close to Burke's Station. Was he really going to leave this group of men who had become like family to him and trust that Hadley would take him in?

He had less than an hour to consider what to do. They always made good time on railroad beds, which were relatively straight, level, and you could take a measured stride on every other tie that was anchored in the bluestone beneath them and the shining steel tracks. Sure enough, up ahead he saw the sign for Burke's Station.

Though the station house was dark, it was getting light enough to see the two painted signs over the two doors to the public outhouse there: White and Colored, instead of Men and Women, as it would have been in Elmira or Albany.

"Well, gentlemen," Belden said, "I'm going to make a stop to visit a dear friend in this town. You are of course welcome to accompany me, and I would hope to be able to offer you a safe place to sleep, but I am not completely sure I'll receive a warm reception."

Bill Scearce drew his knife from his belt.

"How do we know you won't tip the Rebs?"

"Jesus God and Mary, Bill!" said McDonald, reaching out to stay his hand. "This is Belden. You know him!"

"And I know dead men don't talk."

"Put your blade away," Col. Streight said. "I suspect a woman. Why else would a young man part company with his good companions and risk his life if not for the fair sex. I don't suppose there's any way we could persuade you otherwise? We are but a night's march from the Potomac and home sweet home."

"I'm afraid not, sir. She has my heart."

Abel reached out and gave Belden a firm handshake.

"You're a good man, Belden Crane," he said. "Look me up when you get back to the Union. If your Southern belle doesn't chain you up down here, I mean. You've escaped the tightest Confederate prison. Don't walk back into another."

McDonald also shook his hand. Scearce stood apart, grumbling. McDonald took the captain by the shoulder and pushed him away. They walked up the tracks and had soon disappeared into the darkness ahead. With a final salute, Abel Streight followed.

Belden felt suddenly afraid. Was he making a terrible mistake? He was now alone in Rebel territory, trusting that Hadley would be able to hide him. Did she still care for him as much as he for her?

Of course she did. A love like theirs weathered all storms. *Amor omnia vincit.*

Now he just had to find her.

* * *

He knew from their conversations that she lived in the house next to the general store. He could just make out the words "Gen'l Store" handpainted on a sign on the building across a dirt road to the south of the station. Beside it and separated from it by a stand of maples stood a large three-story mansion with columns. It was painted white with green shutters.

Another dirt road ran north and south beside the store, and to the east side of it stood another house, less grand, but still substantial, surrounded by tall firs. Burke's Station was a simple crossroads village. While he could just make out a few more dwellings down the east-running road, to the west were open pastures.

He'd take a chance on the mansion.

Belden knew Hadley had a dog and hoped that Sam would remember him. Just in case, he stopped to dig a piece of dried venison from his haversack.

Wary now, he crept past the east side of the store and around its rear. There, just as Hadley had described it, stood the barn.

All of his senses thrumming, he slowly opened the barn door, wincing at its thunderous creak. He stopped to listen. No barking dog or shouts of alarm. He peered into the darkness of the interior. He heard a horse stamp its foot, a cow chewing its cud. His nose picked up the familiar scent of urine and manure in straw. He slipped inside, closing the door behind him, shuddering again at the loud creak. Once his eyes had adjusted, he could make out a ladder on the wall to his left. He climbed up it into the hayloft. Making his way through the packed hay to the back of the loft, he took off his haversack and burrowed into the sweet-smelling hay.

* * *

He had trouble falling asleep. He'd grown accustomed to sleeping days and exerting himself through the night. His body wasn't even that tired. And to think! Hadley was but a few rods away. Why not just knock and present himself?

Well, he couldn't be sure this was the Winfield farm.

He heard the cow in the manger below him expel gas. He grinned. Rebel cows were no different from Yankee cows.

No, better to wait till daylight and take a look-see, size up the situation. Look before you leap, as Pa always said. For all he knew Mosby might be passing the night in the house.

Not likely, with only two horses in the barn.

Jiminy! He hated it when his mind batted around a problem like a cat did a mouse. Just shut up and go to sleep!

* * *

He awoke to the crowing of a rooster, then the creaking of the barn door below him. At first he was disoriented, as often happens when you have slept for too little time. He heard a black woman's voice talking to the cow and the hissing spray of the cow's milk into a tin bucket. He lay still, warm in the hay, and listened to the sounds of what he hoped was the Winfield farm waking up. The huff of a dog— that must be Sam—and the slap of a door closing. The rooster again. Then, piercing his heart like an arrow, came Hadley's clear soprano voice singing:

> *The sun shines bright on my old Virginny home*
> *Tis summer, the darkies are gay*
> *The corn-top's ripe and the meadow's in the bloom*
> *While the birds make music all the day.*

Swimming up out of the hay, he pressed one eye to a crack between the rough-cut vertical boards of the wall and saw her, wearing a blue dress, her redgold hair streaming out from under her straw hat. She was carrying a basket, heading across the back yard toward the chicken coop. His heart was beating so fast he wondered if he was having a heart attack. It was all he could do not to call out to her.

Still singing, she entered the coop and, he guessed, began

collecting eggs. The chickens, big white Leghorns, spurted out of a little door into the fenced run that was attached to the small clapboard building. He saw Hadley's arm with a scoop in it, appear and dump a scoopful of what looked like laying mash into a feeder trough. Flapping their wings, the chickens hurried to the feeder, jockeying for position.

A few minutes later, he watched her carry the basket back toward the house. He heard the barn door creak and saw a plump black woman carrying a pail of milk walk slowly toward Hadley, speaking to her. Belden couldn't hear what she said, nor Hadley's reply.

This must be Jemima, the former slave who had been Hadley's substitute mother, who her father had freed.

Thinking about the creamy milk in her bucket made his stomach roil and his mouth salivate.

The two women linked arms and strolled to the house, chatting all the way. Seeing the black and white arms touching sent an electric shock through Belden's body, surprising him. It was a mix of revulsion and excitement. He wondered if that was what the Southerners couldn't stand to feel.

The two women went up a wooden stairway onto a screened porch and then into the back of the house. Belden marveled at the grayish screening. He'd never seen an entire porch screened and seldom, where he came from, even a screened window. As a horsefly circled his head, he could see they'd be popular in the South. Here it was not yet March and flies already.

At least he thought it wasn't March. He'd lost track of the days since the breakout. To distract himself from the feelings that seeing Hadley had triggered, he tried to cipher out how many days it had been since the 10th.

He thought they had spent six days in hiding in Richmond, or was it eight? Then that first river....How was he going to talk to Hadley without anyone knowing?

Meanwhile, what was he going to eat?

He could smell the bacon frying in the house. He was ravenous.

25

HADLEY

A few minutes after the frying bacon triggered his hunger, Belden decided to explore the barn, assuming that the household would be at the breakfast table. Chewing his last piece of hardtack, he descended the ladder and began looking around the barn.

One horse, one cow, a tack room that held a burlap bag of oats, somewhat pilfered by rats. He decided he wasn't that hungry. He squatted to do his morning business in the straw of the cow's stanchion, using the pitchfork to break up and scatter the evidence. He found a bucket of water and attempted to wash face and hands. He smoothed back his long and tangled hair and his nascent beard. What would Hadley think of such an apparition? A dirty, hairy man twenty pounds lighter than the one she'd met but a few months earlier?

He felt embarrassed at the thought. Maybe she would retch and run.

The porch door slapped and Belden scampered back up the ladder to the loft. With his eye to the crack between the clapboards, he watched a whitebearded gentleman dressed in a well-cut tweed riding suit and a rather jaunty hat, walk toward the barn, a short whip in one hand. The barn door creaked below him and he heard the man—he had to assume that this was Judge Winfield—speaking gently to the horse. Then came the jingle of the bridle and Winfield's encouragement to the horse to stop puffing up his belly as he secured the girth. The barn door creaked closed and he saw the elderly man mount the horse with practiced grace and trot off, posting with an easy motion.

This was a man who had ridden all his life. Belden remembered the draftees into the Union cavalry who kept tumbling off their horses. No wonder the Rebels could ride circles around them.

He knew that Hadley had a brother, Fax, who was a cavalryman. Since there had been only a single horse in the barn, Belden reckoned that Fax wasn't around. With Judge Winfield gone on a ride somewhere, that left Hadley and Jemima. And possibly Jemima's husband. Ezra, wasn't it? There would probably never be a better time to reveal himself.

But how should be go about that? Just walk up to the house and knock? How would Jemima react? Wait and hope that Hadley came to the barn, or at least close enough that he could call out to her?

I must be crazy. If I'd stayed with my companions I might well be in Washington by now, eating fresh beef. Instead, I'm putting my life in the hands of a woman—just a girl, really—whom I hardly know. How will she react to seeing me like this? Will she even know me?

Part of me wants to wait for nightfall and run. But the larger part cannot stay away from her. It's like she's the magnet and I'm the iron filings.

I've heard that the salmon fish return to the very same creeks where they were born, after years of being in the oceans. How is it that they know how to make such a journey, without map or compass? Some mysterious power draws them. I feel like a salmon fish coming home to where I was born. Now that I think on it, I seem to remember that once they've made it, they mate and then die. I'd like to avoid that last part, though I'd sure enjoy the mating part..

* * *

Locating his last piece of jerky in his haversack, he put it in a pocket. As he did so, his hand brushed his knife. He decided that he'd better leave that with his haversack. He went down the ladder, his heart in his throat. He cracked open the barn door and looked out at the back yard and the back porch. The chickens scratched in their run. From one of the chimneys above the house rose a thin stream of smoke.

Going out to the northern corner of the barn, he checked the back of the store and the road. Nothing stirring.

He gulped in a deep breath and ran to the steps up the back porch, went up them, across the gray-painted wooden boards of the porch, conscious of how his footsteps sounded like cannonshots, and knocked at the back door. Without waiting for a response, he pushed the door open and went in.

He found himself in an open mud room full of boots on the floor and coats hanging on pegs on the wall. He could see straight down a long hallway to the front door, a massive affair framed by glass side windows. Slightly to his left, in front, was a door to a room under the stairway, which went up from near the front door. There were also doorways to his immediate left and right, shut.

The one on the left opened, and there stood the former slave Jemima with her hand to her mouth and fear in her eyes.

"Git!" she hollered. "Youal git out this house right now!"

She was so forceful Belden almost left. But he recovered himself.

"I need to speak to Hadley," he said.

Hadley appeared in the doorway behind Jemima, the same fear showing in her eyes. Though he'd just imagined that she might not recognize him, it shook him to his core. Sam, growling, pushed between the women and came at Belden, who held out the piece of jerky. The big dog stopped, sniffed, and began wagging his tail. He whined in greeting and licked Belden's hand before mouthing the jerky. Belden knelt down to scratch his ears.

"Belden?" Hadley gasped. "Is that you?"

"A piece of me," Belden replied, looking up at her with his blue eyes. "Sorry to bust in on you like this."

"Boy, you a walkin' skeleton," Jemima said.

"I am that."

"Shall I fix him a plate of vittles?" Jemima asked Hadley. "Or should I shoot him?"

Hadley seemed to consider.

"Vittles, by all means," she said. "And start heating some water. He needs a bath."

"I hope I am not putting either of you at any risk," Belden said, standing. Sam nuzzled under his hand, demanding more petting.

"Not today," Hadley said. "Poppa is gone for the day, and Fax is off gallivanting around with Colonel Mosby. Get out of those shoes, if that's what they were, and come on into the kitchen."

The name Mosby sent a trill of fear through him. He took a deep breath. Stepping out of his tattered boots and socks, he walked barefoot into the warmth and lovely smells of the kitchen: bacon, onions, and rosemary. Hadley closed the door behind him.

The warmth came from a big cookstove on the right, where Jemima was now frying up bacon and eggs. Her big arms moved with surprising dexterity. Just beyond the stove was a closed door into what must be the formal dining room. The center of the room was dominated by a sturdy table with four straightbacked chairs surrounding it. Beyond it were the sink and two windows looking out on a distant wooded hill on which stood, perhaps half a mile away, another mansion almost identical to the one he was in. To his left a closed door and an open one—the latter leading into a well-stocked pantry. He could see a hanging ham and vegetables preserved in glass jars. To his immediate left stood a tall cabinet holding crockery and cookware. It was a big kitchen, painted a bright yellow, and it was nearly too hot for him. He'd spent a long time out in the cold.

"How on earth did you get here?" Hadley asked.

"Let the po' boy eat," Jemima said, setting the plate and a fork on the table. Belden sat and dug in. He had never tasted anything so good.

"Jemima," he said between mouthfuls, "this is fantastic."

Jemima broke into a wide white smile.

"Don' you be sweet-talking me, boy," she said. "Save it for *her*." She pointed at Hadley with her spatula. "How 'bout some fried taters?"

"I'd love some of your fried potatoes."

Belden forced himself to eat small mouthfuls and told how he had been "shot" and then transferred to Libby Prison, how they'd dug out and escaped, how he'd forded at least five rivers and followed the tracks to Burke's Station.

"I gather that you received none of my letters?" he asked.

"Not one," Hadley said. "But however did you find our house?"

"From your descriptions of it—and the barn. I holed up in the loft there till your father left."

Jemima was heating pails of water on the stove. She opened the door on the left and dragged in from that room a large tub, into which she began pouring steaming water.

"So no one saw you?" Hadley asked.

"Not as far as I know."

"Well, mercy, you do take my breath away. Let's get you cleaned up and into some of Fax's clothes. Get out of those rags and jump in the tub."

"You mean, right now, in front of God and everyone?"

"Time's a-wastin', boy," Jemima said. "In this house there ain't no prudes."

Feeling very uncomfortable, Belden faced away from the two women to strip off his filthy clothing, which Jemima fed into the stove, piece by piece, mumbling about lice. Hadley left and he heard her footsteps going up the stairs. He stepped into the warm water and his feet shouted their gratitude up to him. As he lowered the rest of his body into the tub he was filled with such bliss he almost wept. He couldn't remember the last time he'd bathed in hot water.

Jemima handed him a bar of yellow soap without averting her eyes. She was considering him as she might a prize stallion her mistress might wish to purchase.

"Open yo' mouth," she said.

"What?"

"I wants to look at yo' teefs."

Something about her matter-of-fact attitude made him want to do what she asked. She stuck a couple fingers in his mouth and peered in as if looking for a lost ring.

"At least yo' gots some good teefs," she said, turning away to open a drawer. It occurred to him that many Negro slaves had been examined in much the same manner.

As he lathered up he heard her stropping a razor. Once more he felt a pang at the loss of his.

"Lie back and hang yo' hair over the end a the tub," she said, "and I'll trim yo' hair and beard. Make you presentable for the lady."

"You can take the whole beard off if you wish," Belden said. "I usually go clean-shaved."

He closed his eyes and felt her shearing off a good bit of his hair. When she started in on his face with the straight razor he had one bad moment when he remembered how Agamemnon had died upon coming home from Troy, but he thrust the image from his mind. He realized that, for whatever reason, he trusted Jemima. She shaved him gently and well, never even nicking him. He could tell she'd done it many times before. When she had finished, without cutting his throat, he reached up to feel his smooth face with both hands. He could feel how the cheekbones stood out like angle irons. He ducked his whole head under, then lathered up his scalp.

As he was completing a final rinse, he heard the door open behind him and Hadley come in. He took the towel Jemima had put over the back of a chair and dried himself facing the sink. He stepped from the filthy water in the tub and wrapped the towel around his midriff. He found it strange that he was shy in front of Hadley after he'd become quite comfortable with Jemima.

"I think these will fit," Hadley was saying, as if he weren't naked under a towel. "You and Fax are of a size. I'll put them on the chair backs to warm. Not sure about the shoes, though."

"I want to thank you both from the bottom of my heart," Belden said, turning to face her, one hand holding up the towel. He'd tucked it, but you never knew. He blushed as he felt Hadley's eyes brush his body. He wished she was seeing him as he usually was, which he knew well he wasn't.

"We'll step outside," Hadley said, "so you can dress in privacy."

"Thank you."

When they were gone, he put on Fax's clothes: small clothes first, then a shirt and breeches with whalebone buttons, and finally thick wool socks and a sturdy pair of lace-up shoes. Everything fit tolerably well, though the shoes were a bit long.

Dressed, he fingered back his shorter hair with both hands, then started dipping out buckets of his bathwater from the tub into the sink. The door opened and Jemima came back in, followed by Hadley. Jemima took the bucket from his hand.

"Let me do that," Jemima said.

Hadley held up a brush and pointed to a chair.

"Sit down here and I'll brush the tangles out," she said.

As she touched his head, brushing out his hair with long strokes, Belden felt that if this were to be his last moment on Earth, he would die happy.

* * *

Putting on kerchief and coat, Jemima left them, saying she had a few things to pick up at the store. As soon as she was gone, Belden stood up from his chair and reached out to take Hadley into his arms. Startled, she backed away from him.

"Sir! What are your intentions?!"

It sounded like a line from a stage play. Belden wanted to laugh, but he willed himself to keep a straight face.

"Hadley, you know I love you. I want to marry you."

"I confess I am confabulated. This is a great shock for me. Colonel Wolfe told me that you had been shot escaping. I had grieved your passing."

"Obviously, he lied. After he assured me that he would tell you I was alive and well. Why would he want to....oh, I see."

"I don't believe he would lie, suh. He is a man of honor. Perhaps he was misinformed."

Belden saw red.

"No, he's not a man of honor. He's a selfish, lying sack of shit!"

"Suh! We do not allow that kind of language in this house!"

"Oh...*fiddlesticks!*" Belden shouted, and began laughing. The anger left him as quickly as it had come. He laughed and laughed at the complete absurdity of the situation. Startled at first, Hadley soon joined him in his hilarity. They laughed till the tears were streaming down their faces. They took each other's hands and held on and kept laughing.

Hadley regained her composure first and said, "But what can we possibly do, Belden? You are a Yankee soldier."

Belden shook his head, letting go of one of her hands to wipe away his tears.

"No longer. I am now but a simple man who loves you. I stand before you ready to give up home and family and country to be your husband. You are all that is important to me."

"I am flattered, but how in all tarnation is that going to work? You are a prisoner of the Confederacy on the run, liable to be arrested and put back in prison at any minute. What do I tell my father when he comes back tonight? And even if he consented to such folly, how do we account for you to the local authorities?"

Belden did his best French accent.

"Ve tell them I'm your long-lost French husband, returned from Par-ee, smuggled back to you through zee blockade."

Hadley laughed. He loved to hear her laugh.

"Well, at least you have a vivid imagination," she conceded. "But I don't think that would fool anyone."

"*Alors!* But when I spik with *un accent francais?*"

She laughed again.

"And you keep that up for the rest of your life? Don't be silly."

"Oh, no, ma'am. Gradually ah'll git me a good ol' Southern accent."

Laughing, she made as if to hit him with her free hand. He caught it in his own, drew her to him, and kissed her.

At first she stiffened. Then she went soft and pressed back against him, her breathing turning fast and broken though her nose.

They heard the back door opening and stepped apart. Jemima came in, bearing two parcels. Belden stepped forward to relieve her of one of them, placing it on the table.

"Isn't he gal-lant?" Hadley said.

"How you think you gonna keep him around?" Jemima said.

"That's the problem we've just been discussing," Belden said.

"Onliest way I can think of," Jemima said, "is to put blackface on you and say you the new slave boy."

"You might be onto something there," Belden said.

"I'll talk to Poppa when he gets back," Hadley said, her eyes shifting to look out the window. The way she said it did not inspire Belden with confidence.

* * *

Over the course of the morning, Belden and Hadley came up with a number of fantasies about how they might be together.

"You and Jemima could come to Bradford for the rest of the War," Belden said. "My family would warmly welcome you both. Once there's peace again, we could decide where best to live. You would have had a chance to try out the Lake District, but if you didn't find it suitable, I'd be willing to come down here."

"How would you earn our daily bread?" Hadley asked.

"I can smith or I can farm," Belden said, "and I'm handy in several other ways."

"I am partial to Virginia," Hadley sighed. "It's where my family and my friends are. We could hide you out in the old Hurst place till the War's done with...."

Busy with food preparation, Jemima said little, though she did grunt from time to time.

After a midday meal of cornbread and beans, Belden retreated to the hayloft. An hour or so later, Judge Winfield returned. He unsaddled, curried, and fed his horse. Peering down at him from the loft, Belden decided that he seemed a reasonable man.

What would Pa expect from a suitor of Helen's? Certainly not lurking like a thief in the hayloft.

"Please don't be alarmed, sir," Belden said, bringing himself into view. "I would appreciate a word with you."

And with that, he began descending the ladder.

When he reached the bottom and turned, he saw that Judge Winfield had drawn a derringer and was pointing it at his heart.

"Please excuse my precautions, suh," Judge Winfield said. "Desperate times call for desperate measures."

"I fully understand, sir. My name is Belden Crane. Perhaps Hadley has mentioned me to you?"

"No, suh, she has not."

This response surprised Belden and produced a bad feeling in the pit of his stomach, as if he'd swallowed lead. He tried to push past it.

"Well, sir," Belden said, "I am a former Union soldier, recently escaped from Libby Prison."

"I have read newspaper accounts of that imbroglio."

"Yes, sir," Belden said, unsure what an imbroglio might be. "When I was first captured, I was in the camp nearby, where I was fortunate to make the acquaintance of your daughter."

"Ah, yes. She did say that some Yankee prisoner there could speak French. I did not approve of her forays there."

"That would be me, sir. She was very kind to me and I fell in love with her. I have come to ask you for her hand in marriage."

Belden blurted out this last and fell silent. There was a long, excruciating pause. To his credit, Judge Winfield did not laugh.

"Well, suh," he said, "I fear you may be under a misapprehension. She is just recently engaged to be married."

Belden felt his whole body shake.

"To whom, sir?" he asked, feeling stupid to be asking. Why hadn't Hadley told him of this? How could she have shifted her affections so quickly?

"I do not see that that is any of your concern, suh. But due to your manly honesty with me, I will give you five minutes start before I call out the militia."

Belden stood as if frozen. No, Judge Winfield was fabricating this tale to incite him to run off.

"You will excuse me, sir," he said, "if I ask your permission to hear it from Hadley."

"You will do no such thing. You may run, now, or I will shoot you where you stand."

Belden bolted for the door. And ran straight to the house. He flung open the back door.

"Hadley! *Hadley!*"

He heard Judge Winfield shouting something behind him and his running footsteps across the back yard.

He shut and latched the back door. That would slow the Judge down a bit. Bursting into the kitchen, he found only Jemima, who, clearly frightened, held up the wooden spoon she'd been stirring the pot with as if it were a sword.

"Where is she?!" he shouted.

"You git on outa here, boy!" Jemima shouted back.

Belden went past her into the dining room. A huge table with many chairs shoved in under it dominated the room. Skirting the table, he opened the far door and, finding himself at the base of the main stairway, ran up it two steps at a time shouting Hadley's name. She came out of a bedroom pointing a derringer at him that was probably the twin of the one her father had just been pulled on him.

"Your father says you're engaged to someone else!" Belden spluttered.

"I thought you were *dead*!" she screamed. "I was so confused! I'm still so confused! But now you must fly, Belden! If you love me, run! Run!"

Belden slumped against the wall to keep from falling to the floor. He couldn't believe what he was hearing. At that moment he would have welcomed the bullet from her gun.

He realized that he had been a complete and utter fool. He had conjured up a fantasy built upon his feelings and his desperation. A big part of him wanted to rush her and make her shoot him.

Instead, hearing Judge Winfield's boots on the staircase, he threw himself through the window before him, which opened onto the roof of the back porch.

Fortunately for him, that window was of oilskin rather than glass. He rolled over the copper roofing panels and barely managed to grab the gutter to break his fall, hanging for a brief time before he dropped into the dormant flowerbed. Though the ground was hard with frost, he landed on both feet, well-shod in Fax's shoes. He went down on all fours, then leapt up and sprinted north between the Winfield house and the screen of trees that blocked the store from view. As he came around the front of the house he heard a shot and the ball whistle close by his head. Who had shot? Judge Winfield or Hadley?

Ahead of him he heard the train whistle and begin chugging out of the station.

As he ran toward the accelerating train he saw several men loitering on the front porch of the store staring at him. He put his head down and ran for all he was worth.

While he felt stronger from the food Jemima had cooked for him, he was aware that he was capable of running at perhaps only half his usual speed. And the line of cars was pulling away. He heard shouts and then shots behind him and the nasty whirr of the balls close by. That inspired him to greater effort.

He feared he wouldn't be able to catch the train, but the good Lord smiled upon him—he came up beside it as the last car was passing, a boxcar with its side door open. Running beside it on the bluestone gravel, he jumped, caught the iron handle, and pulled himself inside, rolling across a wooden floor dusty with old straw. Glancing back out the opening, he saw several of the men from the store's porch and Judge Winfield looking forlorn, staring at the train as it curved away from them to the north.

Belden laughed out loud. He took several deep breaths to regain his wind, then collapsed into racking sobs, his face wet with tears.

He wept like a baby who has lost his mother. He had been so certain that Hadley must feel as he did, that she loved him and would find a way to be together. But while he had been dreaming of her, day and night, and making plans for their future, she had gone on with her life. How could she thrust him aside like this? Was she so fickle and changeable?

Just like Cinder, she had abandoned him and replaced him.

What he saw as their infidelities moved him to rage and he beat against the wooden floor of the boxcar with both hands, screaming like a mad man.

He stopped in sudden fear. What if there was a Rebel guard on the train who might hear him? He'd best save his strength for whatever came next. Besides, he was getting splinters in both palms.

He decided that women were no more constant than the wavering moon.

As soon as he thought it, he realized he wasn't being fair. His relationship with Hadley had been fragile from the start. Yes, they had had strong feelings for one another. He was sure those had been mutual. But then he had disappeared and she had had no idea what had happened to him. She had never gotten his letters. She had believed what that lying snake had told her, that he was dead. Why would she wait? She was a young woman with her whole life ahead of her. She wanted a husband she could count on, children, family connections. What had he been thinking?

Cinder had been worse. She hadn't waited for him to get killed. She'd told him she would replace him with Jesse and then been true to her word.

At least she'd been direct about it. Hadley hadn't said one word about being engaged. How could she spend an entire afternoon with him and never mention that?

How had Shakespeare put it? *Frailty, thy name is woman.*

He took a deep breath. He was basing his conclusion on his experience of two women. When he thought of how his mother or his sister would have acted in similar circumstances, he was certain they would have made different choices. Exactly how they would have acted he couldn't be sure, but different nonetheless. He began to cry again.

He was, he realized, thinking only of himself. He was the selfish one. From their perspectives, both Cinder and Hadley had been abandoned by him. He had chosen his "duty" over Cinder's wishes. From where he sat now, that seemed like a terrible decision. And poor Hadley! She'd believed him to be dead. And never getting one of his letters. How had Wolfe arranged that? Was it he who was now her intended? Another wave a rage swept over him at the thought. He wanted to scream.

He must pull himself together. He had been lucky so far. But now he had no food, no water, no weapon, and he was chugging northward toward Alexandria or Arlington or one of those northern Virginian cities, which would probably be teeming with Rebel soldiers and he had no doubt that Judge Winfield would telegraph ahead for them to prepare a reception. He wished he still had his map. And his water bottle. He had a powerful thirst coming on.

The train was now moving at a good clip. Trees flashed by past his door. Then a ramshackle farm. Next, a burnt-out mansion, its tall chimneys pointing to the sky like black fingers. He lay on his side on the floor of the boxcar watching this panorama flash by. The rocking of the car and the rhythmic click of the wheels over the joints between the rails made him soporific. He fought to stay awake, weeping from time to time. It was a losing fight, He slept.

26

THE POTOMAC

The screeching of the train's brakes woke him. It began lurching as it slowed. He scrambled to his feet and peered out through the open doorway that faced what he hoped was north. The sun was lowering in the west. In the distance he thought he saw a flash of water. His throat was so parched he could hardly swallow. On either side of the tracks lay fallow fields. They were flat and even. Therefore the slowing was not due to an elevation but to an upcoming station. Hoping for a soft landing past the bluestone, he leapt.

His left foot scattered bluestones and he fell head over heels rolling into the field. When he attempted to stand, he knew he'd injured his left ankle. He took stock of his surroundings. Trailing a dark plume of smoke, the train was disappearing into a forest. Across this field was another stand of trees. He limped in that direction.

Once in the trees he took off his shoe and examined his ankle. It was turning purple just beneath the inner ankle bone. Thanking his lucky stars that Fax's trousers had come with a bandana in the back pocket, he bound up his ankle as best he could and refitted the shoe. Searching the ground, he found a broken branch he could use as a cane. Going on three feet now, like the old man in the Greek riddle, he hobbled through the forest.

When the trees thinned and then disappeared at a stone wall bordering another fallow field, Belden could see the river in the near distance. It must be the Potomac.

Galloping into the field from his right came a cavalry squadron wearing Union blue as well as Confederate gray and motley. Belden couldn't stop himself; he shouted out to them before thinking about it. As soon as the sound left his lips, he had the ominous feeling that he'd made a bad mistake

The squad wheeled and made for him. Their commander was a small man with long, flowing hair and beard. His eye was as bright as a bird's.

"Are you one a them Yankee escapees from Richmond?" he asked in a soft Virginian cadence.

Then one of his men laughed.

"Whoever he is, he's wearing my clothes!"

Belden affected nonchalance.

"Why, Fax, is that you?"

Fax moved his horse up next to his commander.

"You have the advantage of me, suh. You know my name and I don't believe I know yours."

Belden made as graceful a bow as he could with a branch in one hand.

"Has Hadley never told you the name of her intended?" he asked. It was a gamble, but he couldn't think of another option. But once he'd said it, he realized that the chances of Fax not knowing Hadley's intended were probably slim to none.

"Captain Simon Peters?" Fax asked, saluting. Belden returned the gesture after transferring his branch to his left hand. He felt a big relief that it wasn't Col. Wolfe, and not just because that would have blown his deception.

"The same, suh. I was visiting your family seat and doin' some huntin' with your father when my clothing got wet through. Miss

Hadley kindly lent me some of your clothing. I hope you don't mind. It shall be returned."

"What in blazes are you doin' way up heah, suh? I heard tell you was stationed around Fredericksburg."

"I was on my way to visit my aunt in Alexandria when my danged horse scraped me off on a tree. I busted an ankle and she done run off. I been hobblin' ever since. Youal know any place hereabouts where I could get me another mount?"

The riders in the squad had been grinning at this confession of poor horsemanship. Belden guessed that they were seldom out of the saddle.

"Hitch on up heah behind me," Fax said. "We're headin' back to camp and I'll find you a nag. That okay with you, Colonel Mosby, suh?"

The small man with the piercing eye nodded his assent. Dropping the branch, Belden pulled himself up on the low stone wall and slid onto Fax's horse behind him, clasping him around the waist. With no sign that Belden could detect, the entire squadron moved off to the west as one, like a flight of sparrows.

Belden couldn't believe his luck. How was it possible that her brother had never met Hadley's intended?

* * *

Their camp put Belden in mind of Robin Hood's in Sherwood Forest, at least as he had imagined it as a boy when Ma read him the tale. He'd been ill with the chickenpox, the constant itching driving him half crazy. Ma and Pa read to him to distract him. Nevertheless, he'd managed to give himself a few scars, one on his forehead that he usually brushed his hair over. After sliding off Fax's mount, he touched the childhood scar for luck.

A small freshwater creek ran through a glen in the forest. They'd pitched canvas tents along the swale to stay out of the cold air that would collect around the creek at night. The firepit, however, was down in the glen itself, hidden from view of outsiders. There was a string of fresh horses tethered to a line between two stout sycamores.

"Sit yourself down on one of these heah elegant chairs," Fax said, pointing to the tree rounds that circled the firepit, "and have a plate of pork fat and beans."

"I thank you kindly," Belden replied.

Fax handed Belden a tin plate mounded with pinto beans and a tin cup of chicory coffee, then took his horse, a piebald gelding, to the downstream creek to drink. He unsaddled and curried the gelding before attaching him to the line.

While Belden shoveled down the beans he watched Mosby's Raiders with interest. Stories of their exploits had circulated among the Union troops, promoting the Gray Ghost to almost legendary status. Observing them at close quarters, he was ready to believe every story he'd heard. Among them there was none of the clear hierarchy of rank that seemed so important to the Union Army. This seemed a band of equals. Mosby took the curry comb from Fax to curry his own mount, a sturdy little quarterhorse. There was no saluting and very little siring, beyond what Virginia gentlemen seemed to do with everyone. Yet everything that needed to be done was accomplished with minimal fuss and efficient teamwork. After they'd been watered and brushed, the horses were fitted with bags of oats that they seemed to relish. The men then helped themselves to the huge pot of beans that hung over the embers of a fire. To be sure, it appeared that this meal had been prepared by a rotund man whose skin was a darker hue than any Belden had seen before. Had all the original slaves shipped from Africa been this dark?

He almost laughed aloud at himself. Here he sat, a Yankee and escaped prisoner of war, eating beans with Mosby and his men as if he were one of them. And, for a brief moment, he wanted to be. These free and easy Virginians, gentlemen to the core, were defending their homes and lands and womenfolk by hounding the borderlands and tying up hundreds of Union troops that had tried, so far without result, to capture or kill them.

Fax got himself a plate of beans and sat down on a round beside him.

"It's a pleasure to finally make your acquaintance, Captain Peters," he said.

"Simon, please," Belden said. "And a very great pleasure to meet you as well."

"I must admit, I imagined you as a somewhat older man."

"I hope you won't hold my relative youth against me."

"Not at all," Fax said, laughing.

"I've been admiring Colonel Mosby and youal," Belden said. "You seem to have remarkable camaraderie and efficiency. I'd love to be a part of such a unit."

Nodding, Fax swallowed a spoonful of beans and then said, "We have fun."

"Give me a glimpse into that fun, if you would."

Fax told the story of the capture of Gen. Stoughton and his staff at the Truro Church rectory, which Belden had heard before. When Fax got to "'No, suh, Mosby's got you.'" Belden laughed along with the other men around him.

Fax set his plate down.

"Well, suh, if you be sufficiently fed and watered, let's see if we can't find you a nag that won't be scraping you off on any trees and set you on your way to your aunt's before it gets too dark to see the way. Unless you'd rather spend the night with us."

"I'd love to, Fax, but I fear I am already causing my dear aunt unnecessary worry."

Though Fax gave him the sorriest-looking nag on the string, she was still superior to many he'd seen in Union cavalry units.

"I can't spare a saddle for you," Fax said, "but I'll give you a blanket and you can pretend you're a Red Indian. Can you ride, thataway?"

"I have on occasion," Belden said. "I appreciate your generosity."

"Head east by northeast," Fax said, pointing, "and you'll intercept the Leesburg Pike. That'll take you right into Alexandria. Don't fret about Yankees—there's few this side of the river since Gen. Lee gave them the scare of turning their flank. I'll look forward to seeing you back in Burke's Station. I'll pick up the nag then. Please keep my old clothes as a wedding gift."

Fax helped him up on Daisy, for such was his new horse's name, and shook his hand warmly.

As Belden rode off, he felt a bit smug. He'd outsmarted Mosby's Raiders in somewhat the same fashion that they'd outsmarted General Stoughton. It did occur to him that luck factored greatly in each circumstance, as it often did in war. But was it luck or Divine Providence?

* * *

Belden crossed the Pike and kept heading due north to the Potomac. When he saw it he gasped. It seemed to be about a mile wide. While he knew the story about General Washington throwing a silver dollar across it, he now doubted its veracity. He maneuvered Daisy up alongside a tree stump and used that to dismount. Relieving her of bit, bridle, and blanket, he gave her a slap on the croup sending her to whatever stable she might have come from.

He found another branch to lean on and hobbled down to the riverside. It was getting dark. There, as if waiting for him in the gloom, was a rowboat, oars included. He could hardly believe his luck. He was beginning to believe that a kindly God was watching over him after all.

Pushing the boat off, he pulled himself aboard and fitted the oars. As he rowed out into the current he was facing the south bank, so he could see the Confederate sentries gesturing towards him as they ran down to the riverside. He scrunched down on the thwart and stroked for all he was worth. He was pulling so hard he passed gas. Then the sentries—four of them, as far as he could tell—fired.

He saw the muzzle flashes and the white smoke, heard the staggered reports and the balls whistling around him. He redoubled his efforts to put as much distance as he could from the south bank. The sentries were reloading and hollering for their comrades, who came out of the woods to join them, raising long-barreled rifles.

Time seemed to pause. He was aware of the clean smell of the water, the reports of the rifles, a single white crane flying high in the dark sky. Then he realized he'd been struck in the chest and driven onto his back in the bottom of the rowboat. He was looking up at the crane from where he lay. It felt as though an elephant was sitting on his chest. The crane was circling, circling. He felt himself rising up into the circle. The crane, he knew, had come for him.

Oh, he thought. *So this is what it's like to die. It's not so bad.*

Then everything went black.

27

HADLEY'S AND CAPT.BALDWIN'S NEWS OF BELDEN'S DEATH

The new year brought the Cranes a present in the form of a packet of letters addressed to them in an elegant hand and bearing CSA stamps. After they had sorted out the sequence of these letters by the date at the top of each, they began reading through them:

Monday, May 10th, 1863

Dear Mr. & Mrs. Crane, & Helen Crane,

Please allow me to introduce myself. My name is Hadley Winfield. I live in proximity to the camp where Belden is being held temporarily. Along with several friends of mine, I visit the camp nearly every day to deliver foodstuffs to the Union soldiers, who, in truth, do not receive the kind of rations that betoken true Southern hospitality. We do our best to augment these and to attempt to cheer the men by conversing with them—which we must do through the wires of their stockade fence—and, as you see, writing letters home for them.

I am happy to report that Belden is unwounded and in good health. He wishes that you might be relieved of any anxiety about him and has confidence that he will be exchanged in the near future. When he is, he will ask for a furlough so that he might come home to visit you.

Sincerely yours,

Hadley Winfield

Wednesday, May 12th, 1863

Dear Mr. & Mrs. Crane, and Helen Crane,

Yesterday we were in national mourning for the tragic passing of General Jackson.

Belden seems in fine fettle. Today he ate fried chicken, cornbread, and steamed collards, whilst helping me with my pronunciation of the French language, at which, I fear, I am hopeless.

Sincerely yours,

Hadley Winfield

After that letter, there was a long hiatus. Then:

Thursday, September 24th, 1863

Dear Crane Family,

Belden hopes that this epistle finds you all well.

Today Belden and I had a spirited discussion about the question of involuntary servitude, which he maintains is the primary cause of this terrible war. You will no doubt be surprised to learn that my father, Judge Chauncey Winfield, has, since I can remember, spoken out against the 'peculiar institution,' affirming that it has no place in a civilized society. He freed his own slaves over a decade ago. He has worked diligently to find means of changing Virginia from a slave to a free economy, as have many of our finest citizens.

Belden's perspective, if I understand it aright, is that we should change our economy overnight. I point out that while that might be easy in theory, it is quite impossible in practice. For instance, if all current slaves are made free men, and women, how will they earn their livings? Belden suggests that we keep them in their current employ but pay them wages. With these wages they would then be able to recompense their employers for food, shelter, clothing, medical care, and a comfortable retirement, all benefits which they now receive. Such a plan, I say, would simply turn them into a class of wage slaves such as you have working in the mills and factories of the North, free in name only and lacking the cradle to the grave care we give to our servants.

Although we have not yet worked out all the details of our economy of the future, we have hopes that we shall do so before too long.

Sincerely yours,
Hadley Winfield

And a final one:

Saturday, October 3rd, 1863

Dear Cranes,

I am deeply saddened to have to tell you that Belden was shot attempting to escape from the stockade.

I have this on the authority of the stockade commander, a Colonel Wolfe.

I join you in your tears of grief and wish you peace at heart. Belden was a truly remarkable man.

Truly yours,
Hadley

When Ma and Pa showed her this letter, Helen burst into tears, exclaiming, "It cannot be true!"

"Let us join hands and pray for Belden," Pa said.

After they had prayed, Helen went up the stairs to her room and sat down on her bed to write in her diary:

O black day! I cannot believe that Bel is dead. I have but one brother now. Surely there has been some mistake. Will I never hear his laugh again? It is too sad to bear.

She set down diary and pen on her bedside table, buried her face in her pillow, and wept as if she could never stop.

* * *

A week later they got notification from the War Department that Belden was still missing and had been charged with desertion. They would no longer be receiving his pay until the matter was resolved.

* * *

A few weeks later still a single letter arrived at the Crane farm on one of those bright sunny late winter's days when it seems that nothing can go wrong. Having had no news of Belden in a long spell, except that he was either dead or a deserter, they opened it eagerly in the kitchen.

It was from a Captain Baldwin of the 65th New York.

It began with the chilling words "I regret to inform you..." and William Crane, who was reading aloud to his wife and daughter, stopped, his face going pale.

Both Emily and Helen stared at him in horror.

"Belden is dead again!" he managed to croak. He dropped the letter onto the table and ran from the house.

Ma picked up the letter, scanned it, and handed it to Helen.

"Please read it aloud," she said. "My eyes..."

Helen took the letter as if it were contaminated with the plague. Key phrases jumped out at her.

"... we pulled his boat aground upon the Potomac shore...he had two musket balls in the chest...his last thoughts were of home and family...."

Helen dropped the letter and reached for her mother. Hugging fiercely, they wept.

Finally, Ma wiped her eyes.

"This August 31st," she said, "he would have turned twenty-two."

She stood and walked from the room. Helen rose to go after her, but Ma turned in the mud room and made a push-away motion with both hands.

"I need to be alone, Helen. I'll be all right, don't worry."

"But, Ma!" Helen almost shouted. "We keep hearing that he's dead and he's not! He couldn't have been killed escaping the stockade, as Hadley wrote, because here he is all these months later crossing the Potomac! Probably Capt. Baldwin was mistaken as well. I *know* he's still alive!"

Ma just looked at her with tears running down her face and shook her head.

"We must see to the funeral," she said.

PART V

RESURRECTION

28

LIFE AFTER DEATH

Belden came to with the jolting of his body. The pain in his chest was like nothing he'd ever experienced. He could barely breathe. He became aware that there were bodies, some of them quite stiff and cold, all around him: above, below, to each side. Another jolt. The creak of iron. He was on a wagon! A wagon loaded with bodies.

They'd taken him for dead. And loaded him up on a burial detail like dead meat. He was on his way to a grave.

He felt a momentary confusion. Was this what it was like to be dead? Maybe you didn't go to heaven or hell. Maybe you were stuck inside your body, feeling all this pain—for how long? Forever? He shuddered, aware now that he could feel his whole body as well as the pain in his chest. Or maybe you were stuck in your body for a few days before release? Didn't some of the Red Indians believe that?

But I can hardly breathe with this stiff guy's back in my face. I need to breathe. Wait. If I need to breathe I can't be dead, right? I definitely need to breathe. I'm alive! They just thought I was dead and stuck me in the body cart!

Now I see why the Irish Catholics have a wake for three days.

Sometimes people seem dead but revive. Jesus! I'm now on my way to being buried alive.

Panic set in. He'd always had a fear of being buried alive, trapped inside a wooden coffin with a ton of earth weighing down the lid. Despite the intense pain in his chest, he began squirming against the bodies surrounding him. He tried to cry out and found himself spitting blood. Panic gave him incredible strength and he pushed the body above him up and to the side. Cold, fresh air bathed his face as he looked up at the millions of brilliant stars in a black sky. How could it be full night? He'd been shot at dusk.

Pushing with his feet, reaching with his hands, attempting to ignore the agony in his chest, he wormed his way up out of the stacked bodies as if drawn by the stars. When his head and upper torso, the latter blood-crusted, came up out of the cold touch of his grisly companions, he saw the hunched shapes of a wagoner and his assistant, who held his shotgun off to the side. It took him several tries to find his voice, but he finally croaked out a garbled sound that frightened even him. Two faces, pale with horror, turned to stare at him. He tried to raise one hand in supplication and passed out with the effort.

* * *

Everything was white. He saw a white ceiling, then white walls, and then, sitting beside him, asleep, a man in a white coat who looked a lot like Ira.

Okay, he thought, *now* I'm dead. This must be heaven, and Ira must be dead, too. I *know* I'm dead, because I feel no pain.

But when he attempted to push himself up in what he now saw was a bed, a shaft of pain shot through his chest so forcefully that he cried out.

His cry woke Ira, who leapt from his chair and then bent down over him, smiling with such tenderness that Belden felt tears wet his eyes and run down his cheeks.

Ira put a gentle hand on his shoulder and made the same soothing noise—a kind of "Shhhh"--that their mother had made to comfort them as children.

"I'm alive?" Belden heard himself croak.

"Don't try to talk. Of course you're alive. But you had two musket balls in your chest, one so near the heart we daren't take it out, and the other—"he reached into a pocket—"I palmed it for you as a keepsake."

He handed the sanitized bit of lead to Belden, who stared at it.

"But, Ira, why do I feel so...strange?"

"Oh, that. Well, you have been dosed to the eyes on laudanum, a powerful extract from the opium poppy. It minimizes the pain. It might also give you visions. Nurse Whitman tells me that Mr. Coleridge took a draught and saw the precise lineaments of the pleasure dome that midwifed the much-heralded poem 'Kubla Khan.' You know, 'In Xanadu did Kubla Khan/ A mighty pleasure dome decree:/ Where Alph, the scared river, ran/ Through caverns measureless to man....' etcetera etcetera. I believe, as well, that Mr. Poe made frequent use of the drug to inspire his own creativity. Such are the benefits of modern medicine. Do I babble? Yes, I babble. Please forgive me. I am just so glad you are alive, brother. We had given you up for dead. Do you know that they are arranging a hero's funeral for you up in Bradford to be held in ten days' time? What am I thinking—of course you don't. You've got to heal fast so you can attend it and give the women and children a fright. They'll believe you a ghost."

Belden stared at him. Ira noticed that his eyes were like twin pools. Darn if he didn't look like a ghost.

"Who," Belden asked, "is Nurse Whitman and why isn't she here to cool my brow?"

* * *

When Ira brought Nurse Whitman in an hour later, Belden would have laughed if laughing wouldn't have put him into agony.

Nurse Whitman was not a woman. Nurse Whitman was a man with the bushiest hair and beard that Belden had ever seen.

"Out of the cradle, endlessly rocking," Whitman said, "comes to us another sacred soul, clothed with this fragile body, racked now with the pain of the intrusive metal that brother flings at brother."

"Actually," Belden said, nodding toward Ira, "my brother is helping to heal me rather than shooting me."

"Quite so. Forgive me my penchant for chanting. My name is Walt and it is my very great pleasure to meet you, Belden Crane. Any brother of Ira's is a brother of mine."

"I am rich in brothers, then. Forgive me if I don't attempt to shake your hand just yet. Give me a day or two, when I understand I must be on my feet to travel to my funeral."

"Fortunate the man who can attend his own funeral," Walt said, smiling, or so it seemed. Belden couldn't be certain, but he thought he saw the bushy beard crimping a bit and crinkles around his eyes. "They will tell such pleasant lies about you that you will come to believe them. I firmly believe that we should all have our funerals well before we die so we can hear our friends and family praise us to the stars."

"As you can no doubt tell," Ira said, "Walt is a poet. But not, I hasten to add, a conventional one."

"A foolish consistency is the hobgoblin of little minds," Walt said.

"Hold on!" Ira said, holding up a hand. "You stole that line from Ralph Waldo Emerson."

"I never steal! Though I do borrow on occasion," Walt admitted, nodding. "But I always return my borrowings. Mr. Emerson may continue to employ his line as frequently as he has need or wish. Borrowing is the highest form of flattery. But we digress from the art of poetry. For far too long poetry has been imprisoned by notions of rhyme and meter within a jail of convention. I wish to free poetry from its man-made manacles."

"He doesn't generally use rhyme or conventional meter." Ira said to Belden, who was watching their interaction as if it were a stage play. He guessed they had done this particular performance more than once before. Meanwhile, his wounds were beginning to cause him greater discomfort.

"I have freed my verse from the rigid rules of poesy," Walt continued, unabashed. "I take my rhythms from the sea, the ceaseless sea, the symphony of the waves breaking on the shore. For instance..."

He cleared his throat and Belden saw his eyes get that faraway look that made most people assume that poets were mad, or at least in some kind of a trance. When his voice came forth from the bushy beard it was of a different timbre entirely, as if another man inhabited Walt's body:

> *Beat! beat! drums!—blow! bugles! blow!*
> *Through the windows—through doors—burst like a*
> > *ruthless force,*
> *Into the solemn church, and scatter the congregation...*

God help us, thought Belden. He held up a hand.

"Sorry to interrupt," he said, "but I need some more of that laudanum stuff."

Walt's eye flashed angry fire. Ira looked shocked, and stood up.

"I'll see if I can't get you some," he said.

* * *

Belden spent a week doped to the gills with laudanum. He was expecting hallucinatory visions but had none, although both Hadley and Cinder visited him in his dreams. He could still feel the pain in his chest but it was as if it were in someone else's body. Ira spent as much time as he could with him, reading to him from his penny novels, playing checkers with him, and bringing him up to date on the news from home.

He reacted to the news of Cinder's marriage to Jesse as if he had never heard of it.

"She did *what*?!" he shouted, and felt as if a spear had penetrated his chest.

"Didn't you get my letter? I knew I shouldn't have told you," Ira said, looking guilty. "But Walt has encouraged me to speak total truth. He says—"

"Leave Walt out of this for one minute!" Belden spat. "You're telling me Cinder really married that slimy sonofabitch?"

"Please settle down, brother, or you'll reopen your wound. I thought you knew. Shall I fetch you some more laudanum?"

"I'm sick of laudanum!" Belden roared. "Get me outa here! Get me a pass home! I've gotta straighten this out!"

Walt came in then and helped Ira resettle Belden back into his bed.

"You don't understand!" Belden wept now, tears coursing down his cheeks. "We are married in the eyes of God! This is bigamy!"

"What God hath joined together," Walt's voice boomed, "let no man, or woman, put asunder. We will work through the Inner Light, my boy, and all shall be accomplished. In good time. To everything there is a season."

"Get this---this—*poet* out of here!" Belden yelled. "I want the doctor and I want a pass!"

* * *

It took nearly a week for the Chief Surgeon to pronounce him well enough to travel. In the interim Belden was visited by a young captain wearing an immaculate uniform who sat next to his bed and informed him that he was officially listed as a Deserter.

"How can that be?" Belden asked. "First off, here I am, sitting in front of you. Second, I was a prisoner of war."

"You weren't on the prisoner rolls the Rebs provided for us. A Corporal Belden Crane died trying to escape from a holding pen near Fairfax. There was a Lt. Belden Crane imprisoned at Libby, but that couldn't have been you. You were never elevated to the rank of officer."

"Actually," Belden said, "I was. By the Rebs. Just so they could stick me in Libby. Because nobody had ever escaped from Libby. Until we did. The Wolfe thought he'd buried me."

The captain looked confused.

"Look, Captain," Belden went on, "how many times in your careful perusals of the prisoner rolls have you ever come across anyone else with the Christian name of Belden?"

The captain thought about it for a moment.

"Never," he finally said. "As a last name, yes, but never as a first name."

"What does that tell you?" Belden asked.

The captain thought again. Belden could see that he was a thoughtful young man.

"Well," the captain said, "I suppose we can conclude that Belden is not a common first name in the U.S. Army."

Belden sighed.

"The lieutenant on your roll with my name was in fact me," he said. "They had to assign me rank in order to put me into Libby, which, as you no doubt know, is an officers-only prison. I was therefore a prisoner of war, not a deserter. I am now back in the United States, with no help from the U.S. Army, I could add if I were ungenerous. I have fought and bled for my country, sir, and I would take it as a great favor if you would make it a personal mission to expunge the slur of Deserter from my record and see to it that I am given my back pay. On your way out, would you please request of the nurse that I receive my afternoon dose of laudanum?"

It was to take another six years, more correspondence than the Cranes could count, and the personal intervention of Secretary Seward before the Army would agree that Belden had not been a Deserter. He was never to receive the back pay that was due him.

29

ATTEND YOUR OWN FUNERAL

W hen the Chief Surgeon finally pronounced Belden able to leave the hospital, he asked Ira to put him on the first train for New York that had an open seat. Despite his concerns about his brother traveling with such wounds as he yet carried, Ira obliged.

Ira had written a letter home with the good news that Belden was alive and healing up. He hoped that it would reach Bradford prior to the funeral, but he also knew how slow the mails were unless franked by the War Department, which failed to see an early funeral as a matter of national importance. Nor would they allow Ira to make use of the telegraph wires.

"Military use only," an officious clerk told him. "Next!"

The train left Union Station one rainy winter's morning and was in New York by early afternoon, despite long stops in Baltimore and Philadelphia. Although the car he was seated in did a certain amount of lurching on the tracks, particularly coming into Baltimore, Belden felt good enough to catch a second train up to Albany and then across the northern state through Utica and Syracuse to Geneva.

Belden knew that a large part of why he didn't feel worse was the laudanum, and he knew he had to begin weaning himself from the drug. He had written out a plan for a gradual withdrawal, but he decided that he would begin that only when he'd managed to survive public transportation.

From Geneva he had to wait an hour for the last stagecoach to Hammondsport. During his wait, he bought a sandwich from a vendor with a dime from the money Ira had lent him. The bread was dry and the cheese was old. It reminded him of the meals in Libby. While waiting, he drank another dose of the poppy.

He took the stage only as far as Keuka, where he bid his fellow passengers farewell and got down. He began to walk south. It was a clear night and cold, but with a good moon to light the road. When he looked behind him, there was his old companion Polaris. This dim, constant beacon put him back to the nights of flight from Richmond through the Virginia Tidewater plain, with its forests and swamps and dangerous rivers. He had, he thought, come a fur piece, as they said down South. And now he was moving away from Polaris rather than toward it.

As he walked he was continually aware of the still-tender wounds in his chest, particularly the one that held a Rebel musket ball. His surgeon had assured him that, while he would carry this memento for the rest of his life, his body would accustom itself to it. He was noticing that it pained him more when his lungs were working harder to supply his heart with oxygen. He slowed his pace, took a swig of the laudanum from one of the vials he carried, and decided to focus on Cinder.

He had decided that he had wronged her. She had been willing to be his wife and he had denied her that. While it was true that he hadn't wanted to burden her with widowhood, if he were honest he had to admit that he had wanted to be free. He had seen marriage as a kind of snare.

Now he saw it as a kind of Paradise.

But she probably had married Munsen just to spite him or, if not, would reject him now just to get back at him. She could be vengeful, he knew.

Well, one thing he had learned from war was that you could lose many battles and still win the victory. You just had to have the will to persist. He would persist with Cinder. She was a good woman.

He knew that a piece of his heart would always contain a dull ache for Hadley, or, to be a tad more accurate, for the Hadley of his imaginings. He had misread her, that was for certain, believing her to be as smitten as he had been. He marveled that in so short a time he had gone from feeling that he loved her passionately to a mere dull ache. Nothing like being rejected to temper one's affections. Or being shot near the heart. Was it possible that a musket ball could kill a loving feeling and leave the man alive? As well as serve as a reminder of the pain he reckoned he would always carry in his heart.

He knew that it was about a ten mile walk between Keuka and Bradford, which he had often traversed in two-and-a-half hours' time. He reckoned it would take him closer to four tonight, given his injuries. Well, there was no rush—he'd be making Bradford prior to sunup anyway. Only the most diligent of farmers would be awake then, feeding their stock. He knew his father would be one of them.

The thought of his father brought tears to his eyes, and they froze before halfway down his cheeks. He rubbed them away with his fingers. It was colder than he had thought. His fingers were stiffening up and his ears hurt.

He unwound his scarf from his neck and tied it over his head and under his jaw so it covered both ears, then thrust his hands into the pockets of his jacket. By clasping and unclasping them he hoped to loosen and revive them. They were still very cold. He took them from his pockets and rubbed them vigorously together, which made his chest hurt.

Jiminy. He'd been down South for so long that his blood must have thinned. The Fahrenheit thermometer at the Geneva station had read 26 degrees. A positively warm winter's evening in upstate New York. Well, he'd lost a lot of weight that his week of feasting in Washington with Ira and Walt hadn't fully compensated. He remembered the chicken cacciatore, something he'd never eaten before, which Walt had insisted he try at a small Italian restaurant near the hospital. His stomach rumbled at the memory. What a festive evening that had been. He'd told the story of the chicken he'd arrested as a spy. Walt had mercifully refrained from reciting any more of that drivel he claimed was poetry. In regular conversation he was an intelligent and compassionate man with thoughts about any number of issues. Belden found it perplexing that someone so bright could produce such awful poetry. They'd drunk a robust Chianti and begun with a plate called antipasto, which was mostly olives and peppers and thin-sliced ham—all of it delicious. Now his mouth had begun to water. It had been a long time since the dry sandwich in Geneva.

He stopped and took a sighting on the moon. He reckoned he'd been walking for about an hour. He rubbed his hands together again and thrust them back into his pockets. At least most of his body was warm from walking. Up ahead he saw the turn for Sylvan Beach—he wasn't yet halfway. Got to keep going. One more swig of laudanum and he'd be good.

That's what he'd say if anyone asked him what he'd learned from his war experience: You just have to keep on keeping on, and laudanum helps you on your way. This seemed both a profound and ridiculous aphorism. He giggled.

* * *

William Crane was awake well before sunup, as usual. Seemed that the older he got the less he slept. Especially since word of Belden's death had reached them in Captain Baldwin's letter. Baldwin had sounded like a trenchant observer and his words seemed to carry truth. William often found that he was weeping when he awoke, having dreamed of Belden. This night he had seen his son walking toward him, a red hole in his chest over his heart.

He slipped from bed lest he disturb Emily. He knew that she slept fewer hours than he, though her best sleep was usually in the morning. It was the falling asleep that was the problem for her. Between them they might average the prescribed nine hours that the doctors said were necessary.

After using the chamberpot to empty his bladder, which took longer and longer as each year passed, he went to the wash basin to rinse his hands and then his eyes. He pulled on his clothes and crept down the stairs in stockinged feet, boots in hand. There were still coals in the kitchen stove. He added kindling and soon had the coffee water boiling. He added the grounds and moved the pot to a cooler part of the stovetop. Emily had shown him how a simmer made for less bitter coffee than a hard boil.

Emily had not wept at Belden's funeral. She was a proud woman. But he knew that she wept every day, more than once. He admired that she could hold herself in like that at the funeral, with so many people standing up to say what a fine man Belden had been and how he had touched their lives.

Lighting a candle, he put on his reading glasses and opened the Bible at random, as had been his practice for many a year. Today he was in the Gospels, at the story of Jesus raising Lazarus from the dead. Anger flooded him.

He slammed the Bible shut and found himself wanting to curse God. How could He take Belden from them? Why didn't He raise Belden back up, as His son had with Lazarus? How absurd, to believe that anyone could make a dead man live again!

He lit the lantern and put on his coat and hat. It was a bit early to feed the stock, but they wouldn't mind. He went out into the cold night air and looked up at the moon and then the stars.

You, he thought, who made the moon and stars, allowed my son to die. Why should I even talk to you like this? You saved your own son and let mine perish.

He heard footsteps and turned to see a lean man with a bit of a hitch in his gait walking toward him. The hairs on the back of his neck went up and he almost dropped the lantern. He had never believed in ghosts, but now he was seeing one. Just as in his dream, Belden was walking toward him, smiling now, his face shining in the moonlight.

* * *

They were all crying together with joy in the warm kitchen, bright now with the light of several lanterns. Ma had left Belden's side only to scramble some eggs and warm some toast. She sat on one side of him while he ate, touching him with wonder, as though he were a newborn child. Helen sat on the other, holding him around the waist and resting her head on his shoulder.

"Jumping Jehoshaphat, women!" Pa laughed. "Let the poor starving boy eat!"

Helen jumped up.

"I'll get you more coffee, Bel!"

Ma wouldn't budge an inch. She'd lost him once, twice, actually, and she wasn't ever going to let him go. Her tears ran freely down her cheeks, which, Pa noticed, had begun to get some color back.

Helen poured coffee from the big blue pot and Belden nodded his thanks, still chewing.

"I haven't had food this good for a long, long time," he said, heaping Ma's blackberry jam onto a piece of toast.

"You're skinny as a ghost," Helen said, sitting back down beside him.

"Please don't say that!" Ma protested, hugging him again.

"Well, you're skinny as a fence rail, then."

Belden washed the bite of toast and jam down with the hot coffee.

"My first order of business is to eat you out of house and home," he said.

"Just tell us what you'd like to eat," Ma said.

"You *know* what I've been dreaming of for all these months," Belden said, grinning.

"Fried sheeps' eyes!" Helen laughed.

"Smart pants!" Belden shot back. It was just like it had always been, he thought. He gave Helen a hug around the shoulders, amazed at how she had grown. She was a woman now.

"I've got to feed the stock," Pa said, putting his coat back on.

Belden stood.

"I'll help you," he said.

"You'll do nothing of the kind," his mother said, pulling him back down beside her. "You need a day of rest, if not more."

"Ma's right," Pa said. "Eat up, get warm, and then get into bed and get some sleep. Helen, take the bed warmer and warm his sheets, will you?"

"Love to," Helen said, jumping back up and starting to load the bed warmer with red coals from the stove.

"Youal are spoiling me!" Belden protested.

"Youal?" Helen said, laughing. "Why, Bel, you've gone and turned Reb on us!"

* * *

Belden got out of his clothes and into the warmed bed. It felt delicious. Not just the warmth, and the fact that it was his own bed, but every familiar object in the room, his and Ira's. Their small table between the beds, covered with one of Ma's embroideries and holding a candle in a bronze holder, a Bible, and a book of popular poems. Real poems by men like William Cullen Bryant and Henry Wadsworth Longfellow.

A chest of drawers stood against the wall beside the wall hooks for hanging clothing that was in use. Belden's were the top two, Ira's the bottom two drawers. Ever since he'd outgrown his older brother, who used to insist that the tallest should have the higher drawers. To the left of the chest the glass-paned window was only partially covered by the wispy white curtains Ma had made for it.

A straight-backed chair stood under the window. He and Ira had often argued over who should have the right to use it as a clothing caddy. He remembered the day when, after almost coming to blows, they had agreed to alternate: Belden on Monday, Wednesday, Friday, Ira on Tuesday, Thursday, and Saturday. On Sunday they'd pick up the room and hang all clothing on the wall hooks. They were both surprised that this simple plan had worked to smooth the waters. Belden smiled. He was fortunate, he knew, to have Ira as his brother.

Against the other wall stood the washbasin on its stand with the pitcher of water beside it. How many times had they had to break ice in the pitcher to be able to pour some water for their morning "ablutions," as Ira called them. There was also a gaily painted chamberpot beneath each bed.

This, thought Belden, is what Heaven must be like. Another breath, and he slept.

* * *

He awoke with the midday sun streaming in his window and warming his face. Six hours uninterrupted sleep—when was the last time he'd had such luxury? Even in the hospital some nurse was always waking him to take his pulse or feed him pain pills. Yes, it was the pain in his chest that had awakened him. Well, he'd survive the pain. He'd do without the laudanum today. As long as he could.

The smells coming up from the kitchen made his stomach rumble. With a pang of fond memory he breathed in the rich scents of real coffee and frying bacon. And something else: Ma had already started on his favorite—Yankee pot roast. After a quick wash he pulled on his clothes and went downstairs.

"Good morning, son!" she welcomed him. "Well, I should say, Good afternoon. Sit down and I'll fetch you a cup of coffee. I'm glad you slept late. I'll start heating some water so you can bathe."

"Top a the mornin' to ye, Ma," he replied. He was relieved that she'd returned to her more businesslike self. All that affection had been a bit daunting.

"Oh, I can see you've been associating with the riffraff," she laughed. "I imagine you encounter all sorts in the Army."

"Oh, aye, that we do," Belden said, in his best brogue. "Some of the riff and some of the raff."

It was wonderful to hear her laugh. She brought him a steaming mug of coffee, almost white with cream and two spoons of sugar. He hadn't the heart to tell her that he'd accustomed himself to drinking it black. He sipped and found himself near tears when the creamy sweetness reached his tongue.

"Your impression of a Celtic accent reminds me: We got a lovely letter from a Boston Irishman named Keogh," Ma said. "He was quite well-spoken. And several from a Hadley Winfield."

A pang of pain went through Belden's chest.

"I'd love to see them sometime," he said. Then: "Where's Helen?" he asked, glancing around, as if he might have overlooked her somehow.

"She's teaching at the school now, in the grand tradition of my older children."

Belden nodded.

"Good for her," he said. "Does she keep the whippersnappers in line?"

"I doubt she's as ruthless as you or Ira were," Ma said, "but I see how they love her. All she needs to do is to raise one eyebrow and they stop cutting up and sit with folded hands. She never has to raise her voice. It's a wonder to behold."

Belden smiled, remembering how effective Ma's raised eyebrow had been in corralling him and Ira as children. He'd seen the same phenomenon in the Army: Some officers commanded with loud voices and threats while for others the troops would do anything out of love. While at Libby he had often heard the tone of reverence with which the Rebels spoke of General Lee.

"How's Cinder?" he asked.

His mother turned the bacon with a spatula before replying:

"She's Mrs. Munsen now," she said. "And a baby to prove it."

"A baby?" Belden said, shocked. How could Cinder have a baby?

"She took up with Jesse Munsen as soon as you left town."

Belden sighed.

"She told me she would when I wouldn't marry her before I left,"

"You spared her the possibility of becoming a widow."

"That was only part of it. I also wanted to be free to have whatever adventures might come my way."

He paused, then decided to risk it.

"In fact, I fell for a Rebel gal."

She turned and stared at him, wide-eyed, as if he'd just told her he'd been to the moon.

"The one who wrote us the letters? Hadley?"

"It happened through a barbed wire fence, but I thought we'd fallen in love."

"Well, land sakes!" Ma said.

"The Commandant of the camp was in love with her, too. That's why he transferred me to Libby in Richmond. To get me out of the way. It worked. When I went to visit her..."

"How on earth did you manage that?!"

Belden told her of the escape from Libby and how his escape party had struck the railroad tracks that went right through Burke's Station and of his adventures there.

Ma shook her head slowly.

"You were a poor, lovesick boy," she said.

"I was. But there's nothing like being spurned by your loved one and then shot a couple of times in the chest to affect a cure."

Ma put a plate of eggs, bacon and toast before him.

"Well, it's just as well she spurned you. What in the dickens were you two thinking? You a Northern abolitionist and her a Rebel. You can't mix oil and water. How is your wound healing?"

"The sawbones was amazed at how quickly I recovered from the operation to extract one of the musket balls," Belden said. "He said they had to leave the second as it was too close to vital organs. So they sewed me back up. I now have a permanent zipper. It will be easy for the next woman to get into my heart."

He grinned. She didn't.

"Which hurt you worse," she asked, "the bullets or the betrayal?"

He stopped eating and looked out the window. Pa was coming in from the barn carrying a basket of eggs. He remembered Hadley doing the same.

"You're a wise woman, Ma," Belden finally said. "Mornin', Pa."

"Good day, son," Pa said.

"Where's Eugene?"

"Oh, he's been long gone, back to Canada. Said he was going to join their army in case we invaded. I'm hoping he was trying to make a joke."

* * *

After his meal and a bath, Belden said he was going for a walk. Both Ma and Pa knew where he was walking to, but neither said a thing. He'd put on his suit and a starched white shirt. Both hung on him like the clothes on the garden scarecrow, but he tightened his belt around his now pleasantly full belly and walked down the lane to the main road into Bradford.

It was just under a mile to the town proper. He came in on Switzer Street, poking his head in the smithy to say good afternoon to Charlie Ide, who was hammering away at a horseshoe, one of his principal products. Charlie stared at him in open-mouthed wonder.

"Close your mouth, Charlie," Belden said, "you look like a moron."

"Helen told me you were alive this morning on her way to the school, but I still can't believe it. I was just at your funeral two days ago."

"I fear the report of my death was a trifle premature."

Dropping hammer and gloves, Charlie came toward him.

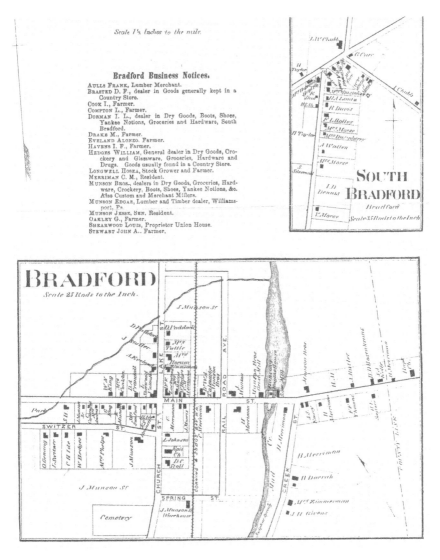

Bradford, N.Y.

"No hugs, please!" Belden said, holding up one hand as if to ward him off. "My chest is not fully recovered yet."

Charlie halted, nodding.

"I heard you were shot."

"Twice. Two balls. They got one of them out."

"Helen told me the other was too close to the heart."

Belden nodded.

"I'm glad you're alive, Bel."

"Thanks, Charlie. Well, I'm off to frighten Cinder."

"Oh, brother. You know she married Jesse Munsen."

"I do."

"And has a baby."

"Yes."

Charlie raised both eyebrows a bit and began re-gloving.

"It's good to see you again, Charlie."

"You as well, Belden."

As Belden left the smithy he passed the Hedges' house and then Mrs. Phelps's large lot, which she gardened with a fierce passion since the death of her late husband. Even at this time of year she had managed green leaves and blooms. The reddish-pink quince stood high and the creeping wintergreen hugged the soil. Mrs. Phelps herself, wearing her hat, apron, and gloves, stared at him with blue-gray eyes from under the hat brim.

"Well, I declare," she said. "Is that you, Belden Crane, or a shade doomed for a certain time to walk the earth?"

In addition to gardening, Mrs. Phelps had a love for the Bard of Avon. The community tolerated her efforts to cajole them into the roles of her productions every summer. When he was only eighteen, Belden had struggled through *Hamlet*.

Belden doffed his cap and bowed, though the latter gesture was quite painful.

"No shade, Mrs. Phelps, but what's left of me."

She came toward him, taking off her right glove, and held her hand out over her picket fence. He took it in both his own and resisted the desire to bow again to kiss it. He had always been very fond of this woman. He'd loved it when she came to the school to read them passages from Shakespeare. Though it seemed a different language to him that he understood only in bits, her tonalities lent it a richness that had touched him deep in his body. And he'd actually enjoyed his brief experience as a thespian under her tutelage.

"I expect you're on your way to see Cinder," she said.

He nodded. She had always been a perceptive woman.

"I always imagined that you two would wed," she said. "If you pledge not to shoot me as a spy, I will deliver to you some intelligence, of which I am privy as her next-door neighbor."

He met her eye and nodded.

"I so pledge," he said.

"I do not believe she is happy in her union with Mr. Munsen."

"What leads you to this conclusion, Mrs. Phelps?"

"I have said enough. I wish you well in this and all future endeavors."

He nodded and turned to go.

"And, Belden. I am glad that you have survived this brutal war."

"Thank you, Mrs. Phelps. I feel the same way."

30

CINDER & JESSE

J esse Munsen's lot was twice as large as any in Bradford and his house proportionate, a blocky two-story white clapboard with redbrick chimneys at either end and a portico in front of the huge double doors so guests could disembark from their buggies shielded from the weather. Belden's heart beat a little faster as he opened the gate to let himself in. He wasn't concerned that he'd have to deal with Jesse yet: The Munsens were nothing if not hardworking. Jesse would be at the mill or the store before the sun rose and he was unlikely to come home until long after it set at this time of year.

He knocked, using the gleaming brass knocker on the right-hand door. When he heard footsteps, his heart beat even faster. He imagined it thumping against the musket ball. It hurt as if it were. The door opened and he stepped back—it wasn't Cinder but a pug-nosed girl in a maid's attire. She had a thick brogue.

"Jesus God and Mary! There you stand, yourself! We heard you rose from the dead like our Lord and Savior, but to see ye in the flesh gives me a start. But excuse me manners—you'll be wantin' to see the mistress. Come in, come in!"

Feeling a bit as he had under his first artillery bombardment,

Belden stepped into the foyer. He'd never been inside the Munsen mansion. He'd heard reports of it, of course, as if it had been some palace from the souk in Istanbul. The foyer was startling, two stories tall, with a wide staircase leading to the second floor directly across from him. The floor was a kind of stone, marble he guessed, and huge dark paintings of somber men in black suits hung upon the walls. It put him in mind of a mausoleum. He shivered—it seemed colder than it was outside.

"This way, sir," the maid said. Inside, she seemed to have regained her professional demeanor. She opened a door on the right that emitted both warmth and a rich yellow light. He stepped into what he supposed was the library. The wall to his left was solid with books, from floor to ceiling. He could tell at a glance that most of them were uncut and unread. At the far end of the room a big fire blazed in a huge stone fireplace, which was flanked by tall windows. To his right, more tall windows. Before them, her back to the light so he could hardly make her out, stood Cinder in an expensive dress that bloomed from her narrow waist like a gigantic flower.

"Thank you, Maisie. Could you bring us some tea and scones, please."

He heard the door close behind him.

"Bel, I am delighted to see you, especially so soon after we attended your funeral."

It was unnerving to be squinting into the light and not be able to see her.

"Believe me, I am very glad to be able to be here," he said.

"Oh, please forgive me. I see you are near blinded by the light. Come this way."

He chuckled, knowing full well that she had positioned herself with her back to the light precisely for this effect. If she heard him, she didn't let on. She swept across the oak floorboards toward the fireplace, before which stood a sofa and two overstuffed chairs. She sat in one corner of the sofa.

Now that he could see her clearly, he noted the new worry lines between her eyes and the shadows beneath them. Helen had told him Cinder had to leave his funeral because she was weeping so hard.

He had to smile. She was play-acting the grand lady to punish him. Well, he deserved a bit of punishment. Did she really believe that all this ostentatious display of wealth over-awed him? He *knew* her.

He sat in one of the big chairs and tried to keep a straight face. There was a discrete knock at the door and then Maisie entered carrying a large silver tray upon which stood a silver teapot, silver sugar bowl, and silver cream pitcher. There was also a silver plate of scones. Belden assumed that the Munsens must have a large account with Reed & Barton silversmiths. The maid set this glittering display down on the low table that stood before the sofa.

"Thank you, Maisie. That will be all."

Maisie made an attempt at a curtsy and left.

"Where did you find Maisie?" Belden asked.

Pouring tea into thin porcelain cups, Cinder shrugged.

"Jesse brought her up from Manhattan Island," she said. "He said she was just off the boat from County Clare, or some such place."

"How old is she?"

"She says eighteen, but I doubt she's a day over fifteen, or else her development has been severely curtailed by a diet of cabbage and potatoes. Cream and sugar?"

"Please."

He watched her hands as she mixed the cream and sugar into their teacups. He had always loved her hands—she had the long slim fingers of an artist or musician.

A big part of him wanted to move beside her on the sofa and take her in his arms and kiss her. But now she was a married woman. He glanced at the simple gold band on the ring finger of her left hand. No ostentation for her.

He tried to imagine how she would react to his customary boldness. Would she stand on principle? Would she push him away, hands hard on his tender chest?

"I'll come sit next to you," he said, rising from his chair.

"I don't think that's a good idea, Bel."

He stopped halfway up, confused by the softness of her tone. "Because...?"

"I made a choice, after you made yours. But our choices are children of the mind and will, not the heart. I will always love you, Bel, but our choices have set us upon very different turnpikes in our lives. As you know, there is a cost to traveling a turnpike. I pay mine daily. When you went off to war, something broke in me. I became a crazy woman. I married Jesse not knowing what I was doing. When I thought you were dead, when the whole town thought you were dead, I grieved all over again. I cried what remained of my heart out, Bel. I had to leave forever the forest path and pay the toll of the pike. Now that you're alive, here, I admit that I am in a turmoil. I'm so happy that you are not dead. But I can't...."

Tears streamed down her cheeks and she turned her head aside.

"...please forgive me...I'm so sorry...for everything. Would you please go now? I can't..."

She rose and stumbled as if drunk toward the tall window nearest her. Every cell of his body wished to go to her, to enfold her in his arms and hold her against his own bruised heart. But he knew where that would lead. He stood.

"I'm the one who's sorry, Cin. I was stupid. Stupid to ever leave you. Stupid to need to run off to a rich man's war and a poor man's fight..."

"Please just go for now. We'll manage...later."

"Okay, Cin. As you wish..."

He stood, intending to take his leave. He wasn't quite sure how it happened—did she reach for him, or he for her? Suddenly they were in each other's arms, hugging fiercely and weeping together, then kissing as if their bodies were defying their intentions. Belden felt the whole room spinning around him.

That's when Jesse walked in.

* * *

Belden had never liked Jesse Munsen, ever since first grade. Nothing since had changed his mind. That was the thing about growing up with people in a small town: Having known everyone all their lives, you had a pretty good sense of who they were.

Not one of the Munsens had enlisted and, when Lincoln instituted the draft, they bought alternates for their male offspring, including the younger Jesse. While these "alternates" fought and died for them, they stayed home and made a lot of money selling shoddy goods to the Army.

In selecting Jesse for her husband, Cinder knew full well she had chosen the one man in Bradford whom Belden despised.

He had to admit that the Jesse who stood before him now, dressed in a black suit and tie with a starched white shirt, lord of the Munsen mansion, seemed a different person than the boy who'd pulled pigtails. The large flintlock pistol in his right hand also lent him a certain gravitas. Belden was feeling a little guilty that he'd been in Jesse's wife's arms when Jesse had walked in. Crying together rather than fornicating, it was true, but nonetheless in a somewhat compromising posture.

"Unhand my wife, sir!" Jesse said, with Scandinavian ice in his voice.

Where had he come up with that line? Belden wondered. Then to his mind's eye came a clear picture of Jesse-the-boy bullying Cinder.

"Get a grip, Munsen," Belden said, separating himself from Cinder. If Jesse took a shot, he wanted it to be at him alone. "We each have a lot to weep about. Mostly that she ever consented to marry you in the first place."

Cinder looked at him in alarm.

"I challenge you to a duel, sir!" Jesse blustered. Had he been watching too much theater down in the city?

"Now there's a great idea," Belden said. "Pistols at dawn atop Mt. Keuka? Who do you think would come out alive? The soldier who's been shooting men or the clerk in his daddy's store who was afraid to serve his country?"

Belden imagined he could see the steam escaping from Jesse's ears.

"Bel," Cinder said, "there's no call to be rude to Jesse."

"Of course there is," Belden replied. "He's being rude to us, coming in here unannounced and implying that a good cry between old friends is infidelity and then waving a pistol about and proposing a duel. Who does he think he is, Harry Hotspur Lee?"

Cinder went to Jesse and tried to take his pistol hand. He snatched it away and stared at her with a poisonous hatred. He then raised his free hand as if to slap her.

"Oh, I wouldn't do that, Jess," Belden said, walking toward him. "Lay one hand on her and you'll need someone to carry you to our duel on a stretcher."

Jesse lowered the hand and glared at Belden. To Belden it seemed that Jesse was trying to look angry when he wasn't.

"Get out of my house!" Jesse sputtered.

Belden sighed.

"Where is our duel to be? And perhaps you would prefer swords to pistols?"

"Get out, and never come back!"

"Does this mean you're chickening out of the duel you so rashly proposed? It seems to me that me killing you fair and square is probably the best way to resolve this."

"Get out!" Jesse hissed.

"Just please go, Bel," Cinder said.

"Gladly," Belden said, "as soon as I've finished my tea." He went to the low table, picked up his teacup, and noisily slurped up the last of his tea. "Good stuff. I can see why the Bostonians would start a Revolution over it."

He set the teacup back on its saucer.

"I bid you both good day. I shall see you soon, Cin."

"You will never see my wife again!" Jesse almost shouted.

"That's up to her, not you," Belden said. "In this country, we are no longer at liberty to own people, or did you miss the whole import of this war?"

This time Belden was sure of it: There definitely was steam issuing from Jesse's ears.

"Please go, Belden," Cinder said.

"I'm going," Belden said, "just as soon as I—" and, moving like one of the timber rattlesnakes in the high fields, he stepped inside Jesse's right arm and grabbed his wrist, taking the pistol from him.

"—take charge of this deadly weapon."

Again, Jesse drew back a hand to strike.

"Don't!" Belden said, leveling the pistol. "Unless you want to meet your Maker!"

Jesse's face had gone as white as his starched shirt. Spittle formed on his lips.

"Would you like to come with me right now, Cin?" Belden asked, keeping his eyes on Jesse.

"I will come to you," she said. "For now, please go, before someone gets hurt."

Belden frowned.

"If you say so. Jesse, if you molest Cinder in any way, or attempt to prevent her from leaving, I will return and kill you with your own pistol. Let us all pray for the state of our souls. And now, *Adieu.*"

31

HEAL THE BODY, HEAL THE SOUL

Belden stood outside the Munsen mansion beneath the portico for a moment. He tucked the pistol under his belt in the small of his back and made sure his shirt covered it. Looking up, he decided he didn't much like a portico—it shut out the sky. He walked from under its confines into the open driveway and felt better. The sky carried a swirl of dark gray clouds blowing in from the north, but it was better than being under the portico or in that house. He shivered, and not just because he sensed the temperature was dropping.

Turning right onto Church Street, he walked the block along Mr. Merriman's large lot with its tall deciduous trees, now stark fingers against the darkening sky. At the corner he walked across Main Street to Dr. Lockwood's home and office and knocked on the door.

Mrs. Lockwood, dressed in her nurse's attire, opened the door and bid him welcome. If she knew he'd been dead she didn't show it.

"Please be seated, sir," she said. She had perfected Prim. "The doctor will see you shortly."

Belden sat. The pistol grated against his back. Removing it, he set it on the table beside him.

He had always wondered why doctors were the only people in

America with a title. He'd been taught that the Revolution had done away with titles. Certainly the ones like King, Lord, and Duke were gone, but Doctor persisted. Why was that? Did they need to put themselves up on a higher level? It was like the officers in the War, who went by Colonel or Captain, and then possibly a last name (but never a first). Would they hold onto those titles after the War? He hoped he lived long enough to find out.

"The doctor will see you now," Nurse Lockwood said.

Then her eyes locked onto the pistol.

"Please don't be alarmed," Belden said. "I had to take it away from Jesse Junior before he shot himself in the foot. May I leave it here while I see the doctor?"

"Please do."

She led him into the office, which was clearly the original dining room of the house, as the parlor was now the waiting room. And, since no one had left, why had he had to wait anyway? Was this a further ploy to make the doctor seem Important? Or had he needed time to finish his soft-boiled egg?

Why this sudden antipathy to doctors? Could it have something to do with the fact that they'd left him with a permanent zipper on his chest and a chunk of lead next to his heart? Ira had told him that one of the musket balls had lodged on the breastbone and was easy to extract. Then they'd probed his chest to try for the other one but didn't dare remove it. They might have figured that out ahead of time and left his sternum well enough alone.

Or was it because some battlefield quack had pronounced him dead while he was still alive?

Now, now, he admonished himself. They did the best they knew how.

Dr. Lockwood stood up from behind his massive oak desk to shake Belden's hand and Belden reminded himself that he'd always liked this man. Now his hair was gray at the temples but as a younger man he'd made home visits to check on Belden and Ira and Helen when they were going through the usual scourges of childhood, from measles and mumps to the chickenpox and fevers. He'd always been gentle and kind with them. Now he assured Belden that he was delighted to see him looking so well.

"Well, it's a tad better than being dead," Belden joked, but neither of the Lockwoods laughed.

"I understand that you still carry a Rebel ball near your heart," Doc Lock (as they'd called him as boys) said.

"Yessir, that's why I'm here. The surgeon in the District released me on the condition that I report to you for follow-up, to keep an eye on the healing."

Doc Lock nodded.

"Let's see it," he said.

Belden glanced at Mrs. Doc.

"My wife is a trained nurse. She will be assisting me."

Belden nodded and took off his shirt. He noticed that there was a bit of red stain on his bandage—and he noticed that Nurse Lockwood took a step back at seeing it.

The doctor had Belden sit on his examining table and brought out a shiny pair of scissors with one of the points blunted. With these he began, very gently, to cut away the bandage.

"I imagine you saw something of the Elephant down there," Dr. Lockwood said.

"A bit."

"And how goes our effort?"

"Well, I can't speak for the entire War Department," Belden said. "All I saw was the trunk—or perhaps the tail. General Halleck could give you a more comprehensive overview."

"Of course. Oh, did I hurt you? Sorry. How do you judge the morale of our troops?"

"Both cynical and high, often in the same person."

"Interesting way of putting it. My goodness, they opened you up like a tin can, didn't they? Well, no sign of infection but we'll dust you with sulfa and refresh your bandages. How does it feel?"

"Like I've had my chest torn open, like Prometheus—but a bit better day by day, although I keep a sharp eye out for eagles. I look forward to when I can resume my normal activities."

"Let me listen to your heart and lungs."

The doctor took his stethoscope from around his neck and placed it near the scar.

"Deep breath," he said. "And again. Good."

Belden remembered now how unstinting Doc Lock had always been with his praise. He gave you a "good" for being able to breathe.

"A bit of fluid still in the lungs, but basically fit was a fiddle," he said, removing the stethoscope. "You'll live to a hundred. Nurse."

"Good to know," Belden said.

Mrs. Lockwood began sprinkling a yellowish powder on his chest, then re-bandaging him.

He felt a rush of warmth for this sweet couple who had taken such good care of him. How could he have ever conjured up such terrible thoughts about doctors in general?

"What do I owe you?" he croaked in a strange, tight voice.

"Not a penny, son. We are eternally in your debt for what you have given for our country and the cause of freedom. You'll need to come by once a day so we can keep fresh sulfa and new bandages on you. And don't even think about trying to pay us."

"Although," added Nurse Lockwood, "if you happen to have a couple of extra eggs out of your hens, we could keep up the doctor's strength."

"Now, Emma..." the doctor began.

Belden laughed—and broke off his laugh when it hurt—and said he'd see if he couldn't talk the hens into a couple extra.

"Emma," said the doctor, "would you give me a minute with Mr. Crane?"

Emma looked surprised but said nothing as she left the room.

Doc Lock stood up slowly, as if the process were painful, and looked out his window before speaking.

"I can't help but notice the tremble in your hands and the odor of laudanum on your breath," he said.

"They dosed me up pretty heavy in the hospital," Belden said.

"And now?"

"I was given a few vials."

"You know you'll need to begin taking less and less every day until you no longer need it."

"I've already started that, Doc, as of this morning. I'm surprised you can smell it on me."

"In my younger days, I experimented with it. I know from personal experience that it's not an easy drug to let go of. If you want my help in so doing, I want you to know I will help."

"Thanks, Doc. But I think I can do it on my own."

"Few can. I'm here if you want assistance."

When he went back out onto Main Street, after returning the pistol to the small of his back, he was whistling "Yankee Doodle."

* * *

Instead of heading west out of town on Main Street toward the farm, he turned left onto Church Street. Old Julius Ide, Charlie's father, waved to him from his rocker on the porch of his little house. Jules had been the blacksmith in Bradford from time immemorial and he still dropped by the smithy to give Charlie a hand from time to time, but he was now "so decrepit that I can't hit a nail on the head," as he put it. Though snow white of both hair and beard, Jules was still mentally sharp.

"You're looking sharp, Mr. Ide!" Belden called, waving back.

"That's cuz I sleep on the edge of town and eat straight razors for breakfast," Julius replied.

Happy that Julius didn't need him to stop and tell his story once again, Belden sauntered down to St. Andrew's Episcopal Church. He let himself in through the front door that was never locked and stood in the back looking at the altar and gold-engraved white marble of the Ten Commandments behind it. He noticed that the lettering was a little fuzzy—were his eyes going bad on him? This is where they must have had his funeral two days ago. He wished he could have eaves-dropped on what they said about him. Helen had said that his ears must have been burning.

He genuflected and then walked up the aisle to the front row, genuflected once more and sat down, a bit gingerly, on the pew that his family usually occupied on Sundays. He took out the pistol and laid it beside him on the seat. What would Rev. Atwill say to his bringing a pistol into church?

The Commandments had become clearer as he got closer. Nothing up there about firearms. Or even swords. He chuckled. He breathed in the faint odors of incense and cleaning wax. He could see dust motes floating in the light coming in through the stained-glass windows depicting the Stations of the Cross. He felt very much at ease. This was his church, where his young spirit had received much nourishment. Reverend Atwill had been a kind and thoughtful spiri-tual guide, never frightening children with images of horned devils and hellfire but gently extolling them toward reason and goodness. He still remembered how that good man had encouraged him to challenge the orthodoxy of the Trinity and the Virgin Birth.

"The Good Lord gave us Reason," he had said, "to question and to come to our own truths. If he'd wanted us to be blindly faithful, he'd have made us without the capacity to think. Use your God-given Reason!"

Belden stared at the communion railing, picturing himself and Cinder taking their first communion together with the rest of their confirmation class when they had been eleven. All the girls had worn white dresses.

Even at the time that had seemed wasteful to him. They would never wear those dresses again. They would languish in trunks in the attics of Bradford. As would their wedding dresses.

That day, Confirmation Day, the knowing had come to him with absolute certainty that one day he and Cinder would be kneeling once again at this railing, she in her wedding dress, to make the vows of Matrimony. Yet she had married Jesse instead. He sighed. He would have to work on being civil to Jesse. The little pissant. Well, it might take a lot of work.

He realized, for the first time, that he had never questioned the fact that Cinder, who was Jewish by birth, would choose to be confirmed into a Protestant Christian religion. There was a lot, he had to admit, that he'd taken for granted. Time to start using his God-given Reason.

Although he was pretty sure she'd picked up his not-so-subtle hint, he was surprised she hadn't gotten here before him. He was certain that, knowing Belden would kill him if he attempted it, Jesse wouldn't prevent Cinder from leaving.

He heard the front door creaking open behind him and, looking back over his shoulder, saw Cinder coming down the aisle carrying something wrapped in a white blanket. He guessed what it must be, and the hairs on his arms rose up. He scooted over a bit so she could sit beside him. She genuflected and entered his pew, slowly lowering the white bundle. A child with bright blue eyes looked up at him from under a pink cap and smiled. She had just the beginnings of tiny incisors, but a lovely smile nonetheless.

He had no doubt at all. She was his child.

He looked from the baby girl into Cinder's eyes and saw the confirmation there. He put one arm around her and tenderly kissed her lips. She sighed, as if releasing a heavy burden, and put her head against his shoulder. He felt her tears wetting his shirt. They sat together in the gentle silence of the church. The child grew restless and Cinder put her down in the aisle. She stood for a moment, holding onto the pew seat, then lowered herself to the ground and began crawling toward the altar.

I've haven't missed watching her learn to walk, Belden thought. To Cinder he said, "She's a gem."

"She is that," Cinder replied. He noticed that her voice was soft, almost timid.

"Can you ever forgive me?" she asked.

"For what?"

"Being such a scold to you, and then marrying Jesse. That was the worst mistake I ever made in my life, and I hope I've learned a lesson."

"There's nothing to forgive," he said, turning toward her and taking her hand. "We were both young and ignorant. We did what we had to, and lived to repent it. The way I see it, we have a clean slate and can make of our life together what we want."

She laid her head on his shoulder and began to cry. He put his arm around her and held her close, but not too tight.

Above the altar Christ hung in His final agony on the Cross, His body twisted in pain but His face serene.

Well, Belden thought, *if You could get out of that, we'll find a way through this.*

32

SILVERNAIL

From the church it was a bit of a walk to the Silvernail residence.

"You didn't bring a bag?" Belden asked.

"I want nothing from that house, except our daughter," Cinder said. "I left my ring on the bedside table."

"He didn't hurt you in any way?"

Cinder looked at him with a strange expression on her face.

"Oh, he hurt me, but not today. He left soon after you did."

"I hope he's serious about a duel," Belden said, smiling.

At first, Belden carried Abby, who kept looking up at him with her big blue eyes in a way that was somewhat disconcerting. He liked her warmth against the wound in his chest. But he also found carrying her tiring and handed her over to Cinder as they headed into South Bradford.

In contrast to the Munsen mansion the Silvernail cabin seemed even tinier than usual. Micah seemed to know they were coming. He opened the door as they came up onto what he called a porch.

"Belden, *bubi!*" he said, opening his arms for a hug, which he administered with great tenderness. "You missed a fantastic funeral!

You should have heard the lies they told about you! They made you sound like such a *mensch*. Come in, come in."

Belden had always liked Micah. He was a small man with a huge bushy beard, a mostly bald head, and a bright eye. He was a bundle of seemingly endless energy. He was always at some project or other, be it studying the Kabbalah or making a toy for a child. Belden still had the dreidel Micah had made for him one Hanukkah.

The cabin contained only two rooms: one big one with two chairs and a table, a cookstove, and a cupboard with a few plates and utensils, and a second with a bed and a wardrobe. Belden remembered that when Cinder had lived with Micah, she had the bedroom and he'd slept on a trundle bed in the big room.

Micah wanted to serve them tea, but both Belden and Cinder said they'd just had theirs.

"Baba," she said, addressing him as she always had, "tell Belden what Jesse did to Uncle Jim's house."

Micah looked at his daughter for a long moment, then turned to Belden.

"Would you believe me if I told you I saw Jesse Jr. tossing kerosene onto Jim's shanty and then lighting it on fire?"

"Did you?"

"The real question is, would the court believe me," Micah said. He opened his arms and took Abby to him. She squealed with pleasure. She knew him well.

"That's not the real question," Cinder said. "The real question is will Jesse want to face you in a court of law, knowing what you will testify to. Or would he prefer to grant me a divorce."

"I'm not sure what standing I would have, as a Jew, in a court of law in the state of New York at this time," Micah said. "However, in the court of public opinion...."

Here Micah made an expressive gesture by waggling his dense eyebrows.

"You're thinking Jesse might cave because the Munsens hate to hear a bad word spoken about them?" Belden said. "He'll deny it, of course, just like he denied bullying the girls back in school. What proof do you have?"

Micah shrugged.

"This and that. What I saw, and that empty kerosene tin with 'Munsen Bros' stamped on the side, just lying there, ten feet away."

"It wasn't kerosene, Baba, it was coal oil."

"Aren't they the same? Simple synonyms?"

"No. Kerosene is made from petroleum, coal oil from candle coal."

"Really? And how did you get so smart, *liebchen*?"

"I had a wonderful teacher, who taught me that God is in the details."

"He must have been one of those mystical Kabbalah crazies," Micah said, smiling. He gave Abby a kiss. "Don't let them ever tell you that your grandfather is a crazy, *bubala*." Abby reached up a hand to grab his nose.

"But the fact that it was a Munsen tin is just circumstantial," Belden said. "Anyone could have one."

"Yes," said Micah, "about that you are correct. However—" and here he paused to remove Abby's hand gently from his nose—"nearby was a handkerchief, crumpled into a ball after being used to wipe kero —er, coal-oil off dirty hands. And, on that piece of discarded linen was embroidered, in blue, the initials JEM, JR."

"Jesse's initials," Belden said. "He liked to have them on everything. Where did you find it, Micah?"

"In the blackberry bush a rod from where the lady detectives found the tin. That is the problem with these privileged people. They think they can use and discard us like dirty linen, and they don't realize other people, whom they call 'servants,' have to pick up after them. This picking up after is an invisible, one might even say a *mystical* process to them. They are too much protected from the consequences of details, and so they believe they can ignore them. They never even carry their own dirty dishes from table to sink."

Abby was squirming now, and Micah put her onto the floor, where she began crawling with determination toward a low box that Belden saw was full of wooden toys. Cooing with delight, she started taking them out of the box and placing them in a semi-circle around her. Belden was amazed by the craft of their design and the warm patina of their much-polished wood.

"Micah," he said, "you are a craftsman. You should open a toy store."

Micah laughed with delight.

"Thank you, Belden, but who would buy children's toys when they are so easy to make?"

Belden thought about that for a moment, then, nodding, said. "Ma and Helen tell me they searched that area the day after the fire. Why didn't they find a white linen handkerchief with Jesse's initials on it?"

Micah shrugged and smiled at him.

"Some of us are better at finding than others," he said. "It is a gift that I have. Besides, by the time I checked it was easier to see through the brambles."

Belden shook his head, but he was smiling, too.

"Where do we go from here?" he asked.

"Not to Jesse," Cinder said. "He'll deny everything and then burn down our house."

Micah laid one long forefinger beside his nose.

"No, not to Jesse *Junior*," he said.

* * *

Belden Crane, William Crane, and Micah Silvernail met with Jesse Senior in the rectory with the Reverend Atwill mediating. The minister was a tall, clean-shaven man with rimless spectacles and a clerical collar. The old State Senator had a shock of white hair and nearly invisible lips whose corners turned down almost perpendicular to his mouth, like those drawn in a pen-and-ink portrait. He listened in silence to Micah's evidence and examined the handkerchief. When he made to pocket it, however, Belden relieved him of it.

"We'll just hold on to this until the divorce decree is signed and notarized," he said.

Jesse Sr. harrumphed.

"That is hardly necessary, sir," he said. "I am a man of honor."

"And a politician," Pa said quietly. "You understand how horses are traded, Jesse."

"As to that," Jesse Senior said, "I expect no more talk of a duel of any kind."

Belden smiled.

"I tried to tell Jesse that it wasn't a good idea," he said. "I have no need for a duel."

"Just so long as that is clear," the senator intoned.

"What is to become of mother and child until the divorce is final?" Reverend Atwill asked.

"She will come to live with us," Pa said. "We have a separate room for them. When sufficient time has passed, and Belden has completed his service, they will be married, by yourself, if you are willing."

"Of course, of course," Rev. Atwill said.

"Might I suggest," said Micah, "that Jesse Junior demonstrate his good husbandry by providing a small stipend, say fifty a month, to the Cranes to cover Cinder's and Abby's room and board with them? Only until the subsequent marriage, of course."

Jesse Senior looked at him with a wild eye. Belden could almost read his thoughts. The Munsens did not like parting with their money.

Pa laid a gentle hand on Jesse's arm.

"Think of it as charity," he said. "And how it will redeem your son's standing in the eyes of the townsfolk."

"Twenty-five!" Jesse snarled.

"That would not redeem anyone's standing," Micah said. "The most we could come down would be five dollars."

They finally settled on $33.33, and everyone went home in some degree of contentment.

* * *

Except Belden.

At the celebratory dinner that night in the Crane kitchen his father asked him what was bothering him. All eyes turned to him. Well, almost all eyes. Abby's were on the scoop of mashed potatoes she was trying to gum to death from where they sat on the tray of her highchair. This highchair was a beautiful piece of Micah's handicraft, fashioned with only glued wooden joinings. Micah sat on one side of Abby, Cinder on the other. Cinder had been consulting Ma about when Abby might be interested in solid food.

"One way to find out," Ma had said, testing the potatoes first to be certain they were cool enough.

Belden sighed, then smiled around at everyone.

"Sorry," he said. "I'm truly happy that we are all together tonight and that we have found such a peaceful solution to the troubles that confronted us. I just can't stop thinking about Uncle Jim. He died a horrible death and the arsonist will go unpunished. Once more, we're overlooking the rights of a Negro. Worse, we traded on his death to secure the solution. I feel bad about that. I fought—and almost died— to create a Union in which Negroes have equal rights. Many brave men are still fighting—and dying—for that principle. Yet way up here in Abolitionist country, a black man is murdered, and the murderer gets off scot free."

There was a silence around the table. Abby looked up with mashed potatoes covering most of her face. Helen tickled her under the chin with a napkin and attempted to wipe some potato off.

"Of course you feel bad about it, Bel," Ma said. "You are a man of conscience. You care about other people. What happened to Jim was awful."

"And we of the Bradford Sleuths had our suspicions," Helen said. "I don't know how we missed the tell-tale handkerchief. Thank God Micah found it." She began playing "This little piggy..." with Abby's bare toes.

Micah cleared his throat.

"Belden, *bubi*," he said, speaking slowly, "the Kabbalah points out that the world is not yet perfect. We must do the best we can with what we have. Think of it from Uncle Jim's perspective. His death, horrible though it was, served many purposes he would be proud of. His death helped free many people. Cinder is free of Jesse Jr. and will be free to marry you, and you her. Abby is free to grow up with her real father in a warm and loving family rather than the *meshugas* of the Munsen mansion. I am free of the fear that the Munsens will burn me up next. And even poor Jesse Jr. is free to find another wife to torment. Well, maybe we should strike that from the docket. He is at least free from my daughter's daily disdain. There is nothing harder for a man to endure than a wife's disdain."

"And I," said Helen, "am free to marry Charlie, just as soon as Ira can get here. We could have a double wedding, if you two would like that."

"I'd love it, Helen," Cinder said, "if the divorce is final by then. How about you, Belden? We double up with Helen and Charlie?"

"Think of the money you will save by combining the wedding feast!" Micah said. "And a single honorarium for the Rev. Atwill. Though he will probably want to do it pro bono, if I know him, and I do."

"Sounds great!" Belden said, laughing.

"Ira wants to bring a friend named Walt," Helen said." Do you know anything about him, Bel?"

"Well, yes, as a matter of fact, I do," Belden said. "Just don't ask him to recite any of his poetry."

* * *

The following day gave signs of spring approaching. The last of the snow was melting off the higher ridges and the first robins were returning from wintering in the south. The oaks and maples were budding, and tender shoots of grass were pushing up out of the dark soil.

Walking slowly, trying to work around the constant pain in his chest now that he'd stopped the laudanum, Belden went alone to the cemetery that had been situated on the bench of flat higher ground just outside town. It contained several new graves. There were large granite headstones for Lewis Whitehead and William Van Auken. It was hard for Belden to imagine those vital young men moldering in the ground. At least, he thought, Lew won't be able to spread the story about how I fell for a lady of the night—and he felt immediate remorse at the pettiness of his thought. If only Lew could still be alive he'd gladly take the teasing he'd have been subjected to. He wondered whether he should tell Cinder about it, then remembered Ma's admonition: "Least said, soonest mended." After all, she'd wisely refrained from telling him about married life with Jesse. And he hadn't wanted to ask how he'd hurt her.

He stood at the foot of Lew's grave.

"You were a good friend, Lew. I couldn't have made it through without you. I hope you have plenty of lady angels to chat with up there."

He stepped over to Will's headstone.

"Will, we sure appreciated it when you kept us informed about the big picture at Chancellorsville. You gave us perspective, made us feel a part of something grand and special. I'm sorry you didn't make it back. I'd have liked to see how you looked in a dress. Funny, how something like that doesn't matter a whit anymore. If something doesn't injure anyone else, why would anybody even care? And if the paintings I've seen are right, everybody up there probably wears a long white dress anyway." He saluted Will, then about-faced and saluted Lew.

Nearby was a third fresh grave. Above it stood a headstone with his name and supposed dates carved into it. He wondered what they had buried there. It made him feel a bit queasy, seeing his own grave. But it sure put things in perspective.

A new life lay before him. What would he do with this gift of life? Could he put aside his wish to wander the world? Though he felt it much diminished, it was still there. He knew that what he really wanted to do was to paint. In fact, he was itching to paint but he didn't feel drawn to landscapes anymore. And he certainly didn't want to recreate what he'd seen on the battlefield. The sooner he could disremember some of those scenes the better.

Then it came to him. He'd paint people. The people he loved, and who loved him. Cinder and Helen, Ma and Pa and Ira. Lew and Will. Abby. Micah. Maybe he'd even have a go at his memory of Tom Rose. He'd never have made it back without Tom Rose.

What about Hadley? He considered it for a moment, then grinned and shook his head. He'd never get the color of her hair right.

"Let sleeping dogs lie," he said aloud, to the gravestones. If they heard him, they didn't let on.

Humming softly the melody from "John Brown's Body," he turned back toward his home.

* * *

When he stepped into the house, he found her waiting for him in only her smallclothes.

"Everyone's out for the next hour or so," she said. "Helen took Abby to visit Charlie so he would be inclined to want one of his own."

"I'm sure he will."

"I thought we might like to get to work on another one ourselves."

Belden smiled.

"You do realize that I was recently opened up like a tin can," he said. "You could say I'm quite open-hearted. We must be very gentle."

"That's the way I like it best," she said.

The End

ACKNOWLEDGMENTS

To my mother's family, the Ides-Cranes-Knapps, who have had a singular role in shaping American history, thank you for your many sacrifices, your integrity, and for preserving the documents that form the backbone of this mostly true story. Of course I have had to imagine certain parts to fill in the gaps in the records you left me, but I hope that I have been able to do so consistent with the remarkable men and women who lived it.

To W.W. Clayton, author of *The History of Steuben County, New York* (1879), much appreciation for your detailed descriptions of Bradford and the campaigns of the 107th. I can appreciate that you left Belden out of the rolls because the records you had access to probably still listed him as a deserter. Thankfully, the National Archives and Records Administration, General Reference Branch, in Washington, D.C., does indicate that he served honorably, or at least picked up his pay, and was absolved of that slur, which fills me with gratitude that I live in a country that so far keeps pretty good records of fact.

To the many historians of the Civil War, and, believe me, they are multitudinous, thank you for your labors of love in gathering and presenting such a trove of evidence of what really happened. While your books take up most of one wall of my study, floor-to-ceiling, and your names are far too numerous for a non-academic to mention, I do wish to single out the following superlative works that have guided my effort: Shelby Foote, for his three-volume classic, *Civil War* (1958). James McPherson, for *Battle Cry of Freedom* (1988). Stephen Sears, *Chancellorsville* (1996). Douglas Freeman, in the Richard Harwell abridgement, *Lee,* (1961). Joseph Wheelan, *Libby Prison Breakout* (2010). Charles Adams, *When in the Course of Human Events* (2000). Drew Faust, now President of Harvard College, for *The Creation of Confederate Nationalism* (1988). Bruce Catton, *Civil War* (1984). Col. John Mosby, *Mosby's Memoirs* (1917). Paul Angle, *The Lincoln Reader* (1947).

And in a nod to the Department of History & Literature, Harvard College, I must mention two of the works they much admired, F.O. Matthiessen's *American Renaissance* (1941) and Vernon Parrington's *Main Currents in American Thought, Volume Two: The Romantic Revolution in America* (1927). I confess that I still haven't read either work all the way through and probably never will.

To my creative writing mentors--Nelson Algren, Vance Bourjaily, Jose Donoso, Robert Fitzgerald, William Cotter Murray, Peter Taylor, and Kurt Vonnegut—many thanks for your tutelage and support. I was fortunate to know you.

To the Berkeley Poets' Cooperative, and especially Charles Entrekin, thank you for your many years of compassionate criticism and inspiration, as well as the publication of my first chapbook.

To my dear friends Dr. David Glaser and George Sidney, many thanks for your invaluable feedback, both historical and literary.

To my wonderful wife, Dr. Yashi Amita Johnson, thank you for giving me two uninterrupted hours to write every morning over our almost thirty years and for the countless cups of Smart Coffee created by your loving hands.